Claire McGowan grew up in a small village in Northern Ireland and now lives in London, where she runs an MA in creative writing at City University. *Blood Tide* is Claire's sixth crime novel and the fifth in the highly-acclaimed Paula Maguire series. She also writes women's fiction as Eva Woods.

Praise for *Blood Tide*:

'A delicious spookiness is added to McGowan's customary mix of complex characterisation and sweat-inducing excitement, offering a new level of chilling thrills' *Sunday Express*

'A brilliantly executed thriller with a haunting and atmospheric setting. Spine tingling' *Sunday Mirror*

'A complex, disturbing, resonant novel that remains light on its feet and immensely entertaining' *Irish Times*

Praise for the Paula Maguire series:

'*A Savage Hunger* is a taut, compelling thriller that merges ancient beliefs with a very modern crime' Elly Griffiths

'I read *The Silent Dead* with my heart in my mouth . . . brilliant' Erin Kelly

'In Dr Paula Maguire, she has created a wonderfully complex character' *Irish Independent*

'A breathlessly exciting and intelligent thriller with a brooding atmosphere' *Sunday Mirror*

'It's a gripping and gory read and shows McGowan to be a thriller writer of exceptional talent' *Irish Independent*

'McGowan's book is bloody and brilliant' Angela Clarke

'McGowan's style is pacey and direct, and the twists come thick and fast' Declan Burke, *Irish Times*

Praise for *The Fall*:

'There is nothing not to like . . . a compelling and flawless thriller'
S.J. Bolton

'She knows how to tell a cracking story. She will go far' *Daily Mail*

'The characters are finely drawn, and it's concern for them, rather
than for whodunnit, that provides the page-turning impetus in this
promising debut' *Guardian*

'Hugely impressive. The crime will keep you reading, but it's the
characters you'll remember' *Irish Examiner*

'Highly original and compelling' Mark Edwards

By Claire McGowan and available from Headline

Paula Maguire series

The Lost
The Dead Ground
The Silent Dead
A Savage Hunger
Blood Tide
Controlled Explosions (a digital short story)

Standalone

The Fall

BLOOD TIDE

CLAIRE McGOWAN

HEADLINE

First published in 2017 by
HEADLINE PUBLISHING GROUP

First published in paperback in 2017 by
HEADLINE PUBLISHING GROUP

1

Cataloguing in Publication Data is available from the British Library

ISBN 978 1 4722 2821 5

Typeset in Sabon by Avon DataSet Ltd, Bidford-on-Avon, Warwickshire

Printed and bound by CPI Group (UK) Ltd, Croydon, CR0 4YY

Headline's policy is to use papers that are natural, renewable and recyclable
products and made from wood grown in well-managed forests and other
controlled sources. The logging and manufacturing processes are expected to
conform to the environmental regulations of the country of origin.

HEADLINE PUBLISHING GROUP
An Hachette UK Company
Carmelite House
50 Victoria Embankment
London EC4Y 0DZ

www.headline.co.uk
www.hachette.co.uk

To Jillian

Prologue

Margaret

Ballyterrin, Northern Ireland, 1993

Dear Paula. By the time you read this, you'll see that I am gone . . .

No. It was all wrong.

She threw down the pen, angry, and it rolled away over the sheet of paper and clattered onto the kitchen floor. It was no good. How could she explain? She couldn't. Was she really going to do this? It didn't seem real.

She glanced uneasily at the clock: 3.17 p.m., getting dark already. He should have rung by now. He'd promised to ring, tell her what to do, say when he was coming to take her somewhere safe. Because mad as it seemed, her kitchen, with its old seventies units and tiled floor, was not safe any more.

3.18 p.m. Her hands clenched, thinking of Paula, of PJ. At least they'd be safe, if she was gone. She could come back, surely, once it all died down. It was nearly over again, they all said it, the peace process creeping ahead, back one step, forward two, back again. She just had to finish this letter, try

I

to explain it, why she had to run now, today. Explain she might still look exactly like Margaret Maguire, mother of Paula, daughter of Kathleen, wife of PJ, but she wasn't. She was someone else now. The things she had done. The lies she had told. But no, she couldn't explain any of that. Not if she had a week to write the letter.

3.19 p.m. Outside, the cough of a car engine in the street. The gun-crack snap of a door. Her hands began to shake. Not Edward, surely – he never parked near, in case they traced the car. Not PJ, he'd been called out on some case before dawn, something so bad he hadn't even told her what it was. Voices outside. Men. Two or three. Her heart rose up in her throat, and she scrabbled on the floor for the pen, scratching down the last few lines in the seconds she had left. Trying to find the words to explain what could not be explained. Failing.

3.20 p.m. Footsteps, coming to her door. They were here. It was too late.

Chapter One

Ballyterrin, Northern Ireland, February 2014

'Mummy. *Mummy!* A bad man's at the window!'

Danger. Up. Run. Paula was on her feet before she knew it, heart hammering as she surfaced from sleep and realised where she was. In the doorway stood a small figure in My Little Pony pyjamas. Paula's heart slowed. 'There's no bad man, pet. It's just the big wind outside. It makes the trees scratch at the window, see.'

'Don't *like* it.' Maggie, almost three now, had started sucking her thumb again, something Paula herself didn't much like. The child's breath was hitching in her chest; her top rucked up to show her little rounded tummy.

Paula patted the side of her bed – cold and empty for nearly eight months now. 'It's just the wind. Come on, get in with Mummy here.'

Maggie climbed up, so light the bed might as well have been empty still. Paula pushed the damp red curls off the child's face, as her tears subsided into hiccups. 'There now. You're OK. There's no bad men. Just the wind.'

'Daddy'll get the bad men,' Maggie mumbled, from the edge of sleep. Paula said nothing, as she felt the child uncurl and sag beside her, and outside the wind howled and worried at the house like a boat tossed on the ocean. How could she explain to Maggie that it wasn't true – that she'd lied to her? Of course there were bad men, lots of them, and Aidan – 'Daddy', as she called him – wasn't around to get them because he was one himself.

The child was asleep now, her chest rising and falling. Paula got carefully out of bed and went into Maggie's room, which had been her own for eighteen years, and then again for a year when she'd moved back in with her dad in her home town of Ballyterrin. Twelve years in London, only to find herself here, back to the beginning as if in some crazy real-life version of Snakes and Ladders. Her old desk was stacked with Maggie's soft toys, and the glassy eyes watched Paula as she knelt down and opened the bottom drawer. No need to hide it really. Maggie couldn't read and Aidan was gone, and PJ and Pat were unlikely to go snooping. But just in case, she'd filled the drawer with some little vests of Maggie's. It felt wrong, somehow, those innocent clowns and ducks so near to the horrors at the bottom of it.

Paula reached under the vests and took out the folder. Plain manila, a little worn. On the front, a name – *Margaret Maguire*. The same name as her child. She and Aidan had talked about what to call her, whether to add O'Hara or not, but then the wedding had never taken place and it seemed now Maggie's name would not change. Sometimes, on nights like this, she'd lie awake and wonder if it was for the best. It would have been a lie, after all.

Paula knew the contents by heart. The handwritten reports, the interviews, the picture of her mother on a beach.

She'd taken that herself, playing at photographer. Margaret's red hair whipping in the wind, laughing against the gale and rain that constituted an Irish summer day. The August bank holiday, 1993. Two months after that picture was taken, in October, Paula had come home from school to find her mother gone, the house cold and dark. And there had been no sign, no trace of her for a further twenty years. No body. No answers.

Until the previous summer, tidying up after builders had finally redone her kitchen, Paula had found her mother's note. An innocuous scrap of lined A4 – torn, she was fairly sure, from her own school notebook – but it had changed everything. And now, six months later, she had still told no one. How could she? Her father PJ had remarried, finally declared her mother dead. And she might be, Paula had to remind herself. Even if her mother had gone of her own accord, as the note suggested, she'd gone for a reason, and it didn't mean whoever was hunting her hadn't found her soon after. Either way, Pat was PJ's wife now. And Aidan was Pat's son, and anyway Paula couldn't talk to him at all at the moment, because he was gone. Saoirse, Paula's best friend, was busy trying and failing to get pregnant, and she and Pat saw each other all the time. It was too much of a burden to place on anyone. There was only one other person who knew the whole story, knew the weight of it. And he was gone too. She touched the note lightly, mouthing its short lines by heart.

Dear Paula. By the time you read, this you'll see that I am gone. You won't understand why, pet, and I can't explain, but I have to go now. There are bad people after me and I need to keep you safe. I'm so sorry, pet.

If you hear things about me, please try to understand I was doing it for you. Someone had to try and stop the killing.

I love you. If I had any other choice I would take it, but I just can't stand it any more.

Look after your daddy, pet, and be good.

Mummy

Look after your daddy, and be good. Well, she hadn't done either of those things. She'd run away to London as soon as she could, and now here she was, a single mother with a fatherless toddler. Who of course had a father – but one she couldn't know about. Who thought her father was a different man, currently sitting in a jail cell several miles down the road.

Paula stood and looked out the window over town, the lights winking against the dark of the surrounding mountains. Some nights she convinced herself she could see the beam from the prison, a bald white laser over a hulk of concrete, but she wasn't sure it was even true. He was there – somewhere out there, anyway – and it was eight months since he'd let her visit, or anyone bring Maggie to see him, and Paula was alone, swimming hard against a current that kept dragging her back, back into the dark.

She pushed the folder angrily away, and rubbed at her tired eyes. What a mess. What a bloody mess she'd made of everything.

Fiona

Looking back, it all began to go wrong on the day Jimmy Reilly cut Manus Grady's throat. Or maybe it was sooner, maybe it had been growing and metastasising long before that, the way a wave will rise to the shore in a gentle green curve before suddenly cresting, battering you down, raking you over the stony bottom. But even if it had, I only realised how wrong things were going, how badly something on the island was awry, when Jimmy walked into Dunorlan's pub with that old knife in his hand. It was one you'd use to gut fish, the Guards said later. Rusty, bent, but still sharp enough to kill a man.

Manus and Jimmy had bad blood, of course, everyone knew that. Most people on the island had bad blood with someone or other. In Jimmy and Manus's case it was that Manus had sold some land Jimmy thought rightly belonged to him. It had been sold, like most of the spare land on the island, for what I hear was more than enough to keep even Manus in whiskey. This was several years ago, when the company first came over. It was old news. Not something that should have ended with Manus on the spit-and-sawdust floor of that beer-soaked pub, gasping and spasming like a slashed fish on the deck of a boat. But it did.

It was a clear day in January, rinsed out and shining from the usual rain squalls. Before I came to the island, I didn't realise there were as many types of rain as there are days in the year. Patchy rain. Drizzle. Thick showers. Freezing rain that soaks through any layers of clothes you care to put on. Jimmy had encountered Manus in the village Spar around eleven. (I heard all this from Bridget who works at the post office counter and was in to see me about a persistent cough.

Never underestimate what you can find out when you have
a government post and a letter steamer.) Jimmy asked Manus
had he filled in some forms from Jimmy's solicitor. Looking
for compensation or some such. Manus said something
along the lines of, don't be bothering my head with that old
shite now, I am off for a pint. And words were exchanged
about the moral character of their respective mothers, before
they were kicked out by Oona who owns the shop, much to
Bridget's chagrin.

Then Manus set off across the harbour to Dunorlan's,
skidding on wet seaweed thrown up by the overnight storm.
Shaking, no doubt, from his morning whiskey. He'd been in
to see me already about early-stage liver fat, and I'd told him
he had to stop or he'd die, but there is no reasoning with an
Irish alcoholic – and Jimmy walked the twenty minutes back
to his farm, and found the knife in a drawer in the kitchen
(or so Bridget said). Even though most people on the island
buy their fish ready-gutted in the Spar these days, they also
never throw anything away. Jimmy took time to sharpen the
knife, then walked back to the pub. Several people claimed
to have seen him with the knife in his hand, but thought
nothing of it. He might have been going to mend a fence, or
cut wood. He entered the pub and approached Manus, who
was on his usual bar stool, watching a hurling match on the
TV. Meath versus Tipperary, I believe. Jimmy said something
like, are you going to fill in those fecking forms or not.
Manus repeated his earlier comment, with some added
swearing. At that, Jimmy lifted the knife and caught at
Manus's head like he was shearing a sheep, and drew the
blade along the man's neck. The bar and the TV and the
packets of Scampi Fries and the barman, young Colm
Meehan – nice lad, brought his mammy in to me last week

– were instantly sprayed with Manus's blood. Although at that point it was probably mostly whiskey.

People said afterwards, enjoying the drama of it all – oh, if only you'd been there, doctor, you could have done something for him. And maybe I could, if I'd pressed my fingers right to where the blood gulps out, quick and hot, if I'd stopped him up like an old leaking boat, but as it was, everyone stood gawping and Manus was quickly dead. Colm, who is that rare thing, a fast-thinking islander, took Jimmy and locked him in the bottle store, where he sat quite docile among the crates of Harp and boxes of Tayto crisps until Rory came to fetch him to the mainland. And that was it.

In statistics, two points are just two points. They signify nothing. But three points, that's a line. That's a pattern. And after the incident with Manus and Jimmy, I began to think about the thing at the primary school, and that awful business with the Sharkey baby, and I started to draw some lines. I wonder now, after the blood in the sea and the boat and the box full of dead things, whether I could have stopped it all that day. Pressed my fingers to it like I might have pressed them into Manus's gaping neck. Or whether things were already too far gone by then. I don't know, but I've written it all down anyway, at the very least so I can try to understand myself. To see what exactly it was I did wrong. For what it's worth, I, Dr Fiona Watts, date the happenings on Bone Island from the date of Manus Grady's death – 5th January 2014 – but if you look back, no doubt you will find that this was only the moment when the building wave began to crest.

Chapter Two

'Well, pet. That was a powerful gale last night. Are you all right?' Paula's stepmother Pat opened the front door, dressed in yoga pants and a lemon sweatshirt. The previous year she'd been diagnosed with breast cancer, and Paula tried not to take it for granted that Pat would be there every morning, up and about, well as could be expected. But she was. Even her hair had grown back after the chemo, soft as a baby's.

'We're fine. No harm done.' At least the house had just been renovated when everything went wrong. At least she didn't have to worry about bits of it falling off in the storm – even if it had been done in the hope of selling the place, moving to a new house that wasn't full of memories.

'Graaaaaanny!' Maggie ran over and Pat scooped her up, struggling gamely.

'Oof. There's my wee pet!'

'A bad man was at my window.'

Paula met Pat's eyes over Maggie's red curls. She shrugged. 'Nightmares. Where's Dad?'

'Still upstairs. The ould wind makes his leg play up.'

'I'll leave him be, then. Saoirse's getting her from nursery today, yes?'

'Aye. I've my follow-up appointment.'

'I know. Tell me how it goes, yeah?' It was always a worry, that they'd find something else on the scans. Paula didn't know what she'd do without Pat's presence in her life – her own surrogate mother, and the only grandma Maggie had. So how could she ever tell her father about the note without destroying the two of them?

Maggie's head drooped against Pat's shoulder, which wasn't like her. Usually at this hour of the morning she'd be running round full of beans, while Paula would trail after her, hollow-eyed with insomnia. Pat jiggled her. 'What's the matter, pet?'

Paula stroked Maggie's foot in its little furry boot. 'She was up in the night crying.'

'Scared of the wind? Poor wean.'

Yes, the wind, and imagined horrors Paula knew came from the real, terrible things this family had been through. Too many to bear, she sometimes thought. And yet they did bear it, somehow. She looked at Pat – her stepmother, almost mother-in-law, and many other things besides. She'd be going to see Aidan today after her scan; Paula was sure of it. But she could never bring herself to ask outright how he was, this man who had so nearly been her husband. And so for yet another day, she didn't mention him, or the note, or any of the other stones that sat in her heart, weighing it down.

'It's a shambles, so it is. Half me gutters came down in the night.'

'Bloody sea wall's in bits, too – council are shite at maintaining it.'

As Paula made her way to her desk in Ballyterrin police station, all talk was of the storm. Not one for chit-chat or office friendships, she steered clear, hoping for a quiet morning of emails and reports. She hadn't slept again after re-reading the file, lying awake with her head full of questions and worries.

'You didn't get blown away, then?' A fair-haired woman appeared, coffee cups in both hands, the seams in her grey trousers sharp as the folds of an envelope. DI Helen Corry, head of the local Missing Persons unit, had been Paula's boss before a spectacular career plummet. Her punishment – for not realising that the man she was sleeping with had hacked her emails, derailing a murder case – had been harsh, slamming her back through the ranks she'd fought so hard to climb. But if Paula knew Corry at all, the other woman wasn't going to stay down for long.

'Maggie was a bit upset by the wind, is all.'

'Poor wean.' She handed over a coffee. 'Here you go, you'll need one when you hear what I've got for you.'

'Do I have to? I'm propping my eyes open here.'

'You'll like it, I promise, or your money back.'

Paula sipped the hot liquid, feeling it hit her bloodstream. She hadn't even drunk coffee before Maggie was born, existing only on tea like a true Irish person, but these days she couldn't seem to remember what it was like to not be exhausted all the time. 'Go on then, tell me.'

'Feel like a trip down south?' said Corry casually.

Paula arched an eyebrow. 'Yeah, sure. Perfect time for a getaway, seeing as half the Atlantic coast's busy falling into the sea.'

'I've got a juicy one, though. You know you love a good missing persons'. We've had a request for you to consult.' Corry was pushing her buttons, and Paula knew it, but she'd still bite.

She sat down, as Corry leaned against the dividing wall of her cubicle. 'So?'

'So, there's this English couple living out on some god-forsaken rock in the Atlantic. Bone Island. You know it?'

The name sent a ripple in her stomach like a stone falling into a well. *Bone Island*. The last stop, the last lighthouse in Europe, before the cold gulf of the Atlantic. The end of the known world, for a long time. It was narrow and thin like a bone, but the name didn't come from the shape, rather from the Irish word for 'white'. She turned to switch on her computer, trying to keep her voice light. Corry was nearly impossible to lie to. 'Off the coast of Kerry, yeah?'

'That's right. Only a wee place, a few miles off the coast. Couple of hundred people. Lovely beaches. Anyway, these two are renting the old lighthouse out there. She's the island doctor, didn't turn up for her surgery yesterday. Fiona Watts. The fella's Matthew Andrews, Matt. When the local Garda went out there to check on them the lighthouse was all locked up, no sign of them.'

'Did they go away or something?'

Corry shook her head, a faint gleam in her grey eyes. 'Locked from the *inside*, Maguire. But empty. The Garda broke the door down.'

'Empty. How?'

Corry shrugged. 'Yours to find out, if you want. I've cleared it with Willis. Inter-force cooperation is all back in style again. Next thing you know someone will suggest setting up a cross-border unit.'

Paula didn't smile. It was still a sore point that the cross-border missing persons unit – the MPRU – she'd come home to work at had been scrapped after a year. Leaving her in limbo, back in her home town, tied down once again by all the bonds of family and friends she'd managed to sever at eighteen. 'I don't know . . .'

'Your mate's the one who asked for you. Quinn.'

'Fiacra? Is he in Kerry these days?' Detective Garda Sergeant Fiacra Quinn, once a fresh-faced recruit to their unit, was rising fast through the ranks of the Irish police, moving around the country on a fast-track scheme, different departments, different cases. Hungry for it, the way Paula used to be.

'He must be. You'd go over to the island with him, if you want.'

Paula began to consider it. She'd maybe go for a jaunt if Fiacra was there, catch up, have a look. But there were other things to think about. 'How long would it take?'

'Day or two. Just check it out, see if there's anything untoward. The local fella thinks they've gone into the sea, but that locked door is a bit off. Can someone mind Maggie for you?'

'I suppose Saoirse would keep her, and maybe Dad and Pat . . .'

'Right. You said she was doing grand after the last chemo?'

Why did Paula ever tell Corry anything? The woman forgot nothing, stored it up to use when she needed a favour. 'She's not too bad.' But the illness was not Pat's only problem, of course.

'Grand. Will I tell them you'll come, then? They've only one Garda there, and I think he's a bit out of his depth.'

'I'll have to see. This weather's not the best – what if I get stuck out there?'

Corry gave her a look. 'Not you as well. Met Éireann says the storm'll pass by over the Atlantic. Fly down tomorrow, get a boat out there to the island and just have a look. Your wee pal Quinn will meet you at the airport.'

'All right, fine. But can someone else finish that O'Donnell report? I'm about to put myself to sleep with it.'

'Fine, fine. Wright!'

The young blonde detective came over when called, her own black suit pressed and neat. 'Yes, ma'am? Hiya, Paula – sorry, Dr Maguire.'

Corry said, 'Can you help Maguire here finish her homework?'

'If you like, ma'am. But the switchboards are going crazy. There's a woman on the line thinks she heard, or so she says, "a loud bang, like a bomb going off".' Avril made air-quotes.

Paula frowned. 'A bomb?' Although the Troubles were officially over, a handful of diehards refused to accept that, and it wasn't entirely beyond the bounds of possibility.

Corry snorted. 'Honestly. It's the wind taking their guttering off. You'd think these people hadn't lived through an actual war. Send some uniform down and give them a bollocking about wasting police time, then you finish off this report. I'm sending Maguire over the border.'

'Yes, ma'am.' Avril turned, and Paula saw the flash of the ring she'd worn about her neck since she got engaged at Christmas. Paula's own engagement ring sat in a drawer at home, stuffed away with all the rest of the things she wasn't thinking about right now. She flexed her fingers over her keyboard. Now was not a good time for those thoughts. 'Let me just check with Pat and Saoirse,' she said. 'As long as it's only one night. Two tops.'

'I promise.' Corry understood. After all, she and Paula were both single parents now. She looked at her watch. 'Right, time for my daily tête-à-tête with Willis, better get my garlic and crucifix.' There was no love lost between

Corry and DCI Willis Campbell, the Head of Serious Crime, a fussy stickler of a man who lived for the TV cameras. 'God save us, here he comes.'

DCI Campbell was striding across the office, throwing vicious looks at any members of staff eating cereal or rapidly minimising computer windows or still going on about the bloody storm. 'If we could have some work around here, *thank you*, everyone. Ah, DI Corry, time for a little chat?'

'Just briefing Dr Maguire here on the Bone Island case. I've said you've *kindly* agreed to let her consult.'

Again the name stabbed at her. *Bone Island*. So many years since she'd heard it. The sound of it made her limbs cramp, remembering the grip of icy water around her. Waving back at a white sand beach, so far away.

'Hmm. I suppose you can go, if all your work's finished here?' It looked good for the force if she was working on high-profile cases, but Campbell was not Paula's biggest fan.

'Of course, sir,' she lied. 'Intriguing case.'

He tutted. 'They'll be in the sea, as any eejit could tell you, but just because they're English the Guards have to make a fuss. The press over there have got hold of it already. I'll be in my office if you need me. Monaghan! Can you join us, please?'

He clicked his fingers, and a tall young detective stood up from his desk, buttoning an expensive-looking grey suit. Gerard Monaghan, another former colleague of Paula's from the missing persons' unit, and also Avril's fiancé, was fast becoming Campbell's right-hand man. 'Do you think Willis took him shopping?' Corry whispered to Paula. 'He loves himself in that get-up, doesn't he?'

Paula stifled a laugh as she saw Gerard brush imaginary lint from his shoulder. Passing Avril, he gave her a small wink. Corry made a noise in her throat. 'God save me from men in suits, Maguire. Come back soon from Bogtrotter land, OK?'

As she went, Paula turned back to her computer, gratefully clicking out of a deadly dull report on a missing person from a month ago – the woman had clearly done a runner from her abusive husband, and well done to her – and googled Bone Island. Her mind was already whirring. A lighthouse locked from the inside? Had the couple fallen into the sea? Been pushed? She was itching to take a look, find the clues that had surely been left. But she couldn't just go haring off any more. She had to make sure Maggie was OK.

On the screen, pictures came up of bleached-white sand, deep green water, rocky cliffs. It could have been the Maldives or somewhere. But all the same Paula couldn't help but feel it coiling in her stomach. Bone Island. She knew it, yes, of course she did. She'd gone there years ago, for a day trip, on her last ever holiday with her parents. The famous white sand of Bone Island was the backdrop to that picture where her mother stood, laughing into the wind, her red hair whipped about her. The very last picture ever taken of her.

Fiona

The first time I saw Matt, it was underwater. We were on a diving trip off Sharm el-Sheikh – a place it turned out we both hated for its plastic tourism and armed guards, but loved for the reefs that still darted and teemed, oblivious to all that. I'd been dragged on an over-thirties singles tour by my friend Karen. Karen was a lawyer then, doing something with trusts, and she was desperate, I mean *desperate*, to find a man. She was thirty-five, I was thirty-three, and uneasily starting to realise that maybe it wouldn't happen for me either. Maybe singles holidays and book clubs and pottery weekends were going to be my future. Karen spent a lot of that trip, in between applying factor fifty sun cream and spilling it onto her self-help books, talking about ovarian reserves. Was it too late for us? Did we need to freeze our eggs? I scooped bacteria-ridden ice out of weak cocktails and worried. What if she was right? Karen's now two kids and a banker husband up, living in Guildford and no longer working. We haven't talked in a while. Funny how things turn out. On that Egypt holiday, I wouldn't have thought it was possible I could ever feel jealous of Karen. But here we are.

Especially after what happened on the dive trip on the fourth day. Karen wouldn't come with me – the saltwater might mess up her hair, and she wanted to flirt with some bankers who sat by the pool all day drinking vodka with grim determination. So I was there, buddied up with some nervous girl from Swansea on her first dive, and I ran out of air. Twelve feet down on the reef. I actually didn't check my tank quite as often as I should have, because my God, this reef. Turtles drifting by. Fish like Skittles spilling through the water. The sun playing round the coral, and now and again the light brush of a kelp or fish, like the touch of your lover tempting you to bed.

We saw the shark about ten minutes in. Time seems longer underwater, of course. I was watching an eel poke out of some coral when the world darkened. I knew it. Somewhere deep in my reptile spine I knew and I froze. I'm not scared of them, of course – reef sharks, usually harmless – but my brain didn't know that. And neither did that of Bethan from Swansea, who kicked for the top like a panicky seal, gurgling and shrieking. I heard her muffled voice – *Shark! Shark!* – and the shark, only a little thing, unaware of its terrifying shape, darted off into the gloom. That's when I realised I was *actually* in danger, because the next breath I took was little more than spit and fumes. My buddy had swum for it. And the surface, the sparkling surface where people kicked and floundered, it suddenly seemed a really long way away.

Some of us like near-death experiences. It's why we watch scary films and ride rollercoasters. But when your life is really in danger, that little pleasurable lurch of fear doesn't go away. It just grows and grows, drowning your grown-up modern brain like a crashing wave. *Help. Help. SHIT.* I had no air. I began to kick up, which you're not supposed to, the weights on my ankles feeling a hundred times heavier than they had before. The surface seemed to move away. I didn't. My lungs began to burn and my reptile brain was screaming and my modern brain was thinking *shit I'm going to die here and I never did anything with my ovarian reserve and maybe I should have married my ex-boyfriend Pete even though he was bad in bed and only ever talked about football and SHIT* – and then I saw Matt.

He just appeared out of the vast shadowed darkness of the sea, black-clad and flippered, and then he was shoving his mask in my mouth, almost violently, bruising my lips the way a hard kiss does, and I was sucking in that sweet air, that life, and he held my hand – I felt his warm skin even in the chill water – and we went up, step by step, sharing the mask between us, so I knew that I was breathing him. The feel of his mouth on mine. I could see his eyes through the water. I couldn't even tell their colour, but I knew he wouldn't let me go. And so even before we got out and I sucked some breath in and thanked him and saw his face and his stocky body under the wetsuit, and his sandy hair and blue eyes, I knew this was the man for me. Why else would he have saved my life? Already, even before we reached the surface, relief was popping into my blood like oxygen. I'd found him. I'd found my man and everything else was going to be OK.

The next time I felt that fear, the one that grabs hold of your brain and hijacks it and tells you to for God's sake run – your amygdala, we learned in Anatomy – it was on the island. And Matt was there again. But instead of feeling saved by him, his big, warm hands, his sure eyes, I was running from him. The part of your brain that tells you, phew, false alarm, everything is cool, now survive another day on the savannah – well, it never did kick in this time.

Funny how things turn out, as I say. But I can't blame myself for what happened, not really. There are laws that go way beyond the ones we made in the light and on the dry land, for regulating our little modern lives. Laws like – get the hell out of here or you're going to die. Laws like – fight, Fiona. Fight back or you've had it, and this time, this time as you're drowning among all the pretty fishes, and the weight of the ocean is crushing you, this time Matt won't be coming to save you, because he's the one that's holding you down.

Chapter Three

'Coffee for me. Three sugars. What buns have you?'

The girl behind the counter of the Costa Coffee, a teenager with four rings in her ear, waved a disinterested hand at the display in front of her. Davey took a full twenty seconds to decide, standing with his lips pursed. Paula waited. 'Give me the doughnut then, love.'

'You getting OK?' The girl turned to Paula, who shook her head. Seeing Davey Corcoran choke down a bun was enough to put her right off. Around them, the small concourse of Belfast City airport was constantly in motion, people landing and leaving, running into their family's arms, waving them goodbye.

She turned to the man as they sat down. 'I haven't long, sorry. I've to go down South on a case.'

'That English couple on the island?'

How the hell did he know that? It meant the Bone Island case was likely on the news already. Maybe it would turn out to be a decent one after all. 'Yeah. Though I could do without it, in this weather.' There was a small lie in there that she was allowing herself. Pretending she wasn't dying to get down and see what was going on.

'They'll have gone in the sea, like as not. You'll have a wasted trip, so you will.'

Paula narrowed her eyes, but she didn't have time to

argue it with him. 'Have you anything for me?'

Davey Corcoran, private eye. About a million miles from Tom Selleck, more was the pity. He had ketchup stains down his beige jacket, and his stubby fingers were stained with fag ash. But he seemed to know his stuff, and that was all that really mattered. He came recommended by Colin McCready, the solicitor she'd hired to work on Aidan's case, who had also once, in a different life, been her mother's boss. Davey knew about the note, and he was the only person who did.

He was hoovering up his doughnut, lips shiny with grease. 'Which one do you want first? Now or then?'

'Then, I guess.' Of the two cases he was looking into for her, that was marginally less painful, if only because she'd had twenty years to get used to her mother's continuing absence.

'Subject One.' He always called her that, not *Margaret*, not *your mammy*, and Paula was glad of it, despite the ridiculous pomposity. Oh, how she liked the comfort of official language. He was leafing through his file now, leaving oily prints on it. 'Here we go. A recently uncovered note suggests subject left of her own accord on Thursday, 28 October 1993. Possible reason: fleeing IRA retribution . . .' He droned on, reducing the raw facts of her mother's life to dull paperwork.

It was true the IRA had been watching Margaret Maguire, had come to the house that day looking for her. But a convict called Sean Conlon had told Paula her mother was already gone when they got there. Maybe a lie. She couldn't ask him again, as he was dead, and Aidan awaiting trial for his murder. 'I know all this,' she interrupted. 'Have you anything new for me?'

Davey looked miffed. 'I did find a wee record of an official car going from Larne to Stranraer on the ferry that week. No passport check done. They knew they weren't meant to look too close at some of them, if you see what I mean.'

'So they could have got her out. Her contact.' Whoever it was her mother had been working for. There was an alphabet soup of undercover agencies in Northern Ireland at that time, the lines blurred and changing on a daily basis.

'Could be. And this name you gave me – this Edward. He was real, all right. One of the top spooks in Army Intel back in the nineties.'

The mysterious man in the hat. Her mother's contact for passing on the information she stole from her job. Also her lover, if rumours were to be believed. 'Do you know where he is now, this Edward?'

Davey shook his head absently, eyes on his doughnut. Of course he didn't, that would be too easy. 'He'll be living under some other name, if he's even in the country at all. Lot of ex-spies go overseas, where it's safer. The Ra would still love to put a bullet into anyone who touted back then.'

Tout. One of the worst words you could call someone, during the Troubles. So many theories, questions, mysteries. All Paula knew for sure was this: Margaret Maguire had disappeared sometime on the afternoon of 28 October 1993. And she had left a note for her daughter, then thirteen. Except the daughter would not find the note – knocking it down the back of the washing machine, carelessly sweeping her schoolbag onto the kitchen counter – and for almost twenty years she would think her mother had been abducted and murdered. Maybe by the IRA. Maybe by someone else. Sometimes Paula could hardly believe she'd found it – the first real solid thing in so many years. Maybe that was why she hadn't told anyone but Davey, who couldn't have cared less unless she'd coated it in sugar and deep-fried it. As soon as she did tell someone, as soon as she saw that knowledge on the face of someone she loved, she'd have to feel the full impact of it. And she wasn't ready. Not until she knew more.

'So what now?'

Davey was picking up bits of sugar with a slabbery finger. 'Still trying to trace your man. The Edward character. Got a few leads. Might have to go to London and do some digging.'

Meaning, presumably, she would have to pay for it. So far, Davey had been suspiciously cheap, and Paula was just waiting for the huge bill. Maybe she'd have to sell the house after all to cover it. She nodded, noting with distaste how he'd spewed out sugar grains as he spoke. 'Anything else?'

'Medical records.' He said it so casually she almost didn't hear him at first. 'The subject's, that is.'

'You found her medical records? Er, how?' They hadn't been in the police file. She'd never been sure why, and her sneaky attempts to get them through other means had always failed.

Davey shrugged and slid a piece of yellowing paper across the table. Paula scanned it quickly, seeing nothing of significance. 'So she had some tests done the week before she vanished. What does this chemical name mean?'

'Dunno. I'm not a doctor.'

And Paula knew someone who was, but she couldn't ask Saoirse without arousing suspicion. She picked up the sheets of paper, covered in the scrawl of their old family doctor, Dr Adams. Long dead now, even if he could have told her something. This didn't tell her anything new, and the frustration of it made her want to tear the papers up, scatter the pieces. *Where did you go?* Why bother leaving a note at all, when it told them nothing? 'So what about the other thing?' she asked, as Davey signalled for another sugar-silty coffee. He seemed to run entirely on caffeine and refined carbs.

He burped gently, into his hand. 'Oh, right so. Subject Two.' Otherwise known as Aidan O'Hara, possible love of Paula's life. Not her husband, though he should have been by now. Not Maggie's father, though Maggie believed that he was, and to all intents and purposes he was the only one available. 'This is a sensitive one now, very sensitive. Tricky to get these Provo fellas to talk.'

Tricky was another code-word for 'it'll cost you'. Davey had a reputation for digging up answers to such questions. Alibis, where it seemed there could be none. Witnesses, who miraculously remembered everything about the incident in question when previously they'd been sure they weren't there, or equally miraculously realised they knew nothing, and indeed had been fifty miles away at the time, and furthermore that they really valued their kneecaps. That was why she'd hired him. Because if Aidan could be saved – if it could be proven that someone else had come to that piss-soaked car park and kicked the man to death – Paula was sure the answers would lie deep within the Republican movement. But how to even start proving it?

'I know it's tricky,' she said. 'Aidan – Subject Two, that is – already confessed to beating Conlon up that night, for a start.' Her mind still gave a shudder of horror when she thought of it. Aidan, celebrating his stag do and off the wagon he'd stayed on for two years, attacking Conlon – the man who'd likely killed Aidan's father – kicking him and smashing his head off the tarmac car park. Aidan had come home with bruised knuckles and a bloodied T-shirt. She'd seen those with her own eyes. Paula was getting frustrated with the tangle of clues, every end leading back to the fact that Aidan was about to be in prison for a very long time. 'So what can we do? How can we prove someone else went there to kill him that night?'

There was no CCTV in the bar, and the clientele were all selectively blind or blind-drunk, and wouldn't have seen someone slip into the back car park. Davey didn't look too cast down, however. 'What we need is a tout.'

She flinched at the word – memories of her teenage years, rumours spreading round school that this was why her mother had gone. 'What do you mean?'

'Some fella who's being done for something else, who'll give us a name. Who'll talk.' He leaned over the table for another packet of sugar. 'That's if you really believe Subject Two is innocent.'

Did she? She believed there was a chance he'd left Conlon alive, and someone else had come and finished the job. She also knew how easy it was to kill someone in a fight, the wrong punch or kick shattering the brain, held in its cradle of bone like a ripe plum. 'There's a chance,' she said. 'But how would we find someone? Willis Campbell won't allow any further investigation. He thinks Aidan did it.' Willis did not want the scrutiny of the world on the town – after all, if the IRA had disbanded, how could their members still be executing old grudges? – so he was happy to take the obvious culprit, standing there with blood on his hands. It was a world of trouble otherwise. And there was enough evidence to convict Aidan all right, more than enough, and Aidan himself had confessed, given up.

Davey said, 'Just need to wait for the right person. And Colin's the boy they'd go to, you see, if they need help. As long as the PSNI would listen, there's a chance.'

It seemed the slimmest thread of hope imaginable. 'Is that all? We just have to wait and see if someone gets caught?'

'Well. There's this too.' Casually, Davey slid over another piece of paper, slightly dog-eared.

Paula looked at the official stamp. 'The autopsy report? On Conlon?' She'd never seen this before. For obvious reasons she was not allowed anywhere near the case file.

'Look at the cause of death there.' He pointed with a greasy forefinger; she pulled the page out of his way.

'Asphyxiation? But . . .' She thought Conlon had died of a cerebral haemorrhage. Beaten against the tarmac until his brain exploded. His liver had also been bleeding from where it was stamped on – Aidan's distinctive Converse sole print clearly visible on his body. Her mind was racing. It didn't necessarily mean anything. It could mean he'd choked on his own blood. It could mean he'd suffocated, with broken ribs weighing him down. But it could mean . . .

Davey explained. 'See if someone's lying there on the ground, seven shades of shite kicked out of them? You come along, and instead of helping them up, you just put your hand like so.' He brought his towards Paula as if he might demonstrate, and she moved sharply back. 'Only takes a few seconds, and they can't get a breath, and then they're gone and nobody even knows you were there. See?'

She did see, finally. 'So maybe . . . Aidan didn't do it?'

Davey shrugged. 'There's a chance. That's all. If you want to take it.'

'I want to take it.' What else could she do?

'All right so. Just so's you know, it won't be easy.' He nodded to the departures board. 'You better go and get your flight. Though like I say, they'll be in the sea.'

'We don't know that,' she said, annoyed. 'So you'll keep

looking? For this Edward and for . . . someone to inform on the other case?'

'Aye, I will. On you go now.'

Paula gathered her wheely case and passport and scarf and coat, hustling to the security gates. She just wanted to go, scratch the itch of this case, and come home and sort her life out. Help Aidan, if any help was possible. And hopefully overturn another of the stones that covered her mother's grave. If she even had one, somewhere, anywhere.

Bob

'What did she say?'

Davey Corcoran broke into phlegm-ridden smoker's coughs, and Bob Hamilton held the phone away in disgust. The man was a wreck, but he was meant to be the best. He could find things out, they said, like a ferret in a rabbit warren. Things people would really rather you didn't know. 'She'll go for it. I told her we need a name for who was after Conlon. That we'd have to try and get it from a tout.'

'And you didn't tell her I'm involved?'

'I'm discreet, Sergeant Hamilton, like I told you.' Bob was not a sergeant any more, not since he'd retired two years before, but he still liked the sound of it. As if he still had authority, and power, and knew something or anything at all about what was going on. 'You'll let me have those names then?' Davey said.

The silence stretched. Of course he would, or there'd have been no point in starting any of this. Working through the PI, feeding him information, so that hopefully Paula would never find out what Bob knew. But now it came down to it, Bob found it was hard. So hard to break a promise, after twenty years. 'I'll need to look for the list. Not sure where it is.'

'Soon as possible, then, she wants me to get started.'

'Aye. Right. You'll have to let her pay for some of it, or she'll get suspicious. But not a lot, aye?'

'Aye, aye.' Davey made a sort of snorting noise by way of agreement and they hung up. Bob stood holding the phone, lost in memories.

In his time, police work had been a bit like chess. You couldn't keep everything. You couldn't possibly win with all your pieces safe. Friends were going to die; murderers were going to walk. Everyone was informing on everyone else, half the police were corrupt and half the terrorists secretly MI5 agents. So you did what you could. You held firm, to your own rules. And what you did was you kept a list of people who owed you a wee favour. It was what got you through the nights of black terror, crouched in the armoured jeep as it rocked with bullets and hoping to God the people outside hadn't got a rocket launcher. It was what got you up every day, checking under your car for a bomb, looking over your shoulder for a gunman, saying goodbye to your wife knowing you might not make it back that night. You kept a wee list of favours, and you hoped that when it was needed, enough of the right people would owe you one.

The clock ticked. He found he was haunted by her – the red of her hair, the smell of lilies on white skin, just as he had been these twenty years. *You promised.* Aye, he'd promised, and so far he hadn't broken it. He waited for a moment, to be sure Linda wasn't back from church, and then he went down on his knees and pulled out the bottom drawer of the sideboard. Where they kept the fancy cutlery, for if people came over. A wedding present, stored clean and tidy, even though no one had come since Ian was born, over thirty years ago. He took the drawer right out, and there it was, in the space between the frame and the carpet – a creased white envelope, and on it a scribbled list of names, written in the hand of a dead man.

Chapter Four

'Are you allowed to do that?' Holding her in-flight copy of
Psychology Today over her head against the driving rain at
Cork airport, Paula peered into the police car, which was
marked *Attending Official Business* and parked in the taxi
rank.

Detective Sergeant Fiacra Quinn turned down the car
stereo, which was pumping out something waily with guitars
(Paula couldn't seem to keep up with young people's music
these days). 'Amn't I picking up our very important expert
on missing persons? Have you a bag?'

'Only a wee one.' She hefted it into the back of the car
and got in the front. 'What's this you're listening to? Johnny
and the Whingers?'

'It's Kodaline, duh. Kind of famous.'

'These days, if it's not on CBeebies, I won't have heard
of it.'

Fiacra pulled out of the car park. 'How is the wee one?'

'She's grand. Nearly three now.'

'And what about . . . you know. Everything else?'

She stared out the window at the rain. 'No change. The
trial'll be next year sometime.'

'Right.' She felt Fiacra's awkwardness. How did you,
a police officer, broach the matter of your colleague's fiancé
– and was he still that if the wedding had been cancelled? –

being charged with murder? 'And have you heard from the boss at all?'

Meaning Guy Brooking. When the missing persons' unit was disbanded, Guy had gone back to London, working on gang crime. Fiacra's tone was light, but Paula wasn't fooled. Everyone knew she and Guy had not been able to keep their relationship strictly professional. 'Not for a while, no.' Last time she'd seen Guy, he'd offered her a job. London, a new start, more money, a chance to take Maggie away from Ballyterrin, a town that to Paula was like stepping in a puddle that turned out to be a chasm going down and down forever. But then she'd found the note, and so she was still stuck, unable to go, unable to make sense of her life there.

He cleared his throat. 'How's everybody else up there, then?'

'Well, Avril's getting on great in CID. And . . . did you know they'd the wedding planned?'

'Aye, I did. Great news.' He wore his fair curls short these days, and it made him look harder. Older. There was no sign on Fiacra's face that he'd once been in love with Avril, or that it had been him who'd broken up her first engagement. Maybe he still was in love with her. Paula herself knew how stubbornly these things could linger, long past the point of any hope or sense.

She changed the subject. 'Tell me about this case, then. Will we be able to get over today?'

'Ferries were running this morning. They don't mind a bit of rain, but if the wind picks up we'll be in diffs, so we will. Latest forecast said the storm'd go over us, so fingers crossed we can get there and back.'

'Let's hope so. How long have they been missing?'

'We think since Monday. Fiona Watts was seen getting

her shopping in the Spar out there Monday night. Then she never turned up for work yesterday, so Rory McElhone, that's the local Garda, he went to their place to check on them. The lighthouse was all locked up, so him and a few fellas broke in.'

'Any signs of disturbance in the house?'

'Nothing except for the bulb of the light itself. It's been broken.'

'Broken how?'

'Shattered, I'm told. I've not been over myself yet. You know the place was locked from the inside? The key was sitting in the lock and everything.'

She thought about it. 'Whose key? I assume they both had one.'

Fiacra gave her an appreciative look. 'No flies on you. It was his key, had his company keyring on it. Her key's not there.'

So maybe she hadn't even been home that day. 'Nothing else weird?'

Fiacra shook his head. 'There's been search teams all round the island – with the weather, we were thinking they'd maybe had some kind of accident, slipped into the sea or that, but, you know. That doesn't explain the door. Their boat's gone too. They'd a wee dinghy, normally kept it pulled up on the shore near their lighthouse.'

'Have forensics been in?'

'We're taking someone over with us today. Had to fight for it – if it's an accident all the energy needs to go on searching for them, not preserving the scene.'

Paula looked at the side of his face. 'But you don't think so?'

'Dunno. It's weird, is all. That's why I wanted you down.

You live for this kind of thing, aye?'

True, it was the kind of puzzle Paula's mind loved to worry at, like a dog with a chew-toy. She was already running over possibilities. Was there another way out of the lighthouse? Could someone have locked it from the outside and made it look like the opposite? Most of all, the question that tugged her down like a drowning current – *where are you?* And once she'd asked that, she could never stop until she knew. As they drove the trees buckled alarmingly in the wind, and Paula for a moment thought – *I better tell Aidan to check our gutters.* Then it hit her again, a loss so bone-deep she had to turn her face to the window, gasping in air. *Stop it, Maguire.* He was gone, she couldn't see him any more, and she had to just deal with that and get on with her life. Still she couldn't help the niggling guilt: was she wrong to go away – could Maggie cope with more disruption just now?

But Paula knew she had to. A lighthouse. Locked from the inside. How? She'd been snagged now, and she'd have to follow this ball of thread to the centre of the labyrinth.

'This is the ferry?'

'It's only a wee island, Maguire, what did you expect?'

They had now arrived in the harbour at Dunquin, which was little more than a stone wall against the sea, down a steep one-track lane. The roll-on roll-off ferry rose and fell alarmingly with the swell of the waves. A queue of anoraked travellers were already waiting to get on; islanders, probably, plus a few hardy tourists trekking out for the day. On the slope of the dock was a small cafe selling teas and bacon rolls. It was basically a Portakabin with a steel roof attached, making a semi-sheltered waiting area that was next to useless in the horizontal rain. A man with a bum-bag collected cash and issued paper tickets on the deck of the ferry. Fiacra parked. 'It's backed up because they stopped early yesterday. But I'll get us on.'

'More Garda privilege, eh?'

'Well, we need to get out there. Fiona and Matt could be in a bad way if they've had an accident.'

'What happens if the ferries don't run? Is there another way over?' Paula got out, pulling a knitted black hat over her flying red hair, and wondering why she'd thought a hot-pink raincoat was a good choice with her colouring.

Fiacra had to raise his voice over the drumming of the rain on the car roof. 'Nope, you're basically stuck. Islanders are used to it – there's a pub on the quays will put people up if they need it. Or some have their own boats – but if it's not safe it's not safe. And there's the police helicopter for emergencies. That's about your lot.'

It seemed so strange, in this world of instant updates and ubiquitous Wi-Fi, to be somewhere you could genuinely get stranded. Across the rainswept bay, several hulks of dark rock sat in the mouth of the sea. The furthest one, Paula knew, was their destination. Bone Island. As she looked, cold rain ran down her neck, and a marrow-deep chill seemed to settle into her own bones.

Chapter Five

The forensics officer they'd met at the ferry was an older woman with a sensible haircut and even more sensible raincoat. Paula regretted the hot-pink choice again (never let a toddler pick your clothes was the lesson). She'd also brought along a little tool-kit, which now sat by her feet on the Bone Island quay. The hour-long journey had been turbulent, with waves licking over the prow of the boat and soaking the deck, and several people puking in the chemical toilet, but apparently this was nothing out of the ordinary. As they waited to get off – you had to dash between the waves that swamped the ferry's ramp on each swell – Paula was shivering. It seemed several degrees colder out on the island. But it was stunning, even under roiling grey skies and with an uneasy sea tossing the boats in the harbour, so they scraped together with a rusty sawing noise. The white sand which gave the island its name was like sugar, and the water in the harbour a deep, clear green. Fiacra examined his phone. 'No signal. Thought as much. The local fella's meant to be meeting us.'

Sure enough, a very muddy jeep was drawing up to the harbour and a ginger-haired man was getting out of it, pulling a navy Garda fleece around him. Paula was always pleased to see a fellow redhead, and felt well-disposed to him already. 'Hiya,' he called over. 'Youse are from the mainland?'

'Aye. Detective Sergeant Fiacra Quinn. Don't think we've met – they have me in Killarney since the New Year. Doing the country stint.' Fiacra was angling for a transfer back to Dublin once he'd served his time. He wanted the big glory cases, and down the country you mostly got drunken fights or accidents with farm vehicles. A juicy double missing persons' like this wasn't common – he must be feeling like he'd won the Lottery.

The other Garda shook Fiacra's hand. He was wearing wool gloves. 'Ah, sure, some of us like the country stint so much we stay.'

Fiacra said, 'You know Anne Malone?' The forensics woman, who Paula still hadn't heard speak, nodded to the Garda.

He turned to Paula. 'And this must be the expert I've been hearing so much about?'

Paula resisted the urge to put herself down. 'I've done a fair bit of missing persons' stuff, yeah. Fiacra and I were in the MPRU together.'

'Well, I hope you've not had a wasted journey. Like as not they've had an accident.' Rory McElhone had a firm hand-shake, and was tall enough to look five foot ten Paula right in the eyes. His were warm and brown, like those of a loyal dog, and his face was lightly sprinkled with sandy freckles. 'Come on, get in the car before this wind blows you away.'

Anne got in the front with her little box, and Rory drove off at a great rattle into the island. They passed a huddle of buildings, a Spar and a shuttered-up craft shop, a pub signposted DUNORLAN'S, its umbrellas flapping forlornly in the wind. Paula recognised it, though she'd been here only once, twenty years ago. A sunny day then, between skiffs of rain. They'd gone to the pub for a drink. A coke for her, a pint for her dad, and a juice for her mother. Strange, the things you remembered.

The interior of the island was a winding stony road, and the Jeep wheels kicked up muddy water as they drove. They passed teams of people in anoraks trudging across the fields, whacking at long grass. Looking for any sign of Matt and Fiona. 'So tell us about the missing couple?' Paula leaned over, looking at the pale back of Rory's neck. She wondered how old he was – maybe thirty?

'Fi and Matt moved over here three, four months back. He's an ecologist, so Enviracorp hired him to monitor the puffins and that on the island.'

'What's Enviracorp?'

Rory glanced in the mirror, as if Paula ought to have known that. 'Seaweed processing company. They've a base out here, north side of the island. And Fiona's a doctor, and we didn't have one since our old one died last year, so it was kind of handy enough. They seem to like it over here. Sort of outdoorsy types. Surfing, climbing, all that jazz.'

'They weren't married?'

'No, but they seemed tight enough. I think they were together three years or something.'

'How old?'

'Fi's thirty-six, and Matt's, he's like thirty-eight, I think?'

'You know them pretty well, then,' said Fiacra, scrubbing at his fogged-up window to look out. 'Do you know everyone here?'

'Aye, it's only a small place, you know. We don't get many outsiders. I liked having a chat with them, I guess. We'd have a drink the odd time in the pub – they loved all that diddly-dee and pints of Guinness.' He'd switched to the past tense, Paula noticed.

Fiacra said, 'So what you're saying is, it's out of character they'd be gone like this?'

'Yeah, it is. Fiona never missed a day of work before. Probably in her whole life, she's one of those real diligent types, you know.' He parked up. 'Anyway, we're here, so youse can see for yourselves.'

When they got out of the car, Paula could feel the press of the wind, and almost staggered against it. Rory McElhone caught her eye, but didn't offer help. This side of the island looked right into the Atlantic, with no shelter or buffer against its rage. Once inside the lighthouse – which stood high on the western cliffs, white and slender against the grey sea – Anne sprang into life, issuing orders and passing out foot covers. 'Though no doubt you've already tramped all through the place,' she said to Rory, somewhat fiercely. Her voice was dry and precise, posh Dublin.

'Aye, well, we had to check they were OK first. Anyway I don't carry a boiler suit or anything like that. Not much call for it out here.'

'Who else was in here? I'll need elimination prints.'

'Seamas Fairlinn, he owns the pub, and the young fella who works there. Colm Meehan. That's all.'

The lighthouse was built with two small rooms on each floor, on either side of the spine of a winding stone staircase. On the ground floor, just inside the cheerful red-painted door, was the kitchen and a utility room filled with raincoats and boots, walking poles, a surfboard, and even a wetsuit, sprinkled with sand. The place smelled of damp and salt-water. Fiacra said, 'So what happened, Garda McElhone? Can you talk us through it?'

Rory stood in the small hallway between the rooms, hovering as if reluctant to go in. 'Fi's first patient called into my office yesterday morning to say she wasn't in work. I went to check on her, she wasn't in her surgery, so I came out here. When I got no answer I went down to Dunorlan's, asked for some volunteers. Came up again with young Colm and Seamas. He's out leading a search party right now.'

'And you broke in?' Paula moved past him to the kitchen. It was clean and tidy, a flowered tea towel hanging over the back of one kitchen chair. Fiona and Matt were either very organised, or they'd had time to get sorted before they disappeared. On the draining rack stood one blue mug.

Rory sounded slightly defensive. 'Aye. We forced the lock. We were worried about them, see. These old doors are flimsy anyway, one good boot will get you in.' Outside, the splintered lock had been bolted over with a new padlock, and a bit of police tape fluttered ineffectually in the wind.

Anne was poking about the kitchen, spraying things and taking little samples from the furniture and windows, which looked out on the green sweep of the Atlantic. She opened the cupboard doors, and Paula saw the kitchen seemed to be stocked with pre-packaged supermarket food. Gluten-free, dairy-free, nut-free. The kind that cost a good two pounds extra per packet.

'Some view they had up here,' said Fiacra, his voice floating down the stairs.

'Aye, but it's fierce cold and exposed,' said Rory, his eyes following Anne as she worked. 'Lonely, you know.' Even inside the thick walls they could feel the wind rocking and moaning, licking its way into every little crevice. The place was freezing, Paula thought, huddling her jacket around her.

The next floor up had a bedroom and living room with an open fire, the ashes cold in the grate. Everything was neat here too, the bright red duvet pulled flat, books and magazines in tidy stacks beside the two armchairs. Bowls of candy-striped stones had been set around the place, as if someone had been aiming for what magazines might call a *relaxed beach house vibe*. The place was full of little touches, scented candles and wooden bowls and prints of Irish seascapes, the kind of home-making decoration Paula had no knack for. Her own house still contained all her parents' tacky seventies pictures, from the Sacred Heart of Jesus to the framed shot of the Pope's visit. It was cosy, romantic. As if arranged by someone who thought people might be seeing it, judging them by the smoothness of their duvet. Paula's best friend Saoirse would be sticking it on her Pinterest board. She asked, 'Would anyone know if things were missing – their clothes, toiletries, that sort of thing? Anyone a regular visitor?'

Rory shrugged. That was a shame. Paula went in to look closer. There was a small bathroom off the bedroom, with seventies fittings. Again, everything was clean, even spotless. Paula looked for obvious gaps and found none – two tooth-brushes, toothpaste, some items of make-up, lots of vitamins and supplements, electric razor. A woman's gold watch sat on the bedside table, beside a framed photo of Matt and Fiona. A white middle-class couple, her with shoulder-length dark hair she wore tied back, and a calm, capable smile. Him taller, fair hair, stocky build. They were wearing North Face jackets – hers lime green, his red – and smiling in a selfie from the top of a mountain somewhere. 'They look so happy.'

Rory didn't reply. What could you say? Happiness didn't protect you from winding up in a case file. Smiling faces in a picture didn't mean the truth wasn't lurking behind them, dark and coiled. Paula had seen more such photos on

Instagram. Fiona had started an account – @islanddoc – three months before, and filled it with shots of seals on the rocks, white-topped waves green as glass at their core, fishermen landing their catch in the harbour. The two of them posing in their small boat, which they'd called the *London Lass*. All hashtagged *island nature rurallife* and so on. The kind of thing Paula really couldn't be doing with, but she had to admit it helped with the investigation. In a missing persons case, when all that was left behind was silence, you could sometimes find a clue in the chatter people put online. A nugget of truth among the hashtags and one-upmanship and bragging. According to Fiona, their life together had been perfect.

'What's up there?' Fiacra gestured to the next floor, snapping at his gloves. Above their heads, the dome of the building soared, a skeleton of metal beams.

Rory nodded his head. 'Lighthouse.'

'It's still running?'

'Oh aye. All automated these days, but a fella comes in every so often to check the bulb and that. It runs on a generator. That's how we knew something was up with Matt and Fi, you see. It wasn't just her being late to work – the light had gone dark.'

Paula was already starting up the stone staircase. 'We heard it was broken?'

'You'll see. Go on up.'

The floor of the third storey sparkled, even in the low grey light. Smashed glass, ground in places into a fine powder, as if someone had walked all over it. The great bulb was empty and dark, and around it, in the wider glass bubble they stood in, you could see nothing but sea and sky, the edges smudged with mist. Paula felt dizzy just looking at it, the space, the light. It was warmer in there, the meagre heat of the day trapped under glass. Outside, a thin strip of balcony ran around the lighthouse.

'Someone smashed it?' she said.

'Aye, we found it like this, so we didn't touch a thing.'

'We need Anne to take a look at this. There might be foot impressions.' Fiacra called down. 'Anne, would you come up here a wee second?'

Her voice floated up, dry and professional. 'I think we should focus here for now. There's blood in the kitchen.'

Fiona

'Bone Island,' I said. 'You seriously want me to go and live on a place called Bone Island? There wasn't one called *Scary and spooky island of death*?'

Matt never rose to me. Sometimes, many times, I wished he would. 'It's from the Irish, babe. It just means White Island – *Eilean Ban*. They have this amazing white sand there, and a coral beach, even. I'll show you pictures.'

'How long have you been planning this?' I was in the living room of our London flat, on the stained grey sofa the landlord had provided. Matt was in the kitchen. The place was so small we could have a full conversation like this. It was one of the many things I missed about our old place, our lovely two-bed Victorian conversion near Cambridge Heath station – the ability to be alone, to put walls around me. But we couldn't go back there; the police said it was too dangerous after everything that happened, and we couldn't afford a two-bed now. In the past few years, house prices had risen around our heads like floodwater.

'I haven't been planning it,' he said placidly. 'I just thought I'd see what they were offering. And it's good. It's really good, babe.'

I drank some of my herbal detox tea. It was disgusting. 'A job?'

'More than a job. My dream job. Environmental impact study. The company are harvesting seaweed, extracting minerals, and they don't want to hurt the seabird population out there. There's puffins! You love puffins!'

Yes, I'd loved them on our trip to Iceland, peeping out from rock faces while I sat safely on a boat, but that didn't mean I wanted to live with them. Matt went on, 'So they want me to head that up. Protect the wildlife. And there's a relocation package, and a housing allowance, and they'll even give us a boat! Our own boat, babe!'

'What about me? I can't do nothing on an island while you crawl about looking at bird nests all day.'

Matt smiled. He wasn't a guileful man. He just got happy about things. 'They said their old doctor died last year. Since then they just have someone visit once a week, and it gets tough in winter when they're cut off. So . . . how would you fancy being the island doctor?'

The island doctor. Sounded like an HBO miniseries. I pictured myself in the cold, clean air, steering a boat around some rocks, clutching my medical bag as people looked to me for salvation. 'I don't know if I'm even allowed to work in Ireland,' I tried.

'Babe, of course you are. They need doctors everywhere. And what could possibly come up on an island that you haven't seen in central London?' (It almost kills me, remembering that. But we couldn't have known, at that point.) 'You know, it might even be good for you, get away from . . . everything.'

He didn't say it. He never reproached me for it, for Anika and what happened after, even though we'd lost our house and had to move to this crappy rental and I was making so much less money now; even though he'd been interviewed by the police; even though we'd had the stones and graffiti and one time, the lit firework through our letterbox. He never said a word. But it was always there between us, like a pebble in a shoe, the sharp edges of it pushing us apart.

I said I would think about it. Usually that meant no. But Matt had to leave early the next day, for a survey of the Highland otter population. This was the way jobs worked when you were a London-based ecologist. He went, and I stayed, and I tried to ignore the feeling between us, that he was always pulling away from me, kicking to the surface while I was weighed down. I took the bus to work in Stepney – I'd given up cycling when I'd been knocked off my bike by a bin lorry the month before. I wasn't hurt beyond a sprained wrist and all the skin scraped off one palm, but the lorry hadn't even stopped. That day I saw thirty-six patients. Thirty-seven if you counted the baby in Ruma Suntharalingham's stomach. Her eighth. Ruma is thirty-five and nearly died having the last one, pre-eclampsia, and I tried to tell her all this again, through the nurse that speaks Bengali, that she needed to use contraception in future, and it didn't matter what her husband said, that if she didn't she would die and leave her children motherless, that she might not even survive this one, and she just looked at me with her hand on her belly until I sent her off with her ultrasound appointment and vitamins. If it hadn't been for the Anika mess I'd have put her on the pill anyway as soon as she had the baby. She'd never think to check what the brand name meant. I didn't think she could even read, and it could have saved her life. I wonder what happened to her, sometimes.

When I finally got time for a loo visit, four hours later, I passed Sharon Cole and her daughter Meegan waiting in the corridor. Sharon was twenty. Meegan was four and I'd referred her to social services three times for strange bruises and once a broken arm. Not enough evidence. Must keep familial bonds where possible. And when Meegan gets killed one day by Sharon's latest boyfriend, the media will ask why didn't the doctor see? Why didn't the social worker stop it? Never, why did the mother let this happen? Why do some people have children so quickly and so easily, and others can't? Others who would be good parents, and make organic food and get vaccinations and who know how to do the Heimlich manoeuvre – why can they not?

In the loo I did what I do every week (because you never know), peed on a stick, set my phone alarm for two minutes (people tried the door four times but tough, they could wait). Negative. I knew it would be negative – we'd not found time to have sex in three weeks, of course it would be negative – but all the same I felt another alternative future die inside me. The one where I'd already planned my maternity cover and thought about moving out of London, even had a quick look on Rightmove. It wouldn't happen, now.

Later, home alone with an M&S ready meal, watching as people on TV made elaborate cakes in competition with each other, then going to bed with the sirens and street lights outside, I suddenly sat up and googled Bone Island. It was just as Matt said. The beaches were like sugar, the water so green and clear. *Population – 276*, I read. And I thought – if it was just me and Matt out there, and 276 people, well, surely that was giving this whole baby thing the best possible shot?

When I went to sleep the traffic noises melted into the sound of lapping waves, and I woke with a smile on my face, which didn't fade despite the hour-long bus ride in the traffic without a seat, and Dr Khan who threatened to report me for even daring to hint that someone with seven kids might consider an abortion, and the way London smelled of old fried onions and armpits.

So that's how it happened. How Matt and I somehow went from being one of those couples who talk all the time about jacking in their jobs and having adventures, to actually doing it. Enviracorp were true to their word, arranging a house – a lighthouse! – flights, shipping, and even a job for me in the tiny island surgery. I'd see patients three mornings a week, and the rest of my time was my own. Time! I hardly knew what I'd do with time. Back then, when I barely had a moment all week to phone my mother or wash my hair, time seemed like the greatest luxury of all. Of course, a wiser person might have pointed out the old Irish proverb – *idle hands are the devil's playground.*

Chapter Six

There were traces everywhere. A dab on the shabby-chic green cupboards, a streak on the stone-tiled floor, even a small drop on the ceiling. Anne had sprayed Luminol and closed the blinds, so the splashes of blood glowed white, like phosphorescence under the waves.

'That's a fair bit,' said Fiacra, in his calm way.

Anne nodded. Her voice was muffled inside her white suit. 'You'd need a spatter expert over to be sure – could be a false positive – but it's a fairly serious injury, I'd say. More than a knick when you're chopping vegetables.'

'Life-threatening?'

'Maybe. We can try to get scrapings for blood type, but it's been washed off, as you can see. Though they never get all of it. I don't know why they even try, to be honest.'

Over the years Paula had learned how impossible blood was to clean, working its way into every small groove and crevice, lurking like the truth. Somebody had bled in this kitchen, and somebody had tried to clean it up. That told her this wasn't a simple tragic accident, a drowning in the storm, a fall. She could almost smell it, with that instinct you picked up after thousands of missper cases. Which ones were your standard domestic – a teenage row, an absconding husband, a wandering grandma – and which were something else. The ones that when you plunged into them just kept going, deep and dark as the sea. And despite the weather, despite all the talk of accidents, she was almost sure this case was one of those. 'I guess you'll be a while here, Anne. In the meantime, can we see outside?'

It wasn't much, the island. No more than three miles along, most of the shoreline grey jagged cliffs, with the odd beach of that pure white sand. The waves were picking up as she and Rory peered over the cliff. It was a sheer drop down to the water, boiling restlessly, and the ground around it was all sharp stones and exposed rock face. Paula had to shout over the wind. 'Are those puffins?' Down below she caught flashes of white against the grey. Little black eyes.

'Yep,' shouted Rory. 'Matt was over here to monitor them.'

'For Enviracorp, you said? Can you tell me more about them?'

'Dunno. They do something with seaweed – taking minerals out of it or some such.'

'And do the locals mind?'

'There was a bit of bad feeling about the land sales – some people were canny and got theirs offloaded fast, other people missed the boat – but apart from that, they've been OK. There aren't many jobs out here, as you can imagine, so it brings in money, which we could be doing with.'

'They employ locals?'

'Some. Admin and manual labour, mostly – lifting the seaweed, transporting it. Also they have some foreign labourers brought in, that caused a bit of a stir. Unusual round these parts, you know.'

Paula moved back from the cliff, feeling the fierce push of the wind. She could easily imagine it was strong enough to blow her right over. 'Can you tell me who else is on the island? There's not that many, right – we could get a list of everyone?'

Rory had his hands in the pocket of his black raincoat, his face hidden by the tightened hood. 'Aye, I can try. There's just the locals, really, some execs at the plant, and the odd foreign worker like I said. But they usually come in shifts, sleep at the Enviracorp base, then go off again. They don't mix much.'

'And Matt and Fiona.'

He turned his face away. 'Aye. Matt and Fiona.'

'Any shops or businesses, anything like that?'

'At the harbour you've a few cafes, my station – though it's basically one room in the tourist office – a B&B in the summer, the pub, and the Spar. And the church and community centre, of course, and the primary school is there too. And Fi's surgery.'

'I'd like to speak to anyone who knew Matt and Fiona well. What else did they do?'

He shrugged. 'What is there to do out here? In winter, you go to the pub, or you hunker down and read books, watch films. Wait for spring.'

It seemed a startlingly small life, nothing but the two of you and the wind and sea. They were at the door of the lighthouse again now, and Paula was looking forward to some shelter. She'd already lost all feeling in her ears and hands. But as she reached for the broken handle, she heard the sound of a car approaching. Another Land Rover, like Rory's, was pulling up in such a hurry the wheels threw up gravel. The man driving was about fifty, craggy face, grey hair, Barbour jacket.

He rolled his window down, his eyes skipping over Paula.

'They're over from the mainland then?' Addressed to Rory.

Paula opened her mouth to answer but at that point Fiacra tore open the door of the lighthouse. His fair hair was pushed back by the goggles he'd put on to help Anne. 'Was that a car? Oh, hello.'

Rory did brief introductions. 'Seamas Fairlinn. Detective Sergeant Quinn and Dr Maguire.'

Paula tried to fit him into the picture she was putting together of the island. Owned Dunorlan's. Also one of the men who'd helped Rory break down the door of the lighthouse. 'You better come to the village,' Seamas said grimly. 'One of the search parties pulled someone out of the sea.'

Paula registered Rory behind her, a sudden freezing of his limbs, a brief stilling. Of course, he had known these people, they'd even been friends. She had to remember everything was much more personal out here. 'Man or woman?' she asked.

'Man.'

'Matt?' Rory asked quietly. Paula was thinking hard. If it was Matt, he'd surely be dead by now, assuming he'd gone into the sea sometime on Monday night.

Seamas started his car again. 'Whoever it is, he isn't dead. Follow me.'

Chapter Seven

Rory turned his own jeep sideways onto the paved surface of the harbour. 'They'll have taken him into the pub. It's the warmest place on the island. Come on.'

She could see why as they entered, Fiacra behind, and felt the heat of the huge turf fire. The place was gloomy and beer-soaked as only an Irish pub could be. On the ground, with a middle-aged woman leaning over him while two other men looked on, was a slumped figure who was very definitely not Matt Andrews. The older man with him – weather-beaten, fiftyish, in salt-stiffened overalls and reeking of fish – said something incomprehensible. Irish? English? Paula couldn't tell.

Seamas, who was standing back near the door, said, 'That's Paddy, one of the lobster fishers. Says he pulled this fella out of the sea over by the east beach. He was out searching – thought it was Matt or Fiona at first.'

'We think he came off a fishing boat,' said the woman from where she knelt, taking the man's pulse. 'South American, I'd say.' The man was in a sorry state. He wore waterlogged overalls and a thick jumper, but his brown, gnarled feet were striped with cuts and sores, as were his hands. Older cuts, and shiny scar tissue, which hadn't come from this recent dip in the sea. His eyes were shut but he was breathing, shallow and wet. The woman – large old-fashioned glasses, bobbly pink jumper – stood and sized up Paula and Fiacra. 'Oona Mulvaney. I run the Spar. You'd be from the mainland?'

'Yes, hello.' Paula stared at the man. 'Is he all right?'

The other person standing there was a young lad with a beer towel tucked into the waistband of his jeans, wearing a Kerry football jersey. His handsome face was pale with shock. 'Is he dead, like?'

Seamas tutted. 'Don't be daft, Colm, you can see the man's breathing. But we'll need to get him to hospital.'

Rory stirred. 'I'll ring over. Is your phone working?'

Colm, who must be the barman, pointed vaguely to the back. 'You're sure he's not gonna die, cos you know after last time . . .'

'He's not going to die,' said Oona briskly. 'He's just had a shock, poor man. I'm sure this isn't what they sign up for when they come over to work.'

'They know what they're doing,' said Paddy, in sing-song English, his voice thick as turf smoke. 'Shouldn't take the jobs if they don't want the consequences. What do you expect if you'll work for fifty pee so?'

'Now, now, Paddy,' called Rory from the phone. 'Air ambulance won't come out in this wind. We've to put him on the ferry and they'll meet us at the dock.'

Paula was struggling to follow this, and felt very much out of place. She could see from Fiacra's face he did too, and didn't much like it. He leaned over the half-drowned man and cleared his throat; self-consciously said something in Spanish. He caught Paula's look. 'What? Had a Colombian girlfriend for a while there is all.'

The man gave a low moan, and his dark eyes flickered open. Paula moved back slightly – the last thing he needed was all of them gawping at him as he came round.

She spoke to Oona, who had also drawn back, her hands working at each other in anxiety. 'You said you run the Spar, yes? You saw Fiona Watts in there on Monday night?'

'That's right. She bought some veg and bits and pieces. I thought it was strange, now, to see her in there. Normally she doesn't show her face much and—'

Rory cut across, moving them aside. 'Give him some space there. Colm, go and get the stretcher, will you?'

Then there was the noise of a car sloshing through puddles outside, and the door was thrown open. Everyone but Paula and Fiacra seemed to react as another woman came in; moving back, letting her take over. Seamas and she exchanged a look. She was also around fifty, Paula thought; tall with long, greying hair. Her clothes marked her as an islander – muddy boots, waterproof trousers, and a thick jumper with a raincoat on top – but when she spoke it was with an American accent. 'What have we here then?'

The others seemed relieved to see her, Oona almost giving her a hug (in Ireland this passed for breaking down in tears in someone's arms). 'Came off the boats, we reckon. One of yours, maybe?'

'Not that I know of, no.'

Without taking off her coat, she bent down to the man and pressed a large, capable hand to his neck. 'Tachycardic.' She glanced at Fiacra. 'What's he been saying?'

'I can't get much sense out of him, I don't really speak—'

The man fluttered his eyelids again and all of a sudden tried to sit up with one big salty roar. Seawater spluttered down his front. Paula jumped – so did the young barman – but the newly arrived woman took it in her stride, patting his back as if he was a colicky baby. 'There, there. We'll look after you now.' She looked up and frowned. 'Where's Seamas?'

Paula looked round, realising he was gone, the door swinging. Strange. Colm said, 'Away home, maybe, to check on wee Sammy. Grainne's sick today, like.'

The woman nodded. 'Well, we have to get this man off as soon as possible. I've asked our captain to bring the company boat around, with our on-site nurse too. We'll get him over to hospital.'

Fiacra looked cross. 'Ma'am, we've already arranged to take him on the ferry. I'm Detective Sergeant Quinn and I—'

'Looking for Matt and Fiona, yes? Good, good. Everyone wants them found, soon as possible. We've sent as many staff as we can to the search effort.'

'And you are . . . ?'

She blinked for a moment, as if she'd expected him to know already, then clasped his hand in a firm grip. 'Dr Monroe. Head of Operations at Enviracorp.' She glanced at Paula. 'This must be your colleague.' Paula waved quickly, hoping to avoid a bone-crushing handshake. 'We're glad you've come. If we can find Matt and Fiona before the worst of the storm hits, there's a chance it might not be too late.'

'You think they've had an accident, then?' asked Paula. Everyone out here seemed to lean that way.

'I can't imagine what else it could be. We'll do all we can to help. Now, let's get this poor man sorted. Is he trying to talk?'

He breathed some words out through his cracked lips, and everyone else leaned in too, though they didn't understand.

'He did come off a boat,' said Fiacra. 'I think that's what he said.'

Paddy the fisherman nodded, as if to say he'd told them so. 'Blow-ins is what they are. Taking the jobs from decent Irishmen.'

'Whist now,' scolded Oona. 'Did he fall off in the wind, is that it?'

Fiacra said something in stumbling Spanish and listened to the response. 'He says . . . he jumped off.'

'He jumped off? In those seas?' Paula didn't know much Spanish, but she recognised the sign of the cross the man was making. Of course, he was probably Catholic. Fiacra frowned, listening, as the man continued to cross himself. Over and over. And over.

'What's he saying?' The nervous barman licked his lips.

'He says . . . the men on the boat were mad. They started to . . .' Fiacra frowned again, and repeated what he'd said for confirmation. He sounded doubtful. 'He says he had to jump off, because they were going mad. They were . . . I think he said possessed.'

Here the man sat up a little, and repeated a word in Spanish for emphasis, which they all seemed to recognise. 'Diablo. *Diablo*.' His voice came out used up, almost drowned altogether in his throat.

Paula didn't understand the rest. But it didn't matter – she got the meaning. The man was saying the devil had been on his fishing boat, and whatever had happened was so bad he'd flung himself into storm-tossed seas rather than stay on it.

Dr Monroe cleared her throat. 'Poor man, he's delirious. Saltwater will do that to you. Come on, let's get him onto the stretcher. The sooner he's in hospital the better.'

Bob

1986

When he thought of her, it was always at the Christmas party, 1986. A year of hopes raised and dashed, as the Troubles seemed to settle in for the long haul. No one wanted this now, surely; no one wanted twenty years of killing. And yet the end was so long in coming, in that final decade. Another death, and then another. Another shooting, another bomb, another colleague gone. The last? No, another, and another and yet another still.

The RUC Christmas party was a strange tradition. He'd never felt happy with it. So many years an empty seat where one of your colleagues had got blown up or shot. They had to sweep the hotel function room for devices before they could have their meal, but they went ahead with it anyway – hats, and cracker jokes, a showband playing Culture Club and Wham!; some kind of defiance, maybe. That Christmas, Bob had found himself sitting beside her. It was the first time they'd met, though Bob and PJ had been partners for a while. You kept your family out of work, that was the understanding. A woman didn't need to know the kind of things you were facing every day. Despite their differences, there was a wary sort of respect between the Catholic Belfastman PJ and himself, Orange and staunch. Best person Bob had ever worked with, if he was honest with himself. Maguire like a dog with a bone when he knew something wasn't right; himself slower, more measured, thinking it through. A trust, that was it, an understanding between them. That would be dead within a few years, of course, lost with Margaret Maguire. Only seven years after that dinner, Bob would betray his partner. He would tell a lie and keep it for twenty years. But back then, in 1986, none of them knew what was to come. They only knew they were deep into a bloody and intractable war, and the normal rules didn't apply.

Bob turned to Linda. 'Nice food?'

'Aye. Not bad.' He could tell she was worried about the babysitter they'd got for Ian. What if he stopped breathing again? Choked on his mushed-up dinner? The worry was between them, pushing them apart like an inflating balloon.

'We can ring if you want.'

Linda said nothing. They sat in silence until he couldn't stand it any more and turned to the woman on his right, as they ate their starter of melon with a glacé cherry. A vague impression of red hair and a black sparkly dress, her skin white against it. 'Bob, is it?' Friendly tone.

'Aye.'

'Margaret Maguire.' She nodded across the table to PJ, who was embroiled in conversation with a lad from the Bomb Squad. He looked to be using his glacé cherry to represent some kind of detonator. Bob was amazed. This was PJ's wife? She looked like a film star.

She was polite. She looked past him to Linda, who was pushing her melon around her plate and glancing at the big clock on the wall every five seconds. 'Hello – is it Mrs Hamilton?' Linda barely nodded. 'You've a wee boy, is that right?'

'Ian. He's six.' Her voice was flat. Saying Ian's age always hurt, because it was meaningless. He may as well have been a newborn, for all he could do. But Margaret didn't know that. She smiled.

'Same age as my Paula, then. Did you manage to get a

babysitter? We had all manner of tantrums in our house about that! Thinks she should come out with us, so she does.' Bob smiled automatically as she rolled her eyes. He'd never know what it was to fight with a stubborn child.

'Get a wee picture of you all?' said the photographer, butting in. They'd hired one for the event, as if anyone would want to remember the overly bright lighting and anaemic chicken.

Margaret reached across the table and tugged on PJ's arm, then smiled at Bob and Linda. 'Come on, let's all get in.'

Bob knew, rather than saw, that Linda was not smiling as the flash went off, leaving ghosts in his eyes for a few seconds.

PJ went to turn away again and Margaret stopped him. 'Enough of the fighting talk, Macho Man. Be sociable.'

'Sorry, sorry.' PJ was like a coiled spring back then – always on. Bob had never seen him relax. 'Happy Christmas, Bob, Linda.' More nods. More clock-gazing. Bob felt shame suddenly – the drabness of Linda in her old brown velvet, her face so tired, nothing to say for herself, no healthy, rebellious child at home. And there was PJ, his wife making a face at him – Bob caught the scent of lily from her – her red hair falling over her face. It was like fire, like autumn trees, he thought muzzily, his hand twitching on his glass of orange juice. Bob hadn't had a drink in his life, but tonight he could understand it, the need for something to steady you, dissolve you away from this shaky awareness of everything. And of her. Always her.

They were halfway through their chicken when some officer came running over, face grey. Bob dropped his fork – you always knew what that meant. The questions that had to be asked. What, where, how many dead. The officer –

what was his name? Took a heart attack in '97 and died –
whispered in PJ's ear, and Bob watched as his partner heard
the news, and stood up, very slowly. Beside him, Margaret
tensed. 'What?' she said, quietly, across the table to her
husband.

'John,' he said, briefly. 'They're saying John O'Hara's
been shot.'

Chapter Eight

'What do you make of that?' Paula murmured to Fiacra, as the sailor – they'd ascertained his name was José – was being loaded onto a stretcher the pub seemed to keep out the back, presumably for drunken accidents. They were standing outside now, the rising wind whipping the pub umbrellas. 'Anything to do with Matt and Fiona?'

'Doubt it. I reckon he jumped off because he couldn't hack it. We've busted a fair few fishing boats with illegal workers. They don't even let them sleep on some of those trawlers, and they hang onto their passports to stop them quitting. It's brutal.'

Paula believed him – immigrant labour was a big problem in the fishing and farming industries. The dark side of the Ireland the tourist board liked to promote, all happy cows and fishermen landing their catch. Even here, apparently, on this remote island with no phone signal, there was slave labour running the boats. 'And what about your woman barging in like that?'

'Seems she runs the Enviracorp plant out here. Lives on the north side of the island.'

'Why would the company care about a random sailor, though? Enough to send their boat away when there's supposedly a big storm heading in?'

Fiacra shrugged. 'Dunno. Corporate responsibility or

some such. Anyway, we should go too soon. Next ferry's gonna be the last today. Search's been called off for the night.'

Paula pushed back her hair as they looked out across the harbour, where the boats clinked together as the wind rose. 'But we're none the wiser about Matt and Fiona. We didn't even see round the rest of the island.'

Fiacra huddled up his shoulders against the cold. 'We've done what we can for now. I want to dig around a bit back home, find out a few things. We'll come back tomorrow – that's if we can convince everyone they've not just gone into the sea.'

'You don't think that. The locked door, the broken light? And that blood? That wasn't catching your finger doing the carrots. That's real bleeding. You know that.'

He looked at his watch again. 'Aye, I do know, and I'm not buying the accident angle. But we can't get stuck out here. I mean it, if that storm turns about we could be out here for days. Don't you have your wee girl to get back for?'

She did, of course. But there was something about this island, backing so bravely into the deep expanse of the Atlantic, that made her want to stay. Turn over more of its stones. Find some answers. 'What time's the ferry leaving?'

'An hour or so. Why, where are you going?'

Paula had turned and set off across the harbour. The stones were slick under her feet, but whether from rain or the sea it was impossible to tell. She shouted back, 'You go with Rory and help Anne finish up, and I'll meet you back here. Promise. I just want to see Fiona's surgery before I go.'

The key to the doctor's surgery was left under the flowerpot outside – a place that small couldn't stretch to a grumpy receptionist and a queue of people outside by eight a.m., which always seemed to be the way in London surgeries. Inside was warm and dry, with a cosy antiseptic smell, and she shut the door gratefully on the wind. The place was tiny – two plastic chairs by a coffee table with magazines three years out of date, and behind a flimsy partition wall, a space barely big enough for Fiona's desk and one other chair. This was where she'd seen patients. What illnesses would people have on the island? Fishing injuries, maybe, or farming accidents. The odd pregnancy or two. Paula imagined it was very different to inner-city London, where Fiona and Matt had been living until three months ago. Fiona had another framed picture of the two of them on her desk – smiling on a background of brilliant white snow. A ski trip. On the wall there were posters about the usual vaccinations and washing your hands, and a tub of bright sunflower stickers on the side, maybe for kids. How many kids could there be on an island this size? It was very tidy, no dust on the computer screen – Fiona must have been here very recently. Paula had to remind herself this was why she did missing persons. When you looked at the person's things, when you delved into their life, there was every chance they were still coming back to claim it. That they weren't dead and stopped and never to return. So you had to treat their life with respect – it might be needed.

Putting on gloves, she checked in the drawers – office supplies, medical books, nothing remarkable. Inside the top one was a piece of printer paper with a name written on it, in neat bold capitals. *Andrea Sharkey.* And beneath that name, others – *Jimmy Reilly. Niamh Ni Chailean.* And then, one that Paula recognised. *Matt Andrews.* Followed by a question mark.

She looked at it for a moment. The point on the question mark was deep and dark, as if someone had pressed the pen hard into the page. *Matt Andrews?* Question mark why? What was the question? Sitting on the desk was a manila file with the name *Andrea Sharkey* on it – as if Fiona had been called away in the middle of something. Paula flicked it open but it was empty, the notes missing. The address and date of birth were on the front – Andrea was thirty and lived just out the road, if Paula's sense of the island was correct. Glancing at the clock, she decided she had time to walk to the house. Perhaps there was an innocent explanation for why this woman's name was on the list, and also on an empty file. At the very least she could rule it out.

As Paula set off down the coast road, rain stung at her face, and the air she breathed was so pure it almost burned her lungs. She remembered the smell from that holiday, the last one. That west of Ireland tang of seaweed and salt and the smoke from turf fires, rare as some precious perfume. Along the side of the road, separated only by a strip of white sand and a rocky tumble, was the sea, green and foam. Paula tried to shrug off the memory of how it had pulled at her that summer, so cold and so irresistible at once. She'd been twelve, almost thirteen, all legs and hair, feeling constantly stretched by the world, body and soul. Young enough to still go on holiday with her parents, old enough to want something more. What, she hadn't known.

The number of the house, 23, hung on the huge concrete doorposts everyone in Ireland seemed to favour, topped with stone eagles. Every farmer was king of his own land out here, with acres of space and no one to tell you what to do. With some trepidation, she walked up the tarmacked drive and rang the doorbell. The house was seventies' pebble-dash, and for a moment as she waited she held her hand against the hard stones stuck into the wall. No answer. And yet she was sure that, as she peered in the stippled glass of the door, she could see the flicker of a TV.

She wandered round the back of the house, feeling rude but reminding herself this was perfectly acceptable in Ireland. Growing up, her friends always came to the back door to call for her. Front doors were for weddings and funerals. 'Hello?' Nothing. She rounded the side of the house, then jumped back with a small yelp. Something flung itself at the side of a small shed, with a sound of chewing and snarling. Dogs. A kennel, a big one, full of them. At the front of their paddock of barbed wire and chain link, she saw them gather. Two, three. Three Dobermans, or something like that, staring at her intently. Mouths slavering. She took a step closer and a furious barking chorus went up. At least she'd announced her presence.

A small child stood in the back door of the house. About four, she guessed, and still in blue Thomas the Tank Engine pyjamas although it was now the afternoon, snot plastered to his face and a nasty red rash on his cheek. One hand was wrapped in a white bandage that needed changing. Poor kid. 'Hi,' Paula said, over the noise of the dogs. 'Is your mummy or daddy here?'

'Daaaaaaaddy,' he called, not taking his eyes off her. 'There's a lady.'

Paula tried to smile at him. 'Did you hurt your poor hand?'

He just watched her.

'Those doggies are noisy, aren't they?'

'The doggies are bad,' he said in a small voice.

A man banged out, holding a baby in his arms. No more than a few months old, in pink pyjamas this time. Her face was shrouded in a blanket, also pink. 'What?'

Paula held onto the plastic edges of her ID as if it was protection. 'I'm sorry to land in on you, but I'm with the police – we're over for the missing persons' investigation. Did you hear about that?' He nodded, once. 'I was just wondering, sir, is Andrea here?'

'Andrea.' He gave her a long look.

'Yes. Is that your wife?'

The dogs still barked. 'Fucking shut it!' he shouted, and they stopped, leaving a sudden silence in the air. 'You're from the mainland?'

'Yes. They just brought me in for—'

'Where did you get Andrea's name? Did McElhone say to come here?'

'No, he didn't mention – um, no, I saw it in Dr Watts's surgery. Andrea's file was out. Dr Watts is missing, as you probably know, so I went to search her office.'

'Good bloody riddance. Meddling bitch.'

'Um . . . so Andrea isn't here?'

'No, she isn't fucking here, it's just me with two bloody weans and a farm to run and TOMAS!' Paula jumped. The little boy, barefoot in the dirty farmyard, had strayed too close to the fence, his small hand almost at the spikes of it. He withdrew, and the dogs started to bark again, silenced to a whine when the man gave a guttural, wordless yell. The baby in his arms was disturbed into a strange, choking cry, and Paula felt a cold tide wash over her.

Mr Sharkey put his face close to hers, so close she could smell his unwashed body and see his eyes yellow with tiredness. 'You listen to me. You've got no right to come round here asking questions. I don't want to hear a word about that bitch of a doctor. I hope she's dead. I hope she fecking drowned. Now get off my land. *Tomas*!' The boy trotted into the house, obediently, and as the man hefted the crying baby the blanket slipped, and Paula had one searing image of the scar that bisected the child's face.

Chapter Nine

Paula was trotting hastily back down the road when Rory splashed up in his jeep, shouting out the window. 'Where've you been? Quinn says you've to come now, they're loading the ferry. What were you doing?'

She climbed in, pleased to get her face out of the blinding drizzle. 'I wanted to see where Fiona worked. I found a patient file sitting out, so I went to the house.'

'You went to the Sharkey house? Jesus Christ. Was Peadar there?'

'Is that the husband? He was, yeah. What's the matter with them? He was pretty hostile. And what the hell happened to that child?' Paula was turning it over and over in her head, trying to see the connections. A list of names. An empty file. A missing doctor.

Rory muttered something. 'Why don't you tell me what you're doing before you run off, Dr Maguire? This isn't London. Everyone knows each other, and things can be – tricky.'

'Tricky why? Look what else I found.' She showed him the list, which she'd bagged up and put in her pocket.

Rory took a look. 'Where did you get that?'

'It was in her office. In the desk. What is it?'

A drop of rain fell off his hood and onto the bag, trickling down. 'Bollocks. Well, I don't know, could be anything.'

'Do you know these people?'

'Aye, of course, they're all islanders. Matt obviously is Fi's boyfriend. Jimmy Reilly – he's a farmer. Niamh lives in the village.'

'And Andrea? What's the deal with her? Her husband wouldn't tell me anything.' Paula had a horrible thought. 'Oh God, she's not dead, is she?'

Rory pushed back his hood, dripping more water. 'She's not dead, but you shouldn't have just gone round there. Andrea – she got sick a while ago. She's over on the mainland still, in hospital. And the baby – well. There was a wee accident.'

'So this is, what, a patient list?'

'I don't know, I said. We need to go now, Dr Maguire. Please. The ferry won't wait.' He turned the wheel hard, rounding into the harbour again, where the boat bobbed uneasily on the waves. The ramp was still down, rocking as the waves spilled over it.

She put the list away again. 'All right, but I'd like to look into it. Don't you think this is strange, having her boyfriend's name on a piece of paper?'

'How would I know? Is that not the kind of thing women do, doodle names on things?'

'Er, when we're twelve maybe.' She looked at him curiously. 'What's the matter?'

'I just . . . it doesn't feel right looking through her things is all.'

'But we have to! She's missing. We might still be able to help her, if we can find out where she is.'

'I *know*.' He almost pushed Paula out the door of the car. 'I know, and you're right, but for now you need to get on the boat. They're waiting for you.'

She could see Fiacra waving her over from the deck. It was hard not to feel a certain relief at the sight of the boat – and she picked up her pace, seeing the last passenger step on – as a way off this soaking, freezing island, but all the same, when she got on and the ramp raised up behind her, she couldn't help looking back to where Rory stood on the dock, a lone figure all in black, receding further and further into the darkness.

'So, do you not think that's sort of weird? That he was so angry? And he shouldn't have those dogs around young kids.'

Fiacra leaned on the side of the boat. Their faces were numb and wet with spray, but the inside waiting area was full of islanders and day-trippers making their escape, and this felt like the kind of conversation you didn't have in public. 'I don't know, Maguire. You shouldn't have just gone. This place – it's not like the mainland. There's sort of a different code.'

She sniffed. 'It's got the same laws as everywhere else. I want to know why Fiona had her own boyfriend's name on a list in her office. And why Andrea Sharkey's husband is so pissed off.'

'Did you find out what was the deal with the other names on the list?'

'Islanders, but McElhone wouldn't tell me much. What do you think of him?'

Fiacra shrugged. 'Dunno. Seems good enough.'

'You don't think he's keeping something back?'

'Aye, maybe. But don't be mistaken, Maguire – we need him, out there. People wouldn't tell us a thing if we didn't have a local with us.'

'But he needs to help us, not keep things back. Two people are missing!'

'Aye, and they're not locals, either. Let's not forget that.'

'Fine,' she sighed. 'But I want to come back out here tomorrow.'

'Thought you were going home?'

'I can't go home when we still don't know anything. That list and the blood in the kitchen, the broken light – that's enough for me. I can get a flight back tomorrow night.'

Fiacra was shaking his head. 'Like a terrier with a rat, you are. I forgot.'

'I'll take that as a compliment. Anyway, how come you're so keen to get home? Got a hot date waiting for you tonight?' She elbowed him through his layers of raincoat and jumpers. 'Another South American beauty?'

'Ah no, I wouldn't have the time for that sort of thing now. Too busy catching crims. Anyway, who'd I meet stuck out here in the arse end of nowhere?'

'All those dangerous country crims. What is it, petrol-stealing and drink-driving?'

'Hey, sometimes we get the odd bit of sheep-rustling too.'

'This case must be a nice change. That why you wanted me down here – grab a bit of excitement while you can? Take your one chance of a proper investigation?' She was pretty sure Fiacra had also got hold of that smell – the one that told you this was one of those cases where everything wasn't tied up for you in a nice bow – but she wanted to be sure her instincts were right. Part of her wished it was simple, so she could get off home to Maggie. But a bigger, deeper part knew that it wasn't, and was gearing up to meet it head-on.

He scowled. 'No. I mean, aye, it's interesting for a change, but that's not why. There's just something strange out there. Did you not feel it? Like – I don't know, we were just the thicko outsiders, and nobody was telling us the whole story? I dunno about you, but I didn't fancy staying the night, case or no case. I don't think they wanted us there.'

Paula looked back as the island faded into the horizon beyond them. It was almost gone now, hidden in spray and waves and the darkening sky. 'I've been here before,' she heard herself say. 'Holiday with my parents. Way back. Before my mother. You know.'

Fiacra was squinting at her, his fair hair plastered to his face. 'You have to find them all, eh?'

'I have to try at least.' Fiona Watts had left that list behind, an unwitting message from her to them, now that she couldn't speak for herself. And Paula intended to find out why. 'Those names on the list – any of them ring a bell, anyone you might have a file on?'

Fiacra considered it. 'I've hardly been here a month. But . . . Andrea Sharkey, was it?'

'Yeah. Anything?'

'Maybe. I'll look into it.'

She pulled her coat around herself. 'I'm going in before I freeze to death. And listen, Fiacra – humour an old mumsy lady, will you, and get yourself back in the game?'

'Ach, I don't know. Maybe. I haven't really felt it, past while.'

Because of Avril, she imagined, and the disappointment of it all. Paula knew what that was like too. 'I know. But sometimes you just have to let people go, and trust that there's someone else out there.'

He raised an eyebrow. 'You're one to talk about letting things go.'

'Never mind me. Go on a date, for God's sake. The women of Kerry deserve it.'

Fiona

The sea is full of blood.

That was the phrase Matt used, back when we first met. He was telling me about Japan, a dolphin hunt he'd tried to stop, back when he was young and idealistic. Of course, Matt never stopped being idealistic. That's the tragedy of it. *The sea is full of blood, Fi, and I'm in this little boat, and the blood is everywhere, slopping in the sides, and it's all over the oars and my clothes and my skin, and every time I touch something I leave these big bloody handprints on it. Like I'm guilty too – like we all did this terrible thing. Do you understand?*

And me – thirty-three, and still dressing like I thought I could pass for twenty-five, nodding madly. *Of course. Jesus.*

We'd been on the island for fifty days when Matt started saying it in his sleep. He'd come home early, refusing dinner, and I'd caught him glugging Gaviscon in the kitchen before bed. Stomach ache. Tired. Going to bed early.

I woke him from his sleep-talking. 'What's the matter? Were you dreaming?'

And him, confused, sweating in his sleep although it was December: 'Don't you see? The blood. It isn't safe. Don't you see it, Fi?'

Me, soothing: 'Of course I see. I see it, babe.'

I didn't. But now I do. Now that I've also had blood on me, leaving a trace on every surface you touch – doors, light switches, your own skin. I understand that feeling, the thing Lady Macbeth was on about. That you'll never be clean again.

When he started to say that phrase in his sleep – *the sea is full of blood* – I knew things were about to get very bad.

I've always been a good diagnostician. What I don't know in every case is how to cure the ill.

The sea is full of blood. I was thinking that as well when it all ended, as I sank over the side and into the silky black water. How remarkably little blood there was this time, but what a stain it leaves all the same.

Chapter Ten

'Can I help you?'

Paula directed a hopefully professional smile to the nurse on reception. 'Hi, yes, I'm looking for an Andrea Sharkey? I think she's a patient here. Could you tell me what ward she's on?'

'Let me take a wee look for you.'

On reaching the mainland after a fairly hair-raising boat ride, the waves rising higher and higher and the loos out of use after ten minutes as people puked their guts up, Paula had asked Fiacra to drop her at the hospital while he went to the station to do some digging. A quick trip to A & E told her that the fisherman was stable but out cold, so she'd decided to dig a bit herself. On the TV in the waiting room, a drenched reporter did a to-camera from Bone Island earlier that day, dodging waves on the dock. The words scrolled across the screen: *search suspended for missing couple.* Meaning everyone thought they were dead, drowned. Which made sense. Except that it didn't, not to Paula.

The nurse, a freckle-faced Kerrywoman, had gone to her computer affably enough, but when she pulled up the record she frowned. 'Oh. Andrea's on restricted visits, so. Are you family?'

'I'm with the police.' Paula hoked out her ID, with its underexposed photo that made her look like the Bride of

Frankenstein. 'Can I ask, what's the matter with Andrea? Is she sick?'

The receptionist bit her lip. 'You better go to the ward and they'll explain. If they'll let you in. Second floor, turn left at the lifts.'

'OK, thanks.' Mysterious. Paula took the stairs instead of the lift – she still hadn't lost that last stone of baby weight and the baby was nearly at school now – then walked briskly down the yellow-painted corridor, glass-walled wards going off on either side. Outside, the rain still washed the windows, and the hospital seemed almost cosy, evening drawing in fast. This impression was almost, but not quite, carried up to the last ward in the corridor, which had no glass, and thick security doors. Paula stopped, puzzled, and counted again. Yes, she'd come the right way. And now she was standing in front of a sign that read: PSYCHIATRIC INPATIENTS.

'Why is it you want to see Andrea?' A doctor, white-coated and severe, had been summoned from the depths of the ward. She looked as if she hadn't slept in about two years.

'I've just come from Bone Island. The local doctor and her boyfriend are missing, and I found Andrea's name on a list in her surgery. So I need you to tell me what happened to her, please. I think it could be connected.'

The doctor once again scrutinised Paula's ID, but could apparently find nothing wrong with it. 'All right,' she conceded. 'You really know nothing about the case?'

'I work up north mostly. Why, what happened?'

'Well. Andrea came in just before Christmas, and I diagnosed her with post-partum psychosis. Do you know much about that?'

Paula had read several studies, but understanding of the condition had changed a lot since her research days. 'An extreme form of post-natal depression causing dissociative episodes, hallucinations, that sort of thing?'

'More or less. They're really quite different illnesses, but you're not far off. I actually spoke to the island doctor about it on the phone – Dr Watts? She's the one who's missing?'

'That's right.' Paula's pulse began to quicken. So there was a connection. 'She'd diagnosed the condition?'

The doctor, a brisk woman with a lined face that spoke of deep exhaustion, shook her head impatiently. 'Not at all. She said she'd seen no signs – she'd actually been on a home visit to Andrea and her baby the week before it happened. Well, you can imagine I had to report it. It's easy to miss this kind of thing, especially if you have lots of patients and you aren't familiar with the condition. It's sufficiently rare that you might not be. But Dr Watts was adamant. There'd been no signs, Andrea was fine when she saw her. But then it happened.'

'I'm sorry. What happened?'

The doctor raised her eyebrows. Her glasses were smudged, her eyes tired. 'You really don't know. Huh. OK. Well, Dr Maguire, Andrea tried to kill her baby. She put her in with the farm dogs. Into their kennel.'

Paula stared at her. She couldn't help thinking of Maggie, how helpless she'd been as a newborn, totally dependent on Paula to keep her alive. 'And the baby . . . ?' Was that what had happened to the child she'd seen, with the ravaged face?

'Oh, wee Mairead survived, somehow. Her older brother heard her crying and dragged her out – got a nasty bite himself in the process. When I say older, the wee boy is no more than four. Terrible thing, he'll likely be traumatised for life. And then they found Andrea round the back of the farm, calmly feeding the chickens.' The doctor took off her glasses and rubbed them on her coat. 'All the signs were there – confusion, delusions, dissociation. It's my belief that Dr Watts missed it, and was trying to cover her tracks.'

And now Fiona Watts was missing. Paula thought of Andrea Sharkey's husband, the spitting rage of him. 'I see. We'll look into that.'

'I hope someone does. You can speak to Andrea if you want, she's pretty lucid now. I'm not sure she'll ever get over it, though. Mairead will have permanent facial scars, and I doubt Social Services will let Andrea anywhere near the kids again.'

'Was this reported in the press?' Paula couldn't believe she hadn't heard about it.

'It was hushed up. There were kids involved, so they didn't release the full names. And they're close-knit on that island. No one would breathe a word to the press. Anyway, she's over there by the window if you want to see her. You're a psychologist, you said?'

'Yes. Forensic rather than clinical, but I did psych rotations while training.'

'OK. Don't upset her, then. She's made a lot of progress since she's been here. With a bit of luck, she might still be able to have some kind of life again one day.'

The psychiatric ward was sparsely populated that evening. A TV played the news, watched by a teenage girl with bandaged wrists and a sad older man, and over by the rain-soaked window, a woman sat looking out. She looked even younger than thirty, with pale hair pulled back from a smooth, blank face. In her blue dressing gown, she was gaunt. But someone had brought her things. The magazine that sat on her lap, unread, and the pretty flowered pyjamas she wore. Someone still cared for Andrea, even though she'd done the worst thing society could imagine.

'Hi, Andrea. I'm Paula – I wonder if I could ask you a few questions.'

Andrea seemed to stir herself. 'Oh! Hello, sorry, I was miles away. Are you a doctor?'

'Yes, but not medical. I work with the police, actually.' She saw the look in Andrea's eyes and said hastily, 'I'm not here about you, though. I've just come from Bone Island.'

'Did something else happen?' Andrea turned her eyes to the window again.

'Well, yes. I'm afraid Dr Watts is missing, and Matt too, her boyfriend.'

'Oh no.' Andrea whispered it. 'I got her in trouble. It wasn't her fault, any of it.'

Paula sat down on the padded chair opposite, hands in the pocket of her coat. 'Whose fault was it, Andrea? Do you know?'

She shook her head slowly. 'I don't remember any of it. They said I hurt Mairead – but I can't remember that day at all. I just remember loving her, feeling happy, glad I had my wee boy and my wee girl too. Then – I don't know. It was like a red fog.'

'You don't remember thinking anything bad about Mairead?' Paula tried to ask the questions gently. She knew that in these cases mothers often thought their children were evil, or sometimes the opposite, that they were sacred, that whatever you did to them they'd not get hurt. She tried to push away the thought of Maggie's limp, warm body in her arms, trusting, helpless.

'No, but – they read me what I said when they came to the house. I was feeding the chickens, they said. I don't know how I could do that if I can't remember anything, but – there you go. And then Garda McElhone came and I said – I said . . .'

Rory had been the first on the scene? Why hadn't he mentioned that? Why hadn't he told her the woman she was asking about had tried to kill her child? 'What, Andrea?'

'I said the baby was the devil. I said I had to get rid of the devil. With dogs and fire. I said the dogs would eat her and we'd be rid of her.' Andrea's voice was small.

Paula stared at her, the thin, meek woman, with her hands folded on her *Take a Break*. She still wore her wedding ring. 'But you don't remember?'

'No. Nothing from the day before that, till I was in here.' So she had amnesia. Was that a feature of post-partum psychosis? There was a blankness about Andrea that told Paula she was heavily medicated, and she pitied the woman, for the inevitable horror that would descend when she could fully feel what she'd done. 'Mairead's out of here now, God love her . . . they said the plastic surgeon did a good job. I can't see her. I won't be allowed.'

'I'm so sorry, Andrea. Thank you for telling me.'

Andrea beckoned her closer. 'Doctor? Will you be going back over there? To the island?'

'Probably, yes.' How could she not, now? When the first person on that list had such a terrible story?

Andrea was whispering now. As if she might be overheard. 'Shh. They'll hear. They listen, you know. They won't let me see my kids – not Mairead, not Tomas. I need to get a message to them. Will you tell my husband – tell him he needs to get them off there. Off that island. Tell him it's not safe.' And now she was leaning forward, Paula could see what it was Andrea had been looking at out the window. Through the fogged-up glass, across the car park, was the distant gleam of the bay, and in it, far away, the dark hulk of Bone Island could just be seen.

Chapter Eleven

The local Gardaí were putting Paula up at the pub in the harbour, the place where the island folk crashed when they missed the last ferry or it didn't run. The tiny room had swirly red carpet that didn't quite hide the stains, and a shower that dripped. When Paula opened one of the little cartons of UHT milk they'd left beside the minuscule kettle, it poured lumpy sludge into her tea. Disgusted, she rinsed the lot down the tiny sink and checked her phone.

A picture message came through, slowly and expensively – roaming charges took no account of the fact it was the same country to many. Saoirse's big husband Dave, crashed out on the sofa beside Maggie. Her red curls were a tangle and she had juice stains on her top, a normal state of affairs. Paula smiled – Dave, a big rugby-playing bear of a man, was fast asleep wearing a pink plastic tiara. Then her smile faded. Aidan had often been made to wear the same one. Princess Bogtrotter, he called himself, a name Maggie found endlessly hilarious. Paula could stand most things, but not thinking of the two of them together, Maggie and the man she called Daddy. She pressed the Facetime icon on her phone and after a while staring at her own pale, tired face, Saoirse answered, saying, 'It's Mummy, Maggie.' Saoirse was wearing jeans and a baggy grey jumper, her dark hair loose.

Paula could see the top of Maggie's red head and hear the film they were watching – inevitably, *Frozen*. The scene with the fella and the reindeer in the shed, which she couldn't help but feel was a little suspect. 'She has you on the *Frozen*, then? God love you.'

'I kind of like it. Dave's gone to sleep in protest. How's it going?'

'Mmm. Not sure. It's a strange one.'

Saoirse had known Paula a long time. 'It's fine if you need to stay longer.'

'No, no, I'll be back tomorrow. Probably. How is she anyway?'

'She's a wee dote. No bother at all.'

Paula highly doubted this. 'Will she talk to me, or can she not tear her eyes away from that bloody film?' The phone was passed over. Paula tried not to mind that Maggie's gaze kept skipping back to the TV. 'Hi, pet. I miss you.'

'Mummy, Auntie Saoirse let me have ice-cream.'

'Aren't you lucky? How's Granny and Grandda?' Of course Maggie called Pat Granny. It wasn't like she had any other grandmas popping out of the woodwork.

'Mummy, the ice-cream melted like Olaf.'

Olaf? Of course, the bloody snowman. 'Well, you have to eat it quick, pet.'

'OK, Mummy. Bye.' The phone was dropped, and Saoirse only just grabbed it in time.

Paula said, 'I see I'm competing with Elsa and Anna here – I'll give you a buzz tomorrow, let you know what happens. Listen, eh, bad timing on this question, but . . . what can you tell me about post-partum psychosis?'

Saoirse sighed. She knew better than to ask why Paula wanted to know. 'Always the cheery stuff with you. I've seen it a few times. Usually the mother tries to kill the kid and herself. Pets too, for some reason.' She'd lowered her voice.

'They always kill themselves?'

'They try, yeah.'

But by all accounts Andrea had calmly carried on with her chores after putting her baby in with the dogs, and she certainly hadn't killed the pets. Paula shivered at the images. Slavering farm dogs, and the child in there with those yowls and teeth . . . And Andrea had used the same word as the poor sailor: *devil*. 'OK, ta, Glocko. Hope the storm's not doing too much damage up there.'

'Och, it's desperate. Dave says the roof of the shed might go. Say bye to Mummy, Mags.'

'Byeee,' came the voice. Paula could see Maggie was now engrossed in the My Little Pony Canterlot Castle Saoirse had got her for Christmas, which was so big they'd not managed to move it up the road yet. She was fine. She was in the best place she could be.

'Bye, pet,' Paula called. 'And bye, you, Glocko. Take care of yourself, OK? Don't be running around after Miss Maggie there.' She'd not asked about it for a long time now, but Saoirse's main goal in life was to have a baby of her own. Paula hoped it wasn't upsetting, looking after Maggie, whose birth had been so spectacularly unplanned and chaotic.

'We're fine. Don't worry.'

Hanging up, Paula got up to try and distract herself from missing Maggie, raking the curtains back to look out across the bay towards the island. The sea had calmed now, milky with moonlight, and it was hard to believe she'd been almost afraid of it on the way back. If only she could calm her mind too, tossed as it was by so many questions. Did she tell Guy

Brooking he was Maggie's father? Did she keep paying Davey Corcoran to look for her mother, and then maybe find her, and risk overturning that last stone? Risk destroying her father and Pat, who likely wouldn't be able to stand another blow? Did she try to get Aidan out of prison, or leave him to the mercies of the police? Hope they would look harder, see beyond the neat solution that offered itself? She just didn't know. And out there in the bay was Bone Island. She remembered Andrea's whispered words – *tell him it's not safe.* She could hardly give credence to the paranoia of a sick woman, but still. Weather or no weather, she was going back to Bone Island the next day.

'Maguire? Are you decent?'

Bleary-eyed, Paula pulled back her door to see Fiacra Quinn in the hallway, scrubbed and suited. His lilac tie was pulled tight against his shaved throat, but she noticed with some affection he'd missed a small patch. 'Just about. Why so early?'

'Press conference. They're all over it for some reason – I'd have thought the storm would keep them busy. Even some of the English nationals have sent people. Like as not they came over to report the weather – it's their lucky day with a nice juicy missper.'

Paula wasn't surprised. People disappeared every day in the UK – 600,000 a year or thereabouts, one every two minutes on average – but only a handful ever made the news. A middle-class English couple, though, and an isolated Irish island – that was enough to pique the interest. She followed Fiacra down the stairs of the pub, noting the dust in the corners. She hoped she wouldn't bring bedbugs home to Maggie. 'Any word on José the sailor?'

'Doing OK. He'll live, at any rate, though chances are he'll be deported as soon as he can walk onto the plane. Coastguard picked up the rest of the fishing boat's crew last night.'

'And?'

'Same. All raving, one of them with quite bad wounds to his arm. Doctors think they're dehydrated and exhausted.'

'What kind of wounds?'

Fiacra answered reluctantly. 'They look like . . . well, they said bite marks.'

Paula stared at him. '*Bite* marks?'

'Aye. Maybe your man wasn't mad after all. Anyway. The boat sails off the mainland here but it's owned by an islander, a Brendan Meehan. Someone else we'll have to question when all this dies down. You saw Andrea Sharkey?'

'I did. Fiacra – she tried to kill her baby.'

'I know, I looked it up. And guess what – there was a murder on the island a few weeks after that happened and all.'

Paula stopped in her tracks for a moment. 'Connected?'

'Not so's anyone could see. It was before my time, but I do wonder why it didn't come up sooner. Like, isn't that the kind of thing you'd expect a local Garda to mention, when you're out investigating a missper on a wee tiny island?'

'It is, yeah. What happened?'

'Some ould boy cut his mate's throat. In that pub, Dunorlan's. Guess what his name is?'

It took her a second. 'Jimmy Reilly?' Another name from the list.

'The very same.'

'Jesus. I think – I wonder if something's going on out there.'

'Like what?' He was ushering her out the door – clearly there'd be no time for the pallid sausages and eggs she'd seen the other guests eating.

'I don't know. Fiona has this list and one of them's her own boyfriend, one of them's a murderer, and one – well. Andrea nearly was, too. It's just a bit weird, like you said. I want to go back out there today. The storm's dying down, right?'

'They say it's gone out across the Atlantic for now. Should be fine for your flight.'

Her flight back to her daughter, and her own safe, warm home where the milk was never on the turn. She should be itching to get on it. 'So we can go over?'

He squinted at her. 'You got a theory?'

'Maybe. Fiona Watts totally missed the fact Andrea was psychotic. How do you think those islanders would feel about that? Andrea's husband was raging. Then there's that blood in the kitchen.' Not that this accounted for the delirious sailor or the murder in Dunorlan's. Coincidence, perhaps. All Paula knew was she was getting the feeling strong as ever – something wasn't right out there. Her searchlights were trained on Matt and Fiona, and whatever or whoever had caused them to be gone, with blood in their kitchen and a strange list of names left behind.

Fiacra scratched at his stubble. They were in the car now, heading to the hotel where the conference would take place. And why the Gardaí couldn't have put Paula up there she didn't know. It even had a swimming pool. Tight-wads. 'The blood's Fiona's, they think,' Fiacra said. 'Same type, anyway.'

'Right. And someone cleaned it up.'

'Anne found some blood round the back of the lighthouse

too, outside on the rocks. Smears of it. She said it looked like someone maybe fell onto them from a height.'

'So . . . maybe one of them went over the side? Could explain how the bulb got shattered. A fight or something, they fell off . . .'

'Or they were pushed,' said Fiacra quietly, watching the road as he pulled out.

Bob

1986

The crime scene – until an hour ago just the offices of the *Ballyterrin Gazette* – was quiet. The quiet ones were bad. That meant there was no point rushing, no point shouting, no point at all. No hope. The uniformed officer on the door – Frankie Davies, good fella, only twenty years old – shook his head briefly and Bob's heart sank. John O'Hara was dead, then. 'Forensics?'

'Held up. Bomb scare out the road.'

'OK.' They were whispering, though no one could hear them. 'Don't let anyone in after me, all right?' Bob started to take a step forward, then turned back, grabbing Frankie's arm. 'I mean it. Don't let Maguire in, whatever you do. Not if someone puts a gun to your head. OK?' He gathered PJ had gone first to check on John's wife – widow now. The hopelessness of it all dogged his steps.

He moved in. The place was so quiet. Nothing even knocked over. He had his gun out, just in case the killer was still here – the Provos would love to take out an RUC man, especially one with an Orange sash at home in his wardrobe. Another step forward. His foot crunched on something, and he jumped. Just a pen. Cheap plastic one, shattered under his boots. Then he saw the hand the pen had rolled from.

The head, caved in. The puddle of blood spread out on the dusty floorboards. A large footprint in the middle of it, man's size eleven or so, with a strange ripple pattern. Bob recognised that from somewhere, he was sure, but couldn't think just now. Careful not to add another footprint to the mess, he bent, felt the cold neck for a pulse just in case. No hope. John O'Hara was a man he'd had little time for – always whipping the town up, crying corruption and cover-ups, exposing the RUC and IRA alike, as if they were remotely the same – but Bob grieved for him anyway. A good man, quiet and dry and stubborn, now just a shrivelling body on the floor. Those stains'd not wash out. The pointlessness of it.

Voices in the doorway. 'DC Maguire, I can't—'

'I'll see you out for this, Davies, swear to God I will. Fecking let me in.'

'But DS Hamilton said—'

PJ swore, loudly and horribly. '*Move.*'

Bob went back the five paces to the door, putting himself between PJ and the blood. 'Maguire, man, you don't want to see. You don't.'

'John—'

'He's gone.'

'Shite. SHITE. The wee lad. Where's the wee lad?'

Bob didn't get it. 'Who?'

'His wee boy. Aidan. I went to the house, neighbour says Pat O'Hara's in the hospital so John was minding the boy tonight. Where is he?'

Bob had thought finding the man dead was bad, but he realised as his stomach sank further there were levels beneath bad, miles of them. A wee boy. And not a sound in the place. 'They don't hurt weans,' he said, trying to sound sure.

'Unless they get in the way. *Aidan.* AIDAN! It's me, son, it's PJ, Paula's daddy. You're safe now, son, come out!'

Nothing. Not a sound. Bob grabbed PJ's arm, was shaken off. The eyes of his partner so cold, shoulders vibrating with rage under his dinner suit. 'You do that side. Come on, man. Please.' Meaning the side of the room away from the body.

PJ tensed for a moment, then went. He was ranting, more or less to himself. 'Margaret's fecking raging, why didn't they *call* us if they needed help, she'd have minded the wee lad, for Christ's sake who cares about the fecking Christmas do . . . Aidan! AIDAN!'

Bob had reached the last desk. No sound. No small dead body either.

'*Aidan*!' PJ's voice roared, cracked. Bob pushed a chair aside. Eyes. He'd seen eyes, down there in the dark beneath the desk.

'He's here! He's here!' He stood up to call his partner, and too late realised PJ was bounding across the room.

PJ stopped. He was staring down at his feet. Bob turned away from the child – who was motionless, but looked unhurt – and saw PJ frozen beside the body of his friend, up to his ankles in John O'Hara's blood.

Chapter Twelve

'Sergeant Quinn, is it correct you found blood in the couple's home?'

Fiacra was very assured answering the press questions. Paula had assumed Rory McElhone might do it, but he was nowhere to be seen. On the island still, she assumed. She'd been roped into sitting on the panel too, though she wasn't planning to speak. It was too soon to say what she was thinking – she didn't even know what she was thinking. Some vague sense of half-formed unease was all she had so far. Blood. Shattered glass. *Diablo*. She looked around the shabby room with irritation, annoyed at the heavy drapes and cheap laminate floor that must have seen the first dances of a thousand brides. She didn't want to be here. She wanted to be out on the island, hunting for Matt and Fiona.

Fiacra was explaining carefully that yes, they'd found blood, but it could have an innocent explanation. No one in the audience looked convinced, and Paula could see the reporters making avid notes. They always reminded her of Aidan, press conferences. He'd have been the first one in with the difficult questions. 'At the moment we're keeping an open mind. The bad weather means an accident is extremely likely.' Again, Fiacra didn't sound like he believed that for a second. 'The search will resume today if the weather holds. At the moment that's our main line of enquiry – an accident of some kind.'

'So why was the light shattered, then?' A clear Dublin voice cut through the throng. One Paula recognised. At the end of the row was a blonde reporter with a walking stick.

'Ms Cooley, isn't it?' Fiacra looked down at his papers. 'I'm afraid I'm only going to say what I said before. It's likely that, sadly, they've met with some accident, and we'll keep searching for them as much as we can in this weather. We'd like to thank the islanders who've been looking so hard in such inclement conditions and urge you all not to attempt a trip over, as it's highly likely you might not make it back again. That's all I have to say for now.'

'Well, you can't blame a girl for trying,' the reporter said pleasantly, and a gentle laugh broke up the conference.

'Well, Cooley. Always throwing a spanner in the works, aren't you?' Paula greeted Maeve with a hug. They were close still, somehow, despite the fact Maeve was really Aidan's friend, and Aidan and Paula hadn't spoken in months, and also despite the fact that the last time Paula had seen Maeve was at her own stupid hen do. Maeve wore a trouser suit, as usual, and underneath, a flash of red Converse.

'It's what I do. You OK?'

'I'll do. Need to get back to Mags, but as you were quick to point out, I don't really buy the accident idea either.'

'Nah, I don't think anyone does. They just have to say something, toss us a few bones. Listen, have you looked at Enviracorp yet?'

'I know they have a base out there on the island – minerals out of seaweed, is that right?'

'That's what they say. What they don't say is what else they're releasing into the ecosystem.'

Paula frowned. 'Meaning?'

Maeve smiled slightly. This was in her blood – cover-ups, scandals, lies. 'Well. About a week ago someone sent an anonymous report into my paper. Didn't want to be named. Blowing the whistle big-time on Enviracorp.' Maeve's paper was a rackety operation which was known to be fearless in its reporting. Terrorists, politicians, and big corporations alike were all fair game. It made sense that a whistle-blower would contact them.

'So?'

'So, it's clearly someone who works for the company. Knew all the protocols, had all the data. Seabird deaths. Birth defects in seal pups. Chemicals in the soil. It's all there, Maguire – that company has messed up in a big way. And whoever wrote the report, they called themselves Puffin the Magic Dragon.'

Paula still wasn't following. 'What's that got to do with my case?'

'Matt Andrews – he's an ecologist, yes? Studying puffins?'

Paula got it. 'Don't tell me you think it's some kind of Erin Brockovich situation, and you're Julia Roberts?'

'Julia Roberts doesn't have my winning ways,' said Maeve, flicking her blonde ponytail. 'Do you not think it's worth looking into, though? We get this report in, and then their ecologist goes missing?'

'Yeah, I do. I want to get out there and talk to them anyway.' For a start, she wanted to know why they'd had such a fit of kindness in sending their boat to help an unknown illegal worker.

'Great. And seeing as I can't go . . .' Maeve indicated her

leg, which had been injured in a petrol-bomb attack a few years before. 'Maybe you'd follow up on some of my questions for me?' She produced a piece of paper and a dazzling smile.

'You're terrible. You know I can't do that.'

'Nothing you wouldn't ask yourself, I'm sure. And you can just tell me whatever you think is ethical.'

Between her and Corry, Paula was surrounded by manipulative women. 'I'll see. Anything you know that we don't?'

Maeve smiled wider. 'Bit of quid pro quo, is it? Fair enough. Well, here's a thing. Have you pulled Fiona Watts's medical records?'

'I don't know.' Paula wasn't sure how it worked. Did doctors treat themselves or did they go elsewhere? 'Why?'

'She was at the hospital over here four times in the last few months. Not exactly normal for a healthy young woman, is it?'

'And you know this how?'

Maeve was as bad as Aidan at digging the dirt. But Paula shouldn't have thought of him. The needle of pain was always there, a stabbing in her lungs that seemed to take her breath away. Once, not so long ago, they'd all been friends, her and Aidan, Maeve and her wife Sinead. Now Paula was alone again. Maeve said, 'Never mind how I know. But has no one mentioned her allergies yet?'

Chapter Thirteen

Fiacra drove like the clappers to the ferry, while Paula clutched her seat and tried not to say anything. The rain never seemed to stop, only ease off and then come on again, heavy, stinging drops that ran down your neck and leached into your shoes. 'Come on, we need to get over and back as quick as possible. I don't like the look of that sea.'

'Are you going native on me? You said the storm'd moved off.'

'Look.' Fiacra pointed to the quay, where soapy grey water slopped up between the side of the boat and the harbour wall. 'Don't tell me that's not a bad sign. Anyway, we'll risk it.'

'Did McElhone mention anything about Fiona's medical condition?' They joined the huddled queue to give their money to the ferryman, Paula dragging her silly wheeled case behind her. She noticed a MISSING poster taped onto the Portakabin, the picture of Matt and Fiona on the mountain, all smiles. It struck her there'd been none on the island. Maybe there was no need, when everyone knew each other.

'No.' Fiacra eyed the roof above them, which was made of flimsy corrugated iron and lifting and groaning in the rising wind. 'That yoke up there's not wild stable.'

'Well, apparently she was severely allergic to loads of things. Shellfish. All nuts. Dairy. It was so bad she had to have her own food shipped over, pre-packaged. I guess that explains all the stuff in the kitchen.'

'That's a bit extreme, no?'

'I don't know if it was a real problem, or she was just careful – I've left a message for her specialist anyway. He was in a case conference when I called.'

Fiacra shepherded her forward, still looking up at the roof. 'Is this another one of your famous theories, Maguire? Or did you get it off that hack pal of yours?'

'Um . . . does it matter? It's easy to check. Think about it. If she was very allergic, there's a strong chance she ate the wrong thing and had a bad reaction. If she couldn't get help in time, she'd have died.'

'McElhone never mentioned that?'

'No. Even though they were the best of friends, supposedly. He also didn't mention Andrea Sharkey trying to kill her baby or Jimmy Reilly cutting his pal's throat.'

Fiacra glanced up again. 'OK, we'll have to . . . Jesus!' There was a tearing, cracking sound, like metal scratching on metal, and Paula felt herself flung to one side. She stumbled, righting herself, in time to see the corrugated iron roof detach itself from the Portakabin, sail a few feet across the parking lot, and catch Fiacra right on the ankle, knock him to the ground.

'Bollocks!' The bellow came out of the depths of him, and then he was down on the wet stone ground, clutching his leg, while the roof skipped lightly off and flattened itself against the boat, passengers scattering. 'Ah Jesus, that hurt!'

Paula raced to him. He was on his back in a puddle, and red was already blooming through his jeans. 'Fiacra! Are you OK?'

'Stand back there, lassie.' The ferryman had come over, like a bear inside his all-over black anorak and trousers.

Despite the irritating 'lassie', she let him kneel down to Fiacra and roll up the leg of his trousers. Blood was leaking fast from a long gash on his calf. 'Aye, you've a wee scratch there all right, son.'

A wee scratch? He'd need stitches at least. 'Should we call an ambulance?' she shouted, over the wind.

The ferryman squinted up like she was mad. 'An amberlance? Sure we'll stick him in a car and take him down to hospital. Brian. Brian!' A similarly anorak-clad man detached himself from the queue and came over. 'Have you a car?' Brian and the ferryman had a brief discussion about this, of which Paula didn't catch more than one word. Fiacra was at least still conscious, swearing like a trooper, his face a pale green. All the while the rain drizzled over them, soaking through hair and shoes and clothes.

'You'll be grand, son.' The ferryman clapped a large hand on Fiacra's shoulder, threatening to injure him further. 'We'll get you stitched up so.'

Wincing, Fiacra beckoned Paula in. 'Listen. You should still go.'

'Don't be daft. I have to come with you to hospital!'

'No, you don't. I'll just a need a few stitches or something. I'm hardly going to lose a leg. Get out there and do the interviews. We can't let this one lapse; they've been missing two days already, and this weather . . .'

'But . . .'

He scowled. 'Maguire, you've spent the last two days trying to convince me something's going on out there. I'm convinced. So get out there and look into it.'

He was right. 'Fine. But I'll phone once I get there.'

'I'll come later if I can, or I'll send someone else. McElhone's there anyway. Just do the extra interviews and come back as soon as you can. It's not going to be safe out there in a gale.'

Paula nodded, shoving her hands in the pocket of her coat as Fiacra was helped into Brian's car – she hoped he wouldn't develop sepsis from the dirt on the back seat, which looked like a large shaggy dog had been living on it – and lurched off to the hospital. Then the ferryman took the rest of the tickets in a leisurely fashion, and she piled on with the rest and sat in a window seat. Back to Bone Island. In her pocket were two lists. Maeve's questions, which she hadn't had time to look at yet, and the list of names from Fiona Watts's surgery. She'd learned who Andrea Sharkey was, and her sad story, and the tale of Jimmy Reilly the murderer, but still nothing made sense, her mind tossing around theories like the sea tossed the ferry. As her fingers touched the damp crackle of paper, Paula turned her face to the island, looming out of the sea fog like a sleeping monster. Hoping she might find some answers there.

Once again, Rory McElhone was there to meet her on the windswept pier, deep in his coat. 'No Quinn?'

'He's had a wee accident. Storm damage. He'll be over later today, maybe.'

'Later?' McElhone pushed his hood back a little, so she could see his freckled face. 'Don't know if there'll be a later. They're saying this might be the last ferry.'

'It can't be! I've a flight booked for tonight!'

He shrugged. 'Look at the sea, Dr Maguire.' He was right – it was boiling like a witch's cauldron, waves breaking on the shore. So green at their centre, cresting for one perfect moment, then crashing down.

'It might settle down,' Paula said stubbornly. 'They said it was passing over.'

'They get stuff wrong. Trust me, out here we learn to look at the sea, not the weather forecast. Anyway, who do you need to see? Come in the car and tell me. We'll go to Enviracorp first.'

She chucked her bag in the boot, moving aside a long coil of rope, and climbed in. In the relative shelter of his draughty, smelly jeep, Paula took out the list. 'So I know who Andrea Sharkey is – she tried to kill her kid last month. How come you didn't mention it?'

Rory started the car, squinting out as the wipers cleared the rain. 'Oh. Well, I didn't think you'd need to know about that. Poor woman.'

'I do need to know about it, and anything else strange that's happened out here. Jimmy Reilly, for example?'

Rory glanced at the list, changing gear. 'Well, Jimmy Reilly, I thought you'd know about that already. Him and another islander had a . . . scuffle just after the New Year.'

'Didn't Jimmy cut the other fella's throat? Some scuffle. Is that kind of thing normal on this island – a murder, an attempted child-killing, and a disappearance, all in a few months?'

'Life can be hard out here,' he said, pulling onto the main island road. It wasn't really an answer. 'It's not like in the city. It's raw, it's tough. It's freezing and lashing most of the time and everyone lives on the edge. Half these farms would go under if it wasn't for the EU subsidies. It's no surprise if people snap sometimes.'

'But I mean, *Christ*. Where is Jimmy now? Jail?'

'Psychiatric facility in Tralee. He'd gone a bit – well, he'd lost the head.'

You'd have to, Paula thought distractedly, to cut someone's throat. 'Rory, did you not think to tell us about these other incidents?'

He shifted gear. 'I didn't think they had any bearing on this case, no. I've told you I think Fi and Matt have had an accident. The Coastguard will turn up something, I reckon, but I doubt it'll be good news after all this time. God help them.'

There was another thing too. 'You also never mentioned that Fiona had severe food allergies. Is that true?'

He scrubbed at the window, which had steamed up with their breath. 'Oh aye, she was a wee bit fussy about what she'd eat. Again, why would that have anything to do with them going missing?'

'Well, someone with serious anaphylaxis can be killed by even a tiny bit of their allergen. Is that why Oona said it was strange to see Fiona in the Spar? She didn't normally shop there? She ordered her food in?'

'Aye, I suppose so.'

'So, there you go. Something had changed. Maybe she ate the wrong thing, and they were out in their boat and she had an attack.'

'Maybe.' Rory was steadfastly unreadable. He'd pulled up now at a set of heavy grey gates, at least twelve feet high. Paula had to peer out through the rain to see the sign – Enviracorp. A green logo shaped like a plant. 'Listen, Dr Maguire—'

'Ah, call me Paula, will you—'

'OK. But listen. People on these islands, they're close-knit. We have a certain way of living and outsiders have to respect that. Matt and Fi, they – well, they came from inner London, right? All those rules and so on, for how you're supposed to do things. Laws. Reporting. And Fiona's a doctor – she's used to being in the right. So she didn't always know to mind her business. Do you catch my drift?'

'Not really, no. It sounds kind of like you're saying we shouldn't investigate.'

'Ah now. I'm not saying that at all. Amn't I doing my best to help? They're my friends, I want to find them. I'm just telling you, both of them liked to interfere in the way things are here. But that doesn't mean you should, too.'

'I don't follow. And what's this got to do with Enviracorp?'

'This company, they came out here a few years back. Built the plant. You know how many people they employ? Eighty. Some of those are from outside, yeah, but the rest are locals. There's admin, packing, transport, the boats they use, and even the work that went into building the place. You may not realise this, Dr Maguire, but it wasn't so long ago people were talking about abandoning these islands for good. It's already happened in the Blaskets. No work, and this bloody wind and rain day and night. Life is hard. There's never a let-up. But Enviracorp might have saved us, and that's not an exaggeration.'

'So you're saying I need to be nice to them?' Paula rolled her eyes; this was indeed turning into an Erin Brockovich situation. At least she had red hair. Julia Roberts could play her in the film.

'No, I'm saying nothing. Just letting you know the context.'

The context. Huh. She thought about the anonymous report Maeve had mentioned. 'Was Matt happy, working for them? Any problems there?'

Rory shrugged, as if to say he was humouring her but she was way off. 'He said this was his dream job. No word of a lie. He could spend the whole day poking about on the cliffs and on the beaches, and helping make sure the puffins and seals and that were all grand. He was happy as Larry, so he was.'

'But what if they weren't grand?'

'Well, all I can say is the company went to the trouble of hiring him to check they were doing things right. Why would they do that if they didn't want the truth?'

Paula looked out at the plant. A squat white building, out of place on this island with its weather-beaten cottages and dry-stone walls. 'I hear what you're saying, Garda. I'll be tactful, I swear.' Well, as tactful as she could manage, which usually wasn't much. In the pocket of her coat, Maeve's questions seemed to crackle and burn.

Fiona

The first time I met Rory it was in Dunorlan's, a week after we moved. At that point, we were happy. Or Matt was happy, at least. I was pole-axed by the cold, the silence, the fact our phones didn't work and it took weeks to get the internet put in. That the only entertainment available was this smelly pub. But Matt was just charmed with the place, everything from the incomprehensible sports on TV (what is hurling anyway?) to the dubious stains on the seats. It was 'trad' night, meaning a circle of musicians had started up a racket on instruments I didn't even recognise. Everyone seemed to know the music except us, singing along in drunken slurs.

'Isn't this great!' Matt was grinning, his face flushed from the turf fire. He loved all this. He was happy, settled, out of the city. I could feel the pressure between us, the pulling away, had eased. I should have been pleased. I was leaning against the bar sipping a bottle of water I'd brought from home – too risky to drink anything from there, I doubted they'd be allergy-compliant. I looked around me twitchily in case anyone was eating nuts nearby; they sold them over the bar, a hanging line of packets that looked as if they'd been there since 1972.

That's when I felt a breath on my neck, and some kind of tingle ran up me. Not pleasure exactly. Awareness, really. That someone was watching me. I half-turned to see a ginger-haired man with a wide, freckled face. 'Like it?' he said. He was drinking Guinness. I could see the foam on his lip. 'The music. You like it?'

'Mmm. What's that big flat drum thing?'

Matt turned slightly; saw I wasn't talking to him, turned

back to the music. I could hardly see past his broad back in his blue fleece.

'A *bodhran*,' the man said. 'And that's a tin whistle and a squeeze box and a wooden flute.'

I sipped at my water. 'Well. I suppose it's better than Justin Bieber.'

I felt him laugh then – more breath on my neck – and we left it at that, and at some point later in the night I was introduced to him as the local policeman – a Garda, they call it here – and we shook hands, and it was all very polite but I knew it was there between us, the awareness, and I knew he'd been watching me all night, and he knew that I knew it too.

Chapter Fourteen

'Hello there! Welcome!'

Paula and Rory had barely arrived in the reception of Enviracorp – flourishing plants; a rolling video showing slow-mo breaking waves, women lowering themselves into seaweed baths, smiling housewives feeding seaweed to their in-no-way fussy families – when they were tag-teamed by a young man and woman in suits. Everything was so clean, so corporate. A shiny iMac sat on the reception desk, which was unmanned. Only the driving rain outside reminded you you were on a tiny island in the Atlantic.

The woman who greeted them had curly russet hair and a snub nose. 'Ellen,' she said, smiling. American. 'I'm sorry, we're kinda short-staffed today. The storm, you know. Most of the workers wanted to leave yesterday so we ran a boat over.'

Paula frowned. 'Your staff left the island already?'

'Well sure, we can't keep them out here if the weather's bad.'

Of course, they were perfectly within their rights to come and go, even if Matt and Fiona were missing. But it struck her as somehow off, like no one was really taking this seriously.

The man with Ellen was an erring-to-chubby type with a smiley, likeable face. He announced himself as 'Dara'. Irish. From Galway, she thought. Neither of them older than thirty.

'How can we help so?' said Dara. 'Matt's dead popular at Enviracorp, he's been doing a brilliant job. Is it looking like they've had some kind of accident?'

They were walking now, down a sealed-in metal tunnel that linked two of the company buildings. Lashed by rain on both sides, it gave the impression of being on a ship at sea. 'Can we talk to the Head of Operations – Dr Monroe?' asked Paula. 'We met her yesterday briefly. I have some questions.' Mainly, why were they so generous to random half-drowned sailors.

Dara soothed. 'Of course, of course. We thought you'd like a bit of a tour of the place first. Get an idea of how we work, how Matt fitted in. These are the research labs.' Behind porthole windows, rows of microscopes. No one in sight. 'So in here's where they find uses for the chemicals we extract.'

'You see,' Ellen enthused, in her all-American accent – Texas maybe? 'There's a lot more to seaweed than meets the eye. There's the well-known uses, of course – thalassotherapy, edible weeds . . .'

'Agar jelly,' chipped in Dara.

'. . . but we've also identified many uses in manufacturing and even biofuels. Seaweed is an excellent source of iron, iodine, and many other materials. Best of all, it's eco-friendly and all there for the taking.'

'We really have a garden under the sea, that's hardly being used!' Dara grinned. What were these two on? No one was that excited about seaweed. 'Of course, Irish people have eaten seaweed for years – dulse is one kind – but it's fallen off the menu a bit. We think the time is right to rediscover our underwater harvest.'

Underwater harvest? Paula gave a sceptical look to Rory,

who was examining the labs with a blank expression. She said, 'Your workers aren't all islanders, I take it?'

'No, we bring most of the research staff over on a boat during the week. Some of them actually fly in from all over the world, through Shannon airport. But we employ locally where we can – from builders to drivers to canteen staff.' Dara looked at his watch, which Paula noticed was a very nice one. 'Like Ellen said, though, most people have gone early today.'

'And Matt Andrews? What was his role?' She might have imagined it, but she thought she saw Ellen look to Dara for confirmation before answering.

'Oh, we had Matt in to do some environmental impact studies. We're very keen to work in harmony with nature here. Matt was keeping an eye on the seabirds, and the fish and seals . . .'

'It's a very diverse habitat!' enthused Dara.

'. . . and making sure they were all happy. We wouldn't want our extractive technologies causing any problems.'

Paula thought of the questions in her coat pocket. She had to tread carefully, avoid putting them on their guard.

They passed labs and greenhouses, everything almost deserted. In one large, hangar-like room, a single worker in a protective suit was hosing down what looked like empty growing beds. 'They've not all gone then,' said Paula. Why was the place so quiet? It looked like a ghost town, not a functioning plant.

'A few of our workers live in,' said Dara easily. 'We've dorms on site, so we do. But I'm afraid most of them don't speak a whole lot of English. You know how it is. Overseas. Anyway, shall we keep going?'

Paula had seen the nurseries, the education centre, and

even a prototype seaweed bath when she decided she'd had enough. 'When can we see Dr Monroe?'

'Just a minute. Would you like to see the drying and packing bays? Dried seaweed accounts for . . .'

'I'd like to know if Matt Andrews found something,' she said. 'In his environmental impact studies. Did he find some impact?'

Dara and Ellen exchanged a lightning-quick glance. Paula recognised it – it was like the one she and Guy Brooking used to share, the ability to communicate whole thoughts without a single word. 'Why don't you come into the coffee room?' Dara said, giving nothing away. 'It'd founder you outside; nice warm drink'll sort us all out.'

Paula followed them down the corridor, mostly because she was thirsty and dying for some tea, and they went into a bright, warm room with windows looking out on the Atlantic. The walls were lined with watercolours and it smelled of coffee. Ellen went to the water cooler and filled a jug, then poured it into the kettle. 'Coffee? Tea?' Paula asked for tea, but Rory just shook his head at the offer.

'So . . . did Matt report any concerns?' she asked, sitting down on a comfortable armchair. Enviracorp looked after its staff.

Ellen blinked. 'As far as I know, Matt was satisfied that we met EU standards, isn't that right, Dara?'

'That's right. I wasn't aware of anything wrong at all, now.'

'So if we needed to, we could see his reports, his data and that?'

Dara screwed up his face. 'Aye, well, of course you could in theory, but the thing is, he didn't keep his stuff here.'

'Then where did he keep it?' She narrowed her eyes.

Ellen shook her head. Paula could see a smudge of foundation on her chin covering a reddish rash; she looked tired and stressed. 'He has an office here but he worked by himself mostly, all over the island. Sometimes he came into the canteen to say hi. Like Dara said, he was real popular. But recently – he didn't come in so much.'

'Maybe Dr Monroe would know more. When can I see her, please?'

Another little glance between them. 'Oh, I'm real sorry,' said Ellen in tones of aw-shucks sincerity. 'I guess we didn't explain. She's not working today.'

'Then where can I find her? Does she live on the island?'

'She has a house here, yeah, but we don't know if she's about right now. She's been helping the search teams, you see.' Dara's face was wide and guileless. 'I can leave her a message.'

Paula looked round her at the coffee room, painted a pale apple green. There was free Nespresso, and baskets of wrapped chocolate biscuits, and the air was warm and cosy. She was trying to conjure the missing person, as she had so many times before. How could a six-foot-tall man, strong and healthy, be one moment safe here in this room with its sachets of UHT milk, and then the next just vanish? Be . . . nowhere? But he had to be somewhere. That was what kept her coming back to these puzzles, time and time again. People didn't just vanish. They were always somewhere, and someone, some place, would know where. And why. And she'd done this long enough to know when she was being fobbed off. Outside, the wind had picked up, and the sound of it worrying around the flimsy tunnel was like banshees howling.

Chapter Fifteen

Paula buckled herself into Rory's car, scowling at the building. 'Is it normally that quiet in there?'

He started the car. 'Must be shutting up shop for the weekend. Which way now?' She felt he was humouring her again, and a small acid-blast of anger flared up in her chest.

'Well, what do you think, Rory? Given the evidence. The blood in the kitchen – Fiona's type. Missing couple, missing boat, smashed bulb? Why does nobody seem remotely bothered over here?'

Rory yawned. He actually yawned. 'Because. We're used to it. The sea, it takes people. Every year, usually. It's sad but it's the way of things. Why did you ask about Matt's data?'

'Just wondered if he had a bolt-hole somewhere. Might give us some clues.' She didn't want to name it, even to herself, the vague niggle in the base of her spine that made her keep things from him. 'I guess what we need is . . . God!' She jumped as there was a thump, and a hand appeared outside the fogged-up window of Rory's car, banging on it. Paula rolled down the window (budgets weren't high in the island Gardaí, clearly).

'Hello?' A high, nervous voice. Female. They could barely see her face behind the scarf she wore. 'You're the police? I need to talk to you about Matt.'

* * *

Mary O'Neill was from Cork, she said, though the accent had almost been schooled out of her by stints in MIT and Cambridge. She was a research chemist for Enviracorp. She sat nervously in the back of the jeep, in her black puffa coat and woolly hat. 'I've a place on the north side of the island. I don't like staying in the dorms on site.'

'Why not?' asked Paula, wondering what the woman wanted.

'It's just . . . you can't say anything against the company while you're in there. Not even a moan about the canteen or the computer systems. It's almost like a cult, they all love it so much. Like they've drunk the Kool-Aid. Isn't that what people say? I need a bit of space sometimes.' Her eyes darted around the jeep. Rory hadn't even turned to look at her, but was staring out the blurred windows at the fogged-in landscape. They could have been on the surface of the moon, for all they could see.

'What did you want to tell us?' Paula checked the time on the dashboard. The last ferry was in three hours. She had to be on it, to get back to Maggie. Home seemed a million miles away right now.

Mary bent over in a lung-rattling cough before she answered. Paula winced; she really couldn't afford to catch a cold. 'Well, Matt and I were friendly. We'd chat about work and that, have a coffee. So it was me he came to when . . . he found things.'

'Things?' Paula tried to stay calm. Everyone on this island seemed terminally afflicted by talking-slow disease.

'The research he was doing. It's not true what they're saying, that everything was fine. He found abnormalities. Puffin eggs, too fragile for the chicks to stay alive. A seal pup with no eyes. And the seaweed . . . well, the levels of phosphate and nitrite were off the chart. He was afraid of a bloom, even.'

Paula looked to Rory for support: none came. 'Can you explain that a bit, Mary?'

She spoke impatiently, as scientists often did to lay people. Paula was sure she was sometimes guilty of the same. 'An algal bloom. We're pumping all these nutrients into the sea, you see – all the by-products of the processes we do here – and Matt thought it was causing . . . something.'

Rory cleared his throat. 'Mary, listen, maybe you can cut to the chase for us. What is it you're on about?'

She blinked, then set her jaw. Her eyes were fierce and beady behind her steamed-up glasses. 'Matt thought there was something wrong. On the island. That it had to do with the plant, with the chemicals we were using.' She looked at them.

Paula wished she could ring Maeve. 'I see. Mary – does the name Puffin the Magic Dragon mean anything to you?' From the corner of her eye, she saw Rory frown.

The scientist smiled, automatically, a warm and unfeigned smile, and Paula wondered exactly how friendly Mary O'Neill was, or wanted to be, with the missing ecologist. 'That was Matt's little joke. Hiding his identity. He loves the puffins, you see. He hated to see them suffering.'

'He wrote a report, yes? An anonymous one?'

She nodded. 'I think so.' Another cough tore into her for a moment. 'Sorry. I'm coming down with something, I think.'

'Tell me, Mary – why would he send it to a paper, instead of telling his bosses? That was his job, wasn't it, to look for abnormalities and monitor them?'

'Well, that's the thing. He did tell them.'

'And what, they didn't listen?'

'Oh, they listened all right. Why do you think they've shut the place down? Trying to clear out any trace of whatever chemicals we've been using. Cover it up.'

Paula digested that. Matt, knowing more than he should. Matt, now nowhere to be found. 'But why would he use a code name?'

'Because,' Mary said matter-of-factly, 'they listen in. They're tracking our emails. Why do you think I'm talking to you out here? They can hear everything in there. It wasn't safe.'

Paula glanced at Rory, who gave a small shrug. Outside, the wind was worrying around the car, and in the back of her mind an anxiety about the ferry was growing. *They listen.* What to say to that? It was the same thing Andrea Sharkey had told her. Who did they think was listening? 'You mean . . . the company are spying on you?'

Mary nodded emphatically, making the bobble on her hat nod up and down, throwing herself into another short coughing fit. It would have been comical if Paula didn't feel an uneasy chill crawling down her spine. She wished Fiacra had been able to come with her. 'I see. So Matt wrote the report, and then – what?'

'They've taken him,' she said, as if this should be obvious. 'They want to keep him quiet. About what he found.'

'And Fiona?'

Mary wrinkled her nose. 'Oh, her. I don't know about her. Maybe she knew something too. But she didn't believe him, you see. Even when it was staring her in the face.'

Rory was no help, looking out the window again and clearly communicating without saying a word that he felt this whole thing was ludicrous. Paula didn't know what to say. 'Right, Mary. Thank you for this. Can we . . . come to you again if we find out more? You'd be a witness?'

She hugged her coat around her like a bird fluffing up its feathers. 'A witness to what? I didn't see anything. I just know Matt was worried and he planned to blow the whistle. I better go, I can't let them see me with you. What you need to do is find his work.'

'His work?'

'He had samples, data, that sort of thing. It's in his boatshed. Have you not found that yet?'

Rory shifted in his seat. He knew where it was, clearly. Why hadn't he suggested looking there?

'We'll go there next,' Paula said firmly. 'Just in case we need you, though – you live on the north side?'

She nodded reluctantly. 'Pebble-dash cottage on the beach. You can't miss it.'

'Thanks. Are you going back to the mainland tonight?' asked Paula.

'No, I'll be staying, helping with the search. I consider here to be my home. Though I don't think the islanders agree. Please find Matt. Please help him.' Mary opened the door, letting in a blast of icy sea air, tinged with rotting fish, and vanished into her own car, a lime-green Honda that seemed more suited to a city than this bleak countryside.

Rory turned to Paula, leaving a moment of eloquent silence. 'Be handy if you'd have told me about that report.'

'I needed to check it out first. Think she's telling the truth?'

'Dunno. She sounds like she's away with the fairies. Load of nonsense.'

Paula wasn't so sure. Why would Andrea have said the

same thing? And would Matt really have fabricated a whole report? 'How come it's not been searched already, this boatshed?'

Rory gave his trademark shrug, the one that suggested if he was any more laid-back he'd have trouble staying upright. 'Didn't think we'd need to, it's only a wee damp place. I'll take you there now if you want.'

Bob

1986

'Well, Sean. How you doing?'

Sean Conlon – twenty-five but looking more like forty, surly and watchful as a fox. He lolled in his chair in the interview room, very much at home. Quite the ladies' man by all accounts, but all Bob could see was the arrogance, the slackness, the straggly hair and pierced ears and tattoos up his arms. 'I'm saying nothing till my lawyer gets here.'

He'd engaged Colin McCready as his solicitor, of course, like all the Republicans did in Ballyterrin. And Bob happened to know that Margaret Maguire worked for McCready, as a receptionist. The thought of it made his chest sore. 'Aye, he's on his way. Just wanted to have a wee word with you first. Man to man.' PJ Maguire was off the O'Hara case, luckily. Too close to the family, though he was raging about it, had barely spoken a civil word to Bob in weeks.

Conlon sneered. 'Look, I know nothing about O'Hara. I've an alibi.'

'Aye, Sean, I'm sure you found some woman to alibi you. But maybe you'd like a wee look at the footprint we got at the scene.'

Some stirring then, a vague wariness. He glanced at the two bits of paper Bob slid over the table. 'So? You'll not find any pair of shoes on me that match those, Sergeant.'

'No, I'm sure I wouldn't. Long burned or bucked in the canal, I don't doubt.'

'No comment.' He smiled. The wee bastard.

'See that print on the left, though? That's not from John

O'Hara's murder. That's from another wee case we had a few years back. Do they look like the same shoes to you, Sean? Because they do to me.'

'No idea. I'm not a detective.' But Bob had seen it, the involuntary curl of the feet under the table, even though he'd be wearing different shoes today.

'Know what case that was, Sean? You remember some-body shot Paddy Dunne during the Hunger Strikes, 1981? Remember the big riots? Dunne was about to come out against the strikes, and somebody didn't want that, so he got shot. His wife found him when she brought his youngest back from nursery. Four, he was, the wee lad.'

Conlon didn't react. These kinds of details did not work on hardened Provos. They'd learned to believe it was all justified, gunning men down in front of their children, blowing up kids who got in the way. All part of their tinpot war.

'Now, what I'm thinking is, Sean – there's a lot of Republicans in this town would love to know who killed Paddy Dunne. Popular fella, he was. Not to mention that prolonging the hunger strike killed off another six men. So if the same person who did that was also at the scene of John O'Hara's murder, I'm thinking someone could join the dots quite easily. Someone who knew exactly which man was sent to shoot John O'Hara the other night, for example.'

Silence. The man's eyes narrowing over the table, focusing now, although still not sitting up straight. 'No comment.'

'I can help you, Sean.'

'I want a lawyer.'

'Aye, you'll get one. I just want to know your thoughts about this wee matter first.'

'No. Fucking. Comment. Are you deaf?'

'I'm not, no, and I'm not blind either. Those are the same shoeprints.'

'Doesn't prove anything. Not if the shoes are gone.'

'What if I said there was a witness? To the O'Hara killing.'

Sean opened his mouth, then shut it again. *Careful, careful.* 'If you'd a witness, Sergeant, you'd be doing this right, with a lawyer and another pig in here and the tape recorder running.'

'Maybe you're right, Sean. It could be we can't prove it. It could be there's no point even trying, as you'd only get a sharp lawyer and walk. So here's what I'm thinking – I can make this go away. This . . . link.' He laid his hands on the two bits of paper. 'The lab might spot the connection, but even if they do, we don't have a name for the 1981 killing. So what would be the point? And who has the time? Sure aren't we up to our eyes in murders, never mind trying to find who shot some Provo five years ago? No, we're not too bothered about Mr Paddy Dunne. But I think some fellas in this town are *very* bothered. I'm thinking they'd love to see these bits of paper I have here.'

Conlon licked his lips. He didn't know where this was going and didn't like that one bit. His voice was low. 'What do you want?'

Bob leaned back. Job done, and the joy that flooded you when you'd broken them, it was so bright and harsh he was nearly afraid of it. A man could get hooked on that. 'Oh, nothing much, Sean. We can't prove it, as we both agree. I'm thinking more of a wee favour. One favour and I'll make sure no one follows up this wee link I'm after spotting here.'

'A favour. What?'

'Oh, I don't need one right now. Who knows when I might? Just be ready, Sean. Just be ready and remember it was Sergeant Bob Hamilton made this all go away.'

Chapter Sixteen

It didn't seem possible, but the north beach was even windier than the rest of the island. Paula could hardly close the door of the jeep when they parked up. It was a white, wishbone-shaped arc of sand, the sea that ate at it grey and forbidding. Beyond, nothing but the Atlantic.

They made their way to a small collection of wooden sheds, soaked in decades of saltwater and rain. Paula and Rory didn't speak as they crossed the beach – it wasn't possible to be heard over the wind. The white sand crunched under their boots. The shed was unlocked, and inside was at least slightly warmer than the beach, if dark and comfortless. The wooden walls and floor were damp, and the seaweed-slippy place for a boat to rest was empty. Rory turned on a small torch and they took in the rest of the room, as the wind moaned outside – a desk made from an old door, an upturned paint tin for a chair, and, incongruously, a small laptop sitting on the desk, with a thin layer of dust on it. 'They never kept the boat here,' he explained. 'It was on the beach near their place, usually. But it's gone now.'

Paula had spotted a sleeping bag in the corner, a thermos beside it. 'Look,' she nodded. 'He must have been staying here. I wonder why, it's freezing.' A row with Fiona, perhaps? Or hiding out in the days since they'd gone missing? She peered in the corners, the light of the torch failing against the dark – silted-up sand, a few shells, a discarded loaf of the local bread. Fish bones. A thought was crystallising in her head, nasty but clear-edged. He'd killed her. Matt had killed Fiona – in the kitchen of the lighthouse, maybe some argument or accident even, that explained the blood – and then he'd hidden here, before giving up and taking the boat out. To where? Could you make it to the mainland in this weather? But what did that have to do with Enviracorp?

Something else was registering on her senses. 'Um . . . can you smell that?'

Rory's jaw had tightened. 'A dead fish, maybe.'

But it seemed more than that. An animal stink. Paula felt fear run through her, anchoring her to the earth. 'Where's it coming from?'

Rory ran his torch around the walls, casting crazy shadows, and the beam fell on a large plastic container, the sides closed with clasps. The kind you'd use to keep files in, or children's toys. He hesitated a moment, and she nodded him on: open it. The noise of the clasps was loud in the small place, like gunshots. He took something out, turning it over in his hands, as if trying to figure out what it was. Paula heard the rustle of plastic. 'Jesus,' he said.

Paula went closer to look. Inside the trunk were lots of small plastic bags, ziplocked and neatly stacked. Inside those seemed to be . . . she could only describe them as specimens. What looked like a dead mouse, its features pressed flat against the plastic. A puffin, stiff with saltwater, its colourful beak grotesque under the wrapping. Something bigger underneath, that Paula was afraid to look at. 'Is it . . . ?'

'A cat,' said Rory faintly. 'Etta Baxter lost hers two weeks back.'

'Is he meant to keep these here?' *Calm yourself, Maguire.*

Matt was an ecologist. Taking samples was probably part of his job. They were obviously dead when he found them. Of course they were.

'No. They're meant to be at Enviracorp.' Rory stepped back, putting down the bag, wiping a hand on his waterproof trousers, as if disgusted.

'So, what . . . what's the matter?'

Rory had frozen, his torch pointing up into the dark recesses of the ceiling. 'Christ. Did you see this?'

She whirled around. In the light beam, the letters looked bold and clear. Red paint – yes, it was paint, that's all it was – on the black walls. She spelled it out to herself, trying to sound calm. 'Blood Tide. What does that mean?'

'No idea. There's more.' Rory moved the torch down to some smaller writing. Again, it was all neat and readable, which made it more disturbing somehow. *A blood tide is coming. The sea is full of blood.*

Paula was willing Rory to say something, anything, explain it away as an island thing, an in-joke, a phrase standing in for something innocent, but he just stood, holding the beam up, explaining nothing. 'Holy Christ,' he said, after a while. 'He was losing it. He'd lost the plot.'

Paula just stared at it. 'Um . . . We'll need to protect this scene until we can get forensics over. Have you any police tape?'

'You don't think we should gather it all up, for safe-keeping like?'

'No. They'll need to take pictures. They'll need to see . . . what it's like.' She wasn't sure a picture would capture how chilling it was, those words on the damp black wood, the wind howling and worrying outside.

'Shh.' Rory caught her arm. Even through the fabric she

could feel that his gloved hands were freezing. 'What's that noise?'

'Shit. Shit, shit, shit.'

It was the first time she'd seen Rory show any emotion. He hadn't even blinked when the half-dead sailor was washed up, but this – the huge grey seal that had crawled onto the beach near Matt's boatshed – seemed to have shifted something in him. 'Is it hurt?' called Paula. She was staying well back, knowing that animals this size could easily lash out when in pain. It must have been two metres long, its huge body a hundred shades of grey and black and white, like the stones scattered on the beach. A low keening sound was coming from it, as it shifted on its front flippers on the wet sand. The eyes, normally inky black, were filmed over with some kind of milky residue.

'Something's wrong,' muttered Rory. 'A seal. A fecking seal this time. This is not . . .'

'What?' She was shouting; she could hardly hear him. The wind was so loud here, down on the exposed beach, and the waves crashed onto it not twenty paces away. 'Has he beached himself?'

'He needs a vet!' shouted Rory. 'Usually we get someone over from the aquarium on the mainland, and they rehabilitate the animal.'

'Can they even get out here?'

He said nothing, looking out at the swirling waves. Paula clutched her hood against her head, hearing her own blood over the roar outside. 'Rory?'

'I'm thinking.' He turned. 'We need to get Rainbow.'

'*Rainbow*?' Who the hell was Rainbow? Was it even a person?

He ignored her, trudging up the beach, feet crunching on the shingle. Paula followed him, the wind stinging any bit of exposed flesh, thinking in the vague depths of her mind: *God, I hope he hasn't lost it as well.*

Chapter Seventeen

'Er, Rory? Where are we going? What's happening?'

He was driving fast, so fast that Paula was pressed against the side of the jeep as he spun round the island's narrow, grass-infested roads. He kept his eyes fixed forward. 'I need to get someone to take care of the seal. He's sick, we can't get the vet over in time – so I need someone who knows animals.'

'And there's someone on the island?'

'Aye. Sort of.' He'd turned in at a gate Paula hadn't noticed on the way over, hidden in overgrown hedge, high and forbidding. He rolled down the window and stuck his arm out, pressing an intercom that was also hidden in the bushes. It looked very swanky for the island. There was a buzz and she heard him shout, 'It's me. I need your help. There's been another one.'

Rainbow, as it turned out, was the first name of Dr Monroe of Enviracorp, as Paula saw when she came shuffling down her driveway a few minutes later. She was bundled up in black waterproofs and carrying a small case, similar to the one that Anne the forensics officer had. Her eyes skipped over Paula, who was feeling thoroughly confused, saying to Rory: 'What is it? A whale?'

'Seal. He's in a bad way.'

Her face was set in hard lines. 'Right. Take me to him.'

As Rory started the car, ramping up to the same reckless speed, Paula looked between them. 'Dr Monroe? I'm sorry, are you a vet or something?'

She kept her eyes on the road. 'I was a marine biologist. A long time ago.'

'And what's the matter with the seal?'

Neither of them answered. They had reached the beach now, and they all jumped out into the sand-blasting wind. Paula felt she should go too, to bear witness somehow, even if she could do nothing to help. The seal was still there, slumped on his side again, eyes shut.

'Is he dead?' Rory asked, over the wind. They all had to hold down their hoods against it, and Paula wondered again about the ferry. Surely it would run. It had to run. She'd get away, back to Maggie.

'Not quite.' Rainbow approached the seal without fear, her bare hand out, and he let her put it on his large, wet head. One eye opened, and the whole body seemed to convulse, as if he was trying to move. A flipper waved ineffectually. Rainbow side-stepped it and examined the large gash on the animal's side. 'He's been fighting. Other seals, I suppose.'

Paula had never heard of seals fighting. 'Is that normal?'

'Well. Normal has quite a wide remit around here.' Rainbow ran some more checks, pressing her face against the seal's side to listen to his breath, opening the other eye. Paula held herself tense, as the seal moaned and twisted, but he didn't seem to have the strength to do anything.

Finally, Rainbow turned to Rory and shook her head. Held her hand out. 'I'll do it.'

Rory sagged slightly, and felt under his coat. Paula was

startled to see him hand over a gun. She didn't even know he carried one; most Southern Irish officers didn't, unlike in the North where they were still routinely issued. Rainbow held it with expertise, as if she was used to weapons, and turned to the animal – Paula suddenly realised what was going to happen but didn't have time to brace herself – and then the bang echoed across the beach, and the seal slumped further down onto the sand. There was very little blood. His eyes darkened, and he was still.

Rainbow handed the gun back to Rory. 'Damn shame. One of the biggest I've seen here. See if you can get Paddy or someone to drag the body out to sea. That's the best way for it to happen.'

Rory took the gun back, and Paula saw with surprise he was almost crying. He glanced at her, defiant. 'It's not fair. They never hurt anyone. They're innocent, and then they have to die like this. It isn't right.'

Rainbow was kneeling down in the wet, yielding sand, pressing her fingers into the dead animal's forehead and muttering something to him. A kind of blessing? An apology?

'What's her deal?' asked Paula, leaning in so Rory could hear her. 'She's done this before?'

'She used to work at Seaworld in the States,' said Rory, his voice thick. 'Till one day she realised what it was doing to the whales. Keeping them in there. I don't know if she ever got over the guilt, so she does her best for the wildlife round here. And if we need to put one down humanely, she's the best. She never hesitates.'

Paula watched the woman. Thinking of the samples in the shed, the shut-up factory, the mysterious report. *They listen.*

'Listen, I don't think we should mention what we found

here to anyone,' she said pointedly, keeping her voice low. 'Or the – rest of it. Not until we can get it bagged up and photographed. OK?'

Rory just shrugged. 'I'll put some tape up. Dunno what else we can do.'

The woman pressed her head, briefly, against the animal's, eyes shut, then stood back up, all business again. 'You should come and have tea at my place. It helps to sit a while, after something like this. Let's go now.' It seemed impossible to argue with that, so they followed her back to the jeep and all climbed in in silence.

Paula looked back at the woman in the mirror, and saw there was a smear of blood on her white forehead.

Bob

1987

'Sergeant Hamilton! You're wanted.'

He looked up from his groaning desk at the young admin girl. He already had two murders and a pipe bomb to deal with that week; he didn't need anything else. 'What?'

'That shooting earlier, the paratrooper killed at the checkpoint?'

'Not my case.'

'But she's asking for you.'

'Who?'

'The woman they arrested.'

A woman?

Then the interview room downstairs, and Margaret Maguire inside. Bob never swore, but he almost did then. Anderson, the arresting officer, was a big ignorant bigot from the Bible Belt. 'Are you mad? That's Maguire's wife!'

Anderson shrugged his meaty shoulders. 'Found her with the body. Just a precaution. Taig, isn't she?'

Bob banged open the door, making clear with a look that Anderson would be back shovelling cow dung in County Wherever for this. 'Margaret, are you all right?'

She was covered in blood. All over her face, her hands, her white blouse and grey skirt. She was staring down at her hands, where it was ingrained around her pretty pink nails. His heart failed. 'Are you hurt?'

'It's not mine. They . . . they shot him. I was going through a checkpoint and I gave him my licence then next thing I know he's down. Only a wee lad, nineteen if he's a day.'

'Was it a sniper?'

'Aye. Maybe. I don't know.' She looked up, her blue eyes fierce. 'He died in my arms. In my *arms*. Asking for his mummy back in Birmingham or wherever. How is this right?'

He felt a stab of fear for her. What she'd done, it was enough for the IRA to start looking at you. In the seventies, a mother of ten had helped a dying soldier, shot on her doorstep, and been Disappeared for it. They'd never even found her body.

'And then your lot drag me in . . . my husband's a police officer, I told them, but they hear a Catholic name and here we are.' Tears welled in her eyes – angry tears. 'They searched me, Bob. I was just going to work.'

'I'm sorry. I'm sorry. They'll be dealt with, I promise.' And when PJ found out they'd probably run back to Ballynowhere by themselves, if they'd any sense at all. 'We should get you looked at. Are you sure you weren't hurt?'

'It's his blood, I told you. That wee lad they just shot, like a dog in the street. He was nice, Bob. He called me madam. It's not his fault he's been sent over here.'

Bob had nothing to say. She got up, her hair falling down, her face so lovely and so angry, splashed with the dead soldier's blood. 'Where's it going to end? They killed John, and they kill wee lads in the street, and John's wee boy, he'll never be the same, and my Paula's crying every night about the bad men and afraid her daddy won't come home one day. Afraid someone'll bomb his car or the house or shoot him in the head.'

He'd nothing to say to that either. The risks were huge, and for a Catholic officer like PJ, even higher.

'It has to stop,' said Margaret, setting her jaw. She moved past him. 'Can I go, then? I'm going.'

'Wait!' She turned in the door. 'What . . . what will you do?' He was afraid for her, a terrible pressing fear that was even worse than what he felt every day, got up with in the morning and went to sleep with at night until it was almost comforting, his old companion. He was afraid because he could do nothing to protect her.

Margaret paused, wiping a hand over her bloody face. Making it worse. 'Do me a favour, will you? Don't tell PJ I was here. Don't tell him anything.'

Chapter Eighteen

'I'd hoped to speak to you at the plant earlier,' said Paula. The nettle tea she was drinking was horrible, so she set it aside.

Rory had gone off on 'police business', or so he muttered, which she hoped meant protecting the bizarre contents of the shed. They were sitting in the kitchen of Rainbow's vast house, which had once been a convent until the last of the nuns gave up on the wind and cold or died off. Paula remembered: they'd come here, she and her mother and father. It was open to the public then, the nuns serving tea and rock-hard scones out of this very kitchen. She'd been bored, wishing they'd go on holidays to Spain or somewhere. Not knowing that would be the last one they'd ever have together, not knowing how little time she had left with her mother. Taking her for granted, as you did when you were twelve. The place still smelled of damp clothes and turf fire, a comforting smell Paula associated with those holidays in the west of Ireland, her in the back of the car, her mother and father in the front. Nineteen ninety-three, the last time they would ever be together like that.

Rainbow swilled her own tea, which she'd served in lumpy hand-cast mugs. 'It seemed more important to search for Matt and Fiona, not sit in work.'

'Looked like the plant was closing up anyway.'

She sipped. 'Like I said. Finding them is our priority. And with this weather, we thought it best to send everyone else home.'

'Except the ones on site.'

'They can hardly go home, Dr Maguire. Some of them are from thousands of miles away.'

Paula toyed with a crumb of oatcake. 'You knew them well, then, Matt and Fiona?'

'I do know them,' she corrected. 'Matthew and I had many areas in common. I may work on the business side now but marine life is still my first love.'

Paula's mind clicked. If Matt had concerns about the wildlife on the island, would he have spoken to this woman off the record, maybe? Would she know if he'd written the report, and what had happened to him after? 'Do you – did Matt talk to you much about his work? What he was doing day-to-day?'

'Of course. He loves it out here, loves talking about the wildlife. It means so much to him, this job.'

'And Fiona? Did she like it here?'

Rainbow considered it for a moment. 'Fiona is more . . . cosmopolitan. I don't know how well she fitted in out here.'

'No?'

'People saw her as sticking her neb in, as they say. Interfering, you know.' It was odd to hear the local idioms in the American accent.

'How do you mean?'

Rainbow lifted a shoulder. 'She's a doctor. It's her job to ask questions. And people here . . . they don't like being told what to do.'

Paula looked at Rainbow, who was dipping her biscuit in her tea, staring into the beige liquid. Her own drink had left a nasty metallic taste in her mouth, as if the kettle hadn't been descaled in years. No surprise: the kitchen was dirty, dust ground onto the floor tiles and into the old wooden table. It seemed a strange place for a businesswoman to live, in this gloomy old hulk that looked like it hadn't been cleaned since the nineties. 'You like living out here?'

'Love it. There's nowhere else like it in the world. And I have roots here.' She saw Paula's surprise. 'Oh yes. My great-great-great grandmother moved to New York in 1827. The women often went first, you know. To work as servants. So when the company wanted to put a base here, I jumped at the chance to come.'

'You don't find it . . . lonely?' That wasn't quite the right word. It was that sense of always being outside, not being in on the secret, that she got out here.

Rainbow set down her cup. 'Dr Maguire – do you know what people mean when they say there are "thin" places on the earth?'

'Sort of magical spots, is that it?'

'More or less. The Celts believed – and lots of people still believe – that in some places, the barrier between our world and Heaven is thinner. Closer. You can just feel it, a sort of atmosphere. This island is one of those places. There's a reason this convent was built here. It's worth putting up with some cold and isolation, anyway.'

It was a strange thing for a scientist to say. With her long grey hair and clever, lined face, Rainbow looked more like some ancient priestess than the Head of Operations in a big company. 'Did Matt and Fiona think so too?'

'Matt did. As I said, I'm not sure Fiona found it so easy to adapt.'

Paula didn't respond for a moment. 'Dr Monroe . . .'

'Oh please, call me by my first name. If you can bear to. Hippy parents, I'm afraid.'

'OK. Did Matt ever tell you he had concerns about Enviracorp? That he'd noticed any strange results in his work?' Thinking of the seal, stranded and blind. The box of dead things. Trying to tread carefully.

Rainbow set down the cup. 'Look. I'm going to be frank with you, Paula. You seem like a frank kind of person. The last time I saw Matthew – and I hate to say this, he's a good man and my friend – but he wasn't making a whole lot of sense.'

'How do you mean?'

'He was . . . angry. Paranoid, I would say. Saying things about being watched and so on. And he hadn't been in the office for days. I was concerned about him, to be honest. So whatever results Matt may have gathered in the last few weeks, I'm not sure if they can be taken at face value. Do you see what I mean?'

'When was this?'

'About a week ago. I asked him to come and see me, and he was ranting and making no sense, and – I can't explain it. I just knew he was off.'

'Off.'

'Yes. Like when an animal is . . . When things aren't working inside, and the behaviour is abnormal. We saw it all the time in the aquatic parks. You force the animals into an unnatural situation, the stress builds up, until finally it explodes in strange directions. I tried to make him see, but he said he had to go as people were probably listening . . . I mean, I ask you. Total paranoia. If I were you, I'd be trying to get his medical records. See if he had a history of mental illness. I even wondered if he'd taken something.'

'Drugs, you mean?'

'Yes. But I would be very surprised. Fiona, you know, she policed him. He couldn't even eat a damn sandwich without her snapping about grains and refined sugars and his glycaemic index.' She sighed. 'I should have done something. I know that. But I thought it would all be all right. You just try to . . . you know how you explain these things away for as long as you can? Because when you do face them, nothing will be the same again. Do you know what I mean?'

Paula thought of that night, before her wedding. The blood on Aidan's bruised hands, the way he wouldn't meet her eyes. How she'd persuaded herself – he'd cut himself shaving. He'd fallen over. Then the next day, in her wedding dress about to walk into the church, and Aidan arrested for the murder of Sean Conlon. Yes, she knew exactly what the woman meant.

She prepared to ask her usual question – the one that was so simple, but could tell you so much about a person and those who knew them. 'Rainbow . . . Where do you think Matt and Fiona are? If you had to guess?'

'Well, my first thought was they went in the sea, of course. It happens all the time. Hence the search, though if the storm picks up again that'll have to be called off. And then I did think, with Matt the way he was, maybe he was hiding somewhere . . . but then why haven't we found them? On an island this size? And where's Fiona? So. No. I think they must have come to some harm. Of one kind or another. You understand?'

Paula nodded, thinking of the words smeared on the wall in that shed. *Blood Tide.* Something wasn't right. A man who was raving, who'd keep dead things in a box, that was a man who was more than capable of hurting his girlfriend.

And there was blood in the kitchen. She was starting to feel in over her head, looking at a surface far above her that was rapidly disappearing. And where was Rory? Why was he taking so long?

'You're a missing persons' expert, yes?' Rainbow said. 'I looked you up. Some very impressive cases you've worked on. They wouldn't have sent you here if they thought it was a straightforward accident.'

'No,' Paula admitted. 'There are some . . . inconsistencies. But nothing concrete so far, so we may well be wrong.'

'Well, I've told you what I know, and I hope it helps. Poor Matt. He's a good guy. But even good guys can snap. And if you find those samples of his – we could really do with taking a look. Making sure things are OK. It's our top priority – after finding Matt and Fi, of course.'

'Right,' she said, non-committal. Did Rainbow know about the boatshed? She might wonder what Paula and Rory had been doing there, put two and two together. If only they'd had the team to clear out the place right away. The forensics, the photographers, the uniforms. Without that back-up she was operating blind, feeling her way on instinct. 'Will you be around if I need to speak to you again?'

Rainbow made a gesture that encompassed her gloomy kitchen, the island around them. 'Where else am I going to go, Dr Maguire?'

Chapter Nineteen

'Can you hear me?' She was shouting over the crackly phone line in Dunorlan's, gawked at by the villagers who'd gathered there for an afternoon pint or something stronger. This was ridiculous. It was the twenty-first century. How could she be stranded on an island with no reception and hardly any landlines? 'Fiacra?'

'Aye, I hear you.' Fiacra sounded grouchy. 'They're keeping me in overnight. The ligament's damaged, they said. Might not be playing any rugby for a while.'

'I'm sorry to hear that, but what am I supposed to do? I can't just leave it, we need some kind of police presence here. There's a potential crime scene sitting open for anyone to tamper with.' She'd already told him about the boatshed, and the seal, Rainbow's description of Matt, paranoid and agitated. And then there was Mary O'Neill's story, of the company hunting him down, covering up their mistakes. *They listen.* She suppressed a shiver that ran down between her shoulder blades. 'And I can't stay out here by myself either. I need to hand it over to someone.'

'You've got McElhone.'

'I know, but . . .' She didn't know how to say she didn't trust him. He was at the bar talking to Colm, not far enough out of earshot. 'Listen,' she said quietly. 'Should he have a gun out here?'

'McElhone? Not Garda-issue. Suppose he might have a private licence but he shouldn't be carrying one, no.'

'So you see what I mean. Someone else needs to come. Someone from outside.'

'They're working on it, far as I know. Weather doesn't help matters. How is it out there?'

'Not too bad, I guess.' By the standards of an Atlantic island, heaving seas and relentless rain were indeed not too bad. 'The ferries are still running, at least. Is there anything else you can tell me?'

'Well, I managed to chat to one of the doctors here. You were right, Andrea Sharkey's family were out for Fiona's blood.'

A common enough reaction. Looking for someone else to blame, so you wouldn't have to believe that the woman who laid her children to sleep at night could be the monster under the bed as well. 'I don't get the impression Fiona was that well liked out here, even before that. Seems like she found it hard to fit in.'

'Right. So that might be a motive for someone to hurt her – getting revenge on the outsider.'

Paula pressed a hand over her ear – the noise in the bar seemed to have risen. 'Did you find out anything else?'

'Maybe.' Behind Fiacra she could hear hospital sounds, voices echoing, the beep of machinery. 'Guess who paid for Andrea's transport to hospital, and who's been shoring up her husband's farm in the meantime? Enviracorp.'

'Why would they do that? He doesn't work for them, does he?'

'Good question. Taking CSR to the limit, isn't it? And that fella from the boat – he's not the first foreign worker from the island that they've had to treat over here.'

'No?'

'They'd three women brought in back in November. Chemical burns of some kind, to the face and hands.'

Paula thought of the worker she'd seen hosing down the factory, in a rubber suit. 'From the plant?'

'They wouldn't say, and they discharged themselves soon as they could walk – the doctor sounded raging about that – but she said she recognised the logo on one of their coats. Enviracorp.'

Overseas workers. Doing the worst jobs, the ones no Irish people wanted, gutting chickens and pulling potatoes out of freezing soil, and yes, steeping themselves in chemicals all day. 'Can we find them?'

'Doubtful. They'll likely be long gone by now, off on another job, fishing boats or factories or who the hell knows.'

She sighed, looking at ancient messages scratched in the metal surround of the phone. 'So we've got islanders angry with Fiona. We've got Matt possibly losing it. And we've got this company with their fingers in everything. So what am I meant to do now?'

'Sit tight for a minute. I'll see where they are with getting someone else over.'

'I need to go home, Fiacra.'

'I know. I'll call them now. OK?'

Paula thought of Maggie, safe, hopefully in Saoirse's warm house. Or cuddled up on Pat's knee watching CBeebies. She was fine – wasn't she? And this was something Paula could do, try to untangle this mystery, even if she couldn't help Aidan or find her mother or do anything useful at all back home. 'OK,' she said, guilt feeling leaden in her stomach. 'Would you do me a favour and ring Maeve Cooley, see if she knows any more about Enviracorp?'

'I won't have to, she's been in to see me already. With a fruit basket, can you believe. Bloody press.'

Paula couldn't help but smile. 'They're still keen on the story then?'

'Aye, well, they're all stuck here waiting out the storm. It's as good a story as any, even if Matt and Fiona are in the sea.'

'They're not.' She couldn't be sure, of course, but she knew there was something else going on. There were just too many lies out here, so many that the clear air felt thick with them.

'Aye, well. You need to get those samples secured and keep Matt's data safe. Otherwise all we have is an anonymous report by someone who's maybe off the rails.'

'I know. All we can do for now is put police tape round it and hope it doesn't blow away in the storm. Get better soon, Quinn.'

She hung up, and stood by the phone for a minute, thinking. Rory had moved away from the bar, into the main part of the pub. She dug out her mobile – next to useless at the moment – and scrolled through to find the number for Fiona Watts's doctor. She fed some more euro coins into the old machine, feeling once again how very far from home she was.

'Sorry, Dr Michaels? You're breaking up a bit.'

Fiona's doctor had the singsong accent of the region. 'Hello, Dr Maguire? I was saying I saw Dr Watts a few times just – she has a specialist in London, of course.'

'So I heard. Fiona was quite severely allergic to various things – her diet was very controlled?'

The doctor made a slight sighing noise. 'Dr Maguire –

you're not a medical doctor, I take it, yourself?'

'No, forensic psychology.'

'Well. I don't wish to speak ill of my profession, but have you heard it said that doctors can be terrible patients? Dr Watts, she'd been tested when she was wee and told she had intolerances to several things. Gluten, seafood, eggs, nuts – most of the common allergens, in fact. I redid the tests when she came to me and told her I thought most of them had cleared up to the point where she could eat normally again. That often happens with childhood allergies. Provided she had an EpiPen to hand, I thought at most she'd be at risk of a reaction maybe once every five years. I'd always lean towards normalising life as much as possible for my patients. It's easy enough to steer clear of nuts and seafood, but the other things – you're looking at buying all your food in ready-made, and it's a wild price and not very good for you.'

Paula's mind was racing. If Fiona had started eating normally again, and it had triggered an attack – they could just be waiting to find her body. 'And did she do what you suggested?'

'Well, that was the strange thing. I thought she'd be pleased. Especially living out on an island, it can't be easy to get the food she needs. But she was furious. Said she could die, did I not realise. She didn't take a thing that hadn't been guaranteed allergen-free, you know. It was costing her a fortune – she had it shipped in from America. Of course, being far away from medical care was a factor in case of an attack, but I thought all things considered there was more risk from the lack of fresh food. Her cholesterol levels were quite elevated.'

Something about it didn't quite make sense, though. 'Dr Michaels – why did she have the tests redone, then, if she didn't want to hear the answers? She asked you to run them?' Paula pressed her finger in her ear; the noise levels were ridiculous.

'She did.'

'But why, if she didn't want to start eating normally?'

'Well now, it was because of the baby, I'd say. She wanted to know if it would be affected.'

Paula frowned. 'What baby?'

'You didn't know?' She heard his voice, solid and unwavering. Just another case for him, sitting safe and warm in his office on the mainland. 'Fiona was pregnant, so she was.'

Fiona

You know how it creeps up on you. You're thirty-five, and you have a wonderful man – admittedly a man you feel straining away from you, always trekking off to remote islands and cliffs and wrecks, a man you know you can't hold in London forever – and you're happy enough. You have a good job. You're respected. You run triathlons on the weekend. Sure, your friends and even your younger sister have, one by one, silently as mushrooms in the night, started to reproduce. You buy one baby present, then another. You go to a baby shower, then three more in a year. Then you realise you are more familiar with the entire range of JoJo Maman Bébé than a childless woman should be. And you start to wonder. Why not me? I'm a person just like everyone else. Why wouldn't I also have a baby, at some point?

You try to discuss it, in a light, round-the-houses way, with that elusive man of yours, who looks alarmed and mutters something about not being sure it's right to bring children into the world. Not when it's like this. War and terrorism and climate change. And you agree. Yes, it's terrible. Children are so awfully unsophisticated, with their dirty nappies and neediness. And what about our nice furniture and our mini-breaks and my pelvic floor. But look, you want to say. Those birds you love so much, they don't stop having babies just because their chicks get eaten by rats and drowned in oil and their nests are swept away by waves. They just do it. They lay those eggs, and sit on them, and fly back and forward with food, and nurture them. It's all they know how to do, however stupid it might be. Why should we, with our Wi-Fi and our wine-of-the-month club, and our weekends away in country cottages, why should we be any different from other animals?

Yes, there were a million reasons Matt and I shouldn't have a baby. But all the same I needed it, with a hungry, voiceless desire I couldn't explain. And I knew more than anyone I was running out of time.

Chapter Twenty

Fiona pregnant. Why hadn't she thought to ask that question? The bloody vitamins, same ones she'd taken herself when she was expecting Maggie. Sitting there in the bathroom cabinet in the lighthouse. Fiona was thirty-six, she'd just moved to the countryside from London. Of course she'd been trying for a baby.

As Paula hung up, she found she was haunted by stats. The riskiest time for a woman was pregnancy. Over twelve percent of pregnant women in Ireland had faced domestic abuse. Twenty-five percent were abused for the first time while expecting. And the blood in the kitchen. And Matt jumpy, aggressive. The silence out here. If you weren't used to it, you could crack. They'd already had a murder and almost another in the past few months.

Frustrated by these inconsistencies, Paula had just turned back to the bar – and that's when the flying bottle hit the wall, just where her head had been seconds before. She ducked, instinct taking over. Behind the bar stank of stale beer. She peered out – somehow, in the few minutes she'd been on the phone, a full-scale bar fight seemed to have broken out. Rory was in the middle of it, trying to separate two bearded fishermen, identical but for the colour of their bobble hats (one red, one green). A middle-aged woman in a huge knitted jumper was screaming and trying to scratch the face of the barman, the young handsome one. 'Get your fecking hands off me!'

'Bridget, Bridget, stop it!' Colm was saying ineffectually. The fishermen seemed to be cursing at each other in Irish. Rory was in the middle, saying nothing but pushing on them both with grim determination, trying to hold them apart. He wasn't strong enough. They were almost nose to nose now. And Paula saw one was holding a dull-bladed fishing knife in his hand.

Panic coursed through her. *Ring the police!* But she *was* the police, and the sum total of the local Gardaí was here in between them. And it hit her – there was no one else to call. No armed response team, no more officers, no ambulance or helicopter. They were alone, on this clump of rock in the middle of the stormy sea. So she did the only thing she could think of. She grabbed the dish-nozzle, the one that was used for spraying water over glasses, and aimed it at the brawlers, and pressed.

For a moment they stopped, shocked, water dripping off their faces. 'Jesus, me good jumper,' said Bridget, straightening her fluffy monstrosity – it had kittens on it, Paula saw, surreally. She hadn't thought this through. What if they turned on her now? Calmly, she said, 'What's this about? Surely there's no need to be knocking lumps off each other, now, is there?'

Green-hat fisherman spoke – she identified him as Paddy, the one who'd rescued the sailor from the sea. 'What would you know about it, lassie?'

'I'm here with the police in an official capacity, so I'd advise you to stop what you're doing right away. More officers are on their way over and arrests may be made if there's any assaults. Oh, and don't call me *lassie*.'

Paddy grunted. 'It's this fella here you should be arresting. The dirty scutter gets his fishing done by foreigners, so he does, illegals, and he pays them like field mice and lets them drown. He should be in jail. I wouldn't treat a dog that way.'

'Don't you talk about my Brendan that way!' said Bridget. 'He's only trying to make an honest living, and that Paki jumped off the boat by himself, isn't that right, Brendan?'

Red Bobble-Hat, or Brendan as he seemed to be called, straightened his overalls. They had the green Enviracorp logo on them. 'He did, so. Lord knows what takes these fellas. They don't want to work, is all. Never done an honest day's labour in their lives. He was looking for a free ride and he didn't get one.'

'So he jumped into the sea because he's lazy? In that storm?' Paula was sceptical. 'And they picked up the rest of your crew anyway, in a similar state.' And if the boat had been doing work for Enviracorp after all – transport or dredging or something – that would explain why Rainbow sprang to look after José the sailor. But why had she lied about it? Was she trying to cover up the fact they used illegal workers?

'The man was pure terrified. He couldn't even swim,' supplied the barman, who was shaking his head, and starting to pick up some of the glasses and bottles shattered in the contretemps.

'Are you calling me a liar?' Brendan squared up to him. 'You wee pup. Good job your daddy was my cousin or I'd punch your lights out.'

'You are a liar,' rumbled Paddy. 'A liar and a murderer, as good as. I don't know what happened on that boat, but thon foreign fella has an interesting story to tell. Isn't that right?'

Bridget made a squealing noise in her throat. 'Brendy, you give him one.'

'Calm down!' Paula held her hands up. 'You need to calm down or arrests will have to be made.'

Bridget sneered. 'You stay out of it, missy. Coming over here, telling us what to do! What are you even doing here?'

'We're looking for two missing people,' she began, her blood boiling.

'That doctor! It's her you should be talking to about murder,' said Brendan. 'Sure Andrea Sharkey'd be grand now if she'd done her job. I say good riddance, and I hope she did go into the sea. I hope she's drowned, the dirty English bitch.'

Paula almost missed what happened next, it was so fast. One minute Rory was breathing hard, smoothing down his thick Aran jumper, and the next he was launching himself at Brendan, punching him over and over in his reddened drinker's nose. Bridget screamed. 'Jesus! He's killing him!'

'Rory!' shouted Paula. 'Leave him. Garda McElhone!'

Rory didn't seem to hear her. He held Brendan – a bigger man than him by at least a foot and thirty pounds – by the hair on his neck, dislodging his hat, and thumped him over and over, with a noise like someone kneading a loaf of bread. Thud, thud, thud. 'RORY!' Paula shot a panicked glance at Colm the barman, who shrugged helplessly. What could he do?

She rounded the bar and approached, arms held out. Bridget was still screaming. Paddy stood, a gleeful smile on his face. 'Stop him, for God's sake!' Nothing from Paddy or the barman. She couldn't stop Rory herself, she wasn't strong enough. But she had to. She grasped his arm, which was swinging like a piston, and felt the muscles under it, realised she wouldn't be able to hold him back, not a chance. 'Rory. Rory, *stop* it!'

There was a bursting sound, as Brendan's nose broke, and finally, Rory stopped.

Chapter Twenty-One

'What the hell is going on?'

The bar was quiet again. Colm had chased Brendan, Paddy and Bridget off home, still slinging insults and Irish curses. She'd been weeping and Brendan's nose had a distinct dint in it. Dimly, Paula wondered if they'd suc.

Rory stared down at his battered hand, which was turning the purple of an over-ripe plum. 'I dunno. I just – saying that about her, when she did her best, and all she ever wanted was to *help* people out here . . . I saw red. And then, I don't know. I couldn't stop. I knew I should stop, but I couldn't.'

'What's going on out here, Rory?' Paula remembered the list from Fiona's office. Jimmy, Andrea, Matt. Two in secure units, one missing. But there'd been another name, hadn't there? 'Who's Niamh Ni Chailean?' she said. 'You never told me about her. Did something happen to her too?'

Colm was suddenly busy clearing glasses, fiddling at the bar. Paula was close to losing her own temper. 'I mean it, Rory. If you know something, you better tell me, or I can guarantee you there'll be consequences. Why didn't you tell me about Jimmy, or Andrea, or that Matt was having mental health problems? What's going on? Who is Niamh?'

He flared up. 'Niamh has nothing to do with it! Jesus, can you not keep your nose out for one second? Do you not understand what's good for you?'

She squared up to him, hands on hips. 'What's good for me is to find out the truth. And for Matt and Fiona, which is all I care about. I don't give a crap about your stupid island politics. They're missing, and they deserve our best efforts to find them. So tell me what you know. *Now*.'

Rory heaved a big sigh, and met Paula's eyes. His were red-rimmed, sunken. 'Fine. Come on then.' He stood up, holding his injured hand awkwardly against himself.

'Where are we going?'

'I'm taking you to Niamh.'

'Driving? With your hand?' And with the wind whipping foam off the harbour outside. 'Can you not just tell me, Rory?'

He was already moving to the door, opening it and letting in a chill blast that threatened to engulf the warm fire. 'No. I need you to actually see it. Otherwise . . . I don't think you'll believe me.'

'This is it?'

A simple pebble-dashed bungalow, on the south side of the island. A washing line tangled by the wind, and kids' bikes stacked against the wall. They'd need to be tied down if things got worse, Paula thought distractedly. Rory hadn't said a word during the ten-minute drive across the island, clods of turf and branches sailing past them in the wind. He stopped the car outside the house and got out. She followed, holding her hood down, feeling the swelling pressure of the wind.

The door was answered by a woman of about thirty-five, with a reddened face and a baby on her shoulder. She was wearing pink pyjamas with a print of cartoon dogs on them, though it was four in the afternoon. 'Ah Rory, it's yourself. I didn't know who'd be out knocking in this weather.'

'Sorry, Michelle. This is Paula, Dr Maguire – she's over with the police, looking for Matt and Fi. Can we have a wee word?'

A look seemed to pass between them, and Michelle paused for a moment longer than normal. The baby made a hiccupping sound. 'All right,' she said. 'You'll blow away out there, I suppose. Sorry I'm in my jammies, I wasn't feeling well earlier.'

Inside the house was warm and noisy, a variety of small children darting about the place. One of about Maggie's age was sitting in front of Peppa Pig in the living room, in just a nappy and vest. It was an episode Paula knew well, which made her miss Maggie even more. 'Hi there. How's Peppa getting on?' Every surface and wall was covered in framed family photos, toys, little children's clothes.

The child just looked at her curiously. 'Cathal, would you take the lady and Rory to see Niamh?' said Michelle, juggling the baby. 'Then go into your room and play, like a good boy?'

He trotted off obediently, eyes still trained on Paula. Rory he seemed familiar with – the Garda greeted him with a grave, 'And how's Cathal? Good boy.'

'Do you want me or . . . ?' said Michelle. 'Only I've something on the stove.'

'If you don't mind, Michelle, we'll just talk to her. We'll take it easy. I promise.'

'Because she's been doing much better.'

'I know. Thanks.'

'On you go, then. Cathal will show you.'

The little boy led them to a bedroom door that was

covered in stickers. Boy bands fought for space with ponies and kittens. Rory knocked softly, then opened the door. 'Hiya, Niamh, can we come in?'

Lying on the pink bedspread there was a girl in pink leggings and a jumper, her hair in loose falling-down plaits. 'Rory?' She got to her feet, nervy.

'Hi, Niamh,' said Rory. Paula tried not to look surprised. It seemed Niamh Ni Chailean, who was on that list with a murderer and an attempted baby-killer, was no more than ten years old.

'Am I in trouble again?' asked Niamh. One foot, with a pink spotty sock, went up to scratch awkwardly at the back of her other leg.

'Niamh,' said Rory, and he sounded so gentle, it was hard to believe he'd broken a man's nose just minutes before. 'How are you?'

'Um . . . OK.' Niamh was hovering by the bed. A slip of a girl, all legs and eyes and ratty blonde hair, hands rolled up in her sleeves. Her room full of toys and the beginnings of teenage things, glitter paints and crop tops and pictures torn from magazines.

Rory nodded towards a shelf. 'Been out collecting?' The shelf had objects arranged on it in a line. A shell, a clump of dried seaweed, a piece of smooth sea glass, milky-green, and what looked like part of a small skull.

'Did you get this on the beach, Niamh?' asked Paula.

'Daddy said it was a dog, maybe. Washed up here. I thought it might be a dinosaur or something.'

'Niamh wants to be an archaeologist,' Rory explained. 'Can you tell this lady what happened to you, back before Christmas?'

'Do I have to?'

'I'm sorry, you do. We're trying to find Dr Watts and her boyfriend – we need you to help us by telling what happened. Can you do that?'

She nodded. 'The thing that happened at school?'

'Yes.'

'Um, well, I don't remember all of it. Mary and Sinead were being mean to me – teasing me because Daddy's away.'

'Moved out to the mainland,' Rory said out of the side of his mouth to Paula. 'And then what?'

'I . . . I got mad. They wouldn't stop laughing at me and it's not fair. So I – hit Mary.'

'What did you hit her with, Niamh?'

Niamh squirmed. 'The thing. For the fire.'

'The poker, is that right?'

She nodded unhappily.

'They have an open fire in their school,' Rory explained. 'It's an old building. And the fire was lit and she got the poker out and . . .'

Paula nodded. A sick feeling spread through her stomach.

'Mary's OK now,' said Niamh. 'Isn't that right? Dr Watts made her better and she went to the hospital in the big helicopter.'

'Well, she's better, yes. They're going to put her glass eye in soon.'

Paula shuddered.

Niamh said, 'Rory? When can I go back to school? I don't like working here, Mammy never has time to teach me.'

'I don't know, Niamh. We'll have to see.'

'Niamh,' asked Paula, leaning forward. 'When did this happen, this thing?'

She looked to Rory, who nodded. 'Before Christmas,' she

said. 'We were learning carols. I like "Away in a Manger" best.'

'Yes, me too.' Paula dredged up a smile. 'And you don't remember it properly, what happened?'

She shook her head. 'It's sort of all red and fuzzy. Like it wasn't really me doing it. Mammy said it must have been the devil got into me.'

Paula waited in the car while Rory said goodbye to Niamh's mother. The ferry would be coming in soon, and hopefully on it would be someone she could hand this case over to, and get away. Away from this island where children blinded each other and mothers fed their babies to the dogs. They'd all used that phrase – the devil. Niamh, Andrea and the near-drowned sailor. Could she really leave, with all this going on? Paula winced at the headache gnawing on her temples. She was dehydrated, probably, only rancid tea to drink all day, and there'd been no time for lunch, what with dying seals and bar fights. She rooted in her bag but found no tablets. Maybe Rory had some. She opened the glove box of his dirty jeep, sifting through car manuals, throat sweets and tissues. No painkillers. She'd be back on the mainland soon, though, so she'd just have to cope until then. She reached down for some papers that had fallen out, hoping Rory wouldn't mind her hoking about, and then she saw the name on the printed notes – *Andrea Sharkey*. These were Andrea's missing medical notes. In Rory's car.

A door slammed, and she hastily shoved them back, clumsily shutting the glove box. Rory dashed over to the car, holding up his collar against the rain. 'All right?'

'Yeah. Um – so did Niamh get any kind of psychological assessment after this happened?'

He started the jeep. 'Fi tried to refer her, but she didn't go. The da's not about and Michelle can't get over to the mainland with all those weans in tow.'

'So no one did anything?'

'We're looking after her. She's in the best place she could be.'

The best place she could be was a children's mental health unit, thought Paula, but she remembered the notes in the glove box and closed her mouth again. 'So what does this mean, Rory? Why did Fiona have this list of names?'

He kept his eyes on the road. 'I dunno. I think maybe . . . she'd spotted that Matt wasn't well. That he was having problems. And so were a few other people. Niamh, and Jimmy, and Andrea.'

'There was a link?'

He shrugged. 'Like I say, life can be hard out here. I don't know what she was thinking. I wish I could ask her but I can't.' He glanced over at her. 'You should go. Ferry's coming in soon. You should be on it. Dunno if they'll run after this.'

'It'll be fine,' muttered Paula stubbornly, even though she could feel the wind rock the car. 'I need to hand over to whoever the Gardaí send.'

'I can do that.'

She said nothing. She didn't trust him, not a bit. She didn't trust anyone on this island. 'No, it's best if I do.'

He looked at his watch. 'Whatever. Mind if I drop you, then? I said I'd help with the search parties, see if we can do one last push before it's dark.'

She looked out the window, at the rain splattering on the glass. Another evening drawing in with Matt and Fiona gone, missing in this storm somewhere. She wasn't sure anyone could survive in that.

* * *

Down on the quay, Paula watched the boat come in. Rory had dropped her off with her bag and gone, with muttered goodbyes. Something primeval in her seemed to be soothed by him leaving, and by the sight of the ferry. A boat, that was something could carry you back to the real world. Rescue. Sanity. Bringing you to where things made sense, and there were doctors and police officers and people in white suits who'd take all the madness and put it in little boxes and bags, give it a name, label it.

She could see on its deck a cluster of people in the rain. Hopefully bringing someone who could help with all this. And maybe then she could hand things over, and leave on the return journey herself, and go back to Maggie and her life. Her life with all its own problems and dilemmas.

Paula shivered, and pulled her coat round her. Maybe the task in hand was easier than all that. Even if everyone on the island seemed to be hiding something and no one, including the policeman, could be trusted. Even as she stood waiting for the ferry she was thinking: just one more night, Maggie wouldn't mind, she was being well looked after by her doting doctor godmother and her adoring grandparents just down the road . . . Slowly, very slowly, the ferry docked, and the burly ferryman leapt off, ushering out the passengers, shrouded against the rain in anoraks and hoods. She was waiting for someone who looked like a Guard. They tended to be strapping, hurling-player types who could wrestle a cow or a suspect to the ground, and so she almost didn't notice the slimmer figure which had stopped in front of her, fair hair lifting in the wind. Grey eyes that matched the sea. 'Paula.' English accent.

Paula blinked, pieces of her mind clicking and whirring

into place like slots on a fruit machine. But what was he –
how did he – *why hadn't someone told her for God's sake*
– and she tried to smile. 'What the . . . eh, what are you
doing here?'

'They sent me to help you,' said Guy Brooking.

Fiona

There were lots of downsides about living on the island, sure. No mobile signal. Crap Wi-Fi. Hardly any TV channels and a social life that consisted of 'trad night' down in Dunorlan's. Not to mention the fact I couldn't even eat if the boats didn't run. And the looks they gave me for having my crates of water and food brought over! Rory even said to me did I know their tap water was the purest in the world. I'm allergic, I explained. Any trace of the wrong thing and I could be dead. Especially as we're so cut off.

But aside from all that, I was looking forward to the change. For one thing, I didn't imagine I'd have to deal with anything heavy at my surgery. A few cases of trench foot, maybe, from working in wet fields, or the odd farm accident (though those can be horrific enough). Not the rickets and inherited diseases and obesity and child abuse I saw in London, though. Peaceful and calm, like a latter-day Dr Quinn Medicine Woman, that'd be me. And of course, with all the extra time Matt and I would have to spend together, I'd soon be rounded and smiling, cradling my bump as the waves crashed behind me. It was bound to happen. Right?

Wrong.

Though I didn't see the pattern at the time, the very first indication was that incident at the primary school, before Christmas. I got a call about ten on the Monday morning. It was the teacher, Lucy Cole is her name, a nervy blonde I always see flirting with Colm in the pub. She wasn't making much sense. 'Oh God, her eye! I think she's – will you come, doctor, please come now!'

I sped up the hill on foot – it's only metres away – with my bag, and when I got there here's this girl, ten or so, and

Lucy is holding a bandage over her eye, which is about the worst thing you can do for a corneal injury, and she's howling, and all the other children are screaming and crying, except for this one little thing – Niamh, that's her name, I had Mum in to persuade her to vaccinate the littlest kid, an uphill struggle – and she's sitting there, smiling to herself. I took the bandage off the injured girl – Mary – trying not to go pale in front of the kids. The poker, the one from the open fire in the classroom, had burned right through the girl's cornea and short of a transplant, she'd never see out of that eye again.

I saw right away there was nothing I could do, but of course I didn't tell them that. Lucy Cole was almost hysterical herself. I called the air ambulance. It was the first time I had to do that – the Trust had told me till they were blue in the face that it must only be used in emergencies, each trip costs ten grand or something like that. I'd listened, so this was the first time. But it wasn't the last.

And Niamh – I referred her for counselling on the mainland, which she didn't go to, and she was taken out of school. I remember being disappointed – London might have been stabby and awful, but I'd never seen a primary school kid put one of her classmate's eyes out with a red-hot poker. Then there was Andrea, of course, and then Jimmy a few weeks later, and Manus, poor old soak that he was. Jimmy was sectioned, taken off the island. But I did start to wonder. What were the chances, two homicidal patients in a population of 276? And I went back to look at the other cases.

I took a lot of flak for Andrea. It's always the doctor's fault, isn't it? But I want to state now that the woman did not have post-natal anything, let alone psychosis. She was coping perfectly fine the week before she tried to kill her baby, a bit tired maybe, which is natural when you've a newborn and small child. I didn't miss it, as there was nothing to miss.

Of course, I missed the wider thing that was happening – or rather, I didn't miss it, but I didn't know what to call it, and it was almost too big to see, and I was too afraid to formulate the idea that the very ground we stood on was crumbling away beneath our feet. But you can hardly blame me for that. In that respect I'm just the same as everybody else.

Chapter Twenty-Two

It wasn't easy, maintaining a professional demeanour. Not when the father of your child – who didn't even know it himself – had just turned up, hundreds of miles from where he was meant to be in London.

'They sent you all the way here?' Paula was pacing in front of the fire in Dunorlan's, unable to sit still. Why was he here? He was supposed to be gone, safe, out of sight and out of mind. Even if he rarely was that, not entirely.

Guy was sitting at one of the tables, perfectly composed in jeans and a thick grey jumper, sipping a latte which Colm had rather unexpectedly made from a machine. 'I was in Dublin anyway,' he said. 'Conference on youth crime. The Met asked me to come over here, seeing as we have all this experience together, and since the missing couple are from London.' He meant experience in missing persons, but they had other kinds too. *Hey, Guy, you know Maggie, my kid? Well, funny story, you're her dad.*

She folded her arms. 'No offence, but I was kind of expecting a team. Detectives, forensics, search dogs, that sort of thing.'

'They won't risk it in this weather. Instructions are to secure the area as much as we can and wait it out.'

'I was going to go home,' she heard herself say. Knowing

it was a lie, that she couldn't leave this case now she'd started.

'Of course, if you have to, you should.' He was polite.

'I would like to try and sort this out, though, before I go.'

'What's the story?' he said. Meaning this case. Meaning, she needed to focus.

She stopped pacing. 'So, this is a bit of a strange one. They briefed you on it?'

'Only the bare details. It's true what they said – the door was locked on the inside?'

'Yeah. And there's blood in the kitchen that's been wiped up, same type as Fiona's. Fiona was pregnant, and also suffered from some pretty serious food allergies. Their boat is gone, and the lighthouse bulb is smashed.'

He frowned. There was a very slight trace of coffee on his upper lip, like the foam you saw on the shoreline when the sea was rough. 'I see. How can that be, that it's locked from inside? They fell off or something? An accident?'

'I don't know yet. But it's even weirder than that. This island – you wouldn't expect much crime, right? But in the past few months there's been a murder, an attempted infanticide, and an attack that took a kid's eye out. And everyone seems to have blamed Fiona – for missing the mother's psychotic breakdown, anyway. So that's one motive – revenge.'

Guy's frown deepened. 'What else have you found out?'

Always the way with them – straight to the crux of things. No time wasted trying to explain it away, or convince her she was wrong. He just trusted her, and she trusted him. She'd always trusted him, she realised. Unlike Aidan. With him, she had spent those two years with her breath held in. Checking the whiskey bottle in the kitchen cupboard.

Sniffing his clothes for cigarette smoke. Feeling in his pockets. And she'd been right, hadn't she? Eventually, he had done something to let her down, tear away the floor beneath them like a slippery rug. So why couldn't she just let him go, as he'd asked her to so many times? Why did the thought of him in prison still fill her with cold pain, icy as the depths of the sea? She said, 'Matt Andrews sent an anonymous report to Maeve's paper – you remember Maeve Cooley, the journalist? – or at least, we think it was him. Saying that Enviracorp, this company with the processing plant here, they're poisoning the ecosystem. Leaking chemicals, and it's got into the food chain, started affecting the wildlife.'

'You think it's true?'

'Maybe. We found a seal, dying, and it looked – weird. And Matt had this boatshed, and I—' She would have to show him that one, so he could really take in the shiver of horror it sent down the spine.

Guy was nodding. 'So maybe he found something. The company messed up, now they're trying to silence him.'

'Maybe. But Matt – he seems to have been losing it. We've reports of him acting strangely, agitated, paranoid. So I don't know if we can believe anything he thought he'd found out. And there's more than that, Guy. The place just doesn't feel right. The way people look at you. Pulling down the hatches, you know? Even the local Guard . . . I just don't trust him.' How to explain the missing medical notes? What possible reason could he have for stealing those? Paula felt that she'd already found a lifetime of strange things out here.

He nodded. 'So where are they, Matt and Fiona? What's your current thinking? Are they dead? Did he kill her, if he was acting strangely? That would explain the blood in the kitchen.'

Paula thought of it, wiped up, but still leaving that ghostly damning trail. Of the words smeared on the wall of the shed – BLOOD TIDE. But each of these neat explanations seemed to slide away from her, out of wet hands. 'I don't know. I just don't know.'

'I guess that explains why you're still here, in the worst storm for a decade.'

She shook her head, frustrated. 'It was locked on the inside. How's that even possible? And why did no one else tell us about these other attacks? Fiona saw a pattern, I think. She had a list in her office of the names. And like I said, she was blamed for missing a woman's psychosis, the island had turned against her . . . what if they all know something and they're covering it up?'

Guy looked sombre. 'What can we do? We can't get a proper team out here till this weather dies down. And there's no one to arrest, by the sounds of it.'

The door opened, bringing in a gust of cold wind. Rory. Paula felt herself put her guard up, scanning the table for any papers or evidence, in a way she hadn't with Guy. She hadn't had time to warn him: *don't trust Rory.*

'Thought you were leaving?' Rory said, frowning to see her.

'I will. Later. Maybe. Rory, this is DI Brooking, he's—'

'Hi,' said Rory briefly. 'Listen, you better come. Both of you.'

'What's happened? We'll need to go to the shed and—'

'Later. The search party's found a body. A dead one, this time.'

Guy glanced briefly at Paula, and they both pulled on

their jackets, and as they followed him out into the swirling air, she found she was thinking about Fiona Watts's face in the picture on her office desk – smiling, tanned, happy. And seeing it beneath the waves, dead and cold.

Chapter Twenty-Three

Paula gritted over shells and hollowed-out crabs, the seaweed wet and stinking, surreally remembering the last time she'd walked on that solid sand. This was it. The beach she'd swum off, on the sunny, blowy day twenty years ago, plunging into the freezing water with her long, pale limbs goose-bumped. Her mother waving from shore, her red hair over her face. Sometimes it felt like that was the only way Paula could remember her. Far away, her face a blur. A stranger.

Near the edge of the water, which was grey and foamy, lay a mass which at first glance looked like congealed blood. Then she realised it was a red raincoat, saturated with water. She remembered the picture in the lighthouse – one of them in a red raincoat, she was sure. But which one? Matt or Fiona? Why couldn't she remember?

As they drew nearer, she saw a man was standing over the body, arms folded, back rigid against the moaning wind. She brushed sand from her eyes. Seamas Fairlinn, the owner of Dunorlan's. Seemingly unperturbed by being left alone with the body of . . . whoever it was.

Seamas acknowledged them with that barely perceptible nod Irish men employed as greeting unless the occasion demanded more (wedding, funeral, drink having been taken). 'We'll need to get this moved before any weans come by.'

Rory was looking down; he hadn't said anything yet.

Guy stepped forward, the wind blowing his fair hair over his forehead. 'Sir, I'm DI Brooking from the Metropolitan police – you're Mr Fairlinn?'

He eyed Guy, whose English accent seemed even more pronounced here. 'Aye. You've had a wasted journey, I'm afraid. Both of you.' Meaning Paula too. 'Anyone from round this way could tell you they've had some accident. No need for any police; it's no great mystery. They drowned. We'll find another body soon, no doubt, washed up.'

Guy kept his voice level. 'Nonetheless. Could you tell me what happened?'

'Was out with my wee lad, and we saw it. In the water.'

'And where's your son now?' asked Paula. No one else was visible anywhere on the shore.

'Sent him home to his mammy. He's no but thirteen years old, he doesn't need to be here.'

Sending a witness away from the scene – Paula knew how that would play with Guy. 'Could you tell us what happened then?' Guy said. He seemed to be assuming control, without anything being said. He was just one of those people. The type men would have followed to war, two generations before.

Seamas cleared his throat. 'We were going round the rocks, helping with the search, like. Thought if the storm had stirred anything up, that's where it would be. We saw something sticking out of the wee cave down there, bobbing along in the tide.'

'What was it?'

'Feet,' he said succinctly. 'So we thought we'd best drag it in and come back here.'

'You touched the body?' Guy was asking. 'I take it you didn't wear gloves or anything?'

Seamas faced him down. 'We don't leave people to float in the sea here, officer. We bring them in, of course we do. Even if they're not locals.'

Guy nodded. You wouldn't expect much else, not out here. Anyway, there was nothing they or anyone else could do now. The sea had taken everything away, leached out the person this had been. Paula was still staring at the face, trying to match it to the one she'd seen in the photos. The eyes swollen shut with water, the skin grey, looking almost nibbled-on in places. The hair dark and matted as seaweed. It settled in her slowly, the recognition, like stumbling into a patch of cold water. Yes, she knew who this was. No one she'd ever met, sure, or ever would meet now, but she felt it all the same, the settling loss that hope was all gone, squeezed out like the last breath in your lungs when you're drowning. Out of the corner of her eye, she saw Rory turn away. Maybe he was upset again, trying to hide it. This had been his friend after all.

The rain had started up again now, and the four living people on the beach looked up instinctively, pulling their coats around them. Drops pattered onto their hoods, making round, damp circles on the sand, and falling, unblinked off, onto the dead frozen face of Matt Andrews.

A short while later, the men had finished loading the body – Matt's body – into Rory's jeep, Paula hanging back, sensing that her help would not be welcome. Rory shut the door, and Paula put a hand on his shoulder. 'I'm sorry.'

'Aye. Well. Always knew it would end this way.'

'We might still find her safe.'

He didn't answer, and she knew there wasn't much chance. Had it really been an accident after all? 'Are you going to take him away?' Meaning the body. There was no chance of getting a pathologist over, and he'd already been moved once, so it made little difference.

'Aye. We'll take him to the pub, I suppose. There's a cold store that locks.'

'OK. Maybe I'll take DI Brooking to see the shed, then, before it gets too dark.'

'The shed? Oh aye. If you like. It's walkable from here.'

'We'll catch you back at the pub?'

'Yeah. Sure.'

She motioned to Guy, and as they trudged over the beach away from the body, she felt some strange kind of relief at putting distance between them and the dead man. And Rory too, of course.

She was relieved when the dark shadow of the little boatshed appeared ahead of her out of the swirling sea fog. The short walk had already left her numb with cold, her eyes and teeth full of sand grit. But she'd be able to show Guy the writing on the walls, and he'd explain it to her, and it would all become less terrifying and more understandable. He always had that ability. She willed herself on, trudging over the wet sand, pushing aside the ineffectual police tape. There was a strong smell of rot on the beach, and she could see at the water's edge the body of the seal still lay there. The waves lapped around its poor dead flippers and she wondered if the sea would come high enough to carry him back out, into the dark depths.

'Come on!' she shouted. Guy hurried after her, bumping against her in the doorway as she fumbled with her phone light. 'Matt used to work in here, his laptop's there and the samples he was collecting and . . .'

'Where?'

She swung the beam. The desk in the corner was empty, a square of dust where the laptop had been. She turned. The sample box was also gone. 'They've taken it! Fuck! I knew it.'

'You think the company did this?'

'They must have. But the wall, look . . .'

That was still there, the crazy red writing. Whoever had stolen Matt's things hadn't had time to clean it off. Guy stood, his own torch shining on, taking it in silently. Paula stood behind him, hearing the shriek of the wind and sea, feeling the cold breath that seemed to come out of the damp wooden walls. After a moment Guy said, 'Come on. There's nothing for us here. Let's find shelter for the night.'

Fiona

'Holy God.' Rory took my hand in his, staring at the cut that ran down the fleshy part of my thumb. It looked worse in the daylight, the edges of it barely knit, crusted in drying blood. 'He did this? Matt did this to you?'

We were in my surgery, my safe place, cosy against the howling winds outside. I'd put up a sad little Christmas tree in the waiting area, not that I or anyone else was feeling very seasonal. I pulled my hand back, ashamed. 'He didn't mean to. He just – I don't know, Rory. He isn't right.'

'What do you mean?'

'He's . . . he's not himself.' I tried again to explain. 'You saw Niamh. And Andrea. The way they just – that isn't normal. And Matt . . .' I was getting frustrated. I couldn't explain, couldn't make him see that Matt was not Matt any more, in the same way Niamh was not herself when she blinded her friend and Andrea was not herself when she put her baby in with the dogs. 'Something's wrong,' I tried again. 'Something is *wrong* here.'

'Fi . . . if he's hurting you, you should do something, you know.'

'He isn't hurting me. Well, he is, but not in the way you mean. Not yet, anyway.' Because it was hurting me every day to live with him, with the ghost of a man I'd loved. Who didn't sleep, who roamed the house staring out of binoculars from the lighthouse desk, who brought home a box of dead things and wouldn't tell me why, who couldn't eat and ached all over and woke up screaming in the night. 'I don't want that,' I tried again. 'I just need your help.'

He answered so quickly. He was sitting where my patients usually sat, where I put them in blood pressure cuffs or felt their necks or listened to their chests. Where I gave them answers, except now I had none myself. He was still holding my hand in his, light and delicate, as if it might break. 'I'll do anything I can to help, Fi. Anything. You just have to ask.'

And that was when I knew what I had to do. Because when you are scared, so scared you can hardly breathe without it hurting, it makes sense to figure out who you can run to for help.

'Anything?' I said.

Chapter Twenty-Four

The fire crackled, spewing out soft hunks of turf that fizzed and died on the hearth. Bits of bog, long-dead things bedded down for centuries, turned into something new. Paula watched it in silence, her glass of whiskey untouched on the table before her. She clearly wasn't leaving now, not when they'd found a body. She'd already called Saoirse to make her excuses. Maggie was fine, and Mummy was instructed to 'stay away longer' so she could keep playing with her 'Auntie Seer-sha house toys'. It was nice to be missed, Paula reflected wryly.

Guy too was staring into the depths of the fire, as if looking for answers, over the remains of the ham sandwiches Colm had scraped up for them. He'd looked up as she came back. 'How's Maggie?'

She couldn't help but wince as he said her child's name. 'Um. She's fine. Grand without me, it seems.' *And you're her dad, guess what?*

'I know the feeling. Katie's at Bath University now. Settled in well, making friends, not a drop of homesickness.'

Paula waited for him to mention Tess, his wife. Their marriage had been fractured by the murder of their son years before, and she was never quite sure if they'd make it. But they hadn't officially split up, as far as she knew. Always a grey area. He didn't mention her. She decided to change the subject. 'So we've found Matt, anyway.'

'Yes. Poor man. And Fiona?'

Paula shook her head slowly. 'Rory said they'd take a boat round the island in the morning, look in all the little sea caves. But if she went into the water too, the tide could have taken her anywhere now.' And with her all their hope of answers.

Guy knew her pretty well, even though they hadn't worked together properly for years. 'You don't like him, do you? McElhone?'

'I don't trust him. He had something weird in his car – medical records, for the woman who tried to kill her baby. Missing from Fiona's office.'

'Evidence he forgot to log in, maybe.'

'Hmm. You really think that?'

'I don't know the man. But you're right – we should be careful who we talk to out here. From now on, we only trust each other with evidence. Assuming we can hang on to any.'

'What did they say about getting a pathologist?' They'd taken their turns on the payphone, its scratchy connection coming and going as the wind grew.

'They won't send anyone over until the storm dies down. Too dangerous.'

'Even in a helicopter?'

'Especially in a helicopter. Those things crash all the time.'

She nodded. And there was no chance of getting back until at least the next day. So it was just her, and him, and a dead body, and an entire island of people who were probably lying to them. 'Is there something we can do?' she said after a while. 'I wish we'd bagged up those bloody samples while we had the chance. Can't believe they're gone.' A doubt was growing in her mind. When Rory had left her at Rainbow's, she'd thought he was going to secure the site. Maybe Andrea Sharkey's medical records weren't the only things he'd stolen. But however much she turned it over in her mind, she couldn't think of any reason Rory would do that. He already knew she'd seen it all. And when she'd told him they were gone, he'd sworn convincingly, his fists balling. She didn't think he was that good an actor.

'You were just following protocol. All we can do for now is sit tight and keep an eye on the body. Try to preserve at least some shred of evidence.' Matt's body was in the bottle store not ten feet from where they sat. 'What did you make of it?'

She tried to recall what she'd seen. 'There was bruising on his head – a wound on the temple.' She touched a finger to her own. 'I was thinking maybe he fell into the water.'

'Or someone pushed him. They need to check his lungs – if there's no water in them, he was dead when he went in. We could also look for obvious rock fall round the island, but with this storm we'd never be able to make sure.'

She nodded again. It was sobering how quickly all your usual weapons – forensics, a back-up team, even police tape – could be put beyond use. On the island, they might as well be investigating a death in the 1950s. No mobiles, a handful of barely working phone connections. She wondered if, living out here, you'd feel beyond the law. If you'd have to make your own. 'So I guess we're stuck out here.'

'For now.'

'Yeah.' It felt wrong somehow. Even though she knew Maggie was fine, and Aidan was miles away and didn't want to see her anyway, it didn't seem right to be out here with

Guy, after everything that lay between them. The secrets shared and secrets held back. The things she wasn't telling him.

'You asked earlier why I'm here,' Guy began.

'You were in Dublin, you said.'

'Yes, and I was keen to see you, of course . . .'

Her stomach lurched.

'But there's more, Paula. The reason the Met sent me over – well, she wasn't unknown to them. Fiona Watts.'

'She had a file?'

'Sort of. About a year ago, Fiona was working in a clinic in East London. Big immigrant community, predominantly Muslim. She had a patient whose parents wanted to take her overseas, to the Sudan. Fiona suspected something was going to happen to the girl there. Female genital mutilation, most likely. Then a forced marriage. But just before they were due to go, the girl disappeared.'

'And – they thought Fiona had something to do with it?'

'Not at first. I was called in, because of my work with the task force, and my background in the MPRU. They thought maybe there was some gang involvement, even radicalisation. I didn't think so. She was a very ambitious girl – Anika, that was her name – even wanted to be a doctor herself. I didn't think she'd risk her studies like that.'

It was the kind of case Paula would have loved to work on. Getting into the mind of a teenage girl, working through her complex network of pressures and motivations, the things that were pushing and pulling her to disappear. 'How come I didn't hear about this on the news, if she went missing?'

He shrugged. 'She wasn't a white middle-class teenager, that's why.'

Paula gritted her teeth. She'd forgotten how things were in London, how the disappearance of a child could be front-page news for decades, or forgotten in seconds, depending on who that child and their parents were. 'And what happened?'

'Well, we found her. She'd made it to a refuge and was hiding out there. The thing was, she said Fiona had given her the details. Even picked her up from school and dropped her off there. So that caused all manner of trouble – the practice had a policy of not interfering in such things. They're obliged to report FGM, but only after the fact. So Fiona was fired. For a while the local force even thought about charging her with kidnap, I believe. Hence the file. I believe there was a lot of harassment afterwards, from the local community. Stones thrown, bike tyres slashed, that sort of thing. Even an arson attempt. Fiona and Matt lost their house, had to move, go back to renting. So when they disappeared, the Met thought there might be a link to that case.'

'So, you came.'

'I came. But now I don't think so. It's something to do with this place, isn't it?'

'And what happened to the girl? Anika?'

'She was only fourteen, so they had to send her home to her parents, and the council didn't want to intervene.'

'So she was taken away?'

'Yes. I believe so.'

Silence for a moment. Then the howl of the wind. Paula knew, in her bones, that should she ever meet Fiona Watts – if she was even alive – she would recognise the woman as her kin. She couldn't promise she wouldn't have done exactly the same, in that situation.

Guy said, 'I thought you should know what kind of

person she was. She wouldn't have sat back and done nothing, if she saw what was going on here.'

'Not that we actually know what's going on.'

'Well. No.'

'What can we do, then?' she asked.

'Only one thing left.' Guy ran a hand over his eyes – he must be exhausted. 'We'll have to interview them.'

'Who?'

He shrugged his shoulders, hands wide to indicate the island. 'Everyone.'

Outside, the wind still battered the windows of the pub. It was dark already, as if the light had just struggled and died against the might of the coming storm. Colm came in from the back room and dumped more peat briquettes on the fire, making it snap and hiss. Paula stared at the warm glow of it, squinting at the tension headache which had coiled up in her temples.

Colm squatted back from the fire and pushed himself up. He looked knackered. 'Getting a bit sick of all this. It's been a bit weird out here since I came back.'

'Back?' said Paula, still thinking about Matt Andrews's dead eyes filling up with rain.

'Aye, I was in Dublin, studying at Trinity. Came back for Christmas was all.'

It was now mid-February, though; surely term would have started again. 'You didn't go back to college? How come?'

He shrugged. 'Wanted to stay, so I took a deferral. Ma seemed a bit . . . off. Like she called me Fintan a fair few times, and that's my brother in Australia. And she was always getting angry. My ma's the softest woman alive, never a bad word to say about anyone, but – she'd changed.

On Boxing Day I saw her – well, a wee mouse came out of the kitchen, and she just – she killed it with the poker. All its blood and brains on the carpet, and she just kept hitting it, like . . .' He glanced at the bar, where earlier Rory had battered the fisherman.

'And there's been more? Andrea Sharkey, is that part of it? Jimmy Reilly? Niamh?'

'Jimmy Reilly killed that man in cold blood. Right in here. It went all over me.' Colm looked around, as if seeing the arc of the blood across the room. Now Paula looked too, there were still faint stains on the yellow paint of the walls. Blood was hard to shift. 'And Andrea – well, they tried to say the doc missed it, post-natal something or other, I don't know. But Fiona didn't seem like the type to miss things, if you see what I mean.'

'Thorough?'

'Aye. God, she asked a million questions when I took my mammy in.'

'So what's going on?' Colm stared at the fire, and Paula felt it acutely, her status as outsider. She repeated, 'What's going on, Colm? If we need help, we can get it.' Her voice wavered, and she clawed at her head as the pain throbbed.

Colm rubbed his face. 'There's something wrong,' he said, almost embarrassed. 'There's something sending people crazy. That's what I think. I don't know what it is.'

She almost laughed at the clichéd phrase – sending people crazy, indeed – but she looked at Colm and he wasn't smiling. 'You mean with Jimmy Reilly, and Andrea and Niamh, and maybe Matt too? Something was wrong with him?'

'Aye, maybe. I didn't know him now, only to have a wee chat with when he came in. But the last while . . . he wasn't in much. He missed trad night on Sunday and all. Loved trad night, so he did.'

Paula looked at Colm. 'You went to the lighthouse that day, when Sergeant McElhone broke the door down? You were there?'

'Aye. Coastguard said the light was off in the lighthouse, and Dr Watts wasn't in her surgery, so Rory went to have a look. But it was locked so he came here and me and Seamas went. Seamas – Mr Fairlinn, that is, who owns this place.'

'And? What did you find?'

He shrugged. 'It was like Rory told you. Locked, but the top bulb all wrecked like. We thought they'd maybe fallen off.'

'But you think something's going on here? Like what?' Guy leaned forward.

Colm shook his head, pushing himself wearily to stand. 'I dunno. Something. Anyway. Need to close up now, folks, go and mind my mammy.' He felt in the pocket of his loose jeans. 'Here. Top of the stairs.' He set down two keys, one on a green plastic fob and one on a red. The handwritten label on one read 1, and the other 2. The sum total of the pub's available rooms. Paula had a memory – another trip to somewhere wild and cold, she and Guy having to share a room, and eventually, a bed. The feel of him beside her, solid and reassuring. It was eight months since a man had shared her bed, but she still woke up groping for Aidan, trying to pull his arm around her in the half-light of morning. Losing him again and again, every day.

Guy took the green one, and she lifted the red. No discussion about it. 'Tomorrow then,' he said. 'We'll start talking to everyone.'

Colm was pulling on his rain jacket. 'Lock the door behind me, OK?'

'Right.' Guy stifled a yawn. 'We could do with your help in the morning, if you don't mind.'

'Aye?' He looked wary.

'I need a list of every single person on the island. Kids, men, women, old people, visitors. Everyone.'

Chapter Twenty-Five

'Quinn? You still alive?' She'd managed to get through to the mainland on the payphone, relieved to hear his voice, a small and tenuous connection to the real world.

Fiacra's voice sounded tired. 'Just about. Still in this fecking place, can you believe it? The consultant's stuck in Tralee with the floods and they won't let me go till I see her. You coping OK?'

'Yeah. You heard about Matt Andrews?'

'Aye.' He grew sombre. 'Sad news. But after all this time, it was always likely.'

Paula hated that. The way people gave up on the missing once they'd been gone for more than a day. Following the statistics, not the story, behind each one. People did come back, sometimes after years. She'd seen it herself. 'I suppose. Is that why the best you can send me over is a Met officer on his holidays?'

'Thought you'd be pleased. You and the boss, back together.'

'Hmph.' It was shaky ground, the subject of her and Guy and their shared history. 'Meanwhile, what are we meant to do with this body? Your evidence chain's shot to shit and someone's been into that boatshed and cleared it out.'

'Aye, I know, bad luck, that. I'll be out there tomorrow if it kills me. It's hit the press over here that Matt's dead so they'll be losing interest soon – it'll look like an accident. Cue lots of phone-ins to RTE about is it safe to go out in storms, blah, blah. Why doesn't the government do more. Is it selfish to live on a remote island still. That kind of shite.'

'I still don't buy the accident theory. There's too much that doesn't add up.'

'I know. But there's nothing we can do for now.'

She sighed. 'OK. See you tomorrow, hopefully. That's two nights away from my wean. You owe me, Quinn.'

'Ah, sure you love it,' he said, and she knew he was right.

She hung up, and on impulse dialled Pat's number. The same one she'd called as a teenager, sneaking furtive chats with Aidan, in the brief window when he was her boyfriend, before he'd cruelly dumped her. She knew it off by heart and always would. Her father answered, in his hoarse, tired voice. 'Maguire.'

That was how he always answered the phone, a hangover from his days as a cop, woken at all hours by what was invariably bad news. Whereas her mother had always answered more politely, reciting the phone number back in elocuted tones. 'It's me, Dad.'

'Och, pet. We didn't think you'd be able to get through in this weather. Isn't it wild?'

'I know. How's Mags, did you see her?'

'Saoirse kept her tonight and gave her her dinner but I called down on my way to the shops. She's grand.'

'How come you're answering the phone?' Usually Pat did the task, since PJ wasn't exactly nimble on his feet.

'She's away to bed already.'

'It's early for that.' Paula had a horrible thought. 'Her scan, it wasn't . . .'

'She's fine. Don't you be worrying about that. Just tired

from the hospital is all.' He changed the subject. 'Is it that Bone Island case you're on, is that it? Saw it on the news.'

'Yeah. Dad . . . we came here, didn't we?'

A small pause, as always when she skirted near the topic of her mother. 'Aye, we did. A good few years ago now.' He knew rightly it had been that last year, and he knew she did too.

Paula could feel it, the weight of it straining the connection between them. The pain of not talking about her mother, twenty years of it. She thought of telling him for a mad moment – *Dad, she left a note, I found it, she might be alive, she went away* . . . But then what? He'd only married Pat, staunchly Catholic Pat, because both of them were convinced Margaret Maguire was dead. Any doubt and they'd never have done it, seized this small bit of happiness for themselves. So Paula couldn't tell him. Maybe ever. And yet she still couldn't stop looking, whatever the consequences. 'I better go, Dad. Take care of yourself.'

Her room was cramped, full of furniture that seemed to belong to different places. The wardrobe was so large Paula could hardly get the door open. At least there was a private bathroom, fitted out in seventies salmon-pink and with a mouldering shower curtain that wrapped itself damply about her legs. She ran some tap water into a grubby tooth-mug, realising she hadn't drunk much all day, which probably explained her headache. But the water came out brown and metallic, and she poured it away again. She got into the sagging bed and tried her mobile, knowing it was pointless. Through a gap in the thin curtains, Paula could see the waves in the bay, still uneasy and white-tipped. She had to get off this place, this lump of rock in the middle of the Atlantic, get home to her child, but at the same time she knew the answers were all here. To who or what had killed Matt Andrews. And why. To where Fiona Watts was.

She tried to shut her eyes, turning everything over in her mind. Niamh, so slight and sweet, holding a glowing poker. Andrea, so meek, putting her baby in the dogs' kennel and locking the door. Cut throats and drowned men and the shattered glass of the lighthouse. Dark spreading out across the seas. And in the next room – so close she could hear him moving around, boiling the stupid too-small kettle – was Guy Brooking. Maggie's father. Always bobbing back up like a cork, when she'd done her best to get away, reminding her they'd be bound together forever and he had no idea. Maggie was getting bigger now; it might start to show in her face. Why hadn't she told him before? She'd argued herself out of it. Maggie thought Aidan was her father, and Paula had reasoned it wasn't fair to add that shocker in on top of everything, not when Daddy had just been arrested and was sitting in jail. And Pat had been ill and Guy was still married, trying to make a go of things with Tess, and how could Paula tell him anyway? How could she tell him she'd let him think, for two years, that there'd been a test and Aidan was the dad? The main reason she hadn't told him, she knew, was that she couldn't bear to see the look in his eyes. He respected her, trusted her even, despite all their difficulties. And now, when she'd already lost so much, she didn't think she could bear to lose that too.

And Aidan. What about him? He'd lived alongside her for two years, and pretended he didn't know he was not Maggie's father. Hid the truth while Paula, and Guy Brooking too, had no idea a test had been done – by Pat, in secret. Whatever else Aidan had done or not done, she still didn't know if she could ever forgive him for that. Couldn't forgive him, couldn't let him go. And telling Guy would mean an end to that lovely lie, that she and Aidan and Maggie were a family.

Every time she tried to find peace, her mind was wracked. And this place, with its memories of her mother, made her feel she was drowning. The beach that day. Her mother's red hair in the breeze. The picnic they'd had, sand in their ham sandwiches and cartons of Just Juice. PJ reading the paper against the sun, and her mother saying would you put that down, leave the news behind for one day. Not that her father ever could. They had that in common.

She tried to sleep, settling her tired bones around the lumps in the mattress. *Sleep, Maguire.* Stop thinking of rotting seals and blood smeared on walls and cold, dead eyes. Gradually tiredness overtook her fermenting brain, and her breathing slowed. She had almost dropped off to sleep when something shot her wide awake. A noise? Someone at the door? Her lungs gave her the answer, as they began to crackle and heave – smoke. She could smell smoke. Then there really was someone at the door, a hammering. 'Paula?' Guy's voice. One she knew well, calm but with an edge of – *let's do this now.* 'We need to get out. The pub's on fire.'

She had to be quick now. Put on shoes, grab jumper, phone. No time for anything else. She wrenched open the door to find Guy with his coat on over dark pyjamas, hair mussed. 'Come on. Stay with me.'

He took her hand, and hers seemed to remember the feel of it, the long fingers and strong wrist. He guided her to the stairs, where smoke was already pooling round their ankles.

'Where is it?' she was whispering.

'In the bottle store, I think.'

'But that's where Matt is!' The body. They had to preserve it. Paula started to pull away from his grasp. 'Maybe we can . . .'

'Paula!' His voice was sharp. 'We have to get out of here, right now. Come on, you know that.' His voice was starting to sound muffled. There was smoke in front of Paula's face now. She couldn't orientate herself – the front door of the pub was directly opposite the stairs, wasn't it? But she moved forward and bumped into the bar. Everything seemed to have turned around.

'Guy?' She'd dropped his hand.

'Paula? Where are you? The door's this way!' He seemed far away suddenly. Why was he far away? He'd been right at her side. She could see an orange glow, and illuminated by it the door of the stockroom. Matt was in there, dead and cold, his body holding the secrets to how he'd ended up in the sea. She had to try. She reached out her hand to the handle, which suddenly seemed to loom large, a round metal knob, and—

'What are you doing?' Someone had grabbed her arm, and was pulling her bodily away. She put up no resistance. What *was* she doing? The smoke was thick now, with a terrible reek of burning pleather seats and synthetic rubber, and Guy was swearing at the front door. 'Can't get the lock open. Bloody hell. See if you can . . .'

See if she could what? She didn't understand. The smoke was making her drowsy. The floor under her boots was starting to get warm. It wasn't unpleasant. Then she seemed to lose her hearing, because she could see, almost in slow-motion, Guy lift up a bar stool and slam it into the glass of the front door, and there was a tinkle of glass – surely it must have been louder than that? – and cold, pure air was pouring in, clearing her head and her mind, and Guy was grabbing her again and shoving her out the door, throwing a coat after her saying *put that on, it's freezing*, glass catching in her coat and hair, and then they were out into the night, the moon glinting on the sea. They were out. Guy was panting. 'What the hell were you thinking? If you'd touched that knob the whole place would have gone up – not to mention you'd have barbecued your hand! Christ, Paula!'

What had she been thinking? It was so strange, almost like her brain hadn't been able to take it in. Paula looked up at him, and tried to explain, and promptly passed out.

Bob

2013

'Sergeant Hamilton.'

Some officers said they never forgot a face – they could pick a criminal out of a line-up, or nab him walking down the street, thirty years after their offence. Bob never forgot a voice. At the sound of his name in that raspy flat tone, he put the sponge carefully back into the bucket – scummy water splashed on his trouser leg – and straightened up from the car. Waiting to feel the muzzle of the gun against his head. When he didn't, he turned, slowly. He hadn't seen Sean Conlon in twenty years. The man had gone inside in 1999, finally caught for one of his many crimes. Waiting in prison, sitting on his secrets. Jail had left him sallow, jowly.

'You're out, then.'

'Aye. Good behaviour.'

Bob shifted his back foot. Ian was at his day-care, Linda was at the library. The man had found his address, although it wasn't hard, when you lived in a small town. 'What brings you here, Sean?'

He scratched his ear. The bravado wasn't as showy now, but he was harder, more compressed, a battle-scarred man of fifty. 'Need a favour myself in return. You ever go back on our wee deal, Sergeant?'

It took Bob a moment to even remember. 'The footprints? Sean, that's so long ago nobody cares.'

'Somebody cares. About Dunne. Word is there's a hit out on me.'

Not unusual, when you'd made a career of murder. The IRA had been finishing each other off for years since the ceasefires, settling old scores, tidying up old witnesses. Good riddance to them too. 'It's none of my doing, Sean. You should know as much.'

'Maybe. But I want – I want your help.'

'My help?'

'I want – away.' He hated having to ask, that was clear. He must be desperate. 'I want away from this town.'

It was almost too much, to be standing in front of this man he'd last seen on the day before Margaret vanished. Had he taken her? Did he know something? Despite their 'wee deal', Bob had never known the truth. You couldn't trust a liar. You couldn't rely on a murderer. But he'd had to, back then. 'I'm retired,' Bob said shortly. 'There's nothing I can do for you.'

'But I helped you!'

'How did you? Told me something I already knew, and the very next day she's gone? You've a funny notion of help.' Bob turned to go, disgusted by the man and the dirt that seemed to cling to himself too. The deal they'd made. All for nothing.

'But – I let her go.'

'What?' He turned back.

'That woman. The one you – the one you were asking about.'

Bob made a noise in his throat, turning to go, to push past the man if he had to.

'Honest. We had her, aye. But I let her go.'

'Prove it, then.'

He said nothing. A ripple of fear went through Bob, all the way from 1993. Of course he'd thought the IRA had killed Margaret – where was she otherwise? He'd spent twenty years holding his breath, every time a body was found. Would it be her? And if so, would her body give up her secret, the one that meant she had to run and never come back? But to have it confirmed, that was a different thing. 'Get off my land,' he said, quietly.

'Wait. We had her. You were right. She was a target. But I let her go. I *helped* her.'

'You're a liar. No one's heard from her in twenty years. Where is she, then, if she got away?'

Conlon shrugged. 'That I don't know. But I'm asking you now, help me like I helped her. Like I helped you.'

Bob stared at the man. 'Who is it that's after you? Give me names.'

He hesitated – a long habit of lying to the police.

'Give me it, man, and if you can prove to me you helped that woman, I'll see what I can do for you. If not, then God help you.'

Conlon took an envelope from his pocket. Bob checked his watch – he couldn't stand to have the man in his house, where Linda and Ian would soon be. Instead he opened the car, stuffy with the heat of the day. 'Get in. Now you're going to tell me everything you know. *Everything*, Sean.'

That was the last time Bob would ever see Sean Conlon. He was dead that same night, beaten to a pulp in a pub car park, and Bob had hidden the envelope with the names and never said a word to anyone. Never said he'd known the man, and he'd helped him once, helped him get away with not one murder but two, all so he could draw on a favour when needed. And he never told anyone what Sean had to say about that day in 1993, about the last known movements of Margaret Maguire. He'd made a promise, and that didn't end just because she'd been gone twenty years. All he knew was he'd had a strange, uncomfortable feeling he hadn't felt in years – something that might have been hope.

Chapter Twenty-Six

When she came to she was lying on her side, coughing up soot onto the wet stones of the quay. Everything smelled of smoke and damp. Guy's hands were on her, firm on her shoulder and hip, holding her safe. 'Are you OK?'

She sat up, still coughing. 'What happened?'

'I don't know. You had a funny turn – I couldn't get you out.' Guy sat back on his heels, his grey eyes wide with worry, soot on his face. He was wearing slippers, she saw. She didn't realise people still owned slippers.

She saw figures scurrying in the smoke from the pub, which seemed to be still standing – they had turned a hose on it. The smoke was black and acrid, but there were no flames left. She'd never had occasion to wonder how fires were dealt with on an island, when you didn't have access to firemen or an engine. By the community, was the answer. She could recognise faces in the gloom. Oona from the Spar, a coat over her pyjamas, and Seamas, fully dressed in his waterproofs, Paddy the fisherman. Working together to save the place. 'What happened?' she asked Guy again, coughing up more soot.

'Your guess is as good as mine.'

'Lightning, something like that?' she faltered.

'I didn't notice any.'

She pulled herself up to sitting, still hacking up soot from her aching lungs. 'The storeroom?'

'Gutted. It started in there. All that booze as an accelerant . . .'

Their evidence, the last that remained of Matt Andrews. 'So . . . his body's just gone?'

'Convenient, isn't it, if someone didn't want an autopsy.'

So this had maybe been done on purpose, by people who likely knew it was just the outsiders in the building. To hide whatever clues they might have taken from Matt Andrews's body, burn them away forever. 'And – do you think they knew we were in there?'

'I think everyone on this island knows what we've been up to.'

She shivered, pulling the coat he'd given her around her shoulders. It felt strange somehow, too heavy. Her legs were full and sluggish, her lungs still burning. A thought occurred. 'Where's Rory? Should he not be here for this?'

Guy rubbed his eyes, leaving a smear of soot across them. 'They went to his house,' he said shortly. 'He's not there, and no one can find him.'

'It's very good of you to take us in,' said Guy, wiping his boots on the mat.

Seamas Fairlinn's wife, whose name was Grainne, she'd murmured, was a colourless woman in a pink nylon dressing gown, her face creased and tired. Seamas was still dressed in his boots and jacket, drinking a cup of tea standing up in the kitchen. In the absence of anywhere else to stay, Paula and Guy had followed him the few paces from the pub to his house. It was so close she could still smell the burning, and knew she would not be able to sleep again tonight, thinking of Matt's body, charred and unrecognisable. Was any of him left, anything of what made him himself – a man who loved birds, and wild places, and surfing – or had that gone too, lost in the instant his life was taken? Paula had always found it difficult, the moment a missing person's case turned into a murder enquiry. The moment all hope was lost.

Seamas drained his tea. 'No bother. Sure we can't leave you out in that storm.'

'I'm sorry about your pub. You must be devastated,' said Paula.

He grunted. 'It's insured. Electrics, like as not. The storm.'

It likely wasn't insured against arson, though. Paula kept silent, wondering who'd started the fire. It couldn't be an accident, could it? So who? Enviracorp, trying to hide evidence? And where the hell was Rory?

'Is there a generator somewhere?' Guy was looking doubtfully at the lights, which flickered with each blast of wind. He'd borrowed a pair of boots from Fairlinn, which were too big for him.

'Aye, community centre has one. We need it out here. I don't reckon youse'll be able to call through to the mainland till tomorrow, though.'

'No?' Paula's eyes widened. They couldn't be totally cut off, surely?

'Phone lines are out – there'll be a tree down somewhere – and there's already no mobile reception, no power like as not soon, too.' Seamas set the cup down with a slap. He seemed to be almost relishing the situation, one of those people who thrived on a crisis. 'Listen to how that wind's picking up.' She could hear it, shrieking round the eaves, making the solid house rattle and shake.

She looked at Guy, panicked.

'A day won't make any difference. She'll be OK,' he said quietly, and she was so grateful for it. He understood. But if they were really stuck out here, what was the procedure, if a crime had occurred and you couldn't get on or off the island for days?

Seamas put his wool cap back on. 'I'm away out to see what we can salvage.' His eyes flickered over Guy. 'You're a strong-looking fella, Inspector, would you lend a hand?'

He hesitated for a second, looking at Paula. She shrugged infinitesimally. She didn't want to be left alone, but it might give her a chance to talk to Grainne Fairlinn, and anyway he could hardly refuse to help out when they were being offered shelter.

When the men went, wrapped in jackets and gloves and heavy stomping boots, Paula smiled at Seamas's wife. 'Thank you again for this. Will we not be in the way?'

Grainne pulled at her dressing-gown sleeves. She had a nervous gesture of rubbing her hands together, as if they were dirty. 'Oh no. There's a spare room as well as the guest bedroom.'

People had a lot of space on islands. 'That's handy. Have you any children?'

Brief pause. 'Sammy.'

'And how old's he?'

'Thirteen.' She turned to busy herself at the sink, washing up Seamas and Guy's cups with a sort of nervous energy.

'Oh yes, he was on the boat with Seamas, wasn't he?' When they'd pulled Matt's body from the water, already compromising all the evidence. 'Is Sammy about, Grainne? I just wanted to thank him for helping us find – the body. Not many kids would keep their heads in that situation.'

She almost smiled, a flicker that was quickly replaced by

her usual look of strained worry. 'He's a good boy. Sammy. Sammy! Come here, will you?'

Sammy must have been in the front room, because he came at once, dressed in Star Wars pyjamas. Paula thought of Helen Corry's teenage son. Connor Corry was a bit older than Sammy, but he had never been known to come willingly without a drawn-out sigh and a pained '*Whhhhaaaaa*?'

'Hiya, Sammy.' She noticed the drag of his left foot right away. Some kind of cerebral palsy, maybe? He was small for his age, with a pinched white face and milk-bottle glasses, and when he turned his head she saw he wore hearing aids on both ears. 'I'm Dr Maguire, from the mainland. I was down at the beach today, after you went home.'

He nodded. The same watchfulness she'd seen in Niamh and the other island children. 'You came to find Dr Watts and her boyfriend,' he said in a small voice. 'She's nice, Dr Watts.'

Grainne Fairlinn gave a tut, which Paula didn't miss.

'Yes, we're looking for her as hard as we can.'

'Is she dead too?' Sammy spoke quietly, as if he didn't want his mother to hear. She was fussing in the porch now, tidying up coats and boots.

'I hope not. It was very sad about her boyfriend, but I'm sure she'd be glad to know you found him and pulled him out.'

'It's not nice in the sea. It's dark and cold.'

'Did you touch him, Sammy? When you – got him onto the boat?' Now was a chance to find out how much the body had been compromised. 'Or did your dad touch him, or move anything?'

He looked confused. 'We touched him to get him in. He was all floppy, and there was all water coming out of his coat and his trousers – we put him in the bottom of the boat then we took him in to the beach.'

'Nothing else? You didn't maybe check to see who it was, in his clothes or anything?'

'We knew who it was.' A small voice again. She wondered if he was close to tears.

So they hadn't gone through his pockets, at least. 'Right.' She heard a silence from the porch, knew his mother was listening. 'Is it nice living here?' she asked brightly. 'Do you go to the mainland for secondary school?'

'If I'm well enough. On the boat. But it's choppy so sometimes I stay here.' He rubbed his ears. 'I get sick.'

'And are there loads of kids on the island?'

'There's forty-three,' he said. He knew the number without counting. 'There was Caoimhe too, but – well, she was grown-up anyway.'

'Caoimhe? Who's that, Sammy?'

Sammy's eyes flickered to the porch. He whispered: 'Mammy's sick, I think. Dr Watts could help her, maybe, but she's gone. Can you help?'

'I'm not a medicine type of doctor, Sammy, I'm sorry. What's the matter with her?'

He lowered his gaze again. 'Never mind.'

Grainne came back in, shutting the door. 'Go and finish your game now, leave the lady in peace.'

Damn. He went off as obediently as he'd come, and she heard the noise of a computer game start up in the living room. She looked at Grainne. 'Caoimhe?'

Grainne turned her back away again, fussing with the kettle, and for a moment Paula thought she wasn't going to answer. Then she said, 'Our daughter. She went off to Australia. She was working over there. Loved it.'

Paula waited. When people used the past tense like that, there usually wasn't a good end to the story.

'A man killed her.' Grainne banged the cupboard door closed, staring fiercely at the kettle. 'Followed her home from a disco, they said, and . . . We never even got her back. They buried her over there. Whatever he did to her, they said – we didn't want to remember her that way. Didn't even let us see her. I couldn't even look at her face one last time. She's half the world away from me.'

'I'm so sorry.' She paused a moment, watching the woman's back. 'Sammy's a lovely boy. Does he – has he some hearing difficulties?'

Grainne nodded. 'He got meningitis as a wee boy. My sister brought her weans over from the mainland, carried it with them. And Sammy got sick. He was lucky, they said – he didn't lose the foot in the end.'

Christ, they'd been through a lot as a family. She shook her head. 'I'm sorry, Grainne. That's awful.'

Grainne's back stiffened. 'We should have just kept them here. They'd have been fine if they'd just stayed on the island! Seamas told her, he told our Caoimhe, it's not safe out there, it's not like this place, where you know everyone and no one would ever touch you, but she wanted to see the world. And I let her go. And Sammy got sick, and I nearly lost him too – so this is my penance. We're all being punished, you see.'

'Punished?'

She was still turned away, so Paula could not see her face. Her voice was dry, cracked on the edges. 'We never should have let them come.'

Careful, careful. 'Let who come, Grainne?' She tried to keep her own voice light.

Grainne turned around, a fierce glint in her eyes behind the smeared glasses. Her hands were held up in front of her, scratching at each other, the skin red and raw. 'Outsiders. We never should have let them come here. They're going to kill us all.'

Chapter Twenty-Seven

Paula didn't know what to say to that, so she was almost glad when the door went and Guy and Fairlinn were swept back in by a gust of wind. 'Foundering out there.'

'Anything left?' she said to Guy. Meaning of Matt. Meaning anything to prove what was going on here. He shook his head, looking sooty and bone-cold. She saw his hands were cut and bruised. 'Need to put something on those? You're hurt.'

'I'm OK. I should wash them off, I guess.'

Grainne was hovering. Her voice was normal again, that of an ordinary tired housewife. 'There's a wee bathroom down the hall.'

In the hallway, Paula noticed several framed shots of a young girl, hair long and fair, with the soft, rosy skin so many Irish women had. She could hear Seamas talking in the kitchen, his voice a low rumble. She nodded to the photo. 'Their daughter,' she murmured to Guy.

'Where's she?'

'Dead. Murdered, in Australia. Her mother says she shouldn't have left the island. And Sammy, the kid – he caught meningitis from some mainland kids. They think this is the only safe place, or something.'

Guy looked at the pictures, contemplative. Caoimhe, in her graduation robes. Caoimhe, smiling with her dad on a boat. Even through the framed glass she looked vibrant and happy, and it was hard to believe someone had deliberately snuffed that life right out of her. 'So . . . you think they'd do their best to protect the place, or something like that?'

Paula was almost whispering. 'Maybe. And if Matt had found out something about the island, something bad – or this business with Fiona and the Sharkey baby . . . Guy, she said they were being punished, the islanders, for letting outsiders come here.'

'Meaning Matt and Fiona?'

'I guess so, but maybe also . . . What?'

He was staring at another framed picture. 'Look at this. Who's that?'

In the picture, Seamas was shaking hands with someone in front of the Enviracorp gates, the logo clearly visible. Paula kept her voice low. 'Rainbow Monroe – I know, mad name, but don't underestimate her. She works for them. The Head of Operations.'

'And why's Seamas with her?'

'I don't know. Maybe . . .' She didn't get to finish her thoughts – not that she was even sure what she was trying to say – because the lights flickered, casting crazy shadows over Guy's face, and suddenly they were in darkness. For a moment her heart stilled, something deep in her brain shuddering in terror – and then she felt Guy's hand on her arm, steady and sure.

'Power cut,' he said, close to her ear.

'Fairlinn was right. I can't even call through to the Guards – the lines seem to be down.'

Guy put down the receiver of the community centre phone. The feeling of isolation was intense. Freezing night fog meant you couldn't even see the mainland, and there were no phones, no internet, nothing. Paula wondered if the radio in Rory's car was still working – but where was he? For now, they were in Bone Island's community centre, with folding beds and a small manager's office that they'd turned into their HQ. Outside in the main hall, which had a wooden floor painted in lines and hoops like a school gym, islanders were starting to gather, as their lights went off and heating packed up. Every few minutes another family came in the door, shrouded in thick coats and waterproofs, greeting each other with stoical nods. There were about twenty people out there now, eight of them children, and Paula could hear the low hum of their voices. The fluorescent lights were still burning bright thanks to the generator, and Paula had spots in front of her eyes from the glow and from sheer exhaustion. Dimly, she was aware that she hadn't eaten or drunk anything since a mouthful of tea at the Fairlinn house, but shock and adrenaline were keeping her going. The community centre had a kitchen, and in the corner of this small, windowless room was a pallet of bottled water. She snapped one out, cracking the seal and gulping it down gratefully. As the coolish water soothed her throat, she asked: 'So what are we going to do?' Because they had to do something. It wasn't in either of their natures to sit and wait for help.

Guy, who needed order in all things, was scribbling on large sheets of a flipchart he'd found in a cupboard, and fixing them to the walls with a roll of duct tape. 'We need to do something about the due process,' he said. 'There's been possible arson, destruction of evidence, maybe a murder, and it's all just going to get lost if we don't start keeping some kind of log. So. What do you think is going on?'

Paula was still wearing the heavy coat Guy had put on

her at the pub – it wasn't even hers. Her hands were sore and red, bits of soot drifting from her hair every time she moved. 'A few possibilities. There's the accident theory. There's a storm, Fiona's got these allergies, and so on. But I don't really buy that. Then there's revenge. We know Fiona wasn't popular here, and Andrea Sharkey's husband in particular hates her, blames her for what happened to his wife.'

'You think he's capable of hurting her?'

She thought of the rage, coursing through him like it might split him open. 'I do, yeah. But it's Matt whose body we have, dragged out of the sea. Seems to support the accident idea.'

'And yet the pub conveniently burns down with the body in it.'

She shivered. The idea that someone had come and deliberately set light to the building, knowing they were in it – it made her want to run and run, get to the harbour and find a boat, as if even the dangerous sea was safer than here. 'Then there's this company – if Matt really did find something in the ecosystem, they could be covering it up. Rainbow was really keen to find those samples. And if she's mates with Seamas, who's leading the search . . . did they even want to find Matt and Fiona alive?' And the company, they'd have the resources to burn the pub down, no doubt about it. They could easily have sent someone to do it. 'So maybe Matt was right. Maybe there's something in the food system here, the water, and it's making people ill. That would explain why they've paid out money to the Sharkeys. Fiona knew something about it, I think. There's that list I found in her office – the names of the people who'd sort of . . . lost it. Matt's name had a question mark after it. As if she'd just started to worry about him.' Paula sighed, realising how crazy it all sounded out loud. 'Or maybe that's too far-fetched. What if she confronts him about his behaviour – he's violent already, maybe, losing it. That blood in the kitchen. And she's pregnant, it's a risky time. So maybe if they got into a fight, and he hurt her . . .'

Guy thought about it. 'What happened to him, then? Why have we found his body and not hers?' He was speaking quietly, aware that just a flimsy partition wall divided them from the islanders.

'I don't know. Suicide, maybe, I suppose . . . but what if someone else killed him? They didn't expect the body to wash up so soon, but the storm saw to that, and so they've set the fire to cover it up. Burn up the evidence.'

'Who?'

'Well, who's conspicuous by their absence right now?'

'Rory McElhone?'

'Right. He's been strange the whole time. Obstructive, even. Didn't tell me about the earlier incidents of violence, or about Fiona's allergies. I think he stole Andrea's notes, too. He's not letting us see the full picture, I'm sure of it. Who even knows where he is?'

'And they can't get anyone else out to us, not till tomorrow at least.' Guy looked round at the claustrophobic little room. Pre-fab seventies walls, bits of tinsel from Christmas still Sellotaped to the ceiling, a box of costumes for a long-ago play piled in the corner. Outside the wind raged and tore at the island as if it might pull it apart. 'So I guess it's just you and me,' he said. A small smile hooked his mouth. 'Still, we've been in worse situations.'

'True,' she said, thinking of some of them. Knives to her pregnant belly and guns to her head. This was just a strange island, and she was only jumpy because she knew they couldn't get off. But the storm would pass. She would leave, and get back to Maggie, and everything would be sorted out.

Guy was still watching her. 'What?' she frowned.

'It's just . . . what are you wearing?' He was looking curiously at the coat she had on, hanging so loose her hands were hidden. 'That's not yours, is it?'

She looked down; she hadn't really noticed. 'No. You gave it to me.'

'I picked it up from the coat stand at the pub door, but it was so dark.' Guy was still looking at her strangely. 'Paula, the coat – it's the one Matt was wearing when they brought him in.'

Paula didn't move for a moment, but she felt her skin retract slowly, stipple into goose-bumps. 'You mean – when they hauled him out?' She was in a dead man's coat. One he'd been wearing in the depths of the cold sea. One he'd died in. Suddenly she was tearing at the stiff red fabric. The lining felt damp, soaked and fetid. She couldn't bear the idea of it, that this had touched his dead flesh. 'Get it off me. I need it off.'

Guy was helping her, his hands warm and capable as she tugged at the zips. 'It's OK. You're OK. Who would have taken it off him? We have to preserve the evidence, surely everyone knows that.'

'I don't know – what's this?' The coat had fallen to the ground, with a strange cracking sound.

Guy stooped to it. 'There's something in the pockets, maybe.' He thought about it for a second. 'Ah well. It's been totally contaminated anyway.' He undid the Velcro pocket of the jacket and pulled out a handful of something, rolling it in the palm of his hand.

'What is it?' Paula squinted in the glaring lights, bright like an operating theatre, or the lights they had in their interrogation rooms in Ballyterrin. He didn't answer, but she could see, because the light hid nothing – it was a handful of stones. The pockets of Matt's coat were full of round grey pebbles, like the ones you found on the beaches of the island.

Fiona

'Matt,' I said. 'Matt. Baby. Are you listening to me?'

He didn't answer. He had the binoculars again, peering out over the sea from the kitchen window. He was supposed to be cooking, but nothing was ready, the counters still empty and clean from where I'd wiped them last night. I tried to think when I'd last seen Matt eat anything. He'd been up the night before again, retching into the loo, nothing but dry bile. I'd run through the diagnostics in my head, weary – ulcer? Food poisoning? Knowing all the while it wasn't that.

He didn't turn round. 'Can you see something out there?'

I looked. I don't know why. There's nothing there, there's never been anything there. 'What are you talking about?'

'The water, it's dark . . . I think it's coming.'

'What's coming?'

'The blood tide.'

I opened my mouth, and then was silenced by a sudden chill of fear, like a dousing with cold water. *The blood tide?* Matt, the scientist, who used to pore over the ordinance survey maps, snort with derision every time an advert made a pseudo-scientific claim. Here he was, talking like a madman. 'Do you want some dinner?' I tried. 'I'll even make you some fish, if you like.' Usually I hated to touch the slimy dead things. But I'd do it for him.

This is how you go in the end. I hated it. I hated how much I was willing to give up, just for the chance to hold onto him, by one desperate hanging thread.

Matt was still looking. Holding my breath, trying to be nice, I opened the drawer and took out a knife to gut the fish with. Matt had caught it the day before, and it had been stuffed into our salad drawer in the fridge, leaking a little pale pink blood, its mouth open and eyes staring. I did it with my bare hands. *Look, I will do anything for you. I will handle dead things. If you can just – stop? Just stop being mad, and come back to me.* 'I think I can see something.'

There was nothing there. Maybe a shadow on the water from the clouds, that was all. 'What did you do at work today?' I said. Like we were still in our flat in London, with the sounds of traffic outside. Here there was nothing but the wind and the cries of the birds.

He didn't answer. That morning, I had peed on a stick that told me I was ovulating. First time in six months, what with all the stress and the Anika business. I knew there was a four-hour window for ovulation, not much more. And under my work clothes – I was still dressing like I was in inner London – I had on sexy underwear. Red, lacy. Bought at the House of Fraser before we left. A woman never feels so pathetic as when she's put on sexy underwear and realises it will not be noticed. I'd even wondered for a while if there was someone else. That mousy little scientist from the plant, who thinks I don't see her watching him when we're all in Dunorlan's. That, I could understand, I could fight. But this – how could I beat something when I didn't even know what it was? Something welled up in me – anger, terror, tears. 'Will you put those down! I'm making dinner, I came all this way for you, and you can't even look at me! Am I invisible or something?'

Matt turned to me, saw the fish. His eyes widened in fear. 'Don't touch that! Don't *touch* it!' It was only instinct, I know that. Paranoia will do that to you, trigger the fight or flight parts of the cortex. But he knocked it out of my hand, and it flopped on the floor, the knife clattering beside it, and I looked at my fingertips and saw they were covered in red. Matt had hurt me. Matt had injured me, drawn blood. And OK, he didn't mean it, but . . . isn't that how it starts? You explain away. You excuse one thing, then another, and it's like a boat with a leak in it and you can never bail out fast enough, and before you know it you are sinking, drowning and gone. Being in a relationship that's dying is like any other kind of ship going down. All the advice is to get off, fast as you can, and not be sucked down, but still we can't take it in. We can't believe the ground that was under our feet a minute ago, solid as land, can suddenly disappear.

Matt hadn't even noticed I was bleeding. He was still staring out that damn window, at nothing. I bent, shaking, and picked up the knife. It was sharp – I made sure they were always sharpened, as it speeds up cooking. I even had a little knife-sharpener Matt's mum had got me for Christmas. God knows what she meant by that. I suddenly thought – that much blood, the spot or two on my fingers, wouldn't convince anyone. But I could easily have been hurt more. Matt wouldn't notice if he'd stabbed me. And that's when I had the idea. If I just pressed the knife against my skin, held it to where the veins run close, there would be more blood. There would be a scar, a wound. Something I could show people – show Rory – and say *look, look what happened, now can you help me, please? Can someone help me?*

I know. I know how this sounds. But you can't imagine it, how it is, when everyone and everything seems to be sinking around your ears. Right before a wave crashes on the shore, there's a moment where it bellies out, where it seems to almost stand on end, defying gravity. I always loved that moment. Full of promise, full of power and anticipation. However, when you're at that moment, that pinnacle, the crash is always just behind. I know that now.

Chapter Twenty-Eight

'Get out of my fecking way!' A voice bellowed out from the next room, making Paula jump and drop some of the pebbles. They clattered on the lino floor, with a noise like scrabbling spiders.

'What's going on?' Guy was already moving to the door, motioning to her to stay where she was. He opened the flimsy partition and Paula heard the babble of voices, a woman screaming, a child crying.

'. . . taking our beds . . .'

'. . . here first . . .'

'. . . fecking move yourself!' She edged over to see two men facing off over a camp bed, both burly and red-faced, with that hardened, weathered look all the islanders seemed to have. The row appeared to be over which family had been in possession of the camp bed first. She saw Guy prepare to shoulder the burden yet again, be the one to keep the peace. A born policeman.

'Sir, is there a problem?' He walked into the room, deliberately slow, holding himself straight and confident.

No one seemed to notice him at first. They had switched to shouting in Irish now, and the woman was still screaming, a harsh, angry sound, and more of the children were crying, including the toddler she held in her arms. Paula followed Guy out. She recognised faces in the room. Niamh, her mother and siblings, watching in fear. Sammy Fairlinn and his mother. Seamas was nowhere to be seen. Bridget from the post office and Brendan the fisherman, the brawling couple from the pub. Colm the barman, and an older woman in a grey tracksuit she assumed was his mother. Everyone was silent, watching the men shout at each other. Gobs of spit flew from their mouths and one already had bruised knuckles.

Guy moved forward some more. 'Come on now, you're scaring the kids. I'm sure we can sort this out—'

'You shut your hole. You've no jurisdiction here! A fecking Brit.'

'Just get out, get out! Mind your own fecking business!' Both men were now shouting, united in their aggression towards Guy. This lasted only a moment, and then they began struggling with each other, in a way that was almost comical, like children wrestling. Except it wasn't. Paula was suddenly afraid for them, all of them, when Grainne Fairlinn stepped forward. Paula saw she was still wearing her pink dressing gown, a man's coat draped around her shoulders, as if someone had placed it there.

'Stop this now. Stop it! Can you not see what's happening? Can you not *see*?' She spun around, so the coat slipped to the ground, unnoticed. In her pink gown, she held her arms out, like a priestess in nylon. 'God help you both, Michael Reilly, Patrick Og. Look to your children and mind your business. There's a storm coming! Can you not hear it? Can you not see it? It's the outsiders we need to fight. Not ourselves!'

The room had fallen deadly silent. Then one of the men, Patrick Og, Paula thought he was, suddenly turned to Guy, and jabbed at him with a vicious punch, catching him on the side of his face. 'Get the fuck out. You don't belong here.' A small cry broke out of Paula's mouth as his gaze turned on her too. 'And you too. You meddling fucking bitch.'

Guy flinched, but righted himself. 'Sir, I have to inform you I'm a police officer and we won't tolerate—'

Then the one Grainne had called Michael Reilly – a relation to Jimmy, maybe? – raised an arm – weedy, slight, but it seemed to make no difference – and caught Patrick Og a terrible blow across the face, so hard he staggered and fell, and his wife screamed again and so did the children, and a cry went up all around the room, a dreadful sound of shrieking and terror over the moan of the wind, and Paula found she was rooted to the spot, unable to look away, until she realised Guy was at her side, pulling her arm. 'We have to get out of here. Come on. *Now*.'

'You have to wear something!'

'I'm OK!' Paula's face was frozen. The wind seemed to be howling right through her fleece, and she'd left Matt's coat at the community centre. They were trudging over the beach, the wind as abrasive as sandpaper from the particles it picked up, roaring up from the sea. Paula still wasn't sure what they were doing. They'd left the community centre while they could, sneaking out the fire door while everyone else was shouting and fighting, and now they were just walking, into the night. But where would they go? Where was safe?

'You're not OK! Look, I've got my jumper. Take the coat.'

She protested, but he already had it off and was draping it round her shoulders. She took it gratefully, feeling the warmth from his body. 'Where are we going?' she asked.

'I don't know. We can't go back to that place, it's not safe. Everyone is – Jesus, I don't know what's wrong with them.'

Paula didn't want to think about it. 'There's the plant. Enviracorp. It's mostly empty now but there might be someone there. I don't know who else we can trust. Not the Fairlinns, for sure.' She shuddered again, thinking of the stones in the pocket of the coat. That someone must have put there to weigh the body down. Not an accident, then. A murder.

'Fairlinn saw you in that coat,' Guy said. She wished there'd been time to grab it from the community centre. Something to cling to, to show they weren't mad.

Paula felt a chill beneath the aching cold in her face and hands. Had someone really tried to kill them, set that fire to get rid of them as well as poor Matt's body? And they were on this island with nowhere to go, no way off. 'Come on. It's another mile or so.'

The beach seemed endless. Paula could hardly see ahead of her with the rain and wind, the sand whipping in her eyes. The waves broke on the shore, licking over the high-water line. The storm on its way back in. After a while she realised Guy was talking to her. She lowered the hood of his coat. 'What?'

'There's a boat!' he shouted. 'Look, on the shore!'

She could see it too, bumping in the shallow water, a small wooden dinghy with its hull pointing up to the stormy sky. Capsized, by the looks of it. 'Is there a name?' But even as she called she knew what it would be. The red sign left no doubt – the *London Lass*. Matt and Fiona's boat. Guy was trudging towards it, struggling to turn it over. Paula had a sudden awful thought – what if Fiona was in the boat, also dead and cold, both of them silenced forever by this island? What had they known? 'Can you get it turned?'

She wasn't sure Guy could hear her over the wind, but he had managed to tip the boat up slightly. He pulled out his phone and turned on the light function. The boat was empty – no dead body. Paula let out some of her breath. But Guy was still pointing the light closer to the wet wood, warped from the sea, and she could see now on the bottom of the boat was a splash of something else, something dark and red and stinking, the same smell she'd noticed in the boatshed. Blood. Matt and Fiona's boat had blood in it.

Chapter Twenty-Nine

The gates of Enviracorp stood open, but the main building was dark, deserted. The perimeter fence ran the whole way along it, warning signs posted up. Beyond they could see equipment, diggers and vats for the seaweed, but all still and empty.

'Should we go in?' Paula realised she was whispering, even though the wind would drown out any sound.

'Isn't it locked?' said Guy.

She pushed on the plate-glass door of the reception and it opened, the door shoved inwards by the wind with a crash. 'Guess not.' They went in, and Paula was grateful for the temporary shelter. The place felt warm, sealed off. 'Hello?' she called. 'Is anyone here?' The cold fingers which had crept down her spine were still there. Blood in the boat. The body burned away. And now here, not a light against the pressing dark of night.

A tapping sound, growing louder. Heels, running down the corridor. Paula realised who it must be just a moment before Ellen burst into reception, her hair wild, still in her suit and shirt from earlier. What was she doing there so late? 'Oh! Dr Maguire! Er, hi! What are you doing here? We're closed, I'm afraid.'

Paula realised she didn't know how to explain why they were there, in the dead of night. The pub had burned down, and they were basically on the run from the islanders? And despite the fact she was fairly sure Rainbow had some kind of role in Matt and Fiona's fate, the older woman at least seemed sane, and she didn't know if she could say the same about anyone else here any more? 'Um . . . I wanted to see Dr Monroe. I know she probably won't be here this late, but . . .'

Ellen blinked. 'Oh, well . . . it is kinda late, I don't know if she's . . .'

Guy stepped forward. Policeman voice again. 'Ma'am, I'm from the police. If your boss is here, we'd really like to speak to her.'

Ellen threw panicked glances between the corridor she'd come from and the door behind them. Then she seemed to sag. 'Look, she's down there. In her office. I have to go.'

'Wait!'

She was already wrestling with the door, trying to get it open against the push of the wind. Paula saw Ellen's face was red and damp, and she didn't think just from the cold. 'I need to go home! I can't do this!'

'But wait – what's going on? Where's Dara?'

'He's – oh God, I don't know. He's gone off. And I'm not sitting around here. I'm taking a boat. It's not worth it, OK?'

Paula caught the door, helping her. 'But Ellen – something isn't right here. What's going on? Why's everyone so scared? You know something's up.'

'I don't know anything.' Her hand shook as she fought the wind for control of her russet curls. 'I don't know what's going on. The bosses have just left me in it – so I'm leaving. Screw this.' She finally got the door open, then shouted back at Paula. 'You should leave too. Get off while you can. Hide out somewhere till it's light. That's what I'm gonna do.'

'We can't just go! There's something wrong here.'

Ellen's face was hidden by her hair, and Paula could barely hear her. 'They don't want us. Can't you see that?'

'But why? Is it the plant? Is something getting into the ecosystem?'

'I don't know.' Ellen turned away towards the company docks, struggling in her heels, and yelled into the wind. 'Look, we didn't know. I swear it. We didn't know.' And she was gone.

Paula and Guy went down the corridor, their feet clanging on the stamped metal floor, echoing in the silent building. Everything was empty, labs, common room, offices. Paula was trying to remember the layout. 'I don't know where . . . Jesus!'

'Only me,' said Rainbow Monroe, materialising out of a dark doorway. She was still in her black waterproofs and practically invisible in the shadows. But her voice was steady. 'Sorry if I scared you. I wasn't expecting anyone to be in. Seeing as we shut up hours ago.'

Paula could feel Guy at her back, inches away. 'We just saw Ellen and we thought – we need to speak to you, Dr Monroe. This is my colleague, DI Brooking.'

Rainbow stepped forward to shake his hand, and Paula felt herself calm down a little. This was fine. This was normal. Just a workplace after hours. Ellen was just frazzled, a long way from home, tired out.

'I'm sorry it's so dark,' said Rainbow. 'Our generator hasn't kicked in. Another reason we sent everyone home so early. I'm afraid we get a lot of power cuts here. I take it you want to speak to me about poor Matt? Come in.'

* * *

Her office was also warm, lit by a dim storm lantern, one large window looking out on the stormy sea, lashed by rain. The roar of it penetrated even the thick walls of the plant. The office was full of books and framed pictures of Rainbow with various worthies, meeting the Irish president, receiving an award. There was also one of her in a wetsuit, many years younger, hugging a huge orca in a pool. The sun slicing bright, a world away from this place of grey. She sat behind her large mahogany desk, pushing her hair back. 'I must apologise, first of all. I wish we could have helped more in the search for Matt and Fiona. But with the weather, and staff shortages . . . Anyway, poor Matt's been found now. If we can do anything for his family, we'll of course help in any way we can. Let's hope Fiona is found too. Put the whole thing to rest, at least.'

Meaning Fiona was dead too. Meaning there was no hope. Was she sure of that, or was she speculating? 'Ellen seemed upset,' Paula tried.

'I'm afraid Ellen will be leaving our employment shortly. Not everyone can take the pace over here. It's understandable.'

'And Dara? Where's he?'

'Performing some tasks for me.' Her face was smooth, unreadable. 'Dr Maguire, I've told you everything I know. I understand this must be difficult for you, being marooned over here, but the best thing to do now is batten down the hatches for the night and wait it out. By morning things may be clearer.'

'The pub we were staying in burned down,' Guy said.

Her brow contracted. Was that genuine surprise? It looked like it. 'A fire? My God, poor Seamas. The storm, I imagine?'

Convenient storm, destroying Matt Andrews's body. 'We

226

don't know.' Guy was adopting the same neutral tone as Paula, and she realised how much she missed this, interviewing with him, no need to even speak or compare notes. They'd always worked so well together. Professionally, if not personally. 'Either way, it's left us somewhat stranded.'

'You're very welcome to stay with me. I have plenty of room, though no power right now, I'm afraid.'

'Thank you,' said Guy, again giving nothing away. 'There's a shelter being set up in the community centre – though we didn't feel particularly welcome there.'

Paula leaned forward. 'Have you ever noticed hostility from the islanders? To you or your workers?'

Rainbow squared off a piece of paper on her desk. 'I've always felt the islanders were very grateful for the work we provide. There's precious little else to do out here. Most of the young people leave and never return. The island is dying – or it would be, if we hadn't come here. I fought hard for it, you know. We looked at several other locations. But it had to be here. Bone Island is . . . a special place.'

'A thin place,' said Paula, remembering their earlier conversation.

'If you believe in that. Are you telling me the islanders don't want us here?'

Guy hesitated. 'There were some comments. Outsiders, coming over and interfering. That kind of thing. We were wondering if Matt and Fiona had encountered the same.' Meaning, did the islanders have them killed. For revenge, for fear. Who knew?

'Not that I know of. They were very happy here.' She seemed to be thinking it over. 'Will you excuse me just a minute? I think we could all do with some hot drinks.'

* * *

As soon as the woman left the room, Paula widened her eyes at Guy. 'What do you make to that?'

'She's lying. They know something's up all right. Seems to me they're desperately trying to cover their backs, discredit Matt as much as possible.'

'Reckon they took the samples, then?'

'It seems likely.'

She shifted forward, whispering. 'When she comes back, let's make our excuses and go.'

'Go where?' He looked doubtfully at the window, rattling in the rain. 'Everyone on the island seems to have drunk the Kool-Aid.' Same phrase Mary O'Neill had used. That gave Paula an idea.

'We have to find someone we can trust. Someone from outside, properly outside, who sees what's been going on.'

'Anyone in mind?'

She nodded. 'We need to get out of here first. Come on.' But when she pushed on the door, it didn't move. She tried the handle – nothing. 'Fuck! She's locked us in.'

'Really?' Guy shoved at it with his strong shoulder. 'Bugger.'

Paula turned to the window, which took up most of the wall. 'We'll have to get out through that.'

'Can you climb?'

'If we knock the pane out.'

Guy moved quickly to the window, pulling over the heavy chair to reach it. 'I need something to smash it.' He pushed at the glass. 'It's only putty, it'll come out.'

Paula cast her eyes about, her gaze falling on a trophy. It was heavy, cast in bronze in the shape of curved hands. The plaque read: *For excellence in business*. She passed it to him, staggering under the weight, and he drew back his arm, and with one sure thrust of his arm, shattered the glass. Half of it fell away, leaving jagged shards still stuck in the putty. She raised her eyebrows at him. He shrugged. 'That's done it. Come on.'

Someone else had heard the glass breaking. They heard running feet outside. Paula let Guy haul her up, wadding his coat around the shards of broken glass, then she plunged through the gap. The cold night air had never felt so good. 'Come on!'

Guy, larger than her, was having trouble squeezing through. His jumper was rucked up about his waist. 'Here,' she said. 'Take it off.' She helped him pull it off, all the while throwing uneasy looks behind him at the door, and over her own shoulder. The beach was only metres away, the sea still rough and glinting. Outside, she could hear the running feet get closer. A door slammed. 'Guy! Come on!'

Now out of his jumper, he managed to slip through, his feet in their ill-fitting boots landing awkwardly on the gravel. 'Shit.'

'Are you OK?'

'Ankle. S'fine. Come on.'

As Guy cleared the window, the door in the room jerked open. Rainbow. 'Dr Maguire? Inspector Brooking? You should stay in here! It's for your own safety!'

Paula looked back at her once – her face an oval in the gloom – and then she turned and ran. Headed for the beach, just metres away, skirting around the low walls of the plant. Rainbow was older, slower. She wouldn't be able to follow them. They'd be able to get away and go . . . where? Was anywhere safe?

They reached the end of the wall, and the beach was right in front of them, beyond a wire fence. Electrified? Not if the power was off, she reasoned. The sea glinted, white with foam. Guy had stopped behind her, looking back. 'What?'

'Do you see that?'

The concrete walls of the plant were set with small high windows, and at them Paula could just about see something pale. Faces. One, then two and three at every window. 'What the hell?'

'There's people in there.'

The foreign workers. Of course, they couldn't send them to the mainland. They'd nowhere else to go. So they too were stuck on this island. 'It's their workers,' Paula shouted, over the noise of the sea. 'They live on-site. They're locked in, look!' At the end of the building was a large metal door, like you'd find on a garage, and it was closed with a large padlock. From the outside. It seemed Enviracorp had a habit of shutting people away.

The people inside had spotted them now, and fists began to go up, banging on the windows. Paula looked at Guy, as pale and wide-eyed as she imagined she was. 'Should we help them?'

'How? It's no safer out here, especially with the islanders closing ranks.'

'But they're trapped!'

'We will be too if we go back in there.' He looked around him, the wind whipping his hair over his forehead. Thinking hard. 'OK. Grab a rock from the beach. A pointy one.'

Stooping in the wind and rain, sea foam stinging her cheeks, she found a large grey stone and hefted it. Guy had one too. They staggered up to the gate, looking round all the time for any sign of Rainbow. 'Bash it!' Guy shouted.

Paula was doubtful, but in the absence of any other plan she did as he said. Bashed it, thudding the rock against the metal clasp of the padlock, both of them over and over until their hands ached with small cuts. Nothing.

'It's no good!' Guy shouted. 'It won't work!'

'But we have to do something! We can't just leave them!'

He set his rock down, and she saw a thin smear of his blood ran along the side. His face was exhausted, pinched with cold. 'There's nothing we can do.'

It hit her. There really was nothing. No one to call, no help coming. No weapons, nowhere to hide. All they could do was run, and leave these people, who were at least safely inside, to their fates. Guy reached for her arm, and she dropped her own stone, which clanged against the concrete ground, and followed him.

As they ran towards the white level sands, a wail went up behind, one voice joined by another, and then another, until it sounded as if everyone in the building was screaming, howling with their last breath. Paula turned her back on it, and ran. The faces at the windows watched them go.

Bob

'Well, son.'

Aidan O'Hara looked askance at the *son*, as well he might. Bob had no particular fondness for the lad. Reckless, like his da, believing the story was more important than your woman and child at home. The truth. Some idea of justice. Bob didn't think the lad would remember that he'd been the one who found him that night in 1986, hiding under the desk in that newspaper office that was so horribly quiet, and then not quiet enough, when they heard the sound of a child trying to cry without making a noise. Aidan hadn't come out from under the desk, where his da had told him to hide, but he was sitting there watching the blood leak out across the floor from John O'Hara's head. He was seven. Bob would have said he was haunted by that night, but in truth it was just one in so many horrors he'd seen over the years, dead children, dead babies in their mothers' arms, men torn to bloody chunks. So no, he felt no particular affection for Aidan O'Hara. Thought he didn't take enough care of Paula or the wean. Spent too much time in scabby pubs. Sure, who wouldn't want to take a drink when you had all that blood in your head, all that pain, if the booze could make it fade for a time? But when you'd a woman and child at home to protect, you didn't. That was Bob's code.

But all the same he was here at the prison, queuing up for visiting day with the worst dregs of the town. He held himself stiff on the plastic chair, wondering what kind of dirt was smeared into this place. O'Hara looked surprised to see him, then rallied into his usual cocksure expression, despite the yellow bruise on one side of his face.

'Sergeant Hamilton! What brings you here? The excellent coffee? Or the top-notch company?'

He'd know Bob was retired; he was using the title as a mockery. Bob nodded to the bruise. 'The Provos?'

'They don't take it too kindly when you knock off one of their own.'

'Son, you should let her help you.' Bob lowered his voice right down. 'There's evidence . . . they were after him. People have long memories in this town. There was a hit on him before he even stepped out of here.'

Aidan looked away. 'She put you up to this?'

Bob almost laughed. 'Are you joking me? She'd lose the head with me altogether if she knew I was here.' He took a deep breath. Had to manage this thing right. 'Listen to me. What's the one thing that she needs more than anything?'

'Better boyfriend,' he said shortly, rubbing his face.

'Son. Come on.'

He sighed. 'She wants to find her ma. Or find out what happened to her at least. You know that.'

'Aye.' He paused. 'I knew her, you know. Margaret.' And how wrong it felt to say her name in here. 'PJ and I were partners back then, for a time.' Before Bob got the promotion that should have been PJ's by right. But PJ was the wrong religion, in a time when being a Catholic RUC man was as good as signing your own death warrant. Another man who'd put an ideal ahead of his family.

'Aye, so?'

'So . . . she . . .' Now that the time had come to say it, the thing he hadn't told anyone in nearly twenty years, Bob found he couldn't do it. The words seemed to crawl back into his throat, treacherous. *Do you really want to do this?*

You promised, Bob. Her face, red hair against white skin. 'I might be able to . . . find something out about it.' Bob let the phrase hang in the air. Waiting for the lad to get it.

He got it. A stillness came over his face. 'If?'

'If you help yourself. At least try to get out. Because, son, she needs that too. She needs you back.'

'I killed a man.'

'You don't know that. You can't. I can . . . find things out there too. There's still people. Lads who owe me favours. I can get names – find out who was after him.'

Aidan was looking sceptical. 'Why didn't you find these "things" out before, Sergeant Hamilton? Paula's ma's been gone twenty years.'

He didn't answer. Plenty of reasons, but most of all that he'd made a promise. But Paula needed his help now. Needed this lad, useless and broken as he was, out of prison and by her side. And since Bob couldn't tell her why he had the list of names Sean Conlon had given him – couldn't explain the twisted bloody path that had led him and Conlon together – this was all he could do.

'So what do you want from me? Why are you here?'

Bob could hear beneath the bald questions that the lad was tired out, trying to keep his head above water in this place. 'I just want you to try, son,' he said, hoping to sound gentle. 'Accept that maybe it wasn't you killed Conlon. Just maybe. Can you do that? If I get names?'

Around them, the other prisoners were starting to get up. Visiting time was over. One of them, a burly man with no hair and tattoos on each hand, bumped into Aidan's chair, sending it rocking. It seemed like an accident, but for the snide look back over his shoulder. Aidan cleared his throat, his face darkening.

'Are you all right in here, lad?' Bob asked, though he knew the answer.

'Am I all right? Well, no, Sergeant, I'm not. It's killing me.'

'So will you try? Will you at least try to get out, if I help you?'

Aidan stood up, and gave a short nod, and then he was gone with the rest, head bowed and not looking back.

Chapter Thirty

'The lighthouse,' Paula shouted. 'It's cordoned off – we can get in there and shelter.'

'Which way?' he shouted back.

She gestured ahead. 'North . . . I think. Which way is that?'

Guy moved forward into the wind, and she followed. It was crazy. The island was only so big, and if you followed the beach surely you'd get back to where you started, but she was finding it so confusing. Was it forward or backwards they needed to go to get there? She tried to remember the island from twenty years back. A changeable sunny day, the breeze calm and clean, coming straight from America, her father had said. Her mother laughing, smiling. No hint that she would be gone in just weeks. But every time Paula tried to recall it, the memories slipped away, tangled and confused.

Eventually, thankfully, the ground rose under their feet, and there was the lighthouse, white and straight at the top of the cliff path. The door hadn't been fixed, and it opened easily, unlocked. Paula flicked the light switch, hopeful, but the power was still off. She shone her phone into the kitchen. Immediately, she frowned. 'This isn't how we left it.' The place was a mess – cupboards open, packets and jars left out on the side. The blue mug from earlier was smashed on the kitchen floor. 'It's been turned over,' she called to Guy. 'I'll look upstairs.'

She ran up them quickly and it was the same – cushions off the sofa, drawers open. Above her, the dome of the lighthouse, the spiral stairs vanishing into darkness. She went down again. 'Nobody there.'

Guy was looking in cupboards, opening doors. 'Just stay with me, OK? There must be candles, or a lantern or something. Have a look.'

She opened a long cupboard in the utility room, holding her phone to investigate the contents, items stacked on the floor and hanging from hooks, fleeces and coats and all the kinds of outdoor gear you needed on an island. Her phone's battery was dying, its only use as a weak torch. 'Here's a camping lantern.'

'Great. Does it work?'

'Think so.' She flicked the switch and a ghostly light came on. She heard Guy come up behind her, then pause, shining his own torch on something. 'See something?'

'Maybe. There's a wetsuit here. Just one. Did they dive?'

Paula mentally scanned the pictures on Fiona's Instagram – smiling on mountains. Smiling in boats. 'I think so, yeah.'

'So where's her suit, then?'

They looked around the small space, but there was no sign. 'Are you having an idea?'

'Maybe.' He shone his torch on something else. A pile of rope, coiled in the corner like a patterned snake. 'Do you think . . . if someone could dive, say, and if they could climb . . . Did they climb?'

'Yep.' She remembered a picture of Fiona dangling from a harness, smiling again. Always smiling.

'So, if you could do both those things . . . do you think you could manage to get down off the top floor here? And off the island?'

She thought about it. 'I don't know. Seems a bit mad, doesn't it? With the storm and everything.'

'Everything about this is mad. So maybe . . .' He stopped, frowning. 'Do you hear that?'

Outside, the noise of a car on gravel. Lights swept over the kitchen. Without hesitation, Guy stepped backwards into the cupboard that held Matt and Fiona's outdoor things, pulling Paula in behind him. 'The lantern. Turn it off,' he hissed. Her hand fumbled, found the switch. In there, there was just about enough room for them to stand, pressed together. She clamped her mouth shut, smelling damp and rubber and him, the warmth of his breath on her neck. Dimly, she thought to herself that once this was all over – once they'd got off this island – she and Guy really needed to have a long talk.

Footsteps approached, and Paula heard voices carried on the wind. She tried not to flinch as the door of the lighthouse opened and someone came in. Seamas Fairlinn, swinging a large torch, stomping in wellies. He looked around in a cursory fashion, shining the torch into the kitchen and up the stairs. Paula didn't breathe. 'Not here,' he shouted back.

Another voice called from outside, almost indistinguishable on the wind, but enough to hear an American twang. Rainbow. The two of them, working together? Finally, they went, shutting the door behind them, and the car started up a moment later. Paula let out all her breath.

'We can't stay here either, I guess,' she said, resigned. 'They were looking for us.'

'Yeah. Not a good idea. Was there somewhere else you had in mind?'

'Maybe. There's someone who might not be part of this, if we're lucky.'

Chapter Thirty-One

Mary O'Neill's small cottage was on the north shore as she'd said, the walls studded in sharp pebbles. But there were no signs of light or movement inside.

'You say she might know something?'

'She knew what Matt was working on. I think she'll understand what's happening here – and maybe not be as badly affected.'

'About that.' Guy's too-big boots crunched on the sand. His arms were folded over his chest, and he must be cold, even though he'd made no word of complaint. 'Have you eaten much, since you've been over here? Anything to drink?'

She thought back. 'Just those sandwiches really. And tea and water and stuff. Like you had. Why?'

'I just wondered – at the pub, you seemed a bit confused.'

She thought back to it, that strange sense of lassitude. Knowing the pub was going up in flames around her, but somehow unable to act. 'The smoke, maybe.'

He was watching her. 'Just be careful. Tell me if you feel sick.'

'You don't think I'm going to flip?' She tried to say it lightly, but heard the note of fear in her own voice. 'Come on. This must be it.' She swung open the gate that led from the beach to Mary's neat front garden. The curtains were open, the windows dark. Guy nudged her and pointed – the front door was ajar. Paula felt a thrill of fear in her blood, thinking of the woman with her fussy measured voice, her big glasses and racking cough.

Guy eased it open, taking up the stance she'd seen him use in raids. All that training, years of learning how to deal with situations like this. You might face danger every day as a police officer in London. This was nothing, she told herself. It was only that they couldn't get off the island. That was what made it feel so frightening.

'Mary?' The door creaked as Guy advanced, talking in a low voice. 'Are you here, ma'am? It's the police.'

Nothing. In the living room, everything was dark. A half-drunk cup of tea and a Jaffa Cake sat on the wooden arm of an easy chair, glasses folded on top of a book. Guy flicked the light switch – also nothing. The power was off still, hardly out of the ordinary on this island. So why could Paula not quell the waves in her stomach, the uneasy tide going back and forth?

She tried: 'Mary? It's Paula here, Dr Maguire. Are you OK?' At Guy's nod, she put her hand on the banister. The carpeted stairs creaked. 'Mary?'

Paula wasn't sure what happened next. She took in a breath, and then there were thundering footsteps and someone was rushing past her, a figure in a black jacket and balaclava pushing against her so she fell backwards in the hallway. Luckily she caught at the banister – steadied – and the figure was out, rushing out the door and onto the beach with big, crunching steps. Guy had shot out from the kitchen and was in pursuit. 'Hey. *Hey!*'

She righted herself, vision swimming, heart hammering. Guy was back, panting. 'Can't catch him. He's bloody fast.'

'He?' She caught her breath.

'You don't think?'

'Yeah.' She felt again the weight of the push, strong arms and legs, heavy breathing. A smell of aftershave, something familiar that she couldn't grasp. Definitely a man. 'Where's Mary?'

'No sign. I'm pretty sure that person had the Enviracorp logo on their jacket, by the way.'

'Oh.'

Together, they looked up the stairs, and Guy moved into position again, creeping sideways up the stairs as he'd been taught. Paula followed, cautiously. At the top the landing was quiet, a window looking out on the moonlit bay. Ornaments, china cats. One had been pushed over and broken, the smiling face smashed. A bedroom door stood ajar. Guy pushed at it. Paula saw patterned carpet, a dressing table with more ornaments. 'Mary! Shit!' He hit the floor suddenly as something sailed past him and into the hallway, breaking. Another ornament biting the dust. Paula heard him call out. 'We're the police! We're the police!'

She wrenched the door aside, only to see Mary O'Neill crouched up in the corner of her room like a trapped animal, a small arsenal at her side – china ladies, a hairbrush, a pot of cream. She stood up, seeing Paula. 'Is that you, Dr Maguire?'

'It's me. This is my colleague. You're safe now.'

Mary looked down at her collection. 'Thank God. I was going to have to throw the orange seller next, and she's my favourite.'

Paula wrinkled her nose. 'What's that smell?' A sour, oily reek filled the room.

'Petrol.' Mary dusted off her hands. 'They had a can of it. Soaked the place. I expect they were going to barricade me in here.' Her bedclothes – chintzy pink – were drenched in the stuff, oily rainbows catching the light from the bay.

Paula blinked. 'They were going to set the place on fire?'

'Oh yes,' said Mary calmly. Just like at the pub. What was going on here?

Guy moved his foot aside, crunching on a broken figurine. Mary's bedroom was in disarray, a wooden crucifix snapped, her creams and perfumes scattered. 'Who would do this to you?' he asked, half to himself. Who indeed? Paula was sure she'd recognised the aftershave, if only she could place it. But her mind was a storm of fire, and blood, and wailing. She couldn't think straight.

Mary stepped forward, her foot snapping the neck of a porcelain figure. 'Any number of people. The whole island. Surely you've figured that out by now, Dr Maguire?'

'What's causing this? You know, don't you?'

They were now in Mary's living room, where sure enough they'd found a plastic can of petrol, filling the place with its stink. 'We were just in time,' Guy said, moving it outside with gloves on. 'If they'd had time to chuck this round, the whole place would have gone up.'

Paula was watching Mary as she looked round her wrecked living room. 'Why is this happening, Mary? Can you tell us?'

Mary straightened a picture, a black-and-white shot of the island. It looked beautiful, peaceful. 'We noticed it about two months ago. Everyone was so snappy – flying off the handle at the smallest thing. And there were fights all the time, physical fights sometimes in the office. A punch-up in the canteen queue. Scuffles in the pub, that sort of thing. And people were starting to be . . . paranoid. Convinced

they'd be cast out if they spoke up about anything, com-
plained about the company. That made things a lot harder
to see. It took me longer to work it out than I'm proud of.'

Paula said nothing – she'd thought Mary paranoid too,
with her talk of being listened to. Same thing Andrea Sharkey
had said.

'You're saying this is some kind of poisoning?' Guy
asked.

She nodded. 'Something's got into the water supply, I'd
say.'

'And it comes from the factory? The seaweed processing?'
Guy spoke calmly, as if he'd already figured this all out.

Another nod. 'I believe so.'

Paula said, 'Was it the company? Were they trying to
cover it up?'

'I think so. Matt, as I told you, reported it to Dr Monroe,
though he hadn't connected his own behaviour to the deaths
among wildlife he'd uncovered. People never do, of course.
Not when they're in the grip of it. I tried to persuade him to
watch what he ate – there are certain plants which absorb
fewer toxins, and of course the further up the food chain
you go, the more concentrated it is. Fishermen were especially
affected. The water is also contaminated, of course, but we
can filter and boil it. I thought it would pass – these things
generally do move through the food chain and out.'

Paula was bewildered. 'But . . . why didn't you do
anything? Why didn't you warn people?'

'I tried. But I was – I was afraid they'd come for me.
After Matt disappeared. But I reported it, of course I did.
And Matt did too, but by that stage he'd had too much
exposure. He couldn't exactly formulate his thoughts. It was
too easy for them to pretend he'd gone mad.'

'Exposure to what?' Paula asked. The power was still off, so Mary had lit some large church candles. In the wavering light, everything looked unsure. Melting into the air.

Mary rubbed her eyes, then put her glasses back on. 'Well, it's fairly technical. We were using corrosive chemicals at the plant to extract minerals from the seaweed. We make food supplements and that out of them. Not very scientific, really, but there's a market for it. Seaweed, as you might know, is a big source of iodine, and also makes good fertiliser. People have been using it on the fields for years – nothing grows out here otherwise.'

Guy nodded. Paula was frantically thinking back to school chemistry.

'It's been known for a long time that heavy metals – mercury is one example – can bio-accumulate in marine organisms. Shellfish are quite vulnerable – they extract it from the water along with their food, and then it gets into the food chain, and carries up and up until it reaches us. When I worked as a research chemist in America, from time to time we'd get reports of towns that had gone – strange.'

'Strange?' said Guy. In the flickering light, his face was full of hollows.

'People acting oddly. Forgetfulness, vomiting and sickness, rashes, that kind of thing. A sort of mass poisoning. The thing is, fish and especially shellfish are not very good at avoiding toxins. Hard to, when it's all around you in the water. So it's usually seaside towns that experience this kind of . . . event. Something similar happens when people ingest ergot.'

'Barley fungus.' Guy was nodding. Paula was lost.

Mary looked at him approvingly. 'Spot on. Shellfish amnesia is another example. Very common, as I've said.

Communities in Japan suffer quite often. Now, we aren't stupid at Enviracorp – we know these processes happen, and we were at pains to stop it. That was the whole point of Matt's job, in fact.'

'But – it did happen?'

She nodded, sifting through the remains of a smashed vase. 'Something happened. I think it was a one-off chemical spill, and we stopped at once, but the damage was already done, a huge surge dumped into the ecosystem. We began to see the effects quite quickly in marine life. Fewer offspring, more birth defects. And then of course it's in the soil, and getting through to the sheep and cows.'

'What is it?' asked Guy. 'Mercury?'

She shook her head absently. 'A lead compound, I believe. The pipes on the island, you know, they're very old. And with such harsh chemicals – we had some nasty burns, at the start. The migrant workers. Hushed up, of course.'

Paula was making the connections now. Andrea, who collected eggs from her chickens. Fiona Watts had been right – Andrea wasn't psychotic at all. Niamh, who liked to beachcomb. And Jimmy Reilly – hadn't Rory mentioned he was a farmer? All of them exposed to it. 'So there's lead in the food chain?' Paula was trying to think back to what she'd eaten. Cups of tea. Water. She felt sick. 'What are the symptoms of lead poisoning?'

Mary said: 'Confusion. Tiredness, lethargy. Rashes. A metal taste in the mouth. Sickness, nausea, loss of appetite . . . then after a while you start to get headaches, you feel sick all the time, your muscles hurt. You might even be paralysed. In children, there's often cognitive deficits. It actually affects their IQ. And the effect on pregnant women is even worse. Very toxic to the foetus – it could even cause miscarriage or still birth. Low sperm counts, too.'

Guy was looking alarmed. Paula tried to think – had he eaten much? No, they'd been rushing about all day, and she'd seen him drink from water he'd brought with him. But she hadn't been so careful, had she? She remembered the cups of tea she'd had at the plant and the commune, leaving such a metallic taste in her mouth, like when she'd been pregnant and everything was off.

'There's another effect too,' said Mary quietly. 'It's caused by more acute poisoning – when there's a sudden spike in the concentration levels of the toxin. I believe that's what may have happened.'

'What's that?'

'Violence,' she said. 'There's good evidence that ingesting lead causes violent and aggressive behaviour. It affects the part of the brain that helps regulate how we act. Studies suggest worldwide rates of violence dropped dramatically when it was taken out of petrol.'

Guy nodded grimly. 'So people are being poisoned. And it's making them violent.'

'Violent, paranoid, withdrawn . . .' She sighed. 'I saw it happening, of course. But the scale of the outbreak – well, I didn't expect that.'

'And you think that Matt had it?' asked Paula.

For a moment her face twisted in pain. 'I knew when I read that report. It wasn't – oh, it wasn't even a report. It was crazy stuff. Ravings about how the blood tide was going to get us all. We'd be drowned in blood, he said.'

Paula shivered. 'A blood tide. Matt wrote it on the wall of his shed. What does it mean?'

'I think he was worried about an algal bloom. It happens when you pump the sea full of nutrients. Very bad for the environment – but what he wrote made no sense. I tried to hide it – he'd have been fired if they saw it, and maybe sectioned too. That Fiona. She'd have had him sent away. I could see it in her eyes. She thought he was crazy. He tried to tell her what was going on, but she wouldn't listen. She always had to know best, of course.'

Paula and Guy exchanged a look. 'We went to Matt's boatshed earlier and his samples are missing.'

Mary stood up and went behind the sofa, tugging out the plastic box they were looking for, with Matt's laptop neatly bundled on top of it. 'I got it. It wasn't safe. They're after it.'

'Who's they? The company?'

Mary nodded, distractedly. 'But I just keep thinking – if only I'd known. If only I'd seen how bad it was going to get. Maybe I could have helped him.'

'Why did you do it, Mary?' Paula was pretty sure she knew the answer. 'Why did you hide his samples, and why didn't you tell anyone how sick he was?'

'Because,' she said, matter-of-factly, 'I was in love with him. I thought I could help him, get him better. I thought Enviracorp were going to deal with the problem, quietly, and it could all be hushed up.'

So it was her who'd hidden the evidence. Not to cover it up, but to save the man she loved. Loved futilely, and with no happy ending. Matt was dead, his life sucked out by the sea, his body burned to a crisp now.

Paula was thinking hard. 'So if someone only ate food that came from off the island, and only drank bottled water, is it possible they would be safe from this? Whatever it is?'

'They would certainly show much lower levels of contamination. Vegetarians too – it's in the fish, you see, and that's what starts it off. But by now – oh, it's in everything. Even if you brush your teeth. I've been very careful, but it was too late by the time I realised. It will be in me too.' Still, she was so calm.

'And someone who never ate anything local?'

'They'd be all right, I imagine. But why would someone do that?'

Paula knew someone who had their reasons. On an island full of people going slowly mad, Fiona Watts had perhaps been the only sane one.

Mary clasped her knees. 'So you see, Matt was afraid. He was right to be, I realise that now. They were after him – do you know where they might have taken him? I think he's still here on the island somewhere.'

Paula looked at Guy again. 'Mary . . .' Her voice faltered. But then, who would have told her? The islanders had closed ranks, and no one knew she loved Matt, and Rory, whose job it would have been to inform people, was clearly not about. 'I'm so sorry, Mary. I thought you would have known. I'm afraid Matt is dead.'

Bob

1993

'I need your help, Bob.'

Margaret Maguire was in his office. Red hair in a bun, neat grey dress like she'd just come from work. Bob blinked slowly. Looked about him. 'Are you wanting PJ or . . .'

'He's out on patrol,' she said impatiently. Bob was a sergeant now, with his own office. PJ, now his junior, was polite, but both of them knew a bad decision had been made and things would never be right with them again. 'I'm wanting you.'

'Right, right. Er – have a wee seat there, Margaret.' What could she want with him? Maybe she'd a parking ticket or something. No, Margaret wasn't that kind of person, who'd ask for favours and short-cuts. She was like her husband, believed in the black and white of it, the right and the wrong, even though here they were living in the kingdom of grey.

'I need your help,' she said. She was speaking briskly, but he saw her knuckles were white as she gripped the edge of the desk. When she lifted off her hands, her prints left whorls and lines on the wood. Her mark. Unique to her, in the whole world. 'I've done – something. These. I've taken these.' She fumbled a file out of her bag, photocopied documents.

Bob leafed, then put it down like a hot stone. 'Margaret, I'm not meant to see this. These are confidential between the solicitor and the client.'

'I stole them,' she said. 'Well. The copies.'

'Why did you . . .'

'There's a man. He came to see me, a few years back.

After the soldier died. You remember? John died, and then the soldier died in my arms. And I just – I couldn't do it any more. This man came to see me and he said, Mrs Maguire, I hear you were very distressed by the incident the other day. And he knew what I did. Where I worked and who for. And he asked me . . . to get things.'

Bob looked at the file. Information inside that would help solve at least a dozen active investigations, he was sure. And yet he couldn't touch it, because if he did her life would be in danger.

'There's things in there. Addresses. Names. People they can watch. Who they should arrest. Maybe to stop more people dying. I've been giving it to him. This man.'

'Dear God, Margaret.' It was all he could say. Taking the Lord's name in vain. 'And what can I . . .'

'They know,' she said crisply. 'Someone knows. I've been made a target.'

Oh dear God, have mercy.

'So. I need your help, Bob.' Her hands were gripped together now, almost breaking the skin she wrung them so tight, and her face was pinched in terror. 'You know what they do. They kidnap you, they torture you – they tape it all – they get your confession. You can't stand up to it. No one can. I couldn't. I'm not – I'm not strong enough.'

'So what are you going to do?'

She bit her lip and he could see she was trying not to cry. 'There's only one thing I can do. I just need you. So please, will you help me?' Bob looked down, at the marks of her fingers that were fading now so rapidly, and he realised that, whatever happened, whether he helped her today or whether he didn't, he was never going to see Margaret Maguire again.

Chapter Thirty-Two

Mary was very calm. She only blinked once, and very slowly nodded her head. 'I see. So they got him in the end.'

'We don't know. His body – he was found in the sea, so it's possible he drowned.'

'He didn't drown,' she said quietly. 'They did this. I knew they would. I should have stopped them.' Her calm was so unsettling Paula felt the hairs rise on her neck.

'We can't be sure. But you're right we need to be very careful, all of us. We have to take these samples out of here. We'll need some way to prove everything that's been going on, and Matt's research is the only record.' Guy put a hand on the plastic box. Inside, the dead face of something was pressed against the side. Paula shuddered. 'Plus, if they've figured out you have them . . . it's not safe.'

'You want to take the box?'

'Please. In the morning the forensics team will be here, I hope, and we'll need to preserve and document all of this. Did you wear gloves when you touched it, by any chance?'

She nodded. 'Of course, Inspector. I don't want to be getting dead mouse on myself, now do I?'

'I imagine you'd want it out anyway, must be stinking the place up.' Guy was smiling, and Paula felt a small easing of the knot of panic she'd carried in her stomach all night.

Maybe this would be all right. They could shelter somewhere till morning – take Mary with them – and then the Guards would come and they could sort out this whole bloody mess. She was already cataloguing it in her head. Who could they charge and what with? Or would they have to write it all off as collective madness?

Mary was nodding. 'All right. Let me get you some tea first, you must be exhausted.'

Paula stood. 'Let me, Mary, you've had a shock.'

'No. I knew he would be dead. I knew it. It's fine.' Mary went out, shutting the door behind her.

Guy leaned back on the sofa, closing his eyes briefly. 'Poor woman. Christ, this is a bad business.'

'I know. I hate having to do that, give the death notice.'

'I'd say you get used to it, but I hope you never do.' One of the things she'd always admired about him was that long years of service, and even the death of his son, had not blunted his compassion, for each and every death. He smiled at her wearily. 'Holding up OK?'

'Not too bad. I wish I could talk to Maggie.'

'I know. The power might be back by tomorrow. You never know.'

'Yeah. Hope so. What'll happen? Can anyone be prosecuted?'

He shrugged. 'The company, maybe. Though if they say Matt wasn't making any sense, who knows. This kind of paranoia has massively complicated things. Are you feeling all right?'

'I think so. I don't have the urge to bash your head in, if that's what you mean.'

'Good. I'm quite fond of my head, battered as it is.'

And she was quite fond of it too, she realised. They'd

seen each other so little in the last two years since the unit disbanded. She liked working with Helen Corry, but it wasn't the same. She and Guy had always had an intuitive connection, and she missed it. It had been something precious, that connection, and because she'd been stupid enough to sleep with him, she'd almost destroyed it. She hadn't even seen Guy in more than half a year, the secret she was keeping from him pushing them apart. 'I'm glad you came,' she said. 'I mean I'm sure you're not – but I couldn't have been out here alone.'

'I'm glad too. I'd hate to think of you here with this . . . whatever it is. This madness.' He shuffled forward and reached for her hand. He'd taken off his gloves, and his were cracked and red from the wind. Hers were too, still frozen through. He rubbed warmth into them, and she let him. No one had touched her like this in months. Not since she'd seen Aidan being dragged away in that police car, still in his wedding suit. After years of being alone, Paula had had to get used to having someone there when she turned her key in the lock, when she rolled over in bed, when she opened her eyes. And she had got used to it, and then it had been taken away, and for months now there'd been a raw emptiness in her. Her heart ached again, thinking of Aidan in prison. Somewhere she could never get to him. No windows, locked doors, slowly rotting away.

She imagined saying it. *Guy. I'm sorry we got it wrong, but you're Maggie's father. You, not Aidan. And I didn't tell you because . . .*

Well, because he was still married. Rockily, but married. And they'd lost their son and she couldn't be the one to break them more. But she'd have to tell him sometime. Maggie would need to know who her father was, for one thing. Yes, sometime. Sometime wasn't now. 'Tess must be worried about you,' she said, as nonchalantly as she could manage.

'She's used to it, sadly. She knows I'd call if I could. I was always away when the children were small. You can imagine how much I wish I had that time back.' He misinterpreted her look. 'But don't worry, you'll be home to Maggie tomorrow. It's only two nights, that's nothing.'

'I've never been away this long.' They'd planned to go on honeymoon, her and Aidan, for two weeks, but of course that had never happened. And Maggie had already lost the man she thought was her father, locked in a prison cell. She tried again, thinking of the job Guy had offered her the year before. The one she'd almost taken, if it wasn't for finding that note in the kitchen. 'Guy. Things have been . . . Since you left, things have been really tough for me, and I . . .'

He took his hands away, his face clouding. 'Paula. I hope . . .'

He didn't finish his sentence. She waited, and he said nothing, and she followed his gaze over her shoulder. To the closed door. Where Mary had not returned from making tea.

'Do you smell smoke?' he asked, calmly.

'Mary!' Guy put his shoulder to the door, but it didn't budge. 'Mary, what are you doing?'

From the corridor, her voice was muffled. 'I can't let you take his things. It wasn't his fault. He was sick. And people will talk about him, say things about him. I can't let you do that.'

He turned to Paula, wide-eyed. The first tendrils of smoke

were creeping under the door. 'The window. We need to get out.'

Dimly, part of Paula couldn't believe this was happening again. Was there no safe place? She looked around for something to smash the window. The hard wooden chair was surely too heavy to lift, and yet she scooped it up and swung it. The window cracked, didn't break. Guy was rattling and pushing at the door. 'Mary. Let us out!'

Her voice sounded thick. 'It's better this way. No one has to know. We'll burn it . . . we'll burn it all up.'

Paula swung again, and the window cracked and shattered, spewing shards of glass over her clothes. She closed her eyes and shouted. 'Come on.'

Guy was behind her, holding his coat over the shards, and they were up and out, into the cold air of the storm. The wind was sucked in, fanning the fire, and Paula saw the door glow red. 'We have to get Mary!'

She raced to the front of the house, where flames were licking now round the door, black smoke pouring out. Through the glass panes of the door, Mary could be seen, slumped in the hallway. A hacking cough came – she was still alive. Paula covered her hands with her fleece and wrenched at the door. 'Mary. *Mary!*' It didn't give. Guy was bashing at the glass with a rock from Mary's garden path, but it wasn't breaking. Bang, bang, bang.

Mary tilted up her face, and for a moment she smiled. '*Matt*,' she shouted, through the fire, and then she was lost in smoke.

Paula howled. 'Mary! Help me get this open, come on.' Her hands were scrabbling at the doorknob, and she pulled her sleeves over her hands to cover them.

Guy was behind her, pulling at her. 'We can't go back in.'

'But she'll – she's going to die!'

'*Paula.*' He held her fast. 'Think of Maggie. You can't.'

He was right. 'Is there nothing we can . . . ?' It was coming home to Paula now, how much had been lost out here. No fire brigade, no police. No one coming to save them. It was just them and the fire and the storm, and all they could do was keep running. But on an island three miles long, how many places were there to run to? She sank into his arms, sobbing. How could this be happening? A woman was dying just metres away, and there was nothing they could do. Matt was dead, Fiona was likely dead too. They'd come to this godforsaken island for nothing, they were being hunted, and she just wanted to get back to Maggie. She wanted to be back in her house with Aidan and Maggie in the kitchen, him wearing Maggie's stupid plastic tiara and singing a stupid song, making the tea towel into a cloak. She wanted that so badly it was like physical pain. Because she couldn't have it. She'd probably never have it again.

'Paula.' Guy was shaking her. She realised she'd slumped down onto the stones of Mary's path, and they were digging into her. 'Come on, it's OK.'

She sat up, shakily, and he wiped the soot from her face. Tender. 'She's . . . she's dying,' Paula choked out.

'I know. I think, maybe – it's what she wanted. To be with him.'

To be with a man who didn't even love her, who like as not hadn't known how she felt. Who was dead too. Both of them dead. 'Fuck.' She was crying.

Guy's hand was strong in hers. 'Please, come with me. I know it's awful but I have to keep you safe.'

She got to her feet, struggling to stand. And they ran

down the beach, feeling the scorch of the fire behind them, and on the breeze was carried the dark tang of soot.

Chapter Thirty-Three

'What do we do?' She was panting, trying to keep up with him. He was pounding over the sand, as if trying to put as much distance as possible between himself and the burning house, the burning woman. Guy's hair was whipped by the wind, his face grim.

'No one can get out here till it's light. That's another four hours at least. There's nowhere safe for us, not on this island. Everyone is . . . well, you can see.'

Her teeth were chattering, her face numb. 'But where can we go?'

'Off. We can go off.'

Paula didn't understand. 'How?'

'The boat. Matt and Fiona's boat. We can take it.'

Back along the shore, skirting the empty boatshed, stripped out by Mary, desperate to keep Matt's memory clean. Both of them gone now. Back past the factory, which was silent too, the windows empty. The buildings dark and lifeless, trees bent to and fro like mourners at an Ancient Greek funeral. The wind keening past their ears.

Paula had been sure the boat would be gone, but it was still there, lying like an overturned beetle in the sand. And someone, someone with the same idea as them, had got there first.

'It's him!' she shouted. 'Isn't it?' The man from Mary's house, shrouded all in black, struggling to turn the boat over in the wind.

Guy paused for a moment, then set his shoulders, and ran towards the man. 'Hey. Hey! I want to talk to you.'

The man saw them and stumbled over, falling in the sand, then tried to get up. Guy had reached him, running easily over the flat compacted sand. 'Wait. Wait!'

Paula raced up beside them, seeing the Enviracorp logo on the jacket, and above it a terrified face she recognised. 'Dara?' she shouted, over the wind. 'What are you doing?'

He had his hands up. 'I'm sorry! I'm sorry! I need to get away from here.'

'Wait! Calm down.' She hunkered beside him. He was breathing hard, his face stung red from the sea spray. 'What's going on? You were at Mary's house.' Had he been planning to kill her, this affable corporate man? Did that mean the company was behind the pub burning, too – almost killing her and Guy?

He wiped his face with the back of one hand, leaving strands of black wool from his glove. 'I had to find Matt's samples. They weren't in the lighthouse, or in his boatshed. She took them.'

So he was the one who'd turned the lighthouse over. 'You knew? About all this?'

He shook his head. 'I didn't know, I swear! Not till that report came out. Jesus Christ, it's a shit-storm. We've been doing our best to clean things up, but it's a mess.'

She remembered how they'd used water from the cooler to make the tea, in the factory coffee room. 'You knew yesterday, right?'

'We don't know anything for sure. Not until we can take

more samples. But people are – Jesus Christ, did you see what *happened*? Her house! She sent the whole bloody place up in flames!'

'You weren't trying to hurt her?' Guy narrowed his eyes.

Dara shook his head frantically. 'I just got sent for the samples. We just needed to clear it all up, make sure no one got hurt . . . Christ. I'd never have hurt her, never, I swear.'

'And the pub?' asked Paula, already knowing the answer.

'No! I swear, we didn't. Christ, I don't know what's going on. It's a fucking mess!' So who'd set the fire, then? Who had tried to kill them?

'You know you can't cover this up,' she said. 'People are sick. Really sick.'

'You don't think I know that? For fuck's sake. Bloody Ellen's fucked off too. Fuck her. Now I'm stuck here.'

He'd managed to drag himself away, and was pulling himself up on the edge of the boat. She shouted back to Guy: 'He's going!'

Guy understood. The man was half-crawling, half-walking to the edge of the water now. 'Wait! We can help you – are you hurt?'

Dara was almost in the sea now. The waves licked round his ankles, and Paula realised too late what lengths someone would go to to get off this island. 'He's going in!'

Guy was running after him, trying to help this time, but the man was terrified, and it just made him plunge further into the waves, and she watched, frozen and horrified, as the waves went higher and higher, grey-green in the moonlight, and soon the small, dark blot of his head was the only thing they could see.

Guy was back beside her, panting hard with effort. 'Couldn't get to him. Can't go in after.'

No, he was right, but could they really stand and watch a second person die in less than an hour? 'The boat!' she shouted. 'Can we get him in the boat?'

'We need to turn it.' Guy was pushing it down the beach, sliding it with effort through the sand. Paula put her hands to the dark barnacled wood and tried to help. He was strong, doing most of the work. Soon they were splashing in the water, and she felt the cold seep through her boots and socks, and gasped. The boat lightened in their hands, picked up by the tide. 'Flip it,' shouted Guy. With much grunting and gasping, the boat turned over in the water, splashing them in cold saltwater. Paula wiped it from her eyes. Guy held the boat steady. 'Jump in. Go on.'

She did, and he followed. The smell of metallic blood was strong in the boat, and she thought that it would be hopelessly contaminated now. After everything that had happened, there might be no evidence left except what she and Guy could testify to. The thought was chilling. They had to get through this night, otherwise no one might know what had happened here.

There was no sign of Dara in the sea now, though she scanned it over and over, and she told herself he'd maybe made it round the island, to a sheltered cove or cave, but with a cold spot in her stomach, she knew this was a long shot.

'Where will we go?' They huddled in the small boat, hearing the slap of waves against the side. It was rocking alarmingly, water still crashing on either side.

'I don't know. I don't think we can make the mainland, not in this. We'll have to just stay out, as close to shore as we can.'

Stay on a small, damp boat for hours, with no water or

shelter? Still, it was better than the alternative, of being burned to death and running for their lives from one crazy person to the next. There might be a house close to shore, somewhere with food and water, which they desperately needed. If the islanders were all in the community centre, perhaps they could find somewhere to hide out till dawn. She nodded. 'Maybe we can go around to the north, where it's more sheltered. Does it still work?'

Guy was fiddling with the outboard motor, pulling and pushing at things. 'Think so.'

'You know boats?'

'A bit. We had one when I was younger, on the Norfolk Broads.' A reminder of how little she really knew about Guy. She knew nothing of his family, his childhood. Nothing of what he'd been doing for two years. And yet she was the mother of his child.

He pulled something, and the thrum of a motor was the most beautiful sound Paula had heard in a long time.

The journey around the island was relatively calm at first. Waves slopped over the side of the boat, spraying Paula with freezing water, and the wind howled past her ears, and she still wasn't sure they wouldn't capsize, but Guy seemed to know what he was doing, guiding the small boat along the craggy cliffs of the island. She felt herself relax, just a fraction. 'So what do you think? Who are we going to pin this on?' Rory, maybe? Seamas? Rainbow? Not Mary. Mary was dead now. She swallowed hard. 'And where's Fiona? Why have we still not found Fiona Watts?'

Guy said nothing for a short while, his large hands guiding the motor. 'I hate to say it, but it seems likely she's dead. Don't you think?'

Paula thought of the list. Fiona had known something was wrong on the island. But what had she done about it? 'The Andrea Sharkey case . . . Fiona was unpopular here, Rory said, because she might have missed the post-natal psychosis. Maybe after that other case in London – if she lost her job and home over that – maybe she was reluctant to intervene again. So Andrea tried to kill her baby. And maybe – if everyone here is so paranoid, maybe they blamed Fiona for what's happening here, everyone being poisoned, and maybe . . .'

'They killed her?' Guy finished. 'It's possible. Or could be Dara was lying, and the company had something to do with it. Maybe they'd kill to cover up what they did here.' They puttered along for a while, thinking of that possibility. Where would you even hide a body on an island this small? Would Fiona surface somewhere, months or even years from now, caught in the Gulf Stream, perhaps, or tangled in the anchor of a ship?

They had now rounded the north side of the island, where Fiona and Matt's lighthouse stood, white against the dark. The bulb at the top in darkness. That would have to be fixed, once the storm had passed. But not everything that was shattered could be put back together.

'What's that?' Guy was suddenly alert, rigid. Again, she saw the beat cop he'd been before years of desk jobs and paperwork. The instincts that didn't die.

In the cove they had just entered, sitting silent in the dark water, was a large white yacht. About four or five times the size of the little boat they were in. 'Is it empty?' Paula could see no lights, nothing to indicate people were there. Guy piloted them closer.

He called: 'Hello? Is anyone there?'

No answer, but a purr of engine as the boat started up and began to move. For a moment she was relieved. Someone to help them, maybe. Rescue. 'Someone's there!'

Stupid. The boat covered the water between them quickly, and Paula saw Guy's face change from relief to a sudden stab of worry. 'They're very clo—'

The ramming took her by surprise, and she almost fell in. 'Christ! What are they . . .'

Guy was gripping the sides of the boat. 'They're trying to knock us over.'

Another shudder. The hull of the boat loomed over them. Still, no one could be seen. 'What? Why?'

'Same reason as all of this! How good a swimmer are you, Paula?'

'I'm OK, I guess, but wh—'

'Take a breath! Now!'

'Wh—'

She understood why a moment later, when the final assault from the hull sent her flying, the boat flipping – she had a moment to feel Guy thrown against her, and to grab for him, and miss – and then the shock of the cold, and sudden blackness with a vague drowned light above, and the water was closing over her head. The last thing she saw as she went under was the name painted on the boat, in letters red as blood: *Caoimhe's Dream*. Seamas Fairlinn's boat.

Fiona

I was in my surgery when I found out about the symptoms. I'd been spending more and more time there, afraid of what I'd get at home. I liked how small it was, how I could lock the door, and the sound of the sea lapping nearby in the harbour. If something happened, at least I'd have a chance of getting to a boat. Not that I had many patients – people were afraid of me, after what happened to Andrea. They'd stopped coming, scared I'd report them, maybe, or that I'd make them worse. That's why things were covered up for so long, I believe.

The webpage was open in front of me.

Symptoms of lead poisoning include: nausea, headaches, tiredness and lethargy.

Matt throwing up his dinner, Matt turning down a walk, Matt refusing to touch me in bed because he was too tired. *I can't be bothered, Fi.*

Muscle pains. Flu-like fever.

I feel like crap, Fi. I can't do anything today. You go climbing by yourself.

Impotence. Male infertility.

The fact we'd barely had sex since we got here. The fact it had actually been worse than it was in London.

Miscarriage. Stillbirth. Birth defects.

That was the point where I stood up from my desk, holding a hand over my abdomen. Thrills of fear were shooting down into my fingers. *Miscarriage. Stillbirth.*

Not now. Not after everything I'd done. I'd been so careful, but had anything got in? Water from washing the dishes? From the shower? I had to start using bottled water for my teeth, like when we went overseas.

Had Matt been right, all this time, when I thought he was going crazy? Was there really something wrong on the island, and Niamh, and Andrea, and Jimmy – and yes, Matt, my Matt – sucked down with it? But maybe I was wrong. It was so far-fetched, so mad. Maybe there was something in Matt's brain, some vessel that had burst, some tumour growing, or something from childhood, lurking there for decades. I remembered he'd had a medical before he came to start this job. Via his GP surgery, which happened to be the one I'd worked in before Anika and everything that happened.

My fingers flexed over the keys. We had online log-ins to the patient records. What were the chances, in that harried, busy surgery, where the Christmas decorations were still up in February, that they'd remembered to delete my account?

What if I could get into Matt's medical records?

Before Matt, I never realised how you can fall in love with someone's body. I don't mean just admire their abs or white teeth or cool haircut. I'd had that before, of course. I'd even had falling in love with what someone did, how nice their flat was, or the fact they'd read all the books on the Booker shortlist and had opinions on them. But with Matt it was different. I still reach for him all the time in bed, blindly, like a baby does. Wishing I could press my face into his back, cup my hands over his scapulae. Stroke his soft earlobes and bristly chin and breathe him in. He was my regulator, I suppose, in very many ways. Until he malfunctioned.

Oh, Matt. I can't explain how it was, how I began to miss you so horribly it felt it would break my ribs, and all the while you were beside me in the bed. Your smell was still there, in every pore of your skin, and your back was the same landscape I palmed my face to at night. Your breathing was the same, even and calm, but you no longer were. And then of course you started sleeping on the sofa, and then at the boatshed, and then you weren't sleeping at all, and your blue eyes grew red and sunken.

I was trying to save you. I know that. I hope you know it too. I'd do it again, despite everything that happened. Because there is only one thing I can't bear, and that's not even being able to try.

Chapter Thirty-Four

Arms were pulling her from the water. She could hear voices, the sounds blurred. A woman. A man. Maybe two men. '. . . shit, I lost him . . .'

'. . . Where did he . . .'

'Bollocks, I think he went under.'

'Shit.'

'Boys, please. Language.'

She felt something rise up in her throat, and she turned her head to the side – everything hurt – and retched up saltwater onto the white plastic surface she was lying on. A boat. Deck of a boat. They'd dragged her on. And the boat must belong to . . .

'Easy, easy.' Someone was holding her wrists as she tried to get up. 'You've swallowed about half a gallon of the Atlantic; you're not going anywhere.'

Paula opened her eyes, which stung with salt, and tried to make sense of where she was. The deck of the bigger boat, yes. Darkness except for one dim light overhead. But it was enough to show her the faces of the three people who'd rammed them, although the light did not help her make sense of it. What were those three doing together? Her brain couldn't take it in. Then another thought hooked into her, pulling her flesh like cold steel. 'Where's Guy?' Her voice was croaky.

'Don't know,' said Rory shortly. He was one of the three, his red hair flattened and damp, his clothes sodden. 'Gone under.'

Paula strained up, trying to see over the side, and was held down again by the strong hands. She blinked at Rainbow, who was the second person. 'What are you doing here?' *Where was Guy?*

'Same thing as us,' said Seamas Fairlinn, who was the third. 'Trying to keep the peace.'

She spat out more water before speaking again. 'People are *dying*.'

He tutted. 'Ah now, Doctor, that just isn't true. Mary O'Neill, that's entirely of her own doing. Poor woman.'

'At the plant – we saw . . .'

Rainbow shook her head, her long grey hair lifting in the breeze. There was a scabbed-over cut above her eyebrow. 'Things got out of hand, that's all. The workers are locked up for their own safety. Nothing strange about that.'

'Matt. Matt Andrews is dead.'

Seamas said: 'Drowned, most likely. Poor fella. Who knows what even happened to him – fell off the top of that lighthouse somehow. Fell, or jumped, or who knows. Poor lad wasn't in his right mind.'

Paula didn't believe any of that, but how could she prove it? 'And someone burned his body. You.' She glared at Rory. 'You did it.' It made sense – that fire had started with alcohol, not petrol. And Rory nowhere to be seen.

He ignored her. He was peering into the water, still speaking to Seamas. 'I didn't see him go down. He could be round the hull somewhere.'

'Then look, for Christ's sake,' Seamas said with irritation. Rory leaned over, shining the torch. That was it, Paula's brain said. Guy would be hiding somewhere, ready to get her out of this, it would all be fine. He would be fine.

'What's going on?' she got out. 'I don't understand. Why did you even call the police over in the first place?'

'You were supposed to go back to the mainland and let us find them ourselves,' said Seamas irritably. 'You weren't meant to *stay*, not during the worst bloody weather in thirty years.'

'You killed them? Why?'

'We didn't kill them,' said Rainbow, also sounding irritated. 'Are you not listening? We'd no more idea where they were than you did. We just didn't want you asking questions. The problem had been dealt with. There was no need to involve the authorities.'

'Problem? You mean your company that's leaking toxins into your water supply?'

'It's been fixed, like I said.'

'It won't be fixed for years! I don't understand. People are getting sick. Don't you think they deserve compensation, even?'

She snorted. 'Is that all you think people need? Money? Dr Maguire, I came to this island for a haven, and I found it. Seamas's people, they've been living out here for a thousand years. We aren't giving it up, not without a fight. Sure, we messed up with the chemical spill, but we've done our best to clean it up. How was I meant to know Matt was right? He sounded like a crazy person.'

'That company's keeping the island alive,' Seamas said. 'The children, they'd have left long ago otherwise. It's jobs. It's lives. It's everything. My daughter, she'd still be alive if the plant was here then. It means my boy can stay. It means we'll survive, for another generation. One mistake is all they made. They'd have fixed it, had Andrews not gone off like a madman, involving the press. Least your woman O'Neill destroyed the evidence. It was all there for you, nice and neat. Their bodies would wash up, sooner or later, and it'd all be clear. The glass, the blood in the house – well, we could explain that away. Glass broke in the storm. Blood – maybe she cut herself. But no, you had to come round interfering. *Outsiders*.' He spat the word.

'Bodies?' Paula was thinking hard, but her mind felt like sludge. *Where was Guy?* 'You mean Fiona's dead too? You killed her?'

'For the love of Pete. We didn't kill her! We haven't killed anyone.' Rainbow shook her head, like a teacher when you hadn't done your homework. 'We told you the truth. Rory found the lighthouse locked up that morning, so he went to get Seamas and Colm, and they broke the door in. No one there, just the bulb all smashed. Both of them gone. Matt must have been in the sea already. She fell in too, I guess. I don't know what happened, but we didn't need you here poking your neb in.'

Paula glared at them. 'Did you know she was pregnant?'

Rory looked up sharply. 'Pregnant?'

Seamas narrowed his eyes at Paula. 'And how would you know a thing like that?'

'I spoke to her doctor on the mainland. So I hope for your sakes you're not lying, that you haven't hurt her.'

Silence. Rory had turned even paler than usual. Seamas had the wheel, and Rainbow was kneeling over Paula, so that her grey hair almost touched the wet deck. She stood up heavily, and went to Seamas. 'She knows a lot,' she said quietly.

'I *know*,' he muttered. 'Let me think. We have to deal

with this.' Paula felt panic rise like floodwater. Where was Fiona, then, if they didn't have her? And what would they do to Paula herself now they'd caught her? They'd pulled her from the sea, that had to count for something. And where the *hell* was Guy?

Rory had come back up, making a scraping noise on the hull. 'Eh . . . no sign of him. But I found this, floating in the water.'

He held his hand out, something in it. Green plastic. A hotel key, with the number 2 on it, the ink smudging in the seawater that saturated it.

Paula struggled out of Rainbow's strong, capable hands, and ran to the side. 'Guy. *Guy!*' Her voice echoed over the water. It sounded like there was nothing out there at all. The water was ink, no swirls or bubbles to show anyone had gone into it. He'd be . . . he could swim . . . he . . .

She turned, wordless, to Rory. He was looking oddly sympathetic, his hair flat and damp. 'Look, I'm sorry. We have to go now.'

'What? No! We can't leave, he's still down there, he's . . .'

'Stop it, Dr Maguire.' Seamas Fairlinn was starting the engine. 'It'll be light soon enough. We need to get this all cleaned up before the rest of your people arrive. We don't have a lot of time.'

'What do you mean, cleaned up?' Stupidly, she thought he meant the blood. The blood and the fire and the stains of this long, terrible night. His hand closed on her arm, solid as a steel bar.

'It was your own fault. You should have gone back. You don't belong here. Neither did Matt or Fiona.' He opened the door of a small dark cabin, and propelled Paula through it. 'That's what no one understands. You can't just move to

a place like this. You have to earn it. Earn it the hard way.'
The door slammed behind her. 'You see, whatever you do,
however hard you try, you'll always be an outsider here.'

Chapter Thirty-Five

There were bones under her feet. White, crunching. Only this time it wasn't going away, it wasn't a nightmare but reality, sharp and clear. The night air was chill, but the storm had calmed now. Paula hardly dared to look down at what she was walking on. It couldn't be bones. *Think, Maguire.* Maybe fish or animals or something or . . .

Coral. Of course. The famous coral beach on the island's south side, near the marina where they'd moored the boat. Last stop before an ocean of dark, cold water, and then America. She was walking over their skeletons, dried out and bleached, sharp as knives on her shoeless feet, Rory pushing her on from time to time, gentle but insistent, as she stumbled. She remembered it – that last summer. Her not even thirteen. Tall, skinny, pale. Legs white as bone. Plunging into the water, cold as it was. A fearless girl, right on the edge of things. Breasts just starting to swell under her conservative one-piece swimsuit. Hair plaited, slick with water down her back. Looking up at it waving like seaweed as she ploughed the depths of the cold sea. It was hard to explain why she'd done it – some crazy impulse, to push herself as far out and as deep down as she could. Feeling the ocean turn colder with every stroke, gripping you. Almost loving, in its way.

Paula. Paula. Her mother, shouting from the shore. A

slim figure in a green print dress. Always so beautiful. Her own red hair flying around her in the wind. Holding up a threadbare beach towel. *Don't go out so far. Come in, pet, come in.* For a moment, which she still remembered almost twenty years later, she'd been tempted to go on. A mermaid, not a girl, among the white fish and the fronds of seaweed. Then she'd turned back, swimming for shore in long, strong strokes. Even from that far away she could feel her mother's relief. The comfort of it, knowing someone was waiting for you on the shore, with a towel and a warm hug and the promise of salty chips later. It was worth it, the icy grip of the ocean, for how good you felt when it ended. How alive you were, now death had touched you all over.

When she got to the shore, her mother was crying. *Mammy, what's wrong?* A sudden stab of fear. All the way through this holiday, there'd been something hovering on the edge of things. Something wrong. Something Paula could not make OK, no matter how hard she tried to be good and behave. She had her own troubles, at almost-thirteen. *I thought you were gone*, her mother had said. *I thought I'd never see you again.*

And the water, the cold green of it, over her head. Something stirred – a memory. Something she could almost grasp at. *Where did you go? Why did you go? Where are you?* Just three words of a question, but enough to drive you crazy. How could you not know where your own mother was? How could a body not have surfaced, after all these years of waiting? Paula was afraid her father would die without ever knowing, was afraid she would too. Didn't know how she would ever tell Maggie that Pat was not her granny. That she had a granny, who was long gone. And Guy. Christ, did he have a mother? What was she like? *Where was he?*

'*Paula*. Get up, for God's sake.' She was being shaken awake from where she'd sunk down on her knees, and she coughed herself out of the bad dreams. They were still on the coral beach, and the bones of dead things were gritty under her cheek. Then she was hauled up, and they were trudging over it again. Her legs had no strength. The sky just beginning to get light, streaks of red like blood across it. The storm was calm now, and that meant they would come, the police and the helicopters and boats, but it would be too late to make it all OK.

'Jesus, what's this?' muttered Rory. Ahead of them were white ovals in the lightening dark. Gleams here and there. Faces. The whole of the island, it seemed, out on the beach in the dark. Brendan and Bridget, Colm the barman and Oona from the Spar, and Seamas's wife Grainne, her boy Sammy pressed to her. The bones on her face showed sharp, as if she was terribly afraid.

'What are you at?' Seamas was asking, impatient. 'Why are you all out here? Go on home now.'

Oona was staring past him, looking with horror at their feet. 'You went through it.' A murmur went up, and people stifled moans, held their hands to their mouths in horror. Paula found herself looking at her own feet, but she couldn't see anything in the half-dark.

'What is it?' Seamas said again. Fear colouring the anger in his voice.

It was the child who spoke. Sammy, with his milk-bottle glasses, and small for his age. 'The sea is full of blood, Daddy,' he said. 'The sea is full of blood.'

Seamas turned his torch to the ground, to his feet and Paula's feet, and sure enough she saw that her jeans were soaked in dark red, right up to the knees.

Bob

1993

The men all gave Bob's car the same look – low, flat, suspicious. They knew an RUC car when they saw one, and for this mostly Catholic factory workforce, that was never a welcome sight. Bob saw Conlon before he saw Bob – thickset, powerful underneath his stained grey tracksuit, laughing with two other men. He gave one of them such a slap on the back the other man nearly fell over. Then he saw the car and his face hardened.

Bob waited. Saw Conlon make a great pantomime of forgetting something, going back for it, *catch you later, lads*, until no one was left at the factory gates. 'The fuck you doing here? I'll be kilt so I will if they think—'

'Time for that wee favour you owe me, Sean.'

'Fuck off.'

'Listen. I just need some intel. Just a yes or no.'

'Just that?'

'I'll ask you a question and you just give me a nod.'

'What's it to you?'

'Just a nod, Sean.'

'And we're quits?'

'Aye.' The man looked suspicious, as well he might. Everything he owed Bob, wiped out just for a nod? A lie. A necessary one. Bob held up the picture. It was one he'd had in his desk drawer for years. Taken at the Christmas party, the night John O'Hara died. He'd bought it on the sly when the photographer sent the snaps round the station, and he'd cut out the rest of them, Linda and PJ and himself, leaving only her, with her red hair and her sparkly black dress and her white skin. The man's eyes narrowed – Bob hated showing her face to him.

Conlon said, 'You know who this is? You know what she's been up to?'

He put the picture away, into his jacket pocket. 'Never mind what I know. Question is, do your lot know?'

'That's your question?'

'Aye. Answer it.'

He seemed to think about it for a moment, and then he gave the nod, a short, sharp jerk. Bob could have pleaded for her – said she was a good woman, a mother, a wife – but it would do no good. This was a war, and she was on the wrong side, and that was that. 'She's a fecking tout,' said Conlon. 'And once they get the name . . .'

Bob understood. She had been marked out, and now it was only a matter of time before they came for her. Not very much time. 'I need your help, Sean,' he said, trying to make it both a warning and a threat and a plea, all at once.

Chapter Thirty-Six

Algae bloom. She was repeating that to herself. Mary had even mentioned it, an algal bloom, feeding off the chemical by-products, turning the water red. She'd heard about such things. Every summer in Ballyterrin the canal turned thick lime-green with the stuff. But all the same she wanted to peel off her wet jeans, be naked even, just to avoid the touch of that red stain. It didn't smell like blood. It smelled of the sea, and rotting things, dark and dank, but not blood. There was a faint blue sheen to it in the lightening dark. Still the jitter of fear ran up and down her spine. Where the hell was Guy? He couldn't have gone under. He was a good swimmer, surely, he was the type, and he knew boats, and the sea had been calm, and . . .

'Where are you taking me?' She found her voice, as she was being marched along the shore, Seamas at her shoulder, Rory and Rainbow crunching behind. On the coral, not bones. What was the matter with her? Seeing death and blood and doom everywhere. Maybe the water she'd drunk since she'd been here, the food she'd eaten. That was all. *Stay calm. Don't panic. Think what Guy would do, but what if he's . . . Oh God.*

Seamas caught at her arm. His breath was harsh in her ear. 'People need to see we've got you, that it's over. They're afraid. You saw how afraid they are. This is your doing, you know.'

She struggled. 'Me! How is it my fault?' And what did he mean, it was over?

'Poking your nose into it. It could all have been dealt with. No one needed to know.'

'They're still drinking the water, eating the food! How can you let this happen?'

'The company knows there's a problem now. They'll stop it, we'll make it all stop. Quietly. No one needs to panic. There was no need to bring the police round here. I told him—' jerking his head to Rory. 'But he rang you anyway. Eejit.'

She twisted her head to face him. 'You're mad. These people are sick. They're sick, and they're terrified.'

He grabbed her harder. 'Right. So I need to show them I'm in control.'

Paula wanted to ask what he meant by that, but she was afraid she might already know the answer. He'd pushed her up off the beach now, and onto the uneven streets of the village. People stood everywhere, in doorways, spilling out of the community centre. All two hundred and something of them. Was it fewer now? Matt was dead, and Mary. Fiona was maybe dead too. And Guy – she couldn't think about that.

Seamas stopped in front of the harbour memorial, the one to lost ships, islanders who had gone out on rough seas over the years and never made it back. He climbed up on the lower steps of it, so everyone could see him. His hand rested on Paula's shoulder, no longer gripping but still strong. 'A chairdre,' he called in Irish. Friends. His voice was low and authoritative, and the worried murmur of the villagers died away. Everyone was listening. 'We've had a hard night,' Seamas said. 'Our houses are damaged. Our weans are afraid. We're afraid. But it's over now. Look, it's nearly light. It'll be over soon. We're safe.'

'But the sea, Seamas!' Oona from the Spar was shouting. 'The sea is full of blood! What does it mean? What's going on?'

The murmur went up again, loud and scared. Down at the shore, a sudden wave splashed, and the people nearest to it began to stumble and run from it, howling in a sort of primal terror. As Paula watched from the steps, she saw a small child go under, knocked by the swell and the crowd, and it seemed no one was going to pick him up, and his mother was running in terror, her baby forgotten, and she almost cried out, but then the child was up, crying. What was going on here? Who were these people?

Seamas was being drowned out. 'Now everyone, just calm down, please . . .'

Someone was pushing their way through to him, thin and nervy as a bird, with the pink dressing gown still showing under the heavy winter coat. Grainne Fairlin. She raised her reedy voice. 'I know. I know what's causing it.' She turned to the islanders, the wind lifting her hair. Her face was lined, making her look much older than she was. She said, 'It's the outsiders. We never should have let them come here. That's what's causing all this.' More moaning from the crowd, murmurs of agreement. Grainne raised her voice, high and cracked. 'It only brings trouble! That doctor . . . we were fine before they came!'

Shouts. Someone shouted, 'I hope she's dead, the English bitch!' Paula looked and recognised Andrea Sharkey's husband, Peadar. He was carrying the baby in his arms, the child with her face marked forever. Paula could hear her wailing across the crowd. Grainne saw him too and called out. 'Andrea was never sick before that doctor came! She loved her children. *Loved* them. Didn't she, Peadar?'

Peadar hung his head, emotions fighting in his face. 'It wasn't her fault. It was that bitch. That doctor.'

More people taking up the shout. '*Bitch. Bitch!*'

Was Niamh here? Paula searched the crowd, looking for the little girl. There were children dotted throughout the crowd, as many as thirty. Dear God, so many kids. And nothing was safe here, nothing and nowhere.

Grainne Fairlinn seemed transformed by the attention, a high priestess in the morning light that burned more with every minute. People's faces stood out in the harsh dawn, every line of tiredness, every crease of fear. Paula saw Niamh suddenly, standing alone in the middle of the crowd, her blonde hair loose about her face. Her eyes were wide with terror.

'It's our fault,' Grainne went on. 'My daughter was killed off the island. She'd be safe and well here if she hadn't left. My son was ruined by the sickness. If no outsiders had come, Peadar, your wean would be fine too. She'd not be scarred for life. Neither would my boy.' Peadar Sharkey was openly weeping, not bothering to wipe it away. 'Andrea could be home with her family right now if we hadn't let them come. So it's time – let's get rid of them. All of them.' Grainne spun, seeking people out in the crowd, where the green plant logo could be seen on jackets and hats and fleeces. 'The company. Taking our land, using it . . . Let's get rid of them. Let's take back our island.' Her gaze had settled on Rainbow, who had a shocked look on her face. Grainne pointed. 'Her. All her people. Bringing shame to this place, using it for money. It's sacred. We have to care for it. And we didn't, and now look what's happening! Blood in the sea!' People were howling now, with fear and rage, turning towards Rainbow, where she stood on the edge of the water.

Rainbow shouted: '*Seamas!*'

Seamas's eyes were darting. Looking at his wife, and then the rest of the islanders, the panic rising up among them palpable as squeezing hands. '*A chairdre*,' he tried. 'We've no fight with the company. They've brought jobs here and . . .'

'*Get out!*' someone shouted, from deep in the crowd. Rainbow began to back away. Down the beach towards the bloody water.

More people were shouting. 'Get out!'

'Get off our island!'

'Bitch! Get out of here, bitch!'

Rainbow was still backing away, her feet stumbling in the blood-red water. 'But . . . I never . . . you know me! I live here! All of you know me.'

Seamas was watching, his jaw set. Paula saw him swallow, hard, then clench his teeth and shout to her across the crowd: 'Run, for God's sake. Get out of here. I can't protect you any more.'

And she was running, an expression of disbelief on her face, sloshing and stumbling in the sea.

Seamas's voice sounded above the crowd, and people turned to him, letting the woman go. '*A chairdre!* I know you're afraid. But we'll sort this. We'll get the outsiders out. Matt Andrews, God rest him, he's dead.' More cries went up. 'He's dead, I swear it, and likely the doctor is too. We'll find her body. I promise it. This woman here . . .' He turned, indicating Paula. She felt two hundred pairs of eyes on her.

'She came here to find Matt and Fiona. But in a few hours, when it's light, the rest of the police will be here and she'll tell them lies about us. She'll say we killed Matthew – lies! You know it's lies, friends. We don't do that here. We're good people. They'll put us off the island, take our children away—' Someone roared. Paula thought it was maybe Peadar. 'No one else knows, no one else has any idea what's happened here. Only this woman.' He stepped back, as if washing his hands of her. She felt the wind lift her hair, sodden and stiff from the water. Her skin ached all over, chafed and icy. And Guy. Where was Guy?

'Tell me now,' said Seamas. 'Should we wait for them to come, and take us away, and put their lies on us? Or will we deal with this now?'

No one said anything. Paula caught Niamh's eyes again, and the girl slowly shook her head.

Chapter Thirty-Seven

'What are you going to do with me? What did you mean? You can't just – the police know we're here! They'll know we didn't just vanish!' But would they know she hadn't slipped into the sea and drowned? Would they ever find her body – or would Maggie never know what happened to her mother either? No. Paula would not let that happen. She'd given Maggie no father, through her own selfishness and cowardice, so she would not let this happen.

She looked round at the crowd in disbelief, the faces turned up to her cold and blank as stone. She wasn't welcome here. They wanted her gone, and with her the story she had to tell. *And where was Guy?*

Someone was catching at her arm, pulling her away. Rory. He muttered to Seamas. 'I'll do it. You stay and sort things here. It's nearly light.'

Seamas gave a nod. He didn't look at Paula, and then Rory was marching her away from the square, towards the harbour. Nobody stopped him, and the last thing she saw as the light brightened, into a bleached-out winter dawn, was the people – the islanders – silently standing and letting her be taken away.

Her feet moved as if automated, and she couldn't think. This wouldn't happen. It couldn't. 'Rory,' she tried. 'You can't do this – you're a Guard! You can't—' She couldn't say the end of that sentence. That would make it too real. Rory didn't answer. 'The press,' she tried. 'People will ask questions . . .' But would they? Wasn't there a nice story ready and waiting – Paula and Guy on the boat, tipped over into the sea, drowned as well?

They were at the marina now. The sea lapped gently at the harbour walls, and Paula could see that half of it had crumbled in the storm. Maybe the morning ferry wouldn't even be able to dock. Rory was getting out a key. 'You're taking me on a boat?' she asked, dazed. It seemed so bizarre.

He didn't answer, just unlocked a small cabin door in a little white boat. Of course. Rory had a boat too. Why hadn't she thought of that? A good place to keep her. Her mind was turning slowly. How would she get out? If he left her there a while she might be able to escape somehow.

Rory propelled her in, not roughly, and she obeyed. The cabin was tiny and dark, panelled in some heavy imitation wood. It smelled strongly of musty food, and human bodies. As Rory pushed her head down, she heard him whisper: 'Help her. Make sure she's OK.'

She almost said, *what*? But he shut the small door behind her and turned the key, and she found herself in a blackness more complete than any she'd ever known. Paula stumbled, putting her hand up to the walls of the cabin. She could hear the sound of water slapping on the sides of the boat. There was something soft too – a bed? Covers? Suddenly she knew it, the way you can feel things in the base of your spine, that instinct that kept us alive in the days of caves and monsters. She wasn't alone in here. 'Hello?' her voice wavered.

A blue light came in the corner, as a phone was held up. A woman with dark hair, wrapped in a blanket and curled up on the tiny sleeping area of the cabin. 'Who are you?' she said. 'You're not from here.'

Paula was going to ask the same, but she knew the answer. She'd seen the picture a dozen times since yesterday. She was locked in the cabin of the boat with Dr Fiona Watts.

Bob

1993

He pulled up outside the house, car parked halfway up the kerb. Too long. It had taken too long to get away from work, trying to do it quietly so PJ wouldn't be suspicious. A terrible day at work. Up before dawn on a hell of a case, the kind that lodged in the back of your throat and made you want to be sick for months after. A woman, a dead child. And then, this afternoon, a report coming in he'd only just managed to whisk away from the despatcher. A Mrs Flynn, reporting suspicious men at her neighbour's house. Possible IRA terrorists.

Bob had known the address like the back of his hand. It was her house. Margaret's. But he couldn't rush off. He had to cover this carefully. Took the report off the despatcher – said he'd file it after he called in. Not something a DS usually did but he made out it was on his way home, and no one was surprised he was going home early after finding a dead baby before it was even light.

He didn't even lock the car. Ran the few steps to the house. It was nearly half three. What time did they get out of school? The wee girl, Paula, she'd be back soon. She was thirteen – same age as Ian, Bob knew it exactly – and he knew Margaret finished work early to be there for her. They didn't want her coming in to an empty house, not when her father was a Catholic RUC officer. Finding a pipe bomb on the doorstep wouldn't be at all unusual. The house was almost dark; the curtains open though the light was fading fast and it was cold, bone-cold already for October. He went round the back. Didn't want the neighbours to see. Hammered on the door, noticing in passing the neat lawn, the roses she'd tended round this drab little semi. 'Margaret. *Margaret!*' Maybe she wasn't at work today. She'd told him she would take the day off. Getting ready for what she needed to do. 'Margaret.'

Nothing. He turned the handle, it opened silently. Not locked. What would he find? Nothing. The kitchen was clean, empty, dark. Dishes draining on the rack. He moved through the house, but no one was there, dead or alive. His heart slowed. She'd got away – or else he'd been too late, and they had taken her.

He remembered what he'd said to her the day before – only one day, but he was already far too late. Story of his life. 'But Margaret, if you tell PJ, you can all go away – they'll protect you, resettle you all.' New names, money to start a new life. Many people had taken that route, once they'd been caught touting on the terrorists.

She'd rolled her eyes, angry. 'And spend the rest of our lives looking over our shoulders? I'm not having that for Paula. Anyway, they couldn't protect a bloody dog, that lot. I have to just get away now, and maybe when this is all over I can come back for her. She has to know nothing, and PJ too. It's the only way.' He knew she was referring to several cases that had been bungled. Informers, resettled on the mainland, tracked down and shot. The IRA had people everywhere. On the ferries. In the DVLA, tracking addresses. Even working for MI5. Nowhere was truly safe.

'But – what do you mean? You have to tell PJ.'

'I can't.' She shook her head.

'But why?' Bewildered. Not understanding one bit of this.

'Because,' she said, and her hand went to the waistband of her skirt. 'I'm pregnant, Bob.'

'But . . .' Again, he didn't understand. God help him.

'PJ,' she said. 'You remember – a few years back?'

He didn't want to. But he did. PJ had taken a week off work. Surprising, because he never did, and the word round the station, the slagging when he got back, was that he was off having the snip. PJ had had a vasectomy. So that meant . . . He stared at Margaret, so lovely, her red hair about her face.

'So you see,' she said. 'I have to get away. I can't tell him any of this. If they don't know anything about it, they'll be safer. I'll leave a note. They'll be fine. So will you help me, please?'

And he'd tried. He'd gone to Conlon, grovelled to a murderer for help. Now, standing in her empty kitchen, Bob found himself saying a fervent prayer that it had worked, and she had got away. But he wasn't at all sure. It was so quiet in the house. As quiet as a tomb.

Chapter Thirty-Eight

The battery on Fiona's phone was close to dying, and she kept pushing it so the light sprang up again. Her face looked ghostly, hollowed-out. 'Tell me again. So he went into the sea? Your colleague?'

Guy was so much more than that word, Paula thought. So much that she couldn't begin to explain, let alone now, to this woman she'd thought dead ten minutes ago. And why had Rory left them there? What was the delay? She was on her feet, feeling around the walls, worrying at the locked door. 'I didn't see him struggle. He couldn't have just gone down. I mean . . . he's a good swimmer.'

Fiona was silent for a moment. She hadn't moved to help Paula find a way out. 'Did he hit his head when you capsized?'

'I don't know. I didn't see.' Paula didn't want to think about that. 'So it was Seamas and that lot? Covering up what happened at the plant?'

Fiona sighed, rubbing her face. 'It's everyone, really. The whole bloody island. I didn't realise how they were . . . connected. Like roots, under the soil. I didn't realise we'd never belong here, not if we stayed our whole lives. I tried to tell Matt – he didn't want to hear.' In the darkness, the ghost of a smile. 'He always saw the best in everyone.'

Past tense. She must know. 'Fiona. You know that he's . . .'

She nodded. 'I saw it happen.'

'Who?'

'Rory,' she said simply.

Paula felt sick – she'd trusted this man, got into his car. 'He said you both probably fell from the lighthouse. That it was an accident, in the storm.'

'Course he did. That's why he called you in – nobody else wanted the police. They wanted to find us first, tidy up Matt's research and hide what they'd done. But Rory – I think it was meant to look like a drowning. Like we fell, or wrecked our boat in the storm.'

'I had Matt's coat. Stones in the pockets.'

Fiona nodded. 'Stage a fall from the lighthouse – maybe even call it a suicide, sink him down, then bank on him not coming up for so long the coat and all the evidence would be gone. If it wasn't for this storm . . . well, it was a solid plan.'

'And you?' They were talking in low whispers. The only sound was the lap of the waves, now calm and quiet. The Gardaí would be on their way already, surely. And why had Rory left them here, her and Fiona, on this boat? 'What happened to you?' she asked again. *How come you're not dead*, she meant. There didn't seem to be a good way to ask that question.

Fiona sighed. 'He knew I'd figured it out. I asked Rory for help, see. I told him what I'd found out, what I was worried about. Little Niamh, and Jimmy, and Andrea . . . you know about Andrea, I take it.'

'Yes.'

'It's not true, about the psychosis. She was fine when I saw her, whatever that hospital says. It was . . . something else. Whatever's wrong on this island.'

'Lead, maybe, I heard.'

'Maybe. But they don't want to face it. Seamas and Rainbow – bloody stupid name, she's got a mind like a steel trap – they know what's going on, they know very well. But they're shit-scared the plant'll get shut down and then the island will die, and they'll have to live in the real world. Seamas is a major shareholder, you see. Took them in exchange for the land. Fucking idiot.' Fiona could still sound scathing, even when trapped. Paula admired that. 'They'd rather hush it all up, lie to people about what's going on. Blame what Andrea did on me, and explain the rest all away, cover it up, hope it stops . . .' She sighed. 'So Rory came to the house. Monday night. He'd taken Andrea's medical notes, and he came to the lighthouse and—' Her voice was swallowed up suddenly. 'He pushed Matt off. He made me watch. I – I couldn't save him. I tried. Then he took me.' Silence fell again, the cold of the sea penetrating through, numbing.

Paula paused in her search for a way out. 'I'm so sorry, Fiona.'

'Don't be. It's all Rory. He did this.'

'He said the lighthouse door was locked from the inside.'

'Lies. Probably wanted to make it seem like we both jumped, killed ourselves or fell or something. What I don't know is why I'm still here, when Matt is . . . I don't know why he didn't kill me too.' The phone was fading again. She pressed it. 'Battery won't last much longer. I guess he was keeping me in case the plan didn't work. In case someone came over from the mainland and solved it all too quickly. Like you. So they have someone to pin it on. Saying the door was locked – well, I'm the only one who could have been in there if it was, aren't I?'

It did add up. Rory getting to the house on Monday night,

not Tuesday morning. Lying about the lighthouse being locked. Rory killing Matt – pushing him off the lighthouse, staging an accident. Taking Fiona and hiding her here. Directing the search, dogging their steps, knowing all the while where Fiona was. Setting fire to the pub, with Matt's body in it. Covering his tracks. Rory hadn't been helpful at all, not at any point, and she could see why now. Like everyone else, he'd been engulfed in this madness. Except Fiona. 'You've not been affected by it? You ate your own food?'

'Always. And I only drink bottled water. I have everything brought in from outside. Matt – he made such a show of eating local, trying the fish, buying the organic veg . . .' Her voice cracked. 'God, he was a good man. He meant well.'

'I'm sorry,' said Paula again. For a moment, thinking of Aidan – locked up somewhere too, only day and night and with little hope of an end, for years and years still – her own voice thickened with tears. *Stop it, Maguire.* If she gave in now she'd never stop bawling, from terror and anger and sorrow. 'I told him you were pregnant. I thought it might – make a difference, if they found you somewhere. That maybe he wouldn't hurt you.'

Silence. 'How did you know?'

'Your doctor. Dr Michaels.'

'Oh.' Fiona said nothing, letting the light of her phone fade down to nothing. Then she spoke, her voice low. 'It's all I have left now. I had everything, you see. I had the man, the job, the life. I had it, and I've lost it all now. Everything.'

'What can we do?' Paula felt a dull ache in her stomach. She too had been there, the months after Aidan went inside. Refusing to believe the life she'd wanted had been just within grasp, and all lost. Maggie was the only thing that had saved her.

'We can't get out. I've tried, there's no point. It's a strong lock.'

'And what will they . . .'

Another shrug, that Paula felt rather than saw. The phone had faded out again, and they sat in darkness. 'If I'm gone too, it makes a better story. I guess he'll put me in the sea. Easiest way. Drowning makes sense, on an island, in a storm. We both drowned, just a tragic accident, no one's fault.' She spoke so dispassionately.

'And me?' Fiona didn't answer, and Paula didn't need her to. The same way, surely. Down with Guy, if he – but no. She had to believe he would be OK. 'But Fiona – Rory said something to me, just there, at the door. He said *help her*.'

'He did?' Paula could feel her think about it, almost sense the wheels turning in her brain. 'Well. I guess he thinks that just because he killed my boyfriend, that doesn't mean he's not in with a chance.'

'What do you mean?'

Fiona laughed, briefly. 'Oh. Rory . . . I think it's fair to say he had . . . ideas about me. He wanted me. Said he loved me, once. I told him it was crazy, I was with Matt, and besides, he was just turning to any woman he could find on the island – not many, as you'll have seen. But then when things started to go . . . weird, Rory lost it too. Said he had to have me, he'd do anything, blah blah. I found out too late. By that stage it was more a question of who *hadn't* gone down with it. It was like . . . like being the only sane person in a mad world. Which makes you the mad one, surely?'

'Could that – is that something that might help? If he

loves you? I don't think anyone else knows you're here. They think you're missing.' The more she thought about it, it all made sense. Seamas, Rainbow, everyone else – they'd just been desperately trying to cover their tracks. They only wanted to find Matt and his research, destroy it. They didn't want the police, but Rory had called them in, to make it all look legitimate. Cover up what he'd done.

'Maybe.' Fiona moved in the dark. 'Where are you?' Paula put out her hand and felt the other woman's, ice-cold. How much it meant, in the darkness, to have another voice. To have a hand. To not be alone with it pressing all over you, cold and black as the sea.

'Listen to me,' Fiona said. 'These people, they are *bad*. Rory killed Matt. He hurt me – cut me in the kitchen with the knife, when I tried to get away. He pushed Matt over, and then got his poor body from the rocks and put him in the boat. Dumped him in the sea. And he'll do the same to us. No one else'll help us, even if they don't know Rory killed Matt. Seamas Fairlinn would see us both dead in a heartbeat. Anything for this fucking island.'

'I won't let that happen,' said Paula. 'As soon as we can we'll call and . . .'

'How?' Fiona almost laughed. 'There's no signal here. Why do you think they let me keep the phone? No one's coming to get us. No, Rory is our only chance. Will you help me?'

Paula wasn't sure what she was asking. She thought of the man, his freckled, guarded face, his red hair. He loved this woman. Maybe that could work. But maybe they would have to do more, hurt him, strike back. She was meant to be on the other side. The ones who helped the hurt, and the lost, and stopped the bad things from happening. But out here, with no armed officers at her back, with no Corry – with no Guy, but no she wasn't thinking about that – what would she choose? She thought of Maggie, back home, asleep hopefully, thumb in her mouth. Of her mother, standing on that shore all those years ago. Those tears. Who or what was she even crying for? Her life was as mysterious to Paula as the depths of the ocean. 'I'll help,' she said, and in the darkness Fiona's cold hand clutched her own.

Chapter Thirty-Nine

The waters had calmed now, just when Paula would have wanted them choppy. Anything to avoid setting sail, now it was light – a pale, used-up winter dawn, streaked blood-red. And just as red, the water lapped on the prow of the boat. She could see it as Rory opened the door of the cabin. She'd wanted to be ready for him, try to overpower him, but Fiona had another plan. And so she'd wait.

Rory's eyes skidded over her as he threw two black holdalls into the cabin. He gestured to her. 'Up here.' He dragged Paula up on the small deck of the boat, and Fiona followed, docile. *Follow me*, she'd said. So Paula went along with it, rather than fighting back. Rory started the boat and headed out to sea. She didn't ask where he was taking them. She already knew. And whatever happened, they couldn't let him get there. *Just follow me*, Fiona had said. *When it happens. Just follow me.* Paula was ready, tensed like a coiled spring. For what, she didn't know.

Rory, who seemed unperturbed by the bloody sea around them, was now ploughing the boat through it. Its white hull was stained a horrible claret colour, like when you spill red wine on a tiled floor. His face was also pale, his clothes soaked in the red. Putting out to sea, the depths of it beneath them, dark and cold. Pulling at her legs again, like when she was twelve.

Paula's breath caught in her lungs. The casual cruelty of what he planned to do. She thought about sinking, deep down, her feet kicking uselessly in the cold water, the feel of it pouring inside her clothes, icy fingers finding every bit of flesh. She looked to Fiona – the woman was tranquil, composed. She must have a plan. Surely she had a plan. Surely Rory did not mean to hurt Fiona, at least, if he loved her.

Rory took the boat out to deeper water. Calmed now, bits of wreckage floating in the dark water, wood and fence posts and branches. Soon the Gardaí boat would be arriving at the island, and what would they find? A community that had torn itself apart, in the dark, and two more missing people. Maybe her body would wash up. Maybe it wouldn't. Christ, her dad! His wife was already gone, with no answers. She couldn't do that to him again. And Maggie. *Maggie*. Rory's eyes flickered over her. She pleaded with him, silently, and he looked away. Cleared his throat. He slowed the boat, stopped it. With the noise of the engine gone, there was dead silence.

Rory went to Fiona, stooped, put a hand to her face – Paula saw her shy away. 'Are you OK? Christ, Fi, you're *pregnant*! Why didn't you . . .'

'Never mind that, Rory.' Her voice cut through him. 'We don't have much time. The police will be coming soon, and they'll want to know where she is.' She jerked her head to Paula. 'If you want me, still . . . we need a plan.'

Rory stepped back. 'She knows. Everything.'

'We can trust her.' Fiona nodded to Paula. This was what she'd meant, surely, by *follow me*. 'We'll say it was Seamas did it, Seamas and Rainbow, and you had to play along to get us away safe. Then you and me . . .'

Paula blinked; she couldn't follow this. Did Rory really believe he had a chance with Fiona? After killing Matt?

Rory said, 'But she knows, Fi.'

She was shocked by Fiona's voice when she spoke. So convincing. 'I know. She knows what happened. But she'll help us, I know she will. Just take us both to the mainland and we'll explain it all. The company, covering it up. And Matt – we can say he had an accident. There's no evidence otherwise.'

His eyes narrowed. 'She won't. I know about her. Always has to do the right thing.'

Paula thought back to her other cases – when she'd had to weigh up the right and wrong on both sides, and sometimes there was no way to tell what side the law was on, but she'd had to trust to it. Trust that it was right, even if so often the outcome was very, very wrong. She cleared her throat. 'I just want out of this, Rory. I'll say whatever you want. My little girl—'

He jerked his head away, ignoring her. 'It's not safe. Too much of a risk.'

'Rory,' said Fiona sharply. 'What's the matter with you? She'll help us.'

His Adam's apple bobbed up and down. 'I just want you, Fi. And the baby! A wee baby. Even if it's not mine, I don't care. I want us to be away from here and safe, with no one coming after us.'

'We can be! There's Seamas, and there's Rainbow and Grainne and, God, everyone else to blame it on. I'll say you helped me, when it mattered. You saved me. You hid me away to keep me safe.'

He was shaking his head. 'Matt,' he said quietly.

Fiona was calm. 'An accident—'

'But she knows. She knows, doesn't she? And then, jail . . . Christ, Fi, we'd never be together again. Waiting for someone to come out of prison? That's no life. I don't want that for us.'

Fiona turned her eyes to Paula. The look of control was gone, and Paula could see her rethinking everything. And then she saw the thought as clearly as if Fiona had said it aloud – *I'm sorry*. And she realised, her stomach shelving away: there would be no help for her here.

Before Paula really knew what was happening, Rory was taking large steps towards her, across the wobbly deck of the boat, and her mouth was open to protest – *Maggie, please, for Maggie* – and then someone was rising out behind the seat on deck, and Rory was down, his mouth open in an 'O' of surprise. Blood seeping from the cut on his forehead. She looked up, stunned, at the person holding the wrench, who had emerged from below them in the boat.

'You OK?' said Guy.

'I thought you were . . . I thought . . .' She couldn't say it, feeling the fear of it seeping into her like cold water, now she knew it wasn't true and he was standing safe in front of her, driving the boat. 'I lost you. In the water.'

Guy's clothes were stiff with saltwater, his hair matted and face red-raw. 'I held my breath. Climbed up the back of Seamas's boat when they weren't looking. Then, in the marina, I saw Rory take you onto this boat.'

'You've been hiding the whole time?'

He nodded. 'I was going mad with worry. I didn't know why they'd taken you, what they'd do.'

She opened her mouth to explain how it had been when she'd thought him gone, the clutching panic of it.

Instead she said, 'You held your *breath*?'

He smiled, lopsided. 'Underwater swimming champ of the Upper Sixth.'

She muttered, 'The name's Brooking, Guy Brooking,' and she felt rather than saw his smile widen.

The hatch of the cabin was pushed up and Fiona came out, stepping carefully. 'Is he OK?' asked Guy. 'I didn't know if I'd judged it right, hitting him.'

'He'll be OK. He's out cold. Concussion, maybe.' She spoke dispassionately. Paula had wondered, just for a moment there, on the boat when all seemed lost, if Fiona had in fact really cared for him – Rory had seemed convinced that she did – but now Paula was sure it was just a very good act. If not she would be down there, weeping over him, pushing his hair back with gentle hands, wiping the blood from his face. The way Paula felt every time she thought of Aidan. Wanting to put her arms round him and never let go, press her face to his back at night, breathe him in.

'I'm glad to see you, Dr Watts,' Guy told Fiona. 'We thought – well, it didn't seem like that was an option.'

'Oh, I'm still here,' she said. 'Not so easy to get rid of after all. Like yourself, Inspector. What'll happen now?'

Guy checked his watch – which seemed like a good investment; it was still ticking after his near-drowning. 'Gardaí boat should be getting in about now. Then, I guess, the clean-up.' Paula tried to think what that would encompass – most people on the island charged with something, the company shut down, and retrieving what they could of Matt's body.

'Rory?' asked Fiona.

'Well. It was him who – he killed Matt?' She nodded. Guy said, 'I'll make sure he goes down for it. A police officer too. The judge will likely go harder.'

She nodded, lifting her face into the growing light. 'I want him gone for as long as possible. Matt – Matt was sick, yes, but he didn't deserve it. It wasn't his fault.'

Paula put an arm around her, and Fiona smiled, weakly, and together the three of them drove towards the rising sun, a bloom of orange-red against the darkness of the sea and land.

Fiona

When I was a junior doctor, I killed someone. It's no big deal, actually. Ask any doctor – ask them late at night when they've had too many gins – and they'll admit they've done it too. Can you blame us? You trust us with the power of life and death, and you can't always expect we'll choose the former.

My first kill was called Gavriel Lemin. An old, old man when he came to me. Ninety. Jewish, born in Poland. Dying slowly, painfully, of a lung tumour. Coughing up bits of himself in blood and bile.

It was one of those cases where someone is so far gone that death is eating them out from the inside like a hungry dog, but they won't let go. They just can't. And it starts to spread out through the ward, through their family if they even have one – how are they still here? How can this be going on still? We have it all wrong in the modern world. Death shouldn't be prolonged. Watching someone die is the most painful thing you can do – better to get it over with. The Irish have the right idea, with their rituals and wakes. Speed the person to the grave, in an exhausting blur of booze and soil. Let them go and then settle yourself on the earth that no longer has them in it. A different place, now and forever.

Anyway, I was on nights, and Gavriel was still with us, still not dead, dying by inches, no, centimetres. He was in so much pain the morphine wasn't even touching him. I could see it in his face, how he bared his remaining teeth. If he was a dog he'd have been put down long ago. And yet we keep humans alive, because we can't bear to sever that link. We can't bear to face our own mortality.

I was checking his pulse, when I noticed tears leaking out of his old eyes. Onto the pillow, leaving round, damp spots. *Are you OK, Mr Lemin?* What a stupid thing to say. Of course he wasn't OK.

I had to go close to hear what he croaked out. He had so little breath left in him. *Please*, he said. *I need go.*

I understand, I said soothingly. *Just let go, Mr Lemin.*

I can't, he whispered to me, in the dark of that ward. Green-lit, like the bottom of the sea. *I can't let go. I don't know how.*

I was feeling the pulse on his wrist, and he turned his arm slightly, and his gown fell, and I saw it, on the saggy underside of his thin arm. The numbers, tattooed in a line. I understood what that meant. What this man had survived. Maybe surviving is a habit like anything else. Maybe sometimes we need to break it.

I can't, he said, more tears of frustration falling from his eyes. *I can't. Please help me. Help me.*

I'd like to tell you I went into agonies about right to die and physician's oaths and responsibilities. I'd like to tell you that the fact euthanasia is very illegal gave me pause. The truth is, I didn't pause at all. I checked to see no nurses were around, and then I gently held my hand over his mouth and nose. I felt his breath flicker against me – warm, like the essence of his life was ebbing away – and then he struggled, but that was just the body's last instinctive fight, and then something turned over in his eyes, and I could tell he'd crossed the border and he wasn't there any more. He just didn't exist. That line is so much thinner and closer than any of us like to believe.

I waited until my hand grew cold again, and then I went to the door and spoke calmly to the nurse. *Nurse, I need to certify Mr Lemin. He's slipped away.* She gave me an odd look, maybe because I was so calm, so unmoved, but no one ever suspected I'd killed him. And I didn't, of course. Lung cancer killed him. Old age killed him. Life killed him. All I did was open the door he was slumped against, scrabbling for the handle.

Chapter Forty

The pier on the mainland, drab and windswept, was one of the lovelier things that Paula had ever seen. The Gardaí boat had sped them over the waters, leaving behind that island with its barren shores and twisted secrets. Later, there'd be questions to ask, and someone would have to be punished for what was done to Matt Andrews and Mary O'Neill and Andrea Sharkey, and the other victims of this, but everyone else was alive and the sun was coming up. Even Dara had been picked up by a fishing boat, half-crazed, clinging forlornly to a buoy, but alive. She'd survived too. And Guy was beside her, wrapped in a foil blanket, eyes tired against the red of the rising sun. She turned and found him watching her, and for a moment allowed herself to lean against him. So warm, so solid. Always there when she'd needed him, despite all she'd done to push him away. Maybe now it was time. Once the dust settled, she would tell him. She would throw the weight of this secret overboard and be free of it, be light and open and unburdened, come what may. And then, if he could forgive her, maybe she'd take that job. Restart her life, as Aidan wanted. Shake Ballyterrin from her feet.

On the shore, police vans were drawn up and she spotted Fiacra, leaning on a crutch. She disembarked, taking a moment to bless the solidity of the ground under her feet –

already feeling the difference when you were used to the movement of the sea beneath you – and went to him. 'Well, Sergeant Hopalong, are you OK?'

He didn't smile. 'Are you all right? Christ, I was worried sick.'

She grimaced. 'You were right to be. I'm OK, though. Thanks to DI Brooking.'

Fiacra was still stony-faced. 'Listen, Paula, we were trying to ring you. We couldn't reach you, but—'

'Sergeant Quinn!' Guy was approaching, hand held out. 'Good to see you.'

'And you, sir, but—'

'You'll want our statements right away, I imagine. Lots of loose ends to tie up.'

'Yes, you're right, but I need to tell Paula – Dr Maguire – I need to tell you something.'

Suddenly, Paula was feeling the solid ground shift like waves. 'What?'

'We couldn't reach you . . . got the call yesterday . . . got a car waiting . . .'

She couldn't follow. 'Fiacra. What's happened?'

He couldn't meet her eyes. 'There's been an accident. In Ballyterrin.'

'Maggie.' Her legs were giving way.

'No, no, she's fine, I swear, Maguire, but it's your—' He didn't know the word to use.

A young, pink-faced female Guard that Paula now noticed behind him started talking. 'It's your husband, Dr Maguire.'

'I don't have a husband,' she said stupidly. Some mistake. Someone else's family in an accident, God help them . . .

It was Guy who explained, who took over, in his 'relatives'

voice, the one she loved but hated when it was turned on her. 'Paula, they're talking about Aidan. Something's happened to Aidan.'

She turned to him. His fair hair lifting in the early morning breeze, turned red by the rising sun. He'd saved her, once again. He'd always been there for her, unlike Aidan, who'd waited till the moment she was happiest and then set fire to their life together, burned it up to ashes. Whereas Guy had held back, quietly offering help. A job. And she still hadn't told him about their child. She was still lying to him. And now, once again, she was going to have to choose.

'I'm sorry,' she said. 'I have to go to him.'

Sometimes Paula could actually feel all the times she'd entered Ballyterrin Hospital, as if compressed into one terrible journey. Going in the ambulance with her father, stabbed by a killer who'd been looking for her. Rushing Gerard Monaghan to hospital, holding her scarf over his stomach while Fiacra drove madly, gouts of blood vomiting onto her hands and front. Then her own dash, Maggie suddenly coming too soon, her terrified and splitting open. But this – this was the worst of all. She knew it, deep in her bones. The journey seemed to take hours. In her head she was dividing it. Boat to shore. Get off boat. Get into police car. Smile mechanically at the young driver, who was obviously mortified she'd been the one to bring the news. Onto the motorway. Watching the miles tick by, every moment of traffic making her hands clench up by her sides. Every red light an hour. Finally, the signs for Ballyterrin, and the road markings changing – they were over the border. The driver – she didn't even learn her name, and later she would have stupid pangs of worry about that – took her straight to the door, pulling up. Paula scrabbled at the handle, suddenly afraid. What ward? What would she find?

'I hope it's all right so,' the driver said in her thick Kerry accent, and Paula was nodding, then out and running into the vacuum of the hospital. Stairs. No time for lift. Looking around wildly for surgical signs. Then spotting a broad, stooped figure she'd know a mile off. 'Dad!' Her voice too small in her throat, he could never have heard her. But he looked up all the same and she saw it written on his face – not good.

'What's happened? Where – oh God.' Curled by her dad's side on the waiting room chairs, wrapped in a pink blanket, was Maggie. Paula bent to her, pushing aside the covers. Maggie was flushed with sleep, out cold despite the noises that came and went around her. Paula didn't wake her, but despite her panic something settled inside her. She had her child back now, and everything else she could stand, she would find a way to bear. 'What's happened?' She lowered her voice.

PJ was staring at his feet, a crunched-up polystyrene cup between his hands. 'Not good, pet. They had to use – that thing, you know, the paddles.'

'Defibrillation?' Christ, that was worse than she'd thought.

'But it's OK now? Where is he?'

'He?' PJ seemed not to understand.

'Aidan! I got the message, he's hurt, they beat him up, in the prison!'

'Oh.' PJ sighed. 'Bloody eejits have got mixed up. There was a wee fight in the prison, aye, but no, pet, he's all right. Broke his nose a bit, that's all. They thought he'd maybe a concussion but he's grand. You see, he heard the news and thought they wouldn't let him out, so he kicked off.'

'So what do you mean? You said not good . . .'

Her father drew in a big, shuddering sigh. 'It's Pat, love.'

Then Paula understood. 'She . . . but she was doing so much better.'

'Aye. Her heart, you know. It puts a strain on. Chemo. Her heart just gave out.'

She'd been so tired the other day. In bed early, which wasn't like her. Pat's heart, so big and full, big enough for a whole town, far too big for the one child she'd been allowed, the one grandchild who wasn't even really that. Paula sank down beside her father, dull with worry, trying to process it all. 'It worked, though, the paddles?'

'For now. You can see her if you want, I had to take the wee one out.'

Paula looked again at her child, sleeping in innocence, red curls over her face. It wasn't right. She'd promised she'd give Maggie as much time as possible with that innocence. Before she had to know the legacy she'd been born to, her missing grandmother and all the lies and pain in between. But what did she have now? One grandmother, dying maybe, and a father who wasn't her father, who would likely be in jail until she was in secondary school. 'Has he gone back inside?' she asked.

PJ shook his head. 'They let him stay. He's in there with her.'

Paula rose, and went to the door. An officer was stationed outside; she recognised the prison guard uniform. He nodded, and she went in.

Aidan was sitting by his mother's bed, his shackled hands holding one of hers. He was rubbing gently at the skin, which pillowed up and didn't spring back. Pat had gotten old, somehow. Paula looked at her first – grey, breathing with a machine, shrunk away even since Paula had last seen her, a mere three days ago. Her own breath caught in her lungs, tears catching in her eyes at the sight. Oh, Pat. Then she raised her gaze to Aidan.

Prison came off him like a bad smell. He looked like a criminal. That same sallow, unlit skin she'd seen in other men, watchful eyes, a puffiness and a starving thinness all at once. His hands, that she'd once loved to kiss, smeared with ink and newsprint, were yellow with nicotine – he'd been smoking too much – and scuffed, the nails cracked. Unloved hands. No one had touched him with care for quite some time, you could tell.

He cleared his throat, not looking away from his mother. 'Maguire.'

'Is she – is she OK?'

He shrugged. 'She's still here. Good you made it, though.'

'I was . . . I thought it was you. They said there'd been an accident, down there. They must have got confused. I came right away.' He turned and she saw his eye – a mess of green bruises, oozing red, like some burst exotic fruit. She couldn't stop the smothered yelp that came out. 'Jesus.'

He touched it wearily. 'Par for the course, Maguire. He's got mates inside, Conlon. Lots of mates.'

She stepped closer. They hadn't been in the same room for months now, and all his little gestures were rushing back at her, the way he cocked his head, always listening for stories, the way he drummed his fingers that meant he wanted to smoke, the way he unconsciously rubbed the front of his head. He kept trying to do it, and the clank of the cuffs pulled him back each time. She'd missed him so much it almost made her stagger on her feet. She said, 'I thought maybe you'd – that you'd been hurt.' That she'd lost him. She'd lost him months before, of course.

'And you rushed back for me.' His voice flat.

'Of course I did, Aidan, I – it's you didn't want me to visit. I'd have come. You know that.'

He made an impatient gesture. 'Why? What's the point? You've your whole life ahead of you, a whole world you can live in that isn't this shitting town and all its fucked-up history. Why don't you leave, Maguire? Why don't you just bloody leave Ballyterrin?'

'You know why.'

'Yeah well, you can get over that, I'm sure. You were always good at letting your head make the choices. Buggered off at eighteen, you can bugger off again now too. Be sensible.'

Paula swallowed. 'That isn't fair and you know it. We were kids, you'd dumped me. Now we're . . . We were almost . . .' She was afraid if she said any more she would cry.

'Almost, but no cigar. I mean it, Maguire. Think about what you're doing.'

'And what about Maggie? I have to choose for her too.'

He almost laughed. 'Aye, and what's here for her – a da who's not even her da, locked away with murderers and men who'd kill you as soon as look at you?'

'You're her dad. You know that.'

'She won't remember me. Few more years, she'll be grand. Find her another dad. Maybe even her real one. He down there with you, was he? Brooking? Very cosy.'

Paula took a deep breath. She wouldn't lose her temper, not when she hadn't seen him for months and there was so much to say. She didn't rise to the bait. In the bed, Pat's chest lifted and fell, while she lay comatose. 'Did she see you like this? Mags?'

Aidan shook his head. 'No. Got your da to take her out. Didn't want to confuse her. She'll be glad to have you back, though.'

Paula took a step forward. 'This doesn't have to be it. We don't have to just give up – there's a chance, a way we can all be . . .'

He gave a twisted smile. 'Even if I was still a gambling man, it'd be too big a bet for me, Maguire. And I'm done saying prayers. Only did that the once since I was a wean and look how it all turned out.'

'When was that?' She tried to keep her voice calm, keep him talking. Terribly afraid that he would go and she'd not see him again for months, maybe years.

He made that gesture again, the fingers groping for a cigarette, a crutch that wasn't there. 'When you were having her. Mags. Prayed you'd both be OK, and promised I'd not ask for anything from you ever again, if you'd only be OK.' He smiled, and she saw one of his teeth was loose and bloody. 'Made a mess of that one, didn't I? Always wanted too much.'

She tried not to look at his mouth. Jesus Christ. 'You know Bob Hamilton? Dad's old partner? Well, he told me – Sean Conlon had enemies. People who said they'd get him, as soon as he was out of jail.'

'Aye, well, there's no need to get him now, is there?'

'But you see – maybe someone else came that night. Maybe he was still breathing when you left him and maybe . . .' She tailed off. 'GBH, maybe, and you'd have done your time by now. Mitigating circumstances . . . Aidan, you could come home.'

'Home? There is no home. Only lies that I told you. You know that. You should put the place up for sale.'

'No. It wasn't lies. There's more to family than just . . . blood.'

'Aye, but blood is a lot, isn't it, Maguire? Blood is a lot. You'd give anything to have your mammy back. Even her bones. Wouldn't you? It calls to something inside you. I have it with my da, and with . . .' He bowed his head to Pat, squeezing her limp hand. 'Blood is a lot,' he said again. 'That man, he's Maggie's father. They both need to know that.' She hesitated and he widened his bloodshot eyes. 'You still didn't tell him? Christ, Maguire.'

'I don't know how! I let him think that it was you, for two years, and that was a lie, so how can I tell him? I lied to him. All thanks to you.'

'You can tell him because you have to. God almighty.'

'I'm not ready. Not yet.' Meaning she wasn't ready to give up. On Aidan, on their family, on that life together that she'd allowed herself to hope for. Hope that still clung by a terrible shred of flesh, like a tooth in a bloody jaw.

Aidan regarded her out of his good eye. 'Still married, is he?'

How dare he. How fucking dare he, after all this. 'Look, you stubborn dick,' she said, as quietly as she could, for fear of disturbing Pat. 'Forget Guy Brooking. Forget you and me and that whole mess. Do this for Mags, if no one else. There's a chance it wasn't you who killed Conlon, an actually pretty bloody good chance, so why won't you take it? Why?'

'Who's gonna prove it? You're relying on Provos to come forward, terribly sorry, officer, but you got the wrong man, it was us did it, not that poor nice journalist who only beat ten shades of hell out of Conlon. It was us came along and finished the job, only nobody saw and there's not a shred of evidence, even if we were feeling nice enough to own up. How in the hell would I ever prove it? They've got me, Maguire. I told Hamilton as much myself.'

She frowned. 'What do you mean? When did you see him?'

Aidan sighed. 'He came to visit me. Said the same – maybe he could help, maybe he knew someone, blah blah. As if it would make any difference.'

Bob had gone to see Aidan? Why would he do that? 'There was other DNA on the . . . on Conlon.'

'Aye, and you know as well as I do half the punters in Flanagan's use that car park as a toilet. Course there'd be other DNA. All manner of it. And there's also my footprints on the man's chest and my knuckles in a state and my T-shirt with his blood all over it.'

He said it so calmly, the facts of the case against him, that it made her flinch. But she had to try all the same. 'But if Bob says he can help . . .'

He snorted. 'Bob. Sideshow Bob, is that what you used to call him? You'd leave it up to him? That man couldn't find his arse with both hands. Couldn't find a trace of your ma, could he, back in the day? What makes you think he could find some Provo that doesn't want to be found?'

Paula flinched. Aidan was lashing out, looking to hurt and knowing just the way to do it. 'I've got a PI working on it. Trying to find someone that might confess. Why won't you try?'

'Maguire. I could easily have killed Conlon, even if by some miracle I didn't. So I'll take my punishment for that, and it's no more than I deserve. Everything good I ever had I ruined. You too. You and the wean. All my fault.'

'But . . .' But Maggie, she wanted to say. But me. Me and you, and the life we had. Instead she said: 'Just tell me why. When there's at least a chance.'

He looked up, his green eyes haunted and restless. 'Because, Maguire. I said I only prayed the one time. I won't stake any more on it – hope. Look where it's got us up till now. Look what I did to you, because of hoping, and to that wee girl. So no, there's no point. I'll do my time, and then I'll get on with what life I have left, and you'll do the same. For her.'

Paula's fists clenched. Damn him. Damn him for winning her back once, and keeping her here in this godforsaken town, and then leaving her here alone. Damn him for the fact she kept on choosing him, stubbornly refusing to go no matter how many other doors opened for her. Refusing to go out through them, while there was even the slightest chance she would get Aidan back. Even in five years. Even in ten. Damn him to hell. 'You can't stop me trying,' she hissed, and turned on her heel and went out.

She paced the corridor, too angry to go back in, too scared to leave in case something happened to Pat. What a mess. What an unholy shit-storm they'd made of their lives. He was right, though. She had to tell Guy about Maggie. She had to go to Guy and tell him and face the consequences. He'd be on his way back to London now, likely. She'd hoped to tell him that night, but fate had intervened. And there would always be a reason not to, a way to be a coward over and over.

Her phone was ringing. Guy, calling to say goodbye? She fished it out, earning a black look from a passing nurse, and looked at the number. 'Davey,' she said wearily, answering.

'Sorry, I can't really talk now, there's kind of a family emergency going on . . .'

He ignored her, his twenty-a-day rasping coming down the line. 'Got some news for you.'

Her heart began to race. There was a smug, victorious tone in his voice. 'Did you – you found something?' Oh God. She couldn't bear it, not on top of everything else, the answers she'd sought for so long. Her mother dead, maybe, while Pat lay hovering on the brink. Paula looked down the corridor, to where her father dandled Maggie by the hand, dancing along the corridor, a man of over sixty doing the steps to a Taylor Swift song. Whatever Davey had found out might be about to destroy them all. 'What?' she whispered.

'Your man Edward. The Army Intel fella. I found him. Or at least, a last address. He retired out to London, in 1993.'

'What month?' She tried to sound calm. Her mother had gone missing at the end of October that year. Almost Halloween, smoke and sulphur in the air.

Davey said, 'November. Stopped working, gave up his commission, pretty much went to ground, changed his surname. But I've found an address.'

She could hardly form the words. 'And did you . . . have you gone there?'

'Not yet. Wanted to check with you, like.' Because if he went, and this Edward was still there, and there was someone else with him . . .

Paula began to tremble, so hard she almost dropped the phone. From down the hall, she heard the sound of Maggie laughing – so high and clear it was almost like a scream.

Chapter Forty-One

Back in her house. Maggie asleep upstairs. Back in the place her mother had last been seen, pacing around the kitchen. Open the fridge, empty now of Aidan's beer. Open the cupboard with the whiskey bottle, which she had checked so often while she lived with him, without asking herself why she felt the need to do this, why she didn't trust the man she was going to marry. She thought for a moment about taking a swig, then closed the door again.

The medical report on Fiona Watts was in her inbox, and she flipped through it absently on her laptop. *Slightly heightened levels of lead . . . consistent with exposure to contaminants . . .* So even Fiona, with her packaged food and bottled water, had not escaped the madness that was seeping out of the very ground on Bone Island. Paula remembered her own sense of dislocation, as if nothing was properly real, the blood-red sea sloshing around her feet. Guy disappearing over the side of the boat. She hoped the exposure was not enough to affect Fiona's baby, that she'd fought so hard to protect. Sometime, when everything had settled – if it ever could – she would like to see Fiona again, the woman who'd kept her going in that cold cabin. She would go back to England, Paula imagined, once she was discharged from hospital in Kerry. Back to her old life, or what was left of it. Trying to make a life with the centre of it hollowed out. Paula knew what that was like. And as for the rest of the sorry mess that was Bone Island – she didn't know what would happen. Rory would be prosecuted, undoubtedly, for the murder of Matt and kidnapping herself and Fiona. Seamas too, maybe. The company would have to pay compensation for what they'd done, poisoning a whole island, trying to bury the truth. And Maeve's paper would no doubt follow up the story. Paula should have been there, sorting it out. Instead she'd dropped everything and run to Aidan. Like she did every time. Never learning, never making a better choice.

She scrolled on, not really seeing the words. *Presence of HCG . . . recommend monitoring of lead levels and chelation where appropriate . . .*

HCG. It stirred a memory in her somewhere, but she was too tired to retrieve it.

Paula sat at the table, staring at the sink and the fridge. The countertop beside it – the units and doors now new and replaced – that was where her mother had placed the note she'd written, maybe sitting in this same spot. The note explaining to Paula that she had to leave, but not why. Explaining that she had to go away, and she knew Paula would not understand, but maybe she would one day. So if her mother had been having an affair with that man, Edward, and if she'd gone off with him, and he was still alive and living in London – was there a chance she had got away? Could be living still? In London, where Paula had spent so many years herself? What if she'd passed her on the street one day, or stepped off a train as her mother stepped on? Would she have felt a shiver, maybe, as if a ghost had walked past?

And Paula felt hope, that terrible thing, flutter inside her like a flame you thought you'd snuffed out long ago. It hurt more than despair. Despair was like reaching the bottom. A comfort in it, your feet on solid ground. Hope was drowning, floundering in the sea, still trying to cling to life, kicking and flailing even when there was no point. Once again she pictured her mother on the shore of Bone Island, red hair flying in the wind, her green dress moulded around her body, for a moment swelling . . .

Paula froze. How strange was the human mind, the way it could know something for weeks, maybe even years, maybe decades, and only reveal itself fully in one moment of blinding clarity. Of course. Fucking hell, of course. It all slotted into place. Her mother off work sick the day before she disappeared. A doctor's appointment.

Her bag. Where was her bag? It had been retrieved from the ruins of the pub, charred but not destroyed, and she'd dumped it in the hallway on her return. It stank of smoke and salt air, taking her back there, the floor heating up under her feet and groping for Guy's hand in the dark. Paula scrabbled through the papers Davey had given her, her mother's medical records, a little damp and sooty but still readable. There was a word she recognised. A chemical name. One she'd also just seen on Fiona Watts's medical summary. She groped for the phone. Luckily, Saoirse was a good enough friend not to need social niceties, and she was used to Paula calling up with random medical questions.

Her friend sounded sleepy. 'Well, what's the craic? You OK?'

'Seersh, what's human chorionic gonadotropin?' She thought she knew, but wanted to hear it, in the hope that the vague ideas fractured in her head might come together.

Saoirse yawned. 'HCG? Can be a sign of some cancers, tumours and that.'

'Cancer?' Her mind was churning, mashing, crashing like waves.

'Sometimes. But that's not what it usually means. Do you not remember from when you had Maggie?'

'Tell me anyway.'

'It's what pregnancy tests check for. A hormone.'

Paula was thinking hard. Seeing her mother on the shore there, her summer dress blown around her by the breeze. The shape of her body. You didn't look at your parents when you were twelve, not properly. And PJ had been working so much that year – the ceasefires had broken down in 1993, and it was back to daily killings for a while, and he'd been out all the time dealing with one murder or another. Even the morning Margaret disappeared, he was out before light on a case. So it was possible. August, their last holiday, was only two months before her mother had gone. A lifetime from the hot summer days to the cold autumn morning when they'd somehow lost her. But not so long in the scheme of things. Maybe long enough to make a decision, or realise a decision had been forced on you, by your own inaction. Paula knew that. After all, she'd done exactly the same.

Saoirse yawned again. 'So . . . you're not going to tell me what this is about? You're not . . .'

'Christ, no. Course not. A case.'

'Right. Always a case with you.' There were murmurs in the background, Dave waking up, no doubt. The two of them in the sleepy cocoon of night, like Paula and Aidan had been, so briefly. 'It's only Paula,' Saoirse was saying.

'Sorry, I'll let you get back to sleep. Thanks, Glocko.' The line went dead and Paula was left alone with the facts, cold and sharp. She remembered it well – she'd hidden her own pregnancy for months, not telling anyone, as she tried to work out what you were supposed to do when you weren't sure who the father was. She'd even puked on Guy's shoes one day in work. And still no one had figured it out. So could you hide something like that? In a house with your husband and daughter? Your husband who was crushed almost senseless by the death he saw every day. Your daughter who was just thirteen and wrapped up in her world of watching *X-Files* and wondering if Aidan O'Hara, son of her mum's best friend, would ever talk to her again now they were growing up.

She was pacing in the kitchen, the familiar anger back. Why had her mother left so many questions? Hadn't she known what her daughter was like, PJ Maguire's daughter, who didn't know how to live with an unanswered question, who always had to know everything no matter the cost? The only thing she'd not found out the answer to was Maggie's parentage, and only then because she must have known, deep down, that the answer was not what she and Aidan pretended it was.

Angrily, in silence, she asked her questions now. In her head her mother was always the age she'd been when she'd gone. Beautiful, still turning men's heads. But Paula realised she would now be much older, if she was alive. What would she look like? Where could she have been all these years, if she'd gone off of her own accord? To hide a baby, maybe. But why?

Now, in the silence of the house, she once again tore her hair out with unanswered questions. They cropped up like the Hydra every time she found something. This time it was a new one. *Oh God, Mum, what did you do?*

She took out her phone again and fumbled a message to Saoirse. *Sorry to wake you and Dave. I need to go to London tomorrow – any chance you could watch Maggie for one more night?*

Fiona

Through the glass of the lighthouse bulb, I could see the sky. A white and featureless dome, like the top of the skull when you peel the skin away for surgery. Rory was gasping on top of me like a landed fish. 'Oh God, Fi. Oh God. We shouldn't have – oh Jesus, Mary and St Joseph.' They really do love calling on the saints, the Irish. I hoped he wasn't going to start with the Catholic guilt thing again.

I got out from under him, looking for my clothes. Trying to sort out my feelings and parcel them into little boxes. I don't know if Rory ever really believed me about Matt. Even the cut on my hand didn't totally convince him. I think he was suspicious, but also he wanted me, so he went along with it. I could see the way his eyes always came back to rest on my hips or breasts. Not so flattering, really – aside from Lucy Cole at the primary school and that crazy researcher from the plant, the one who's so blatantly in love with Matt I can practically feel the death-rays she sends my way, I'm the only woman under forty here who isn't married or raddled. And Lucy is the kind of person who irons her knickers – I know; I've given her a smear test. However, Rory's interest was currently all I had, and like a woman dying of thirst, I'd take what I could get. But like so many men, the ones who paraded through my sheets in the days before Matt, as soon as he'd finished, Rory was already thinking about how to archive the whole encounter. 'What'll we do? Matt's my friend. Oh God.'

I wiped myself off – sticky, cooling – and pulled my jeans back on. 'We don't have to do anything. It's fine.'

'He'll know. I'll have to tell him. Jesus.'

'Rory.' My voice like a gunshot in the glass bubble. 'You

don't have to tell him anything. I don't think he would notice if you did. Unless it's about seaweed, Matt is currently unable to take your call. Please try again later.' But that was no good. I softened my voice, held my arms out. 'Rory, please. Don't go. I need you.' A suggestion of tears in my voice. 'I'm . . . scared.'

With some guys, that's all you have to do. Need them. Rory turned back. 'Hey, it's OK. We'll sort something out. I promise.' And he put his arms around me and I clung to him like driftwood when you're drowning, this guy I wouldn't have looked at twice in London. Because despite myself, I did need him. And I was scared, more than I could admit to myself.

It's easy to judge, I know. I'm basically professionally judgemental. But you don't know what you might do, if you were stuck on an island and your boyfriend had gone crazy and no one believed you. And that little pink line does tend to focus your mind quite amazingly.

Chapter Forty-Two

King's Cross station was frenetic, with rushing feet, squeaking suitcase wheels, and a gaggle of tourists around the Harry Potter display. All a world away from Bone Island, the stillness that seemed to leach right into the core of you. Paula hurried along, huffing from her dash through the underground corridors. They'd arranged to meet at Patisserie Valerie, and before she went up the escalator she paused, trying to compose herself. Trying to be ready. A headline in nearby WHSmith's caught her eye – KILLER COMPANY FACES TRIAL. So someone would pay for what had happened to Andrea, and Niamh, and Mary, and all the other victims of Bone Island. Maeve was on the case, and she wouldn't rest until the whole dirty truth was dragged out into the light.

Her phone was ringing and she dug it out of her bag, her mind still on the island, the ice-pure sea and the sand white as bone. She didn't even see the name of the caller, and so Davey Corcoran's smoker's hack was a shock in her ear. She'd been leaving him messages all morning after her last-minute trip over. 'Davey?'

'Aye. So you're here, are you?'

'Yeah. I just thought . . . I had to come.'

'You've had a wasted trip, so you have. I went to the address. They moved on years back, the neighbour said.'

The hope she'd dared to feel was shrivelling already. 'But . . . they?'

Davey said nothing for a moment, and she could feel him weighing it up, whether to tell her or not. 'Aye. Neighbour said he'd a woman with him when he lived there. Black hair, she said. I asked.'

But maybe she'd dyed it, to cover up the red that was so striking, so unusual. 'OK.' Another question unanswered. Maybe her mother, maybe not. Maybe he'd had a wife the whole time.

'Something else,' said Davey, reluctantly, and Paula knew it as if he'd already said the words.

'They'd a child?'

He sounded surprised that she knew. 'Aye, they did. A wee one. A girl.'

Paula stood holding her phone, Davey's flat Belfast tones in her ear, the rush of a city around her, millions of lives, millions of people who'd never know her mother. What difference did it make to anyone if she'd lived or died, if she'd got away or been caught? Only to Paula. It was only her who could not stop looking, even now, when she was starting to see the shape, the outline of it.

'You want me to keep looking?' said Davey. She could hear what he wasn't telling her: that she might not like what he found. That the answers might be harder than not knowing.

But there was no other answer she knew how to give. 'Yes. Please. Keep looking.' She hung up the phone and went up the escalator, trying to push it back down deep inside her, trying to bury it, the thing she carried with her at all times.

* * *

The woman was sitting there anxiously, her handbag on her knee, looking about her as if she might get robbed at any moment. Susan Andrews – Matt's mother. Since she was coming to London anyway, Paula had decided to use the trip to tie up any loose ends on the Bone Island case. Package it away, neat and solved, file it and close it. She stuck on a sympathetic smile, trying to hide her own turmoil.

'Mrs Andrews, hello. I'm Dr Maguire. I was there when they found Matt. I'm so sorry for your loss.'

Words she had said a thousand times before. She did these visits if the family wanted it, knowing what it was to have unanswered questions about the death of your loved one. At least if you knew all the hows and whats, it might make that giant why somewhat easier to tackle. Or maybe it didn't. Maybe she would soon find out for herself.

Mrs Andrews looked older than her years, her skin pinched and eyes red, wearing an unfashionable lemon twinset. 'Is there anything more you can tell me, doctor?'

'It would have been quick. He wouldn't have known what was happening. Just one moment there then the next . . . peace.' If the family were religious she might say something vague and spiritual at this point. You had to judge it right. It made some people angry – they didn't want the transient comfort of thinking they might see their loved one again. They didn't want any comfort at all, like it would be a betrayal of the lost one. But other people liked to hear the soothing platitudes.

'He was in the sea, they said. For a long time.'

'He had been when we found him. But he wouldn't have known that, I promise you. He was already gone. He hit his head, falling down.' Being pushed, rather, but she didn't say that.

Mrs Andrews clutched her bag tighter. 'Then he burned. They burned him.'

'Again, he wouldn't have been aware of it. He was . . . far away by that point.'

She nodded dully. 'So they say.' She had a flat Glasgow accent. 'That policeman did it, they said. His friend.'

'Yes. He'll stand trial in a few months. If it helps at all, Mrs Andrews, something was very wrong out there on the island. They were all sick, all of them.'

'This lawyer called. Said I should sue.' Her voice was toneless.

'That will be a separate case. But if it helps at all, I got the impression, from my enquiries, that Matt was extremely popular out there. Well liked. He was happy there. That was the reality, you see, not . . . anything that happened after.'

Mrs Andrews was quiet a moment as the waitress, harried, brought tea, slopping a little down on the table. She moved the brown drops aside with one finger. 'She didn't get sick, though. Fiona.' Her tone was hard to read.

'No, she was all right. We think it's because she only ate food from off the island. She didn't even drink the water.' Paula thought of saying something about the baby, a comfort maybe, but perhaps Fiona wasn't ready to tell. It could be too much to take, the emotions of a funeral and a pregnancy on top. 'Have you seen her at all since?'

Mrs Andrews shrugged. 'We're not close, exactly. I doubt I'll see her again now.' So maybe she didn't know about the child. Paula would say nothing, though. Every woman deserved to tell that news when and how she chose.

She changed the subject slightly. 'I'm sorry I never met Matt. He sounded like a really great guy. Did he always love the outdoors?'

'Oh yes. You'd be taking your life in your hands going into his room as a little lad. Frogspawn, baby birds he'd rescued, a toad on the landing one time!' She was almost smiling a little.

'It must have been his dream job, then. It's beautiful over there. Maybe, in time, you'd even like to go. See why he loved it. The seals, the birds.'

Mrs Andrews took a deep, sighing breath. 'He was happy there, I know. Before he got sick. Hated London, always hated it. He was only here for *her*.' She looked round with distaste at the noisy concourse, chill and dirty with spring winds. 'I just wish things had been different. That I could have had something left of him. But it wasn't possible, of course.' She bit her lip, eyes brimming. 'I think that's the hardest part. That I never could have had it.'

Paula didn't understand. 'Had what, sorry?'

'A bairn, of Matt's. He's my only one, you see.'

So she really didn't know about the baby. 'Matt didn't want children, you mean?'

'He couldn't, love. Had the leukaemia when he was a small lad, and the chemo for it. Course they stored his . . . stuff, but he said he didn't want to bring a child into the world. Not when we were destroying the environment.' She recited it listlessly, as if remembering a conversation she'd had many times. 'Suppose they could have adopted or summat. One day.'

Paula frowned. That couldn't be right. 'Mrs Andrews . . . sorry, you're saying Matt . . . he couldn't have children?'

She shook her head. 'She kept on at him to have a baby, but he wouldn't. I don't think Fiona knew. Though when she'd have time for a baby with all her working, I don't know.'

Paula's mind was racing, though she tried to keep a neutral, sympathetic face while the woman talked on about her son, sniffing at times and tearing up, leaving her tea to grow cold. It would be easy to check Matt's medical records. The Guards probably had them already. Had Fiona found out about this, after years of secret trying and hoping? She smiled mechanically as Susan told her a story about Matt's first pet, a grass snake he'd hid in the airing cupboard, but all the while she was thinking: Did Fiona know? What did she do when she found out? How did she feel?

And most of all, if Matt Andrews could not have children, then who the hell was the father of Fiona Watts's baby?

She remembered something. The way Rory had said, on the boat: *even if it's not mine.* That could be taken two different ways, of course. It could mean Rory knew there was a chance the child was his. And what else had he said? *Waiting for someone in jail, it's no way to live.* She'd assumed he meant Fiona, waiting for him. But there was another way to read that too.

Then her mind was turning again, as if someone had taken her by the hand and led her to the memory. The bowls of stones in Fiona's house. Smooth and polished, with pretty candy stripes and seams. Picked up on the beach maybe, for their island home, to look good on Instagram. Lying around in bowls and arranged on window sills and shelves. Except for the glass bowl on the dining room table. Which only had one or two small stones in the bottom. As if the rest had been hurriedly scooped up, by someone rushing, and crammed into the pockets of a coat hanging nearby.

She knew where Guy worked. It had been ingrained in her for so long, kept in the back of her mind, even when she'd

...self he was long forgotten. She'd always known the ...ct station and street where he went every day, no doubt swinging in the doors in his suit and smart overcoat, every inch the successful career detective. Now she was there in reality, on a rain-soaked London street in late February. At four p.m., the lights were already sliding into the puddles, a rainbow of colour. She waited, hands shoved in the pockets of her trench coat, hair already damp and tangled. She could never quite rise to an umbrella. *Come on, Guy.* She didn't know what she would say, or how to explain, and she hoped that just seeing her, damp and bedraggled, he might somehow understand what she'd come to tell him. Tell him about Fiona Watts, about the terrible suspicion that was growing inside her like a dark child, have him make sense of it somehow, but also tell him more as well.

Guy. I need to tell you. Maggie – there never was a test. Only there was, and I didn't know about it, I swear I didn't know – but it said – Guy, you're her father.

And he would be angry, and confused, and she'd have to do her best to explain what had driven her to not find out the answer – fear of the result, a desperate making-do with Aidan, trying to pretend it would be all right, that they'd never need to find out. Stupid. Maggie would need to know, at some point, for her medical history alone. She'd need the truth. Paula had never wanted her daughter's childhood clouded by secrets and lies, as her own had been. But how would she explain to Guy that she had known now for months, and not told him?

I was afraid. That was all she would say. *I was afraid to lose you.* Afraid to see him look at her with disgust, and distrust, and afraid to lose the thing she held most dear – his good opinion. And then maybe they could finally talk, after years of half-promises and half-confessions. Maybe then she could take that job he'd offered, and leave Ballyterrin behind again, wipe it from her shoes like dirt, and make a new life for her and Maggie, in this city, where they could lose themselves.

There was movement at the turnstiles of the police station. Paula straightened up, pushed her damp hair into some semblance of neatness. Her stomach was turning over and over, seasick on dry land. Was that – yes, it was him. She'd know the height and gleam of fair hair anywhere. His long grey coat. He was smiling back at the person coming through the gate after him. A person Paula knew too. Jet-black hair, hooded eyes, guarded face. Though a little more rounded. Tess Brooking. Why was Guy's wife there? Meeting him at the station after work, perhaps?

Paula held her breath. The busy road ran between them, cars skidding up water, and he had not seen her. He was putting up a large black umbrella, sheltering his wife, pressing a hand into the small of her back. Tess turned, a smile breaking onto her lips – Paula had never seen her smile before – and her own coat fell open, and Paula saw it. The curve of the stomach. The bloom in the face. She knew it for what it was, and something stabbed in her heart, and she stood back, quickly, turning her face to the brick wall, in case they would see her.

They passed by – Guy, and his wife, and their coming baby – and Paula let them go, drips of cold city rain running over her face and pooling down on the warm hidden flesh below.

Fiona

Even now, I don't know how it happened. Matt was out on the balcony, where he'd spent so much time recently. He was staring out over the horizon. It was beautiful, though I hated it now. I'd never seen sunsets like the ones there, not even in Bali or Mexico. The way the sea turns blood-red, and the sun dissolves into it like a giant pill, something to take the pain away and make it all better. It would have been romantic, had my boyfriend not been crazy. Had he not been standing in a sea of broken glass, from where he'd shattered the lighthouse bulb. I said, 'What are you doing?'

I'd left my surgery early. I'd gone shopping. I was trying so hard to make it all perfect and nice and good. I'd even bought food, normal food. Hoping against hope there'd been a mistake, that what I'd found in Matt's medical records was somehow not true. My brain was trying to shuffle what he'd said about being sick as a kid. Some echo of his awful mother. A childhood illness. Pictures of him with a shaved head, vague references to hospital stays . . . *But of course, that won't matter to you, Fi, because you work so much anyway, you wouldn't have time for one anyway* . . . I hadn't been listening. I should have listened.

Despite all this, I was making an effort. Because even after everything, I hoped so much he would look at me. Say, I'm watching the sunset, sweetheart. Put his arm around me, pull me close like he used to do. I used to worry so much I would lose Matt's love in the obvious ways. That he'd meet someone younger, thinner, nicer than me. That he'd see me naked and in full light and realise what a terrible mistake he'd made. That I wouldn't get pregnant and he'd leave me for someone who was twenty and fertile. That I would get pregnant and he'd run from the responsibility. Or that I'd lose him properly. Bike into lorry. Ski into tree. Tumour in head or blood or bones. I never thought I'd lose him like this, when he was still standing in front of me, breathing and whole.

His eyes skipped over me. Empty. I'd become invisible, and some terrible part of me wished he would beat me or cut me, anything to feel his mark on me. To know he still saw me.

'Baby,' I tried again. Trying to be nice. 'I'm here. What are you doing? I'm sorry I didn't listen to you, about the company. I believe you now. People are sick, you're sick. Why don't you come down, and we can watch the sunset together, and we can have dinner and you can tell me about it . . .' And what? Make love? Have a baby? Live happily ever after? I don't think I even believed in that any more. A raw sob tore out of me. 'What's happening, Matt? Why are you being like this? Why did you lie to me – why didn't you tell me you'd been sick? You knew I wanted a baby. You *knew*.'

He turned to me. He looked so beautiful. His face bearded, his hair shaggy. So strong and tanned. My love. My saviour. My ending. How could our story have unspooled like this? The sunset glinting off the glass and off his hair, like liquid fire. Everything red and burnished. Like the whole place was coated in blood.

'We can't have a baby,' he said, his eyes flicking every-where. Watchful. Scared. 'I can't, Fiona. How can we have a baby when all this is happening? The blood tide! I had to stop the light, in case they find us! Don't you see?'

The blood tide again. 'What does that *mean*? Why did you lie to me?'

'Never mind that. Can't you see it's happening, Fi? It's coming *now*.'

He was touching me again. It was like water in the desert. His hands on my shoulders, pushing, showing me. And I looked. I tried to see, for his sake. Out in the ocean, nothing but the dazzle of the dying light, and the black shadows it cast. No blood. A vague blur of dark, maybe.

And that's when I realised that it was too late for Matt and me. Even if he stopped this, if we got off the bloody island, I could never find my way back to him. I would always resent it, these nights and days he'd made me suffer. There would always be a tumour of hate inside me, lurking, ready to grow and kill us. Even if I got him back, tore him away from this darkness, there had already been a pink line on a stick, one I couldn't cross back over or explain.

Matt would know. He'd know what I'd done to him. And I couldn't bear that. Going back to London alone, having to explain how our picture-perfect life had rotted from the inside out.

'I'm sorry, baby,' I said. 'I love you.' And then I stood back, and when he leaned over again, trying to see whatever it was he saw, I just pushed. It didn't even take much. His eyes opened in surprise, and he fell, just as easily and completely as I had fallen for him all those years ago. We began and ended in the sea.

I was very calm afterwards, almost like the plan was already there and waiting. You learn this, rushing around A & E with someone's life in your hands. Maybe it's easier for doctors. We're so used to it, that when the time comes, you find you have the skill there and ready, like a scalpel snug in your hand. I locked the front door from the inside, made sure my key was in my pocket. I washed up the mug

I'd used at breakfast. Wanting everyone to see how good my life had been. How well I'd done, before this fucking island. I got my wetsuit and climbing gear. For this to work, it had to seem like I hadn't been here. I'd take the boat out, maybe. I'd been capsized. I'd struggle back to shore in the storm that was coming later that night. The story was there and waiting for me, if only I knew how to tell it right. So I put up my ropes, the way I'd learned, and I climbed down the lighthouse to where he'd fallen. It was easier than lots of climbs we'd done, and the adrenaline was singing in my veins, spurring me on.

Matt looked peaceful. There was only a small amount of blood, spread out on the rocks under his head, but his eyes were open, and he was smiling. I filled his pockets up with small stones, and I got him into the boat, dragging him into it, heavy and limp, and we sailed out to sea, and then I let him slip under and I dived in after him. It was just like the moment we met – under the water, in its cold arms, Matt's hair waving like seaweed, his face carved like coral, and I let him go from me. Nothing left of him but an outline of blood in the boat.

It would have been fine. The boat would drift out to sea and maybe get wrecked in the storm. Maybe I'd have got off the island somehow, or surfaced in a day or two and said I had a sailing accident. Matt must have fallen off while I was away. Or jumped, maybe. He hadn't been well, everyone knew that. I would have thought of something. I'm sure of it. But then I swam back to shore and Rory was waiting for me on the slip, in the dark. *Holy God, Fi, what have you done?* And then it came to me. There was another way to tell this story. Another way to frame it, if only I was smart and quick and sensible. And Rory would do anything to help me.

He'd already said as much.

In the end, I will always do something instead of not doing something. I will always make the wrong choice instead of no choice at all. I will always kill before I let something kill me, as slowly and stealthily as a boat becalmed at sea. And maybe, when my baby is born and grown up and I get out of this place they've put me in, and I explain everything, how I really had no choice but to do what I did, maybe then I will tell her what really happened, what I did for her, and I know she will understand.

Acknowledgements

A big thank you to everyone at Headline for producing such a beautiful book, and to my agent Diana Beaumont for her unstinting help and support.

Huge thanks to everyone who takes the time to read or review the Paula books, and keep up with her ongoing adventures. I couldn't do it without you!

A big thank you to Scott Bramley, for coming all the way to Scotland with me in February, so I could research islands and ferry timetables. The island in this book is not real, but there are many similarly beautiful ones off the coast of Ireland and Scotland – Iona is a good place to start for beauty and eeriness, minus the actual murderous strangeness that happens in this book.

I love to hear from readers, so if you have any comments, please do drop me a line on Twitter at @inkstainsclaire or via my website www.ink-stains.co.uk.

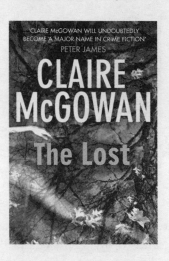

'CLAIRE McGOWAN WILL UNDOUBTEDLY
BECOME A MAJOR NAME IN CRIME FICTION'
PETER JAMES

CLAIRE
McGOWAN
The Lost

Not everyone who's missing is lost

When two teenage girls go missing along the Irish border,
forensic psychologist Paula Maguire has to return to the
hometown she left years before. Swirling with rumour
and secrets, the town is gripped by fear of a serial killer.
But the truth could be even darker.

Not everyone who's lost wants to be found

Surrounded by people and places she tried to forget, Paula
digs into the cases as the truth twists further away. What's the
link with two other disappearances from 1985? And why does
everything lead back to the town's dark past – including the
reasons her own mother went missing years before?

Nothing is what it seems

As the shocking truth is revealed, Paula learns that
sometimes, it's better not to find what you've lost.

978 0 7553 8640 6

HEADLINE

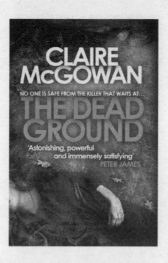

Stolen. Missing. Dead . . .

Forensic psychologist Paula Maguire, already wrestling
with the hardest decision of her life, is forced to put her
own problems on hold when she's asked to help find a baby
taken from a local hospital.

Then the brutal, ritualistic murder of a woman found lying
on a remote stone circle indicates a connection to the
kidnapping and Paula knows that they will have to move
fast if they are to find the person responsible.

When another child is taken and a pregnant woman goes
missing, Paula finds herself caught up in a deadly hunt
for a killer determined to leave no trace, and discovers every
decision she makes really is a matter of life and death . . .

978 1 4722 0439 4

HEADLINE

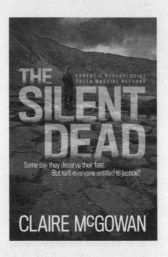

Victim: Male. Mid-thirties. 5'7".
Cause of death: Hanging. Initial impression – murder.
ID: Mickey Doyle. Suspected terrorist and member
of the Mayday Five.

The officers at the crime scene know exactly who the victim is.
Doyle was one of five suspected bombers who caused
the deaths of sixteen people.

The remaining four are also missing and when a second body is
found, decapitated, it's clear they are being killed by the same
methods their victims suffered.

Forensic psychologist Paula Maguire is assigned the case
but she is up against the clock – both personally and
professionally.

With moral boundaries blurred between victim and
perpetrator, will Paula be able to find those responsible?
After all, even killers deserve justice, don't they?

978 1 4722 0442 4

HEADLINE

Victim: Female. Twenty-two years of age.
Reason for investigation: Missing person.
ID: Alice Morgan. Student. Last seen at a remote religious shrine in Ballyterrin.

Alice Morgan's disappearance raises immediate questions for forensic psychologist Paula Maguire. Alice, the daughter of a life peer in the Home Office, has vanished along with a holy relic – the bones of a saint – and the only trace is the bloodstains on the altar.

With no body to confirm death, the pressure in this high-profile case is all-consuming, and Paula knows that she will have to put her own life, including her imminent marriage, on hold, if they are to find the truth.

A connection to a decades-old murder immediately indicates that all may not be as it seems; as the summer heat rises and tempers fray, can Alice be found or will they learn that those hungry for vengeance may be the most savage of all?

978 1 4722 2812 3

HEADLINE

THRILLINGLY GOOD BOOKS FROM CRIMINALLY GOOD WRITERS

CRIME FILES BRINGS YOU THE LATEST RELEASES FROM TOP CRIME AND THRILLER AUTHORS.

SIGN UP ONLINE FOR OUR MONTHLY NEWSLETTER AND BE THE FIRST TO KNOW ABOUT OUR COMPETITIONS, NEW BOOKS AND MORE.